FORTUNATE SON

BY

MELINDA MITCHELL

DEDICATION

To all who could never tell the truth of their love,
to all who had to hide who they are:
you are loved beyond measure.
Your story matters.

THE STAR SYSTEMS AND NATIONS OF THE BETA ARM

aka the "OUTER SYSTEMS"

EUPHRATES SPIRAL GALAXY

Two hundred years after the collapse of the Red Nebula

PYGA SYSTEM (Rumored; contact lost centuries ago)

ETHO CLUSTER: large asteroids and microplanets, one empire under a Queen

BARA SYSTEM: around twenty worlds and moons of various nations from a fallen republic

NACAEN GROUP: twelve nations plus original inhabitants, system united under King Saul

THE BARA SYSTEM

Nations and Worlds

BARA REPUBLIC: Aza

PHENIA: Ilistia and Gerar (Gerar seized from the Bara Republic)

LEKI: Balec

Other nations seeking possible homeworlds in Bara: Modes and Stiners

THE NACAEN GROUP

Nations and Worlds, united under King Saul

(There were at least three nations, known as the Originals, living in the system before the Nacaens arrived)

NIDOS: Tali, Hessan, and Lubez (Hitti: originals of Nidos)

MELAS (moon of gas giant Horeb): Dahan, Jamin, and Sim'ee (Sebuj: originals of Melas)

RICHO (moon of gas giant Horeb): Beneur, Dagael, and Ildan (originals unknown)

SAMAR (moon of gas giant Horeb): Charn, Reshar, and Maire (Rito: originals of Samar)

PROLOGUE

ZAM

His sandaled foot trod over the bloodstained marble steps up the dais. The old prophet leaned on his cane as he reached the top, turned around, and surveyed the damage. Servants were still cleaning up tables and carrying off trays of empty glasses and bottles, though it was afternoon, the celebration in the Great Hall over hours ago. He paid no attention to the signs of debauchery. The lingering scent of incense and the ashes that spilled over the rippled gray stone altar indicated someone had performed the rite of absolution without him, but even that didn't trouble him as much as the blood on the steps.

"What happened?" he asked as the princess approached, but he knew in his bones before she answered.

Princess Kyla folded her arms across her flight jacket, biting her bottom lip. Strands of her dark hair had loosened from its plait. "We routed the Stiners from the system and celebrated our victory, but you never showed up."

Zam's countenance sank. "The king gave the offering in my place."

"Forget the ritual!" she shouted, her voice echoing off the stone of the Great Hall. A tray fell to the floor, clattering as it rolled in a circle. A servant scrambled to retrieve it. Zam arched an eyebrow, turning back to the young woman. King Saul's youngest at eighteen was his spitting image, the sharp angles of her bronze complexion mirroring her father's, along with her temper, but she still held the same idealism that Zam once saw in her father. "He brought the Leki informant from the prisoners and executed him. He *mutilated* him."

His gaze fell from her back to the bloodstained steps. He squeezed his eyes shut, trying to stop the visual of the king stabbing the prisoner's chest and arms, slashing through vital organs, before ultimately beheading him. "I hoped I'd never see such things again. Not after he hunted the goddess worshipers." He ran his fingers down his beard, opening his eyes to the trail of blood the servants had attempted to clear.

Kyla stepped closer, her jacket opening slightly, revealing the holster under her arm. "He dismissed Jon as his advisor and banished him from the Elder Council."

A cough echoed from the west doors. Zam spied the prince, his dress uniform disheveled, running a hand through his light brown hair. The prince who looked so much like his mother that some whispered rumors about his parentage, but Zam knew he was Saul's blood. The same recklessness Saul once showed in his youth emerged in his son's drinking and fraternizing. But when it came to decisions on the battlefield, where Saul would be ruthless in his quest for power and control, Jon took risks to save others. Zam once held hope that Jon's position at his side would temper the king's thirst for power.

The prophet let out a shaky breath that shook his joints. "If he won't listen to his own son, he won't listen to me. His reign will come to an end, and soon."

"Goddesses," the princess swore under her breath. Under different circumstances, he would've admonished her for invoking any other deity than the One God, but her warning was sharp. "Zam, he's had people disappeared for saying less."

The light slanted at the edge of his gaze, and he touched his temple as the pain settled between his eyes. A vision, sharp and bright — far to the south, a field of golden grain, a farmhouse — a place he knew only from history. A red-haired young man strode over a meadow of green, a dog at his heel, sheep scattered in front of him. A man with a song on his lips, charisma in his heart, longing in his deep blue eyes. Zam dropped to the steps, his cane smacking the stone.

He found Kyla by his side, her dark eyes wide with concern.

"Are you okay?" the princess asked, putting her hand out to help him up.

"The kingdom will fracture," he muttered, leaning on her shoulder as she retrieved his cane. Kyla hissed. He ignored her. "You must help."

"There you are," a familiar voice boomed through the Great Hall. The king strode across the marbled floor as servants bowed. His hair was streaked silver, the sharp angles of his bronzed face deepened with lines at his eyes and forehead. His dark blue uniform was unbuttoned, cuffs loose, and he carried a pistol holstered at his side. "Give us the room," he ordered, to the servants as well as his own daughter. Jon had already made his exit.

But she hesitated. Zam shook his head in warning. While Kyla had always been able to turn her father's heart, the prophet feared it was only a matter of time before she faced his wrath.

"GO!" Saul barked, and the princess bowed her head, hurrying out of the hall.

As soon as the door was shut, Saul turned his displeasure toward Zam. "You were not to leave Melas. I gave an order —"

"And I am under a higher authority," Zam retorted.

"This was our hour of need! The one chance I had to make sure that the people see me as their king!"

Ah, there it is. Your ego. Your fear. The two swords that will cut you down.

"The people are united under our God, not you," he replied coolly. "You are but an instrument in the Maker's work —"

"I can't hold it together anymore," Saul interrupted. "The twelve nations, our whole system — I could barely hold our own world in the fight. I had to do it."

"The offering, or the slaughter?"

The king didn't reply.

Zam cocked his head, recognizing that what he was about to say would either change the course of the galaxy, or get him killed. *Probably both.*

"You're not a prophet anymore. You gave that up to become king of the twelve nations, but you keep conflating your role. You cannot force people to believe in you. You cannot undo the damage done by publicly torturing, *murdering* your prisoner. In your act to unify your people you're already causing division, even in your very home ..." Zam's mouth went dry, but he held his voice steady. "You need someone to *help* you. An advisor; an advocate. He will be wise, and strong, and the people will love him — and he will look to you. He will not stand in your way."

"*He?* Who is this?" the king spat.

"There's a young man to the south. He has a way about him — he charms people." Zam recalled the young man with auburn curls, his strong voice. "I have seen him in a vision. But he isn't aware of his ability. He will be fully devoted to *you*, and he will serve *you*, if only you listen to him."

The king's hand twitched, grazing the weapon at his side.

He's chosen to kill me. So be it. Zam closed his eyes, remembering how once, long ago, Saul had been a young prophet under Zam, before he went to war, before he was chosen to become king. In attempting to unite all the nations of the Nacaen Group, Saul turned not only to violence, but vengeance. Worse than the goddess cults.

Zam foolishly once thought Saul would be a king of peace. The vision, however, clearly showed another. Someone who was more than an advisor, but a born *leader*.

When Zam opened his eyes, Saul had folded his hands across his chest.

"Bring this advocate to me. Now."

PART ONE

ONE

ARMAS

"Come on," Armas muttered, pushing the stubborn sheep's rear end up the embankment. The ewe scurried over the rocks, and he leaned against a boulder, wiping his sweaty brow. His legs were caked in mud up to his mid-thigh. The fence had broken in the last storm, and Shane was supposed to fix it. The older brother often shirked his duties, leaving Armas to clean up his mess.

He climbed over the edge, where Roxy kept the rest of the sheep together. "Who's a good dog?" Armas coaxed, scratching the herder under her chin. She nuzzled his palm affectionately as Armas sat down on the ground, leaning against the fence post. He pulled the small tablet from his pocket, the screen cracked. Clearing his throat, he found a note and tapped the voice record icon.

"I long for the one, who frees me from mud ... oh God that's crap," he said, tapping the icon again and turning to Roxy. "You seem to like it," he added as her tail beat against the post. "Lemme try again." He switched over to his pre-recorded tracks and found a high note to descend on as he tapped the voice record: *"You're the only one who knows how I fe-e-el, You're the only one my love for is re-e-al ..."*

Roxy's ears went flat. The low rumble of an engine sounded from over the hills to the northwest. She cowered, whimpering. Armas frowned, turning as the roar grew louder, the shuttle flying low to the ground. As far as he knew, no guests were expected. The shuttle banked slightly, the insignia of a wolf on the shuttle door glittering in the sun.

King's business. *Why is the royal shuttle landing here?*

For a brief moment his heart clenched. But Eliot — his oldest brother, a transport pilot — was home on leave. They hadn't been called up in the last battle. Shane hadn't re-enlisted after his first tour with the Dahan mech regiment. They were safe.

"Let's go, girl," Armas said before whistling. Roxy leaped to her feet, barked, and rounded up the sheep. Armas's mind raced as to what this could be. A chance to serve the king? To get out from under the thumb of his brothers, a chance to prove himself? The opportunity to fight for the future of Melas and all Nacaens? Maybe the royal family heard one of his music tracks on the socials. Maybe he'd be asked to sing for the king, or heck, compose a new national anthem for the unified system.

Pride soared in his blood, lifting his feet as he sprinted across the field. Roxy followed behind, nipping at the heels of a stray sheep.

The shuttle landed in an open field near the barn, but Armas went directly to the pens. His older brother Shane sat on the fence, his wide-brimmed hat shading his face. Armas swung the gate open, hard enough that it smacked the other side of the fence.

Shane smirked. "Whatchya doing back so early?"

Armas leaned against the gate. "Saw the shuttle. Thought I'd take the opportunity —"

His older brother laughed, slapping his leg. Shane was tanned and muscular, his hair the color of sunlight. The girls in town had noticed him for years, and he knew it. Armas ran his fingers through his own auburn locks, a deep reddish-brown. Dirt clung under his fingernails and dust and sweat on his forehead. Both Shane and Eliot were two meters tall. Armas was barely one and three-quarter meters and lacked their muscles.

"This ain't no military delegation. Just the prophet. Came to see Dad for some reason. Eliot's the only one in there with them now. But the prophet's pilot — she's pretty hot."

Armas stepped away from Shane as Roxy yipped at the lambs straggling through the gate, but his brother leaped off the fence, blocking his path. "No, Armas, you're stuck here, shoveling sheep shit. And to think, this was once the headquarters of the Dahan Militia, back in the day. Now, just grain fields and sheep. Dumb luck Eliot will probably get called up to the prophet's personal bodyguard. You and I'll get left behind again."

Shane was an ass, and he was probably right, which made him even more of an ass. Armas yanked the gate shut, almost hitting the last lamb. "Sorry," he muttered to the spotted youngling as it scurried to his mother.

"Shane!" Their father's voice boomed out over the farm.

A wide grin spread across the elder brother's face.

"Well, well, maybe Eliot didn't make the cut, eh?" He cracked his knuckles. "Maybe it's my time to go impress the prophet and get moved into the fortress. Anything to get out of this stinkhole."

Armas sneered as his brother left him for the farmhouse. He wanted to follow Shane in, get in front of him before the prophet had enough of his annoying brothers and left without meeting him, but his father hadn't called his name, and he still had chores to finish up. Armas shoveled feed into the troughs, forcing the shovel so hard it almost slid from his hands. Dad would never let him leave the farm. Eliot had enlisted, and their parents were overjoyed when he was accepted to flight school after serving a tour in the mech forces. Even Shane was encouraged to join the military, and their parents pushed hard for him to re-sign. Armas glanced at his hands, covered in dirt and wool. His dad saw him only as a farmer, the one who would carry on the Lehem-Perez family business started by his great-grandparents.

He longed for the chance to prove himself. He was more than a farmer. More than this. But whatever the prophet was looking for, his father had already decided his fate. Armas wasn't what he wanted.

"Well, Roxy, at least I'll always have you."

Once the sheep were settled, he strode to the barn, singing with Roxy on his heels.

"When I'm pulled down, by troubled voices;
My heart stays glad, my soul rejoices ..."

Armas fell out of tune. Eliot's decommissioned mechanized suit stood in the center of the barn. Armas had promised to help him fix it, but he'd been stuck helping with the sheep and hadn't got to it yet. Sighing, he grabbed his toolbox. The suit was at least two meters taller than he was, boxy with armor patches, painted red though the rust gave the original paint job a run for its money. The Jamin mechs were newly manufactured, with the latest weapons and tech, whereas the Dahan and Sim'ee units were still pulling scrap jobs together. But he'd never get the chance to fight, not even in one of these broken-down Dahan mechs. Eliot's suit had proton rifles mounted on both arms, but the targeting computer was at least two generations old, and the interface was fried.

Armas yanked open the panel on the side and peered inside. The switches were corroded, which explained why his brother couldn't get it working again. The idea had been to reprogram it, and Armas would use it to help with threshing in the barley fields. He'd already taken apart the weapons on the left side, hoping to retrofit with a pick for tearing apart hard soil.

The youngest brother tugged on the wiring, muttering a curse as he pulled harder. *I'm like this wire, stuck here. I'll never get anywhere.*

His father's voice trumpeted into the barn. "Armas!"

He spun around, swiftly making his way to the entrance. His father stood on the porch, hands cupped to his face. "Armas!"

"Coming!"

Rushing to the farmhouse, he panted up the steps to the front deck, but his father Jesse blocked the doorway. Taller than Armas, Jesse's hair was once the same dark auburn but turned silver long ago. His sun-weathered skin made him appear tough, hardened, but the youngest son knew his father didn't want his boys to go to war. Jesse only wanted them to have a better life.

"The prophet wants to see you. But go wash up first."

"Yes, sir," Armas said, his heart pounding.

His dad set his hand on his shoulder. "Son, I'm

counting on you." He'd rarely seen his dad so serious. Jesse cleared his throat. "You're too young, still. But the prophet's looking for someone special."

Armas's jaw dropped. "What for?"

"I don't know. He won't tell us. But Eliot's disappointed and Shane's mouth already lost him whatever job it was." His father jerked his head. "Go wash."

"That won't be necessary," a low voice called from the living room. "Just send him in."

"But sir," his father began, "he's been out with the sheep —"

"And the people need a shepherd. Send him in, Jesse."

Armas's father moved out of the way, letting him pass through. He stepped forward in trepidation into the living room, the mud still caked up his legs. At least his face was clean — or so he hoped.

The old prophet stood in the center of the living room, wearing dark brown robes, leaning on a staff. His forehead wrinkled as he eyed Armas. "You're Jesse's youngest?"

"Yes, sir," Armas responded quietly.

"What makes you different from your brothers?"

"Um ... what?"

"I said, what makes you different from your brothers?"

Armas scrambled to answer the prophet. "I'm the youngest, so I've always had to work hard to keep up —"

"No, that's not what I'm talking about," the old prophet said, pacing around him. The prophet's skin was pale, probably spent all his time onboard ships and not out in the sun like Dahan farmers. A lump grew in Armas's throat. "Why are you covered in mud?" the prophet asked.

"I was out in the creek, our sheep got out of the pen,

and I had to —"

"You were out finding a lost sheep, correct?"

"Yes, sir."

"I smell dog."

"Yes, sir, that's Roxy."

"What talents do you employ?"

"I... um... what?" Armas asked, not following.

The old man raised his hands. "What are you good at?"

"Fixing things. I like to tinker around on machinery."

"Ever fought before?"

"No sir. That is, if you don't count fighting among brothers." Armas couldn't count how many times Eliot and Shane had fought each other, or him.

The prophet chewed the corner of his lip. "Hm. What else?"

Armas wracked his brain. "I like to sing, make up songs."

The old man's eyebrows raised, a smile crossing his face. "Ah. That's more like it. A creative. A dreamer. Someone who sees beyond what is in front of him."

A soft voice called from the kitchen. "I've got your tea, Zam, and —"

The young woman stopped short, carrying a mug of tea. Her black hair was in a single tight braid. She wore a combat flight jacket without a rank insignia, gray fatigue pants, and a Bara Republic Sharpshooter pistol holstered at her side. Her dark eyes were striking against her bronze skin, and her cheeks were tinged pink.

His mother followed behind her, carrying a tray and teapot with four mugs. Nita was just shorter than Armas, her short blond hair shining with silver strands. Her hands shook as she set down the tray.

"Kyla, this is Armas. Armas, Princess Kyla Kishrah."

"Princess?" His jaw dropped. Shane had said she was the prophet's pilot, but no, she was the *princess*. Helping his mother. She handed the prophet the mug she held, the scent of unfamiliar herbs wafting across the room.

"Here's the medicinal tea," she said quietly. Her nose twitched, possibly from the herbs.

Or possibly because Armas stank like dog and sheep.

"Um, I'm sorry, sir — prophet —"

"You can call me Zam."

"Zam, I'd really like to go shower. I'm sorry you had to see me this way."

The prophet chuckled. "On the contrary, this is exactly how I hoped you'd look. You're the one."

"The one what?" he asked, while the princess sat down on the couch, and his mother poured her a cup of tea. He shook his head, not believing the scene in front of him. His mother serving tea to the *princess,* in his own living room.

"The one who is going to help the king."

Armas opened his mouth, and closed it several times before saying, "What?"

Zam raised an eyebrow, as Armas felt his insides turn. "The king needs someone who can help him see the bigger picture, someone who can see beyond themselves. An advisor. Someone who is a dreamer. A poet, perhaps. Your other skills will be needed as his assistant, and I suppose you will learn in time how to fight well. For Dahan, for Melas, for all Nacaens."

Before Armas could reply, Jesse interjected, "You must be mistaken, sir. He's only nineteen. Eliot is better suited —"

"I didn't choose him," Zam countered. The prophet turned to Armas. "God sent me here and showed me that *you* are the one."

Armas's heart began to pound, his palms sweaty. *Please don't let Dad blow my chance.* He glanced at the princess, sitting on the edge of the couch, and quickly averted his eyes. He was smelly and awkward.

"His mother and I need to discuss this," Jesse said.

"Dad, it's my life, I should get to choose —"

"It affects all of us! How are we going to run this farm without you?" His father motioned to their guests. "Please excuse my wife and I."

Nita followed Jesse out from the living room, and Princess Kyla rose from her seat. "What now?" she said to the prophet. "The king will expect us to return tomorrow with an advocate."

"They'll come around, I'm sure," Zam responded.

Armas's stomach twisted. What if they didn't? What if his father insisted he stay behind and convinced the prophet to give Eliot a try instead?

"Excuse me," he muttered, fleeing the living room. He bounded up the stairs and shut the door to his bedroom. Leaning against it, his heart beating fast, he cradled his head. He slid to the floor, closing his eyes.

Voices mumbled from downstairs, before the house shook with the front door slamming shut. The prophet and princess must have left the house. His vision cleared; his heart slowed. Armas rose from the floor and went to shower.

He rested his head against the wall for a long time as the steam rose, until his skin turned pink. He stumbled out of the shower, leaning against the sink as the water dripped down, until his head cleared. There was no roar from the shuttle engines, so they must not have left yet. The house was quiet. After dressing in a button-down shirt and slacks, he stepped with trepidation as he returned downstairs.

"Dad?"

Jesse sat at the kitchen table; his shoulders slouched. Nita washed the mugs in the kitchen sink. Armas knew that rich families had recyclers for everything, but here on the farm they washed and reused without breaking things down by their molecular structure.

"Armas, do you really want this?"

He slumped his shoulders as he placed his hands in his pockets. "I know you need me here."

His father stood, the chair almost tipping over. "Son, I *don't* need you here." Jesse breathed out through his nose harshly. "I want you to stay because I don't want you to grow up too fast." He pursed his lips. "My father — your grandfather — told me stories as a kid of the old wars and the political games. His own parents barely survived. They wanted a different life for their children and grandchildren, and for you. When you were born, we made a promise," he added, turning toward Armas's mother. "We promised that we'd always keep one of our children at home, safe, never to know the horrors of war."

Nita dried her hands and joined Jesse's side. "But this is a chance of a lifetime, a chance no one else will get," she added softly. The skin under her eyes was dark from tears.

"Where's Eliot?"

"He's packing," Jesse answered. "The prophet promised him a promotion; he's flying out in the morning. Shane will return to the Dahan mech forces at Glia next month."

"What about you? What about the farm?"

His mother smiled. "The commission from Shane's enlistment would help us cover hiring a seasonal hand or two, but your commission alone will help us run the farm for years."

"It's not fair of us to make a promise that you can't keep. We agreed in the end it is your decision," Jesse added, "so he's waiting for a direct answer from you."

"Where is he?"

"Outside. The princess wanted to see the barn and Shane agreed to give her a tour."

Armas gave a curt nod to his father and ran outside, leaping down the steps of the porch. The sun had set; twilight spread across the sky. Horeb, the gas giant of the system, hung high above. He'd never been off-world before.

Roxy was on his heels as he ran across the yard. A light shone from the barn, and he slowed, frowning, the hiss of an air compressor growing as he approached the doors.

"Shane —" Armas began, expecting to find his brother messing with his tools, but he stopped short.

The princess was blasting sand out from the crevices on the mech suit, dust filling the air. Armas sneezed. She let go of the trigger, turned around and lifted her mask. "Couldn't get the interface to work with your tools, there's so much sand in there."

"You're ... you're ..."

She pulled her helmet off and killed the power on the compressor, the air still. "A princess?"

"Um ..."

"I'm fixing your mech is what I'm doing. Zam is talking to your brother. He seems to think he should've gotten your job."

"Your Highness, why are you here? Why me?"

Her lip caught under her teeth for a moment, her eyes focused on his. She yanked the work gloves off her hands, tossing them on the work bench. "You're not connected to any of the power players in his cabinet. You're not part of the leadership in Dahan's old militia." The princess stepped closer to him. "You're the model Nacaen, a common farmer's son, and you're humble. You won't accept praise or attention." She stood right in front of him, her cheeks warming to a soft shade of pink. "You're perfect."

Armas swallowed hard, his fear shrinking and some other emotion — a combination of pride, embarrassment, and *attraction?* It all balled up in his gut.

"Think of what this will mean for your nation, for the system ... and for your family."

His chest swelled.

A place in the palace. Moving ahead of Shane and Eliot. Fame. Honor for his family. Everything he ever wanted. His ticket out.

Any fear or hesitation he held crumbled in an instant.

"It's my decision. I'll go."

"Excellent," a voice called out. Armas spun around. The prophet waited at the door of the barn, leaning against his staff. "Let's be on our way, then."

"I need to say goodbye to my family —"

"Of course," the prophet interrupted, "but make it quick. I sent your brother back up to the house."

The princess frowned. "Zam, shouldn't we stay the night in the town? To give him one more night at home with his family?"

The prophet's brow furrowed. "I'm old, and I'd like to sleep in my own bed. Besides, it's not that long of a flight."

Armas raised his hand. "It's okay, I just need to pack," he said, half-smiling. Excitement sprung in his chest.

He raced back up to the house where his whole family waited in the living room. Eliot set his military duffel on the couch, still packing, while Shane sat in a chair scrolling on his tablet, the screen perfectly intact. Armas had grumbled that his father wouldn't replace his broken one, but now, as the King's Advocate, he'd probably get a better one than Shane had.

Nita pulled Armas into an embrace. "I'm so proud of you. You are going to be amazing," she said. "Who knows where this will lead? There is nothing you can't do." Nita pulled back, touching his face. "Now remember to say your prayers every day, and call when you can, and —"

"I will, Mom," he said, squeezing her hand.

"— And keep practicing your singing. I love your voice."

Shane coughed. Armas caught him rolling his eyes, but he didn't care.

"I will make you all proud," he said, turning to his father, relief waving over the old man's face. "I promise, I'll do it."

It only took a moment to grab the few things he wanted, throwing them in a shoulder bag. He packed the cracked tablet — his latest recordings were on it — and his seven-string lyre.

Roxy whined at his feet when he came downstairs. "I know, girl, I can't take you with me. Don't let Shane boss you around."

"We'll take care of her," Jesse said, pulling his son into one last embrace.

"Thanks, Dad. I love you."

His father squeezed him. "I love you too, son."

He glanced at his brothers. Eliot stepped over and shook his hand. "Can't believe you're growing up," he muttered.

Shane gave a mock salute from the couch. "I'll probably end up seeing you, since I'll be in Glia next month anyway."

"Maybe," Armas responded. Maybe someday Shane would stop being a jerk, but he didn't count on it.

Armas stepped outside in the dark and took one last, long look at the farmhouse he grew up in, lit by the outside security lights. His great-grandparents built this house after the war. They'd wanted to raise their family in peace. Now, King Saul needed help, and even though he didn't have the slightest clue how he could help him, he'd have to figure it out. For his family.

He walked back to the barn into the shadows, and around the corner where the king's shuttle had landed. "I'm ready," he said, straightening the strap on his instrument case over his shoulder.

He stopped dead in his tracks. The prophet and the princess were squared off at each other before the shuttle hatch, still closed, only a dim light from the princess's comm casting shadows. "You can't go home, Zam."

"He ordered you to kill me." the prophet said softly, pushing the comm into her hand.

Who ordered whom *to kill?*

The princess's eyes gleamed with tears.

"You're going to have to make it look good, then," Zam said, raising his hands.

"I'm sorry," she breathed, putting her comm in her pocket. "I didn't want to do this, but I couldn't think of anything else."

Armas's eyes grew wide, his heart galloping. *What the hell?*

"You're certain, then, that he wants me dead," the prophet said, his voice flat.

The princess's words were barely a whisper. "I don't have a choice." Her hand went to her side.

I have to save him!

Armas dropped his lyre case and lunged for the princess.

TWO

KYLA

Kyla's torso smashed against the barn wall. She spun her body, shoving Armas with her back and shoulder. He tried to get his arms around her. She twisted out of his grip, slipping low and sweeping her leg, knocking him off his feet.

"What the hell are you doing?" she shouted as Armas leaped back up, startling her with his quick footedness. He must've learned hand-to-hand combat somewhere. She backed up a meter.

Armas's eyes were wide as his gaze skimmed down her body. "You said you were going to kill him," he said between breaths.

Kyla dared a glance at her side. Her weapon was still

holstered, but he'd managed to knock the secondary comm out of her hand, the one she'd used for making the off-the-books transport contact. "Fuck. No, I *didn't* say that. And I'm not going to *kill* him." She locked her eyes on him while she bent to pick up the comm, now cracked in one corner, but still functioning.

"I thought ... you were reaching for your pistol," he said, rubbing the back of his neck. His cheeks were as red as his hair.

Kyla glared at him, noting the freckles blending into the blush on his cheeks. Sure, he was good-looking, and she'd found him charming earlier, but if Saul found out he'd laid a hand on her he'd be lucky to walk off the shuttle.

He raised his palms. "Really, I'm sorry, I just —"

"We're wasting time," Kyla snapped.

The prophet shrugged. "It's all right, Kyla. Another good quality in an advocate — protect the innocent and the weak."

She scowled at the old man.

"I didn't mean to imply you are weak, sir," Armas said.

Zam leaned on his cane. "It's true, though. I've become frailer this past year."

Kyla bit the corner of her lip as she swiped her comm screen. The prophet had seemed to age more rapidly, especially as he tried to shore up support among the priests of the One God, who were fractured in their support of Saul. Zam had done so much for the king, but Saul's power grab — and performing the ritual of absolution for the soldiers — threatened the sovereignty of the religious order. Now, she needed to save the prophet's life.

She stopped on the message from her contact. "I've

arranged a transport for you, but they won't arrive until before dawn and we can't risk you being caught before then. The whole plan depends on us staying tonight — the king doesn't expect us until tomorrow."

"Kyla," Zam said softly, "he was just trying to protect me."

She flared her nostrils and pointed at Armas. "He can't protect you from my father. Saul *will* have you killed, one way or another, unless I can help you. And the best way to do that is to have you disappear."

"I understand," the prophet said, then flexed his jaw and gestured at Armas. "But he can save us all. The king — the system — needs him."

Armas backed up to the barn wall, raking his fingers through his hair.

Her anger cooled, and she dared a step toward the Advocate. "My father *did* order me to kill Zam once we found you." She pocketed the secondary comm. "Obviously, I'm not going to do that, but I was hoping to get Zam a ride off-world without having you complicit, and now that plan has gone to shit. I'm sorry you're finding out this way."

"That the king wants to kill his closest advisors?" Armas spat. Kyla flinched, surprised at his anger. "Yeah, that sounds like something I might need to know." He crossed his arms.

"He won't kill *you*," the prophet said. "He *needs* you. I've challenged his authority in a way that is ... unforgivable to him."

Kyla gave a sideways glance to Zam, because she knew her father would take out Armas if he saw him as a threat. But Armas needed assurance, and her father needed an advocate. "He's right." Kyla took another step closer. "This is a lot to take in. But this isn't about you right now.

This is about making sure my father thinks his orders have been carried out, so I can get Zam to safety."

The prophet folded his arms. "Where are you taking me?"

"I have a contact through Nidos, to Ramah."

Zam threw his hands in the air. "He'll know. I was born there, and I became a priest in the old temple. But the cult of Tana now resides —"

"And the king won't look for you there," she countered. "He believed he destroyed the settlement when he tried to wipe out the Tananites, but he didn't destroy the structures below the surface." She cast a glance at Armas. His eyes smoldered and her heart almost skipped again. *Why does he do that to me?*

Kyla shook those thoughts away and turned her attention back to Zam. "I know it's not ideal, but if you don't go into hiding, he'll know I didn't carry out his orders. You can't come back with me."

The prophet's eyes brimmed with tears. "Then this is goodbye."

Zam opened his arms, and she embraced the old man, squeezing tight, just as he had when she was a little girl. Because she knew he still saw her that way, someone innocent and incapable of hurting someone else. Even if she never embraced the One God he believed in, she had learned devotion, integrity, and humility from him. She'd always looked up to him.

Maybe that was why Saul ordered her to kill him: to test her loyalty, to see if she would be unwavering under her father's will. Jon had warned her that if she really wanted to fly in combat someday, she'd have to follow orders and innocent people might die. She'd have to follow through on her father's commands even if she disagreed. He told her she might not be cut out for it.

He might be right, because she'd do anything to save Zam.

"Dearest princess," Zam whispered. "Do not fail your people." She blinked back tears as he let go of her, keeping his hands on her forearms. "You and I may be on different paths, but we both want to do what is right." He motioned to Armas. "She will help you."

Before she could gauge Armas's reaction, her comm beeped. She pulled it from her jacket pocket and decoded the reply. "My contact will meet you at the southeast edge of the farm," she told Zam. "They'll hide you until the transport arrives tomorrow morning. But you can't be seen *by anyone* after this." Kyla gave the prophet a half-smile. "You'll have to shave your beard."

He chuckled. "Just don't make me get one of the Tananite silver tattoos. That I couldn't live down." The prophet motioned to Armas. "You will go with her, back to Glia."

Armas rolled his shoulder. "How can I serve the king now knowing that he wants you dead?"

Kyla gritted her teeth. "Because you already said yes. There's no going back."

"I have done all that God has called me to do," Zam said, setting his hand on Armas's shoulder. "Trust her. Go with God's blessing."

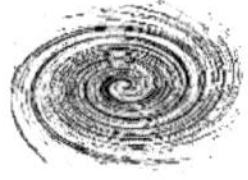

Keep your eyes ahead. She stole another glance at Armas's reflection in the viewscreen, his hands gripping the armrests of the chair behind her. What could she say to him?

The sleeves of his shirt were rolled up past his elbows,

showing off his tanned forearms. He was leaner than most soldiers she knew. He wasn't tall like Jon, either, but right at her height, her age. "You've never flown before?" she managed to ask.

"No."

"I'll teach you, if you want."

Armas didn't reply.

Swearing inwardly, Kyla glided the shuttle over the hills, away from the Dahan farmlands lit by the moonlight. He was obviously still rattled by their departure. She didn't look again, but his face was etched in her mind. When she'd walked into his living room, despite the mud all the way up his thighs, she'd immediately noticed the dark auburn hair, his blazing blue eyes. Cleaned up, he could be a fashion icon from Etho or another far-flung rich system. With his lyre, he looked like he belonged on stage, not in a military command center. He was just a shepherd, a farmer's son. He should've never gotten into this. *Tana curse it all.*

"We have to tell the king the prophet's dead?" His voice caught her off guard.

"*You* don't. *I* do." She stared again at his reflection, relieved he was catching on. "I'm the one who'll tell him he's dead. He'd be suspicious if I let you witness the murder, which is why the plan was for you to not witness any of that. So, you need to tell him exactly what you *saw* regarding Zam, that I ordered him onto a transport, and not what you *know*. Probably of anyone, he trusts me the most." She tapped her fingers on the console rapidly.

He shifted toward her, the leather cushion squeaking as he moved. "You weren't planning to tell Zam tonight, were you?"

She cast a glance over her shoulder at him. "No. But

he wasn't buying my reasons to delay, so I had to tell him. I'm just glad that my contact was able to get here earlier," *though for twice as much as we agreed to,* she added silently, turning back to the viewscreen. "Hopefully, by the time we see the king, Zam will be halfway to Ramah."

They flew for a while in silence. Kyla wiped her palms more than once. She didn't know what to say to assure Armas. Despite telling him Saul wouldn't kill him, he didn't seem convinced. He might blow this, and it would all have been for nothing. *Father would kill him, then find Zam.*

Divine Starre, she prayed, *give him strength to fulfill his destiny and not fuck this up.*

Armas cleared his throat behind her, pulling her mind back.

"The King's Advocate," he stated flatly. "Like an assistant? To get him what he needs?"

"Yes, somewhat. You'll supervise his personal equipment in war, and you will counsel the king at times," she added, recalling what Zam told Saul in the Great Hall.

"Counsel? Help him make decisions?" Armas's laughter, even edged with bitterness, rolled through Kyla's ears. She noticed he no longer smelled like sheep. Something wild and sweet, like honeysuckle.

Focus.

"It's no joking matter," she retorted. "At times, my father — the king — has made rash decisions on the battlefield." She winced, not wanting to admit her father's faults out loud, though Armas was now acquainted with them. "He needs someone who can help direct him back. Not as a challenge, but someone who agrees with him enough to show him the right way to proceed."

Jon's latest blunder flew into her head. Her brother was so much like her father at times, rushing off to do what he thought was right, instead of following commands. Even if he disagreed, Jon ought to have found a way to persuade him, instead of squaring off. *He was born ready to fight the world,* her mother said before she died. Whether she was referring to her father or her brother, Kyla wasn't sure.

She took a deep breath. "My father needs someone to help keep a level head. Sometimes, he has lost sight of the mission for the glory." *Again, just like Jon.*

Kyla glanced in the viewscreen, catching Armas's expression of puzzlement in the reflection.

"Why me, Your Highness?" he shifted, suddenly formal again, as if he remembered who she was. "I know nothing of battle — I'm not even a soldier yet!"

"Zam believes that God chose you, so you must have something special."

His eyes narrowed. Kyla tore her gaze back to the nav charts as they approached Glia. "I'm nothing, just a shepherd."

Kyla sucked in the smile that wanted to escape. Of course he'd say that and be sincere. She'd met enough guys who faked humility, mostly to catch her eye and perhaps her inheritance. However, Armas seemed to have no clue about how handsome he was, no awareness of how strong and yet soothing his voice could be. The perfect man the people would rally around, and he'd point all the glory to Saul. *Good choice, Zam.*

"Keep that attitude, it will help with my father." She glanced over her shoulder briefly.

He set his elbows on his knees, his head hanging low. "I don't know if I can do this."

Kyla touched the carved figure she kept hidden in her pocket, of the warrior goddess Tana. *We need a warrior.* Her father had once been a great leader. Would Armas help restore him to his former glory?

She punched the autopilot control and sat down. She preferred to fly manually, but this part over the plains outside the city was boring anyway, and her family's transport shuttle wasn't anything special, unlike the Bluehawk fighters her father flew or even the old Sparrowing Jon started out in.

Kyla spun around in the chair to face him. "We need you." She tilted her head, frowning slightly. If he didn't start projecting confidence, Saul would reject him. "We'll train you, of course, for battle. As to the king, just be yourself. You've proved yourself already." *At least to Zam.*

"My great-grandfather was the leader of the Dahan militia, then of the council that formed with the Sim'ee and Jamin nations," Armas said, picking something off his trousers. "After him, those who followed didn't lead in the same way. He called the people to work together, to share resources, but the ones after him took bribes, so my father said. Dad turned us back to farming and out of government." Armas chuckled, finding Kyla's gaze. He seemed relaxed for the first time since — well, since he tackled her. "And here I am, running back into the old family business, without a clue."

"It's different now, since my father became king. Zam helped the twelve nations' leaders get behind Saul. And now, he's called you to help."

Armas leaned forward. "Your Highness, if your father's so quick to kill off the prophet, how quickly will he try to kill me?"

Damn. He read my mind. "He won't," Kyla lied, biting

her lip right after. *No one is safe.*

The console beeped, letting her know they were approaching Glia. Armas leaned back in his seat as Kyla spun back toward the controls. "Buckle in," she said sharply. "It's a steep descent into the fortress."

The capital city of Glia rose from the dirt and rock. Surrounded by a stone composite wall that generated a forcefield, cannons protected the outer wall from invaders, and around the periphery, mech patrols stood on guard. Lights glared from the large helms of the strong metal battle suits. The southern third of the city was the fortress and royal palace her father had built long before she was born.

Kyla turned to the east, where the gates to the landing tunnel opened upon recognizing the ship's signal. She caught a glimpse in the viewscreen reflection of Armas falling back into the seat as the shuttle dove into the entrance, gliding into the steep shaft of the landing tunnel. The viewscreens were blank until they reached the landing bay, and the shuttle leveled off to land inside the large underground flight deck, lined with stone and steel. A few flight techs stood at the edge, some pilots chatting with them, and one figure made their way toward the shuttle.

"Who's that?" he asked from behind her, his tone curious.

"Dusted ash," Kyla muttered as they arrived. She'd expected her father to be waiting with his guards on the flight deck.

Instead, her sulking older brother leaned against a Sparrowing fighter.

THREE

JON

Jon's brow furrowed as the young man walked off the ship.

That's who's replacing me?

Granted, the kid was only a few centimeters shorter than him, but he needed to bulk up. Scrawny Dahan farmers. They may have led Melas to freedom once, but they hadn't done their part to keep up. Jon fought alongside Dahan fighters and wasn't impressed — and those were the few who didn't desert the military to run back to the farms when the harvest was in. The system couldn't catch a break, and this was the hero being sent in?

Jon had slept most of the day, trying to get through his hangover and the aftermath of his father's atrocities. Raimi, his friend and second-in-command before he lost his post, had woken him and filled him in on the briefing Saul had called. Some sort of "advocate" was chosen to fill in as advisor to the king. After he stormed out of his quarters, Jon found himself down by the flight deck and spotted Kyla's shuttle on the arrival screen.

The young man carried his bag from the shuttle transport along with some sort of instrument case. *Father does like music. Maybe the only normal thing about him.* There wasn't much on the king's agenda that didn't have to do with politics or war, but Saul did attend the occasional concert, mostly Bylon symphony orchestra or Ramaen classical instruments. Maybe this was more of a cultural advisory role, and Raimi misunderstood?

This was no warrior. *He'll be eaten alive.*

Jon spied his sister stepping off the shuttle behind the boy, moving to catch up to his side. His sister was all flushed, her eyes bright. He'd seen that look before. The Dahan man was tanned like all the other farming conscripts, but the auburn hair was striking, his strong jaw and blue eyes made him an attractive figure. Jon chewed the inside of his cheek. He could see why Ky's cheeks were red. The young farmer would stand out. Everyone would know this was Saul's new right-hand man, an easily identifiable target.

Maybe that was the point.

"I saw your flight was coming in," he said to Kyla. "You're early; we didn't expect you until later tomorrow."

Kyla didn't seem to hear him, her focus on the handsome Dahan.

Jon glanced back at the shuttle. "Where's Zam?"

"He didn't come back with us," she muttered, brushing a stray hair out of her face.

"Where'd he go?"

"He said he had other business to take care of."

Jon set his hands on his hips, frowning. The prophet had gone off on his own in the past, but with Saul's latest deplorable action, Jon was uneasy without him nearby. Especially after the execution. Usually, Zam was the only one Saul would listen to, the only one who could remind him of the bigger picture. The prophet would've stopped Saul from executing the Leki informant if he'd been there, Jon was certain.

But prophets had their own business to attend to, and it was only a matter of time, he reckoned, before Saul would stop listening to Zam and take matters into his own hand. He'd witnessed his father — cold and merciless — kill not only on the battlefield, but also in the interrogation room. It hadn't shocked him the way it had Kyla when the king brought out the Leki prisoner, but it haunted his dreams.

Jon focused his attention to the young man with her. "What's your name?"

"Armas Lehem-Perez, sir,"

The prince extended his hand. "I see you met my sister." Kyla scowled at him, but the crimson tint on her cheeks hadn't faded.

"Oh," Armas responded, seeming a little stiff and starstruck as Jon shook his hand. "Yes. I mean, I didn't know she was your sister, sir — I mean, Your Highness."

His sister's eyes bored lasers into Jon, but he ignored her. "Jon's just fine. You'll need to stick with the honorifics with the king, though. We'll start training with the dawn shift."

"Already?" Kyla startled.

Jon stuffed his hands in his pockets. The situation was not good, as Raimi had filled him in — before dropping the bomb that Saul had already found a replacement for him. "Phenian scout ships were spotted on scanners near Ramah. Recon mission, we suspect, but intel shows they were passing drop ships through the Bara system a couple of weeks ago."

"Mechs?" Armas asked.

Jon blinked, surprised the Dahan farmer would guess that. "Yup. Each one carries a dozen, and at least ten ships were spotted. Maybe more."

Kyla's eyes narrowed. "They're not known for fighter ships."

Jon nodded, impressed at how much she did know. "They've got a couple of Bylon warships guarding them. Our fighters may be able to take out a few drop ships, but we'd sustain heavy losses that way. We don't have the fleet we need for that, so he's ordering preparations for a ground assault."

"He's going to just let them through?" His sister's eyes widened.

"We've got more mech troops than we do pilots right now and he thinks our numbers will stand against them. Besides, he's pretty sure they're targeting Melas specifically."

Armas appeared confused. "So ... what do I do?"

"The king doesn't know you're here yet, which is why he's not here to officially welcome you," Jon said to him. "Something about arriving tomorrow?" he added, tilting his head toward Kyla. "He's been in conference between the Lubez and the Sim'ee nation elders all evening, trying to get them to agree on the warship contracts. He understood you and Zam would return in the morning."

"Plans changed," she snapped. "How long before the Phenians attack?"

"Days if we're lucky. They're going to notice our orbital defenses are diminished if they get close enough." Horeb's magnetic field often disrupted long range scanners and sensors, and they still hadn't gotten everything back online after the last battle with the Stiners and the Leki. When he disobeyed his father and lost his position.

"Then let's get to work," Armas said after clearing his throat, wiping his palms on his trousers.

Jon raised an eyebrow at Kyla, which she returned with a shrug. Armas was certainly trying to be brave. Trying, however, would get him killed. He needed help — and as much as Jon detested what his father had done, it wasn't Armas's fault.

"It's late. I'll get you settled into temporary quarters — not sure where Father plans to have you stay permanently, but right now there's an empty officer's apartment." Jon shook his head as Armas picked up the instrument case. "Gonna have to exchange your gear. It's time for you to become a soldier."

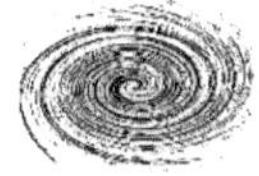

Jon woke early and sober, rising at the time the Jamin soldiers would be up for training, and sent a messenger for Armas. He instructed him to deliver the new Dahan recruit to the armory, where the king's mech suit was stored. The armory was a massive warehouse, four stories tall, where their mech units were serviced and prepped for battle, before moving to the mech hangar. Techs worked on repairs and servicing — some with welder's masks, others with grease smudges on their coveralls.

The mechs ran the spectrum of colors. The Dahan tended to use red or gold paint, the Sim'ee blue or white. Though Jamin often painted theirs dark green, Jon's own mech was black. The king's was unpainted, remaining the dark gray Airysan steel it was made from.

"Any experience repairing armor?" Jon asked the new advocate as he entered.

Armas crossed his arms. Jon noted the dark green standard-issue fatigues made Armas's auburn hair appear brighter, his eyes a darker blue. "I've repaired mechs on the farm. We started rebuilding my brother's suit for farming."

"Hopefully those skills transfer," Jon said, motioning Armas towards his father's suit. At four and a half meters tall, the dark Airysan mechanized suit was the embodiment of power. Like the others, it was armed with proton rifles on both arms and missile launchers at its shoulders, but it carried an electromagnetic sword on its back, capable of cutting through force shields and disrupting almost all known weapons.

The pilot's seat was located in the central compartment behind massive shield armor, protecting the pilot and the control systems. On the top of the torso was the head — mostly decorative, containing some cameras and auxiliary systems, but made to look like a face. Even on Saul's mech, the only markings were the eyes, painted black.

The farm boy whistled. "My brother's suit was a bit

shorter and not nearly this nice. Lots of welded patches. Made with the old Liphes steel."

"Airysan steel is almost impenetrable, but so damn hard to come by in the Outer Systems. We currently have twenty-four Airysan mechs, the remaining ninety are Liphes, including the two-dozen patrol mechs outside of Glia." Which Jon realized they'd have to pull from to match the invaders machine for machine, if their intel was correct.

"What do the Phenians use?" Armas asked as he climbed the ladder up to the pilot's compartment.

"Fairly certain they are mostly Liphes steel. But that's not the problem."

"What is?" Armas peered inside the open mech suit. Jon watched as he ran his fingers along the inner panels. When the redheaded farm boy looked down at Jon, he noticed the faintest hint of freckles below those blue eyes. A flutter rose in his stomach.

What is wrong with me? This is the guy replacing me, not —

Definitely not someone to be interested in.

"The Phenians have a Stiner team working for them," Jon continued, turning his eyes to away from Armas's freckles and back to the suit.

"Mercenaries? Didn't y'all just fight them off?"

Jon folded his arms across his chest, swallowing a smile. Armas's country ways were adorable. *Don't go there.* "Stiners will go where the money is, and Ilistia, the Phenian home world, isn't far from the Leki world of Balec, their last boss. But it's not just any merc team — they hired Ogroma."

The farm boy frowned. "I'm not familiar."

"You haven't heard of *Ogroma*?"

Armas shook his head. Jon ran his fingers through his hair. "Ogroma is a specialized unit of mechs. They have a way of joining their suits together to form a larger mech, channeling their power systems into a destructive weapon, but it's more than that — it's their technology hard-wired into their brain stems to act as one body when connected. Everyone suspects they use outlawed Mode augments. Ogroma have wiped out land forces in other systems, destroyed city defenses. Their suit's at least Airysan, maybe even stronger. No one's found a weakness."

Armas climbed back down the ladder. "What's the weakness on these?"

"Gravity, mainly. A large mech throwing you in one of these. Something heavier crushing you. We had thirty-six originally, and they aren't cheap."

"Did the operators all —"

"Dead, all of 'em. And many more. You realize that's what war is, don't you?" Jon sucked in a breath, stepping closer to Armas. *What is it with me that immediately wants to protect people from what I've seen and experienced?*

Unlike the other soldiers Jon knew, Armas smelled like he'd just come in from outside, as if he wasn't tied to ships and machines and mechanisms of war, the dirt and grime of battlefields and staleness of space. He smelled like wild grass, like freedom.

"You ready to put your life on the line?" Jon continued, trying to ignore every sensation in his body triggered by this close proximity. He wanted Armas to understand the horrors of war in the same way he wanted Kyla to. If he wanted this, he needed to know what he was getting into. "Because that's what it takes. Your willingness to die for your fellow soldiers. In your case, your willingness to die every day for your king."

Jon noticed fear building as Armas's eyes widened. "Not only do you have to be willing to die, but you will see death all around you. No matter what horrors you imagine in your head, it's always worse."

The sound of weapons firing tore Armas's gaze from Jon. "That's the Jamin recruits," he told Armas. "They've been here three weeks. The Dahan and Sim'ee troops will join in soon."

"They train separately?" Armas asked.

"Their training isn't as extensive as the Jamin, unfortunately. It's something we need to work on in our unified military. Same with pilots. The nations on Nidos were supposed to send their warships to back us up, but they're delayed. Why my father was up negotiating with the Lubez last night."

Jon led Armas from the mech armory up a ramp to the firing range, where he spied Kyla target practicing, away from the recruits. The long room was lined with firing stations on one side and targets on the other. Before each firing station was a rack of weapons, ranging from small pistols to powerful assault rifles, and screens above them, currently showing various security feeds from around the fortress. The lights above rippled in his vision — the energy force shield that protected the ceiling and walls from stray rounds. Each targeting station was also separated by a force shield, so those firing next to each other could see, but not cause harm.

Armas put his hands in his pockets, walking beside him. "Have you ..." his voice barely above a whisper, "... have you killed anyone?"

Jon chewed the inside of his lip, not looking at Armas. "Yeah. It will happen. And you'll feel like shit afterward."

He stopped near Kyla, who didn't glance their way, her noise-canceling headphones protecting her. She wore a combat jacket, gray-and-black camo pants, and black boots. Jon surveyed the weapons at their disposal for training at an empty station, and pulled off the rack an Ember 75, a small pistol. "Ever fire a gun before?"

Armas took the gun from Jon's hand. The farmer pulled the magazine and checked the rounds, before snapping it back in place. With one arm raised, he aimed and fired at the target on the other side. His shot was just to the right of center. "Damn. Still pull to the right sometimes."

Kyla stopped, watching Armas fire again, this time hitting the target square with the dinky little gun. She yanked the headphones off. "Stardust. Could you give him a *real* weapon, Jon?"

As Armas worked through their standard array of weapons, Jon reconsidered. Maybe this kid could pull it off. *Scratch that. Armas isn't a kid.* He was a year older than Kyla, and he was a good shot and a fast learner. Maybe he learned to ward off predators or thieves, but he knew how to shoot.

However, the chance that Armas would be killed in a mission against the Phenians was pretty high, even in an Airysan suit. Whatever Zam's thoughts were of Armas's role, the only reason Jon had survived was because his father hadn't put him on the front line. Because he was the heir. *Why he dismissed me — because I risked myself to save the fleet.* The gamble had paid off, but he'd faced his father's wrath and reprimand. The shame still hung in his chest.

Maybe, by helping Armas, Jon's father would see how useful he was. Maybe his father would restore him to at least a position on the Elder Council, if not back at his side. By helping the Advocate, perhaps his father would recognize he still had purpose and potential.

Jon watched Armas fire a proton rifle, taking out half the target. Kyla moved into Armas's station, laughing at something he said, and playfully touching his arm. Jon scowled. But he couldn't tear his eyes away from watching Armas fire again. Even if he didn't have much muscle, his stance was a pleasing form.

"Whatchya looking at?"

Jon startled, crossing his arms, as Raimi walked up. His friend's black hair was freshly cut, keeping it close for regulation, and he was wearing his standard issue uniform, his last name NADAB stitched on the right side. He raised a brow at Jon.

"Just watching the new Advocate," Jon informed him. "Looks like he knows how to shoot."

Raimi mimicked Jon's posture. Jon's friend and former second-in-command followed his gaze. "He's good. Think he'll work out?"

"How should I know? I'm not a prophet."

Raimi raised an eyebrow. "A bit sour about this still, are we? You know my ass got chewed out for letting you follow through on disobeying the king's direct order."

Jon scratched the back of his neck. "At least you didn't get demoted," he said, motioning to the two half-circles above Raimi's surname signifying his rank as captain. "But I'm sorry about that. It was my call. I took full responsibility."

Raimi slapped his back. "I didn't think he'd dismiss

you, though."

Jon shrugged. "I thought getting the comm station back from the Stiners before it was in blackout range was a better call than allowing our fleet to fly into the moons blind." The prince and Raimi had been ordered to monitor the comm station the Stiners had taken control of. Jon had decided taking it back from Stiner control was worth the risk to assure the fleet's success.

He hadn't known then that his father had already paid off the Leki royal family who hired the Stiners, and the war was about to be over anyway. Jon didn't tell Raimi what he knew, either — that the Leki informant slaughtered during the victory celebration was Saul's way of covering his tracks. The king taking on the Call to Orders and the ritual cleansing of the soldiers from the blood of battle was just icing on the cake. Make it seem like God ordained it. That God condoned everything the king did.

"This is the Advocate?" Saul's voice called out. Jon's skin grew cold. He hadn't spoken to his father since he was dismissed from his post. He turned, watching the king approach with his bodyguards. He'd lost track of time, forgetting that his father planned to observe the new recruits around midday. The recruits, standing at the firing range stations, stopped, removed their headphones, and saluted the king, as did Raimi.

Armas put the rifle down, and raised his hand, a sort of half-salute. Jon snorted.

"What's your name?" the king demanded.

"Armas, sir — Your Majesty. I mean. Armas Lehem-Perez."

"Of the famed Lehem Farm?" Saul questioned.

"Yes, Your Majesty."

Saul avoided Jon's gaze, continuing to act as if he wasn't there. "At ease, everyone," he announced, and the recruits moved back to their firing stations. The king stepped forward, swiping on the target control panel next to the firing station, replaying all of Armas's shots, most dead-on. "I see your target work," he acknowledged to Armas. "Impressive. Have you ever seen battle?"

"No, my Lord."

"You will soon. I see my daughter has begun your training today." Jon bit back a curse as Saul blatantly ignored him. "The nation's Elders are preparing to meet for the next briefing soon. I want to see what you think."

"Already, sir — Your Majesty?"

"Zam believes you are sent by God to help me. This will be your first test. I'm counting on you, son," the king added as he placed his hand on the farm boy's shoulder.

Son. The flutters squashed under the pain of his father's rebuke, and the sting of jealousy overtook him. Jon's fists were clenched so tightly his fingernails dug into the skin of his palm. Raimi reached for him, but he shrugged out of his friend's grasp, turning to find someplace to escape, some refuge from his father's verbal destruction and Raimi's pity. Away from the pretty boy who'd usurped him.

He needed a drink, now.

"Speaking of which, the prophet didn't return with you?" the king asked, and Jon stopped on his heel, frowning. He'd wondered himself where Zam had gone off to.

"No, Father," Kyla responded. Jon gave her a questioning look.

"Well, where is he, then?"

Kyla's voice quivered. "He ...he ..."

"What? What happened? Was he not with you both?" the king asked.

The Dahan farm boy didn't flinch. "He was leaving on a shuttle."

Jon's eyes narrowed. He couldn't blame the prophet for leaving at the opportune moment, after the way Saul acted, but he'd hoped the old man would talk some sense into his father. Help him see what a bad example he was setting with torture and execution and assuming the role of prophet.

The king's hand flew to his chest. "Zam deserting us? No, he wouldn't do that."

"I'm sorry to say he did," Kyla said, her eyes on the ground in front of her.

Jon studied his father. He was lying, that much he knew. But his sister's performance was good. *Too good.* She was hiding something. She shifted her weight from one foot to the other, one of her tells when she was nervous.

"Then he is a blasphemer!"

The firing range went silent at the king's outburst. The three-week recruits, the guards — eyes widened, jaws dropped.

"He has abandoned our God and our ways." The king set his hand on Armas's shoulder. "This is the Advocate called by God. He will prove himself tonight, and we shall see if God is still with us. As for our prophet, he is to be caught and brought to trial for desertion."

Jon clenched his teeth. He was setting Armas up for something already? This couldn't be good. Maybe Jon had dodged a worse fate.

"There is no need, Father," Kyla said, her eyes focused now, set on the king. "He's dead."

She pulled a tablet from the inside of her jacket pocket and thrust it into the king's hands. Saul stared in horror, before sliding the image across the tablet, casting it to project on the security screens above the weapon racks.

There was a figure in the video. Jon couldn't quite make out where they were, as the video was somewhat grainy and mostly dark. It looked like a field of grain in the dim light. The figure raised their hands. "Princess, please, I must go," the prophet pleaded. "I will not serve the king any longer." While the quality was poor, the voice was Zam's.

"You know the price for treason," his sister's voice said, and Jon shuddered. She was the one filming the video, from a camera she must've pinned to her shoulder. A gun was raised, pointed at the prophet.

A shot fired.

The prophet fell into the shadows. The camera dipped down, showing a bloodied and broken body.

Zam's face was unmistakable.

Jon tasted bile as he rushed to get away from his father — and now his sister, too. *My God what did she do?* What happened to the little girl who loved Zam like another father? What happened to the sister who wanted to fly so badly, to shoot a weapon — was she willing to do *this* to get what she wanted? Who had she become?

He wasn't sure anymore.

Jon ran back down the ramp to the armory, leaving Raimi and Armas behind. The techs were still working, though he was certain Saul would soon share a security alert with the video, letting everyone know what happened to traitors.

He scanned the large hangar until he spotted her, closing a dark blue mech belonging to the Sim'ee unit. Sharda's blond hair was pulled back under a cap, the top half of her coveralls hanging down from her waist, exposing her black tank top. She slammed the lid shut on her toolbox.

Jon reached for her arm, startling her as he spun her around. "Can you get away for a bit?" he whispered. "I need ..."

He didn't finish his sentence.

She tilted her head "You look like you could use a drink."

The lights flashed in the hangar, and all the screens at workstations flipped to an emergency alert.

"Let's go," he whispered, reaching for her hand and tugging her along. Everyone else's attention focused on the emergency alert and the video he knew was about to play, and not on the prince leaving the armory with a pretty mech tech.

FOUR

ARMAS

Before the briefing began, Armas was escorted to the officer's mess, where the chef served him Jamin-style noodles with beef and sprouts and a spicy glaze. While he was eating, the screens on the walls flickered, switching to an emergency alert feed where the king himself shared a longer statement, that Zam the prophet had turned traitor and had forsaken the Nacaen peoples. He stopped watching when Zam stated he would no longer serve the king, not wanting to once again view the bloodied prophet's body at Kyla's feet. *She didn't do it, but the video looks so real —*

The noodles knotted in Armas's stomach, and he

threw the remainder into the compost bin.

All the officers stood as a man in a dark green uniform entered. He had white hair sprouting around his crown but was bald on top. Deep lines marred his bronze skin at his temples. Armas noted the thin gold leaf above the bars on his shoulder, indicating he was a major. "You. Advocate?"

It took Armas a second to recognize the man was speaking to him. "Um, yeah, I mean, yes sir." He saluted.

The older man's jaw clenched. "Come with me. The king has ordered you to the Situation Room."

He followed the major down the hallway lining the officer's quarters. On the way, he replayed in his head the events of the night before. He'd watched Kyla walking Zam to meet her contact in the field. It'd been dark, the light of the gas giant Horeb behind the barn then — but Zam had been alive when he followed Kyla, dipping out from the dim light over the edge of the field, near the old war bunkers. *The prophet is alive, and at Ramah by now,* he repeated in his head like a mantra, though he kept the lie whispered on his lips, "the princess killed the traitor prophet," so he would not forget and say the wrong thing.

Armas's heart threatened to pound out of his chest as he met Saul, coming the opposite way down the main corridor. He saluted, but the king waved him off, and together, they entered the Situation Room.

The door slammed shut behind them and Armas jumped. He stood with his hands behind his back, unsure of his place. He'd worry about Kyla later. Right now, he was with the king in a long white room, with an oval table, screens on the walls and tablets at each seat, filled with the Elder representatives of each nation of the united system. The screens across from him displayed scanner visuals from Horeb's rings, and orbital views of each habitable moon: Melas, Richo, and Samar. Nidos, the only habitable planet in the system and closest to the Cana Star, was known for its orbital shipyards that constructed the warships sent to protect the other worlds. Jon mentioned it earlier — their nations were delayed sending the new ships.

The twelve national Elders rose when the king entered the room but took their seats as Saul sat at the head of the table. The major who escorted Armas took a seat next to the king, and an Elder began the briefing without introductions. "The Phenians are following the heels of the Leki defeat," she said, pointing to the screen. Her thick reddish-brown hair was pulled into a bun, the crimson sash draped across her black uniform signifying she was the Hessan representative from Nidos. Her expression was stern, but no lines marred her rich brown complexion. "It's no secret they want control of Horeb's fuel mines, but now that we're a unified system, they're gunning for the capital world. Both the Leki and the Phenians have suffered cataclysmic climate change on their home worlds, but Balec still has breathable air for the Leki. The Phenians don't and are desperate. Their drop ships have entered the system — they're coming to take us on the surface."

"As I had foreseen, Elder Diez," the king said, bringing his fingertips together in front of him. "We annihilated the Leki fighters with their Stiner mercenary ships in the rings of Horeb, and the Phenians thought to catch us off guard."

"But if we bring in our fighters to attack the drop ships, we leave our moons vulnerable again," the major who had summoned Armas advised, looking right at him. Armas realized he was the Elder representative for the Jamin. "And we'd lose a number of fighters in the process."

Armas's knees wobbled. He locked his legs into place, trying to steady his breathing. *What the hell did I just get myself into?* The tiny bit of information Jon had given him about the drop ships was all he really knew.

A woman with amber hair and ivory skin, wearing the gold and sea-blue colors of the Lubez nation of Nidos, cleared her throat. "If we would apply to join the Interplanetary Alliance —"

Elder Diez, who began the briefing, pointed at her. "Our people didn't survive crossing the Red Nebula hundreds of years ago to assimilate into the Alliance. As it is, their foothold in the Outer Systems is weak. Even the Leki left them years ago."

The rep from Lubez leaned forward. "We can rush a couple of warships from Nidos, if you give backup with your Bluehawks —"

"Where were your warships in the last battle?" the dark-skinned Sim'ee man across the table demanded, his short, curled black hair streaked with silver. While others wore dress uniforms, he wore a blue flight suit. A thin, three-pronged leaf was pinned to his shoulder — Armas guessed he was also a major, but the Sim'ee had a different design. "You've been promising them for months! We can't sacrifice any more of our own Bluehawks and Sparrowings."

"We're still rebuilding from the prior assault!" the Lubez representative countered.

"Right. That's why we can't depend on Nidos," the Sim'ee Elder said. "This has to be a ground war. We know our landscape better than the Phenians. We know our strengths and weaknesses."

"But their armor is stronger —"

"They've terrorized other nations in the Bara System —"

"They launch a bioweapon and we're done —"

Saul raised his hand, and silence fell across the arguing Elders at the table. The king swiveled in his chair to Armas, who still stood at attention, as best as he knew how, by the door. "This is Armas, of the Lehem-Perez family."

"Your Majesty," Armas acknowledged, all eyes landing on him.

"They were heroes of Melas," Saul continued, "of a time not long ago when we were trying to unite the nations, and here we are again. Armas was chosen by God, so our former prophet said, to be an advocate and advisor. What do you propose, Advocate?"

Sweat broke across his hairline. If only Eliot had been chosen. His older brother at least had combat experience, understood the risks and the cost. All the lives now on the table. But Eliot wasn't here, and Armas had never been one to take the initiative. He ran his fingers through his hair. He had to come up with something, some plan. *Help me*, he prayed.

"Your Majesty," the Jamin Elder began. "Are you certain —"

"Yes, *Abe*." The sharp look from the king caused the Elder to shrink back in his chair. "Do not discount his age. Despite the prophet's betrayal, my daughter confirmed this is the one God has favored. We will listen." The king motioned to Armas. "Go on."

His heart still beat fast. "I think he — I'm sorry, I don't know your name, sir?" Armas said to the Sim'ee Elder.

"Major Milo Barish, representative Elder of the Sim'ee

nation.”

“I think you’re right, Major Barish,” Armas began, stepping forward and setting his palms on the table. *Courage. Focus. You can do this.* “The only way to win this is on our turf.”

Barish nodded. “We try to fight the Phenians in orbit, and we’ll be destroyed. It’s neutral territory but an unequal playing field.”

“On the surface we have the advantage.” Armas added, remembering conversations with Eliot when he prepared to ship out for his first tour.

“Our cities are spread out, and we know where all our old bunkers are,” Major Barish added. “We know our arsenal. We know how to fortify our defenses.”

All Armas really knew were the old bunkers on Lehem Farm, but he suspected that other lands of Melas must be the same. The Jamin and Sim’ee had the same history on their shared world, the same metal bunkers and antiaircraft missile launchers. His great-grandparents hid out in the bunkers on the farm during the Dibon assault, almost eighty years ago.

“What about Ogroma?” Abe, the Jamin representative, interjected. Murmurs broke out among the other Elders.

Saul held up his hand again. “It’s been confirmed the Phenians have hired Ogroma. Apparently the Leki aren’t the only people mercenaries make deals with in the Outer Systems.”

“Your Majesty, I object. We ought to fight them in orbit,” the Elder who argued about their armor said, his accent carrying the brogue often associated with the wintry moon Samar. He was younger than the others, though not as young as Armas, but with a slightly tan complexion like his own. The orange square on his olive-green uniform signified the Reshar nation's flag. "Even if we have the advantage on land, Ogroma will demolish our mechs. Their technology — it's like they meld their minds to the machine and fight as one giant." His face flushed. "I've seen them before when I traveled to the Bara system. We canna defeat them."

Armas surveyed the room. Fear rippled through in a wave that could paralyze them. But what choice did they have? The Phenians were coming, and bringing Ogroma, and the best way to win was in territory they knew well.

"Not unless we force them into a trap," Armas responded.

All eyes focused on him.

"What kind of trap?" Abe questioned, folding his arms.

He thought back to the farm just the day before. "Like my dog Roxy, herding the sheep into their pen."

Laughter erupted. Abe rolled his eyes. "This is what that crazy prophet turned up," the Lubez Elder snickered from the other side of the table.

Major Barish held up his hand. "Maybe you need some bait, some target they can't resist."

The other Elders grew quiet. "Are you serious?" Abe asked.

Barish beckoned him to continue. The tightness in Armas's chest eased. *At least one Elder doesn't think I'm useless.* "Where are they most likely to attack?" Armas asked.

"Either here, to try to wipe out the capitol, or Zek, in the Sim'ee homeland," Major Barish said. "Because we manufacture the Bluehawks. They'll try to destroy our ability to renew our fighter ships."

Armas glanced at the king, but he said nothing, only arching an eyebrow.

"That's where we need to set the trap. Zek." Armas folded his arms. "We need to bait it so there's no way they'll try for Glia."

"That can be done," Saul said. "I will make sure it's known I am touring the Bluehawk facility with an extended stay in Zek."

Gasps broke across the room. "Your Majesty, you shouldn't risk yourself —" Abe began, but the king cut him off.

"We don't have much time," Saul replied. "We must move the troops quickly. What do you have in mind?"

"I need to see what we're dealing with," Armas said, pointing to the screen.

Barish began typing on his tablet. "You'll need every schematic, every blueprint, anything we've got on our assets, bunkers, topography."

The king cleared his throat. "Make sure he has everything he needs." He gave a pointed look to Abe. "It is decided. We move under the cover of darkness tomorrow evening to Zek."

Armas trembled. They were going with *his* plan. A plan that might get them all — and the king — killed.

God, please don't.

The king gestured to Major Barish. "Contact the leaders to evacuate all civilians from the shipyards and move the people of Zek into protective bunkers." He stood, and the Elders rose and bowed to him, Armas following a half-second behind them.

"Armas," the king said. "You work with Major Barish on planning this trap. Every resource you need is yours, every command you give right now has my authority."

"Y-yes, Your Majesty," Armas stammered, breathing out hard in both relief and fear. The king approved. A king who was ruthless, who would do everything he could not to lose, had put his trust in *him*.

And now he had to plan a battle with no training.

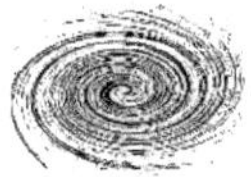

Armas made his way to his quarters an hour before dawn, having spent all evening and night going over the topography of Zek and the surrounding area with Major Barish. At long last, they'd found it — a canyon that would work as a sheep pen. If the Phenians, and especially Ogroma, took the bait.

Frowning, Armas realized he'd taken a wrong turn. He'd been assigned a former officer's quarters, but in the whirlwind tour he'd forgotten if it was two lefts, a right and a left, or two rights, a left and a right. He came to a T-junction with a sign and discovered he was by the maintenance crew barracks.

If he couldn't find his way back to his quarters, how could he find his way around a battlefield? "God, I'm in over my head." He placed his hands on his skull, pressure and pain building up. "Help me."

Laughter rolled down the corridor. Armas spotted Jon: his face beet red, his arms entwined around a long-haired blonde. "Shhhh," Jon said, not even noticing Armas. "Don't tell anyone."

The girl laughed loudly, as Jon drew his finger across her lips, before moving his own lips to her neck, unzipping her coveralls. Armas recognized the mech tech crew uniform from the armory. She pushed Jon gently back, laughing and straightening the top of her coveralls. "Not now, Jonny. You're too drunk."

"I'm not dat drunk," he mumbled.

"You can barely stand ... Jon — Jon!" the girl said,

spotting Armas, and slapping Jon's shoulder.

The king's son looked down the hall, his eyes squinting as if to make him out. "Oh shit."

The girl slid out from his grasp. "I'll see you later, Jonny."

"Bye, Sharrrrrda."

She brushed by Armas's shoulder.

Armas stuck his hands in his pockets, as Jon slid against the wall to the floor, his face still scarlet, his eyes bloodshot. "Stardust and ashes," he swore again.

"Do you need help?" Armas asked.

"No. Yes. Don't tell my father," Jon added, gagging a little.

Armas hadn't meant to stare, and despite his exhaustion and feeling lost in more ways than one, Jon had helped him earlier, and he felt he owed him. "I think you should get back to your room," Armas said, reaching his hand out to Jon. The prince took hold, and Armas pulled him to his feet. "Show me the way."

Drunkenly, Jon pointed out the way to the secret passage that led to the palace, embedded into the western side of the fortress. There were guards along the way, especially as they neared the lift, but they simply nodded if they acknowledged him at all. No one questioned why he was with the prince in the palace, and none offered to help. *Must be a regular occurrence,* Armas thought as he put his arm around Jon to steady him. They walked through a set of heavy metal doors and up a great marble staircase. The prince fumbled, entering his security code three times before he got it right and the door opened.

Inside was a spacious apartment, about the size of the entire first floor of his family's farmhouse. A stark living area with a small kitchen, a bedroom with navy blue linens and dark curtains, and a bathroom. The floors were all white marble covered with thick, plush rugs.

Armas helped Jon to the couch in the living area. The prince slumped forward, elbows on his knees, cradling his head. "Oh God."

"Are you going to throw up?"

"No."

"If it helps, I won't say anything." Armas said as he sat next to the prince. He'd seen Shane drunk plenty of times. Even Eliot snuck a girl into the barn once or twice. They had an unwritten rule to keep each other's secrets. A brother's silent pledge.

Jon rubbed his face. "Thanks."

Armas wasn't sure what to do. The prince probably shouldn't be alone, but Armas needed to sleep before the troops moved out.

"Look, you don't have to be nice to me," Jon said, avoiding his gaze.

Armas frowned. "You were nice to *me*. I know your father ... I know I've stepped into the role you had. You didn't let that get in the way of helping me get started. And I want to make sure you're okay."

Jon's eyes drooped, bloodshot and glistening. He rubbed them with the heel of his hand. "I can't believe she killed him."

So that's what this is about. Armas let out a breath. He'd thought Jon was upset with him. He sat down next to him on the couch. *I have to give him something, some reason to hold on to hope.* "Maybe she didn't."

"What?" Jon lifted his eyes.

Armas swallowed hard. He'd played the part for Saul, but this was different. "I didn't *see* her kill him, that's all."

"But the video?" Jon ran his finger through his hair. "I

mean ... I don't want to believe she did it. She didn't agree with Father killing the Leki prisoner."

Armas exhaled harshly. *What can I say that doesn't give Kyla's secret away?* "The last time I saw the prophet, he was alive."

Jon tossed his head back. "I don't know what to think." He closed his eyes.

Armas gave a silent prayer of gratitude that Jon didn't push any further. He glanced at the door. "I should go — the assault plans and all —"

Jon's lids flew open. "What assssault?"

Armas leaned toward him. "We're getting ready to move out this evening, in preparation against the Phenians. Ground war."

The prince coughed. "Damn fools."

"It's the only way we can win. Lure them into a trap on our turf, in the ways we know how to fight."

Jon looked Armas in the eye. "We'll get slaughtered out there. Ogroma is too strong."

Armas swore. All the confidence he'd mustered for the briefing faded. He sank back, lacing his fingers together on top of his head.

"If Ogroma is made of Airysan steel ... I need to know everything about Airysan mechs." His brow furrowed. "Can you help me? Help me know every shortcoming, every flaw, every weakness?"

The prince shook his head. "You can't stop them from crushing you."

"No, but I can stop them if they have the same weaknesses. You know how on wool sweaters, if there's a thread loose and you pull it, you can end up unraveling the whole thing?"

Jon blinked at him.

The shepherd sighed. "Wool sweaters. Don't tell me only Dahan keep sheep."

"Jamin are hunters. We shoot game."

Armas sat up straight. "There must be a tech weakness, maybe a virus that can bring down a mech suit."

Jon's eyes widened. "Not a virus, but the Liphcs suits have outdated commands. Maybe we could find …"

Jon didn't finish his sentence because he lurched forward. Armas reached for him, but the prince managed to get his feet under him and make it to the bathroom before retching into the toilet. Armas winced, gagging on the stench, before following Jon. He pulled a white towel down from the wall as the prince flushed, wetting it in the sink before handing it to him.

"Thanks." Jon wiped his face, moving to sit down on the cool tile floor. "I'm sorry you have to see me like this."

"Why *are* you like this?"

"He ordered Zam killed, and whether he's dead or not doesn't matter. He's *gone*. The only one who could ever turn Father from his bad decisions. He chose you to replace me. I thought he'd cool off after a while, but he's acting like I don't exist, like I'm nothing."

Armas frowned, and sat down, cross-legged on the floor, the smell fading enough for him to stay. "I need your help, but I'm going to need you sober."

"That's going to take a while, even with detox meds."

"So come with me," Armas urged. "We're leaving in ten hours. Take the detox, sleep it off, then run over all the tech with me in flight."

"I don't think my father will allow —"

Armas tilted his head. "He told me I could have every resource I need. I *need* you."

Something in the way Jon gazed back at him made his chest ache. The intensity in his green eyes even if he was drunk. No one had ever looked at him like that before. His heart beat all the way in his suddenly very dry throat. "I know how to repair physical damage to the outer armor. I don't know the tech — we just had basic farming software we uploaded after wiping the mech's memory clean. I need you to explain it and show me."

Jon's lips curved slightly. "Okay."

Armas helped Jon clean up and found a dose of detox meds in a cabinet. He walked with Jon into his bedroom. "Don't miss the flight. I can't do this without your help."

Jon's eyelids fluttered as he lay down, and Armas pulled up the dark blue bedspread over him, watching him for a moment. Something about seeing the prince broken, seeing who he really was — it didn't bring up pity, but compassion. Armas had heard stories of the king's son, the warrior, but finding him this way made him real. A broken soul in need of healing.

I can't do this without you.

He closed the door to Jon's quarters softly, but as he turned, he gasped, hand on his chest.

Kyla stood across the hall, staring at him, her hand resting on her hip near her weapon. The holoimage of her standing over the prophet's body flashed in his mind.

FIVE

KYLA

“What are you doing?” she asked.

“He’s not feeling well,” Armas said, his cheeks flushed.

Kyla frowned. Her heart still beat fast, seeing Armas against her brother’s door. She hadn’t expected her father to ask about Zam in public, to declare to everyone the prophet was a traitor — she thought she could show him in private and that would be enough.

Only Armas knew the truth, and he stood with his eyes focused on the floor as if he couldn’t bear to look her in the eye.

“Is he awake?” she asked, motioning toward Jon’s door.

Armas shook his head.

Kyla rubbed her forehead. "I have to tell him."

His eyes narrowed as he finally caught her gaze. "I need you to tell me the truth. Again."

Kyla drew breath to speak, but the hallway wasn't the place. She glanced at the security camera positioned above her and Jon's doors and frowned. She knew the double-standard. Her father didn't approve of Jon's choices of partners at times, but he'd get off with a stern warning. She, on the other hand, was forbidden to bring anyone to her room outside of family and servants. Laina, her maid, would be arriving soon with her breakfast and to help her get ready for the day, but for now, they were alone. Normally, security couldn't care less what Saul's children did — the cameras were for their protection — but it only took one person to slip to her father. Even with Armas the Advocate, she didn't trust what her father might do if he found out.

Damn her father's judgments.

She grabbed Armas's arm and pulled him into her quarters, shutting the door behind her. Her apartment mirrored Jon's — a living area, bedroom and bathroom, but hers had a balcony that overlooked the courtyard, and the plush couches and high-backed chairs were decorated with colorful pillows and throws, compared to Jon's minimalist design.

"You know I didn't kill Zam."

"The vid looks pretty real," Armas retorted, crossing his arms and staring back at her.

Kyla shook her head. "How else do you think I can convince my father? I didn't expect him to ask me about it in front of everyone."

"How'd you do it?"

"Zam's idea," Kyla said, noting the dark circles below his blue eyes that searched hers. "I added the blood visuals after we got back, but we staged his death there. My contact even carried Zam off in case anyone was watching in the distance. We had to make it appear as real as possible."

Saul seemed to accept the video's authenticity, and she hoped he found no reason to doubt her. If someone had a reason to dissect the video, they might be able to determine there were added effects. Still, Zam did a good job of playing dead, with his pale complexion and breathing so shallow it wasn't noticeable in the darkness. Part of his deteriorating condition, kept at bay by the strong medicinal tea he drank.

Armas raised a dubious brow.

"I don't know what I can say to convince you. Ramah is where Zam grew up. The temple there is underground, mostly run by Tananites now —"

"The king outlawed their practice."

Kyla rolled her shoulder. "They know how to hide in plain sight, how to worship in secret. Zam's not happy about it, but it was the best place to hide him, somewhere Saul would never look to find him. He's safe."

His eyes narrowed. *He doesn't believe it.* She ran her palm over her hair, tugging on the end of her braid. It was dangerous to share this information, but no one could spy on them from inside her room.

"Here, I'll show you." She pulled the secondary burner comm from her pocket and swiped to the encrypted file of the shuttle Zam had taken arriving at Ramah. There was no satellite imagery because the satellites orbiting that moon were destroyed years ago, but the transponder ping showed the shuttle's last known position. "There. The shuttle is long gone, and they've changed their transponder now, but here's the proof he made it."

"He made it," Armas repeated, his eyes softening. She breathed out in relief that he believed her.

He leaned against the back of the armchair, stifling a yawn as she set the comm down. "Have you been up all night?" she asked, changing the subject.

"Yeah."

"Are you okay?" She took a step toward him.

Armas shrugged. "I'm heading out to plan a battle based on my experience herding sheep with my dog."

Her jaw dropped.

He gripped the back of the chair, locking his arms. She noted the sweat gathering on his brow.

"Hey," Kyla said, recognizing the panic emanating from him. "You're safe in here. There are no cameras, no recording devices. You don't have to be afraid with me."

"I don't know what the hell I'm doing."

"I understand that feeling. It's overwhelming. But Zam *believes* in you, and I trust him." She dared to touch his jaw, the slight stubble grazing her fingers. Armas swallowed under her touch. She cupped the side of his face, forcing his eyes to lock on hers. "If my father is already listening to you, then he believes in you as well."

Or is setting you up to take the fall.

Kyla dropped her hand, averting her eyes. With Zam away safely, her feelings shifted toward protecting this Dahan farmer, the way he'd tried to protect Zam without even knowing him. She wanted him to be safe from her father's rash decisions.

"I've never been in war," he said quietly.

"I haven't either," she admitted, turning back to him. He blinked. "I've gone through basic training and flight school and am confined to the royal shuttle."

"I'm about to get a lot of people killed, even if by some miracle it works. I can't imagine having to ... kill. Or watch people die." He trembled. "I could barely handle the video of Zam, even if — *even though* — it's fake."

Kyla reached for his hand, and he released the back of the chair as she clasped it. "You are a good person. This doesn't have to change who you are inside. My father is ruthless, sometimes cruel. You are not. *Remember* who you are."

A muscle flexed in his jaw. "Jon warned me this morning I might not be cut out for it."

Kyla tugged him closer. "Armas, look at me."

His eyes glistened.

"Jon's seen combat but Dad — my father — tries to keep him out of it when possible. Which makes Jon do riskier things sometimes. But you don't have to be like Jon, or my father." *Please don't be like them.* "You can do this, and I know Jon will support you."

"I've asked him to help me."

"That's good," she said. "He'll feel useful." She shot a glance to her door. *Divine Starre, keep Jon safe. Stop him from doing anything rash.*

"I should go," Armas said, his breath soft on her face. She hadn't realized she'd drawn so close to him.

Heat rose in her cheeks as she let go of his hand and stepped back. "Of course. I'm ..." Her words jumbled on her flustered tongue. "Armas, no matter what happens, out on the battlefield, or with my father — know I'm on your side. If you need anything, just ask."

Kyla went to the door. "Don't let anyone know you

were here." She opened the door and let him pass. But as he crossed the threshold, he glanced back.

"Thank you. And, um, can you tell me how to get back to my quarters?"

Goddesses, he was adorably hopeless. "Officer's section. Go down the stairs and turn right — the guards will let you out the doors to our wing, they saw you come in with Jon — then follow the corridor back around the Great Hall toward the fortress. Officer section will be the first left after the junction."

He nodded to her, stuffing his hands in his pockets as he went down the stairs. She watched him all the way down, until he made the turn for the doors, and exhaled deeply. A warmth spread through her veins. He was everything Zam hoped for, and he was now here, an Advocate for her father, someone to help lift the people's spirits toward their king.

He was perfect, in every way.

"Your Highness?" a voice called from the bottom of the stairs. Laina, who had cared for her since her mother became ill, stared up at her. "I wasn't expecting you up so early."

"I was just helping Jon's friend find his way back," she said. True enough. She never wanted to lie to Laina, but she also knew her maid wouldn't speak out of turn. The tall maid flipped a blond braid over her brown shoulders. She bore a thin silver tattoo on her upper arm, visible from her sleeveless shirt.

"I'll get your breakfast, then," she said, her Tali accent lilting as she reached the top of the stairs. She cast a glance back down and her lips curved slightly. "He is handsome."

"Laina," Kyla said, rolling her eyes at her maid's teasing. "He's Dad's Advocate, and Jon's friend."

"Ah." She shook her head, but her smile didn't leave as she passed Kyla and headed to the kitchenette in the princess's quarters.

"Thank you, again," Kyla said, following her. "For your contact."

Laina raised a brow. "Do not mention it, Your Highness."

Kyla nodded. Her maid's connections to her people on Nidos had helped Kyla find the pilot, though Laina didn't know who was on board or the nature of the mission. Kyla picked up the burner comm from where she'd left it on the table, swiped to the encrypted file, and deleted it.

She pocketed the comm and leaned against the doorframe, staring back down the steps. Armas wasn't interested in her — that was abundantly clear as he never even tried to make a move, though she'd given him every opportunity. Or maybe he was too afraid of what Saul would do. She was the princess. She was off-limits to everyone until her father made a match for her. Yet *another* choice for her own life out of her hands.

Or his mind was on the upcoming mission, in which he might be killed, and all Melas taken by the Phenians. She hoped he was smarter than her father, who'd blindly put his trust in him.

As much as she trusted Zam, Armas was one person. One human being who had the weight of the entire world on his shoulders. Loyalty, ethics, goodness — the qualities that made her heart hum.

Qualities the current king *and* the future king should hold.

Kyla's thoughts went back to Jon, and she frowned. He

must've been drunk when Armas found him, probably in the bed of the mech tech he'd been seeing in secret.

Every time Jon got on Saul's bad side, he'd get drunk, but her brother always came to her, trusted her. This time he'd shut her out. She'd witnessed the burning anger in his eyes when Saul showed the image. Zam had kept things in check, and now he was gone. Who did Jon have left? He'd trusted her before, but Saul's display of her mock vid had ruined everything.

She crossed the hall and gently knocked on the door. "Jon? Are you up?"

He didn't respond.

"It's not what you think," she said to the closed door, leaning against it, her voice low. "I promise you: I'll never betray you."

SIX

ARMAS

A week ago, Armas had pushed a sheep out from the creek embankment it was stuck in.

Now, he pushed on a black Airysan mech while operating his dull green Liphes steel suit out from the rubble on one side of the valley, with the Phenians firing two clicks away from the other side. The enemy had launched from the drop ship the day before, entering the atmosphere above the Sim'ee continent as Major Barish had predicted. The Melas Unified Military, with their mech units, had been waiting for them in the bunkers near Zek, forcing the Phenians into the steep valley. They were matched almost evenly, machine to machine.

"Dark Wolf, you okay?"

"Yeah," Jon grunted over the comm. "Almost free."

Armas wedged his Liphes shoulder under Jon's giant Airysan foot, which was dangling in air, shoving until Jon was able to grab onto a boulder above. He and Jon were supposed to stay off the front lines, but the battle shifted, and here they were, clinging to the edge while missiles launched and rail guns fired above them.

"Got it!" Armas dug into the rock until Jon's other foot, slightly crushed by the rubble, was free. Jon used his thrusters to leap over the rubble to the outcropping above, and Armas scrambled up the valley wall nearby. The Liphes suit was smaller and more vulnerable to damage, but he'd found his response time almost equal to Jon's in the advanced Airysan model. Liphes control systems were also easier for a shepherd-turned-soldier to learn in a week's time to fight in.

The ground shook near them, rocks tumbling past them as the Phenians launched another missile. "We've got to get them further into the valley," Armas shouted over the roar of the return fire.

"Red Lion, this is Gray Wolf, what's your status?" Saul called out. The Jamin used the wolf as their call signs; Sime'ee and Dahan used lions. Jesse had told Armas that his great-grandmother's call sign was Lioness. *Eliot deserves the call sign, not me in this metal can.* Of course, his brother also flew transports, not fighters, and didn't have red hair.

"I'm with Dark Wolf and Wolf Two," Armas replied, as Raimi joined them in a dark blue Airysan suit, scrambling up the same side after him. "The Phenians are hesitating. We've got to get them to chase us."

"Chase you? That will get you killed!" Saul shouted.

"Your Majesty, it's our best shot right now. We surprised them but now they've got the advantage." Armas turned to Raimi. "Any sign of Ogroma?"

"Negative. Satellite image shows they launched, though. Hiding somewhere."

Armas swore. They must've suspected the trap. "What do you think?" he asked Jon, hoping his voice sounded steady and not betraying the fear crawling on the back of his neck.

"We do your plan. It's gotta work."

"But Ogroma isn't on the scopes," Raimi pointed out.

The Advocate bit the inside of his lip. Pull the trigger too soon, and the mercenary unit would still have to be dealt with. The other Elders had told stories about Ogroma to Armas on the trip from Glia. While the Modes in the Near Side systems had augmented their bodies with technology for years, this particular team connected their minds via specialized augments at the brain stem, a practice outlawed among all the worlds of the Interplanetary Alliance in the Near Side Systems. One massive machine, with five brains.

But the scanners on the suit display showed him most of the Phenian mechs were entering the valley. No monsters. Maybe the stories were wrong.

An older Liphes model suit approached, the red paint dulled and patched with unpainted metal, controlled by the Dahan nation representative. "Sir," Major Zeru's voice carried over the comm, "We're prepared to fall back."

Armas looked to Jon, but he pointed back at him from the suit. "You're in command of this mission," the prince reminded him.

"Major Zeru," Armas said to the soldier in the red suit,

"call your units in." He then signaled the king. "Gray Wolf, White Lion: it's time to give the signal."

"Are you sure?" Saul asked. Armas couldn't see him or Major Barish, the White Lion, on his viewscreen.

Armas breathed in deep. "They're coming into the valley; it's go time."

Saul gave the order. "All squads, retreat. Repeat: all squads, retreat."

Major Zeru's suit saluted Armas. "Gold Lions, fall back," she called out. Armas swallowed a lump. Shane was due to be assigned to that unit, normally guarding Glia. But he was safe at home for a few more weeks.

The Melas mech fighters fell back toward the east. Sure enough, the Phenian mechs followed them, but kept their distance and stayed near the rim of the valley a click away, instead of following into the tight canyon.

"They know it's a trap," Armas said on the comm. "We've got to get them to believe they have *us* trapped, in order for this to work."

Armas killed the connection and took off before Jon or Raimi could protest, leaping over the outcropping and running down the side of the valley, where he'd climbed only moments before. He didn't look back to see if Raimi and Jon were following him, knowing they probably cursed his name on the comm.

An orange and black Phenian mech fired, missing only by centimeters, but the force of the blast propelled Armas to the valley floor. Before he could pull himself up, Jon was at his side, tugging on his mech arm, close enough Armas could hear him yelling through his suit. He winced, turning his comm back on.

"What the hell do you think you're doing?" Jon shouted.

"Getting them to follow!"

Sure enough, the Phenian mechs began to descend from the valley's edge, following the Melas Unified Military mechs into the canyon. Some were orange and black; the rest yellow with splotches of gray, the color of the toxic desert landscape of their home world in the Bara System. Armas waited. One second. Two seconds. Three.

"Run!" Armas called out, and Jon took the lead, with Raimi on Armas's heels, running down the valley floor into the canyon, the walls rising up seven hundred meters.

The sharp whistle above let Armas know their diminished Bluehawk fleet had arrived to provide cover. *What if Eliot was up there?* He shook the thought from his head. His older brother flew transports. He would not see combat.

"Red Lion, we're in position," Saul called on the comm.

"We're almost there!" Armas shouted.

The prince stopped in front of him. "I'm prepping the package!"

Suddenly Jon's damaged mech foot slid on a patch of loose gravel, and he went tumbling down. Armas and Raimi stopped to help him when a blast shook both to the ground.

Armas's helm display fizzled and went out.

"You okay?" Raimi asked him.

"Yeah, my system just went down," Armas said, grunting as he moved to one knee.

That's when he realized the lower part of his mech leg was missing.

"Shit, Armas," Jon said, his voice shaking.

Armas bit the inside of his cheek, cutting off the panic.

"I'm all right. I'm not hurt," he insisted, wiggling his toes to convince himself he'd not lost a limb. He'd drawn his foot up while running, and that motion saved his leg from being severed. But with his system down, his shields were also off-line. He was sitting in a metal can with little defense.

Raimi whistled. "You're exposed. We've got to get you out of here."

"No!" Armas shouted back. If he could just get the damn system back online, he could pull up his shields and counterbalance with thrusters the rest of the way.

Proton rifle fire pounded the ground behind him. "We've got you," Jon shouted, and he and Raimi took Armas's mech by the arms. They ran, Armas between them, though his suit refused to reboot. They half-carried him around the bend until they reached the canyon's edge.

Most of the Melas mech team was assembled, their back against the steep rock wall, and the Phenian mechs were closing in by the dozens. Five hundred meters. Four. Three. Two. One hundred fifty.

"This is it," Gray Wolf said. "Dark Wolf, send the package."

"Yes!"

Armas's system finally rebooted, and his shields restored just as he received Jon's widebeam comm message, a call to surrender overtop an obvious corrupted file. Armas still clung to Jon and Raimi's mechs as they raised their arms. The system locked down the virus to purge it, but Armas denied the purge command. "This has gotta work," he muttered to Jon.

"It should. Look."

The Phenian mechs had their arms pointed at the

Melas mechs, their guns open and ready to fire, as they lined up along the canyon floor. They should've received the widebeam by now, Armas thought, but Jon didn't say anything.

"Purge it," Armas urged. They had to take the bait.

Seconds passed, and the Phenians pulled into formation, a semicircle around them only fifty meters away, the guns mounted on their arms aimed at the Melas mechs. A message came from the Phenians. "We will accept your surrender when King Saul comes forward."

Jon's mech rotated slightly. Saul had remained in the bunkers. "They're not going for it."

"Come on," Armas urged through gritted teeth.

At once, the Phenian mechs dropped their arms in front of them, heads falling forward as they purged the fake virus Jon had loaded.

Accepting the message and purging the infected file triggered the actual virus: a command to reboot their systems. Every single mech that purged the file rebooted. For one brief moment, the enemy was shut down.

"FIRE!" Gray Wolf called on the comm.

"Wait!" Armas shouted, but it was no use — his comm link had been cut off.

This wasn't the plan! The plan was to ask for the Phenians to surrender and to accept it. Not to murder them the moment their shields rebooted.

The Melas mechs raised their arms and opened fire, cutting the Phenians to pieces. Armas gaped as the machines in front of him fell over, their shields down. Mechanical fluid and blood intermixed, flowing into the soil.

Jon faced him, bringing the head of his mech close to Armas's so he could hear. "It's no use! This is what he does. He had no intention of accepting a surrender from them."

Armas sank in his suit. Jon let him fall to his severed mech leg. Raimi had already left their side, the weapons fire ceasing, and he moved toward the downed Phenian suits, searching for survivors. "Get me out of this," Armas ordered the prince, not bothering to soften his tone to the royal.

Jon relented, helping Armas open the back hatch. He unhooked the connections from the suit to his helmet and climbed out from the metal frame, ignoring the rope ladder since his suit was already bent at one knee and missing the rest of the other leg. He noted the Bara Sharpshooter pistol, standard issue, tucked inside the right-side compartment of his suit, but left it behind. Unnecessary when there might not be any survivors anyway. The smell of burned flesh and rubber hit his nose hard and he gagged.

His eyes widened as he scanned the valley before him. All the enemy mechs were down. Some fighters opened their hatches, hands raised. Raimi and some of the other Melas mech fighters rounded them up. The Phenians wore half-masks covering their nose and mouth, the oxygen and nitrogen of the Nacaen worlds too rich for them to breathe.

Armas was relieved they weren't all dead, but a sharp pain nudged in his chest. He glanced down and yanked a piece of shrapnel out of his chest guard. He hadn't realized a bullet had pierced the mech when his shields went down. The light armor he wore inside the suit seemed less protective now that he could see just how fragile the Phenians were out of theirs.

The pain didn't cease. He'd seen death on the farm.

He'd seen the doctored image of Zam's body. But this was real.

"You all right?" Jon asked from inside his mech.

"How can this be right? The whole point was to get them to surrender — that was the plan! The king agreed to it!" Armas kicked at a rock in front of him, and it tumbled ahead. He glanced up at the valley walls above, swallowing hard. The other plan, suggested by an Elder to Major Barish just over a day ago, was to blast the steep canyon walls following the command shutdown, burying the enemy alive. He and the major had both objected, mainly because they would lose too many mechs of their own.

The king had kept another plan up his sleeve. Kyla had warned him more than once of Saul's cruelty. "We need to get the survivors out of here."

"Prisoners," Jon reminded him. "The survivors are over there."

Armas wheeled, watching some of his fellow troops crawling out from their damaged mechs. A few bodies lay on the ground near their machines, some grotesquely disfigured. Some with limbs smashed and bowels spilled. The sight sent him over the edge. He spun around, yanking his helmet off in time to retch behind his damaged mech.

But as he wiped his mouth with the back of his gloved hand, fear shivered down his spine. *Ogroma.* They weren't here. There was no sign of a giant mech, no weapons stronger than those carried by the usual Liphes and Airysan suits.

So where were they?

"We've got to get out of here!" Armas shouted as he put his helmet back on, connecting his comm to his bodysuit battery pack. Jon didn't answer. Armas followed Jon's gaze to the three Airysan mechs floating down on their thrusters: King Saul's unpainted dark metal mech, Major Barish in white, and Major Abe Renk, the Jamin commander, in dark green.

"We've taken out the Phenians," Saul said. "Their air forces are retreating."

"Your Majesty — what about Ogroma?" Armas asked, desperate.

Abe answered, "They're not appearing on any of our scopes. It's possible the shrouded shutdown command took them out as well."

Armas folded his arms. "They might have circumvented the shutdown command. With Mode technology, they might be fortified against it."

Major Barish swore over the comm. "We need to get the hell out of here."

"Affirmative," Saul agreed. "Get the wounded out first." The king started to turn, but stopped, his mech towering over Armas's frame, the hilt of the electromagnetic sword sticking out over his shoulder. "What is going on?"

Armas followed the king's line of sight to the Phenian survivors. "We're rounding up the prisoners," he answered Saul.

"On whose authority?" the king demanded.

"Mine," Jon interjected, stepping between the king and his advocate. "I sent Raimi to find any survivors." Armas's chest felt lighter than it had the entire battle.

"They do not deserve our help," Saul spat.

"Your Majesty," Major Barish interjected, "we ought to interrogate the prisoners, find out where Ogroma is. And again, I suggest we hurry out of here."

Armas studied the king. He was silent for a moment but did not look in Jon's direction. Armas knew that Jon had been dismissed because of a disagreement with his father before, and worried what might happen now.

"Send a transport shuttle for the Phenian prisoners. We will interrogate them at the Sim'ee stronghold." The king turned to Major Barish. "Get our wounded back to Glia, all who are able to be transported."

"Yes, Your Majesty."

Relief washed over Armas as the king didn't belay Jon's order. There would be some Phenian survivors, but the hollow feeling in his chest wouldn't leave. If they didn't get out fast, Ogroma might still trap them. Taking time for the survivors were minutes they didn't have. As much as he hated it, Saul had his reasons. There was no time.

While the medical transport attended the wounded, one of their own mech carriers landed. As the loading doors opened, a shadow spread across the canyon.

"Stardust," Jon swore, tearing his gaze to the sky.

A giant figure blotted out the sun, lowering to the canyon floor.

He didn't even have to look. "Ogroma," Armas breathed, as ice traveled through his veins.

SEVEN

ARMAS

The stories the Elders had told Armas on the journey to Zek reminded him of the chaos monsters lying deep in the vacuum of space, part machine and part creature, waiting to gobble up ships and entire worlds — the kind of stories his brothers told him when he was young. From what he heard on the transport, Ogroma was indestructible, cutting down the best warriors and destroying entire battalions of mechs within minutes.

All those images flooded into Armas's mind when the giant mech fired its thrusters and landed. Even with the Phenians defeated and the battle over, Armas's stomach spun with the realization they might still lose this war.

"Oh my God," Raimi said on the channel.

Armas's gasp caught in his throat as Ogroma neared the other side of their mech battle transport. Sun glistened off the blue-tinged reflective steel — probably stronger than Airysan. What that might be, Armas hadn't a clue. The giant mech was at least double the size of their Airysan suits. Size alone was reason enough for soldiers to soil themselves.

"Holy shit." The prince took a step back in his suit.

Sweat poured across Armas's brow.

As Ogroma set down, the panels on its arms and legs opened, exposing its massive weaponry, including hypersonic cannons on its arms capable of bringing down the canyon. Armas's hair stood on end, a physical reaction to the electromagnetic shields in place to protect the beast of a mech. Even if the entire mech division opened fire, Ogroma would no doubt destroy them.

Armas's eyes focused on the mech's signature weapon: the proton cannon. Resting above its right shoulder, the weapon would bring down a transport ship with one blast — he'd been warned Ogroma could destroy an entire city without defenses in less than a minute.

Armas felt faint. Nothing the Elders said truly gave the full picture. Not even Saul's sword could stop that machine. If Armas had known, he would've told them this was impossible.

This would be over quickly.

"We demand the unconditional surrender of King Saul and all his military. Otherwise, we will annihilate you."

Armas's skin crawled at the blended voices of Ogroma.

"Do not think we will stop here — it won't take us long to conquer Melas with your pathetic forces."

"If you fire that cannon down here, you'll destroy all

the Phenian prisoners along with us," Saul belted back on the widebeam, pointing to the canyon walls. Armas could feel Jon's rebuke, though he couldn't hear it, as Jon switched off his comm. His heart pounded against his rib cage, knowing at any moment it might be his last. "Is that really what you want? Let us come to a truce," the king finished.

The voices of Ogroma laughed over the comm. "A truce? You opened fire when your command brought the Phenian mechs down and they surrendered. Any option for mercy has been lost."

"What do you care? You're mercs anyway!"

"He's going to get us all killed," Jon said, having switched his comm back on to a private channel with Armas and Raimi.

Armas swore. If it was him, he'd find something to give them, some way to buy them time or at least allow some of them to safety. To save Raimi and Jon, to save their military. To try to secure the release of Melas. That's what a king ought to do.

"Your shutdown command has been isolated and will not stop us. Negotiate the terms. Or die."

"Your Majesty," Major Barish said on a secure channel to the king, Jon, Armas, and the squad leaders. "We need to consider all our options. If we try to fight back, we will take heavy losses. We should offer them payment, maybe they will come to our side."

Armas's eyebrows raised.

"Paying them off is only a short-term option. Besides, the Phenians may hire more Stiners and be back," Abe argued.

Major Zeru climbed out of her mech suit, damaged in battle. Dust clung to her helmet. "We don't have options.

We don't have much to bargain with, and we can't surrender now," she said over her comm link.

Surrender. The king would never agree. But he was the King's Advocate and could advise him. *Think.* What options hadn't been pursued?

"Your Majesty," Armas interrupted. "We could make an offer of challenge. I've heard it's part of Phenian custom — maybe they will honor it?"

"We don't have a mech that size!" Abe spat.

"We don't have to," Armas insisted. "If someone of importance, of higher rank makes the challenge and they accept, the rest can clear out. It buys us time."

"That's preposterous!" Abe shouted on the comm. "An offer of challenge means we'd have to release the Phenian prisoners. It's not a solution."

"It might be our only shot," Major Barish said. "One the Phenians paying Ogroma might accept."

"Everyone shut up!" Saul snapped.

After a second, Armas received the king's call on a private channel. "Who do you suggest takes up this challenge? And how do we know they'd accept?"

"Your Majesty, they won't accept the challenge unless — unless it was you, or ..." Armas paused, unable to say Jon's name. "It would end any further divisions among the Elders and bring everyone under your authority."

"You'd have me die to save my people," Saul replied, his voice dispassionate.

"Your Majesty, no, listen —"

"Without a king, I don't know how they'll survive," Saul added, his voice soft, sad, surprising Armas. "They'll be a weaker force, and it won't be long before someone else comes and conquers Melas, and the rest of the Nacaens."

Armas remained silent. The king was actually considering sacrificing *himself*? This was not the Saul he'd seen before, not the Saul that Kyla had shown him. A cunning warrior on the battlefield, shrewd in leadership, but this — concerned about his people? This was the kind of king he'd hoped to serve, before his notions of the noble king were shattered with Kyla's revelation.

The fact Saul was considering offering the challenge changed *everything*. He would die, and Jon would become king — but he wasn't ready. Armas had just helped him barely get sober in time for the battle. He knew there was animosity between them, but Armas also knew the king would never allow Jon to sacrifice himself. *I wouldn't allow it, either.*

If the king was willing to die to save them all, then what could Armas do, except die to save his king?

Maybe this was why the prophet chose him: to die for his king and home world. Armas's ancestors established the first unified government, right here on Melas, between the three nations who called this world home. The stories his father told of his great-grandparents, what they'd lived for and what they'd sacrificed — they weren't just stories. If Armas truly believed it, if he believed God was with him — then this was the *right* thing to do.

This was his destiny.

Saul cleared his throat. "But if it will save them to fight another day —"

"No, Your Majesty — I'll go in your place."

This was his role, his job to do, as the Advocate — the Advocate for his people.

Armas continued, knowing they didn't have much time. "If I die, you'll have saved the people. If I live —

you'll be the one who led his people to victory. The first king of the united Nacaen Group, that people will tell stories about for generations to come. It would show the people who have resisted joining with you what they are missing."

Ogroma interrupted, repeating their demands on the universal channel. "King Saul and your pathetic military force must surrender, if you wish to live."

Come on. Armas gritted his teeth. What was worse than knowing death was a few meters away were the seconds wasted while Saul didn't respond. Sweat drenched his fatigues.

"You'll need a mech," he reluctantly said to Armas. "Take mine."

"No, Your Majesty, you need it for your protection!"

"You'll need the electromagnetic sword," Saul countered. "It may buy you some time. You're quick on your feet, faster than anyone I've seen. You can use that to your advantage."

Saul switched to the universal channel. "Here are the terms: In exchange for my troops, I offer a challenge to Ogroma, as King of the Nacaens."

"No!"

"My king!"

"Your Majesty, no!"

The leaders overlapped each other as they shouted on the comm, before it went abruptly silent. Saul had cut the rest from the channel.

"Release the Phenian prisoners, and we will agree to the terms," Ogroma replied. "Come forward to begin the challenge."

"Not until my people are gone."

Ogroma raised its arm, adjusting its cannons. "How

do we know you won't escape with them?"

Armas tapped Saul's comm. "Send them your suit's comm tracker code."

"Affirmative," Saul responded to Armas, before the king switched back to the universal. "Here's my tracker. You'll know exactly where I am, at all times. Only allow me a few minutes of prayer to our God with the Elders of my people."

"You have five minutes," Ogroma replied in unison. "Release the Phenians."

"We will send coordinates to rendezvous with a transport shuttle for the prisoner exchange, outside of the battle zone," Saul replied. "Surely that is acceptable."

The comms were silent for a few seconds before Ogroma replied in multiple voices, "Affirmative." The giant mech lowered its arms with the hypersonic cannons, but the guns on the open panels of its legs would be enough to obliterate them, should they stop out of line.

While the Melas units scrambled onto the battle transports and prioritized the wounded out first on medical ships, Major Barish, Jon, Raimi, and Abe surrounded Armas and Saul. They raised their hands as if for a commissioning prayer. Hidden behind the ring of Liphes and Airysan suits, the king climbed out of his mech and set his hands on the Advocate's shoulders. "Today, you are making a great sacrifice on behalf of your people. May God be with you."

Armas gulped as the king embraced him, and he glanced at Jon. He couldn't see the prince's expression through the suit, but his mech posture was slumped. Jon had pored over every detail with Armas on the flight here, answering every question, helping him to think through the plan with Major Barish. He didn't know what to say to him, to express his gratitude.

Saul slipped away behind Barish and Abe, and Armas thought of Kyla. The princess who'd seen him covered in dirt and muck. He wished he could've spent more time with her, told her something — anything — instead of being so tongue-tied in her presence.

He stole one more look at Jon, who saluted him. A soldier's goodbye. Then he climbed inside Saul's mech.

"Stardust."

He'd glanced at the panels before in the armory, but now he appreciated the sleek design. The Airysan model was far more advanced than the Liphes he'd controlled before. He had only another minute before he faced Ogroma with his last breath, but he still was impressed enough to take it all in — the three-sixty-view camera mounted above the viewscreen, the targeting computers for the shoulder cannons, the full charge on the electromagnetic sword. He'd picked up the Liphes system quickly — if he could manage this, he might last longer than a minute. He tapped his helm connection to interface with the controls.

But this Airysan had been built for Saul, and Armas's helm was made for the Liphes. The connection wouldn't link.

"Try rebooting," Jon told him over the comm, and Armas flipped the switch, but Saul's mech refused to accept his connection. Without helm control, he was simply in a very sleek steel can, ready to be crushed.

"The last transport is loading," Major Barish warned.

"Armas," Jon started.

Armas peered at him through the suit's open hatch. "You have to go."

"No," Jon asserted, his mech hand grasping Armas's

mech arm. "You don't stand a chance without the suit."

"There's no time. Go. Get the rest out of here."

Jon grabbed Armas's mech shoulders. "There's a Bara Sharpshooter on your right. If *you* need it."

Armas's heart pounded in his chest. The Sharpshooter would end things quickly for him if it came to that.

But it also gave Armas an idea.

"Jon, go. I'll make it."

The prince stood motionless in his suit.

"Go!" Armas almost choked. "That's — that's an order."

Technically in the chain of command, as the King's Advocate, he was over Jon. He felt awkward pulling rank, but he had no choice.

Before Jon could reply, Raimi dragged the prince to the transport, leaving Armas alone in Saul's dead mech suit as the clock ran out.

The giant monster mech maneuvered closer as the transport ship took off. Armas grimaced, pulling hard on a lever to manually move the mech's arm into position with its proton rifle, aiming at Ogroma as they began to taunt him on the comms. "Such a beautiful suit. Hardly a scratch on that Airysan steel," the voices hissed as they aimed their proton cannon. "Wonder if anyone will recognize what it used to be when we're through with it!"

Armas pulled the pistol from the compartment and opened the back hatch, leaping as the cannon fired. Pumping his legs hard, his breath heavy and fast, he ran a split second ahead of the explosion. The rush of air from the blast pushed him towards the boulders, as the proton cannon blew Saul's Airysan suit into a crater. Luckily Ogroma wasn't stupid enough to fire at full power and take them both out. They still wanted to get paid at the end of the day.

Laughter times five filled his comm. "You can try to run, but you're trapped, little mouse."

Armas dove behind a boulder, his chest pounding as he held the gun close to his chest. He checked the magazine — there were eight rounds. Jon's words echoed in his head. He could end it right there, relieve himself of any future pain. Take the victory from the Phenian's hands and deprive Ogroma of their kill. But he doubted they would hold to their word. They would catch the king's transport and kill him.

He had to fight with any strength he had left, had to make his shot count. But it was like slinging a rock at that thing. How in the world could he stop that giant mech?

An image flashed in his mind, a memory from the farm. While foxes and wolves were the common predators of his father's sheep, once there had been a bear. The giant carnivore had lumbered into the field after the newborn lambs. Roxy charged the bear, barking at it, then dodging left and right. The bear was quick — had already managed to tear a lamb into shreds — but being smaller and faster, Roxy was able to avoid the bear's reach, zigzagging around it until his father was close enough to take the shot.

He'd have to get close, really close. Even then, what part of that machine was penetrable, with steel stronger than Airysan?

"Come out, little mouse. Come out and play," the voices echoed off the rocks around him.

Armas peeked over the boulder. The four-limb mechs connected to the base seamlessly. There was no vulnerable spot. The rock before him exploded into dust and Armas ducked down, dodging the proton rifle fire.

The beast was playing with him, enjoying the game.

He slumped with his back against the boulder, glancing above the rocky wall at the transport ships, now small dots in the sky. Below them, the canyon curved, eroded underneath by the river that once carved the valley, now dried up.

It wouldn't take much to dislodge the rock outcropping. If he hit it just right, he might trigger a rockslide. But Ogroma could easily use their thrusters and rise above it.

Unless he could figure out a way to blind the mech unit.

Another blast sent him scrambling. "This is fun for me, but it cannot be fun for you, little *rat*."

He stole a glance. The giant mech's head was like the other Airysan mechs, which meant it had a three-sixty-degree helm cam mounted above what appeared to be eyes, projecting to the viewscreens inside. There were other cameras embedded into the suit's metal, and he doubted the bullet would penetrate, but knocking out the main camera was the best shot he had. He dove behind another pile of rocks, knowing if Ogroma fired their proton cannon again, he was done for.

"I am not afraid. I am not afraid," he repeated to himself. "I'm in the valley of death, but I am not afraid." He let out a breath and a prayer: "God, be with me."

He aimed the Bara Sharpshooter to right below the outcropping. A blast of proton rifle fire from Ogroma a few meters off kicked up dust, but he kept his focus.

Breathe. In. Out.

Fire.

The bullet struck the canyon wall, and Armas lowered his weapon. Nothing happened. His heart sank as he uttered an oath. Laughter echoed around him as Ogroma fired their laser rifles again.

"Little rat, little vermin, let us put you out of your misery."

They were trying to draw him out, rather than just crushing him with one blow. Another few seconds' reprieve. Armas squinted, aimed again at the rocks above, and squeezed the trigger.

A crack boomed, echoing to the canyon floor, and Armas leapt to his feet. He ran ten meters toward the monster mech before dodging to the side, then again before diving behind a rock. Ogroma's head focused on the crumbling valley wall, not at Armas. He took another breath, then slipped around the boulder, running another ten meters with his pistol raised, closing in. Ogroma turned its attention back toward him, its cannon swiveling to aim.

Armas fired at the camera on Ogroma's head. The giant mech jerked, its cannon firing directly into the canyon wall and penetrating the rock behind him.

The blast knocked him directly into the mech's torso. Armas's bones rattled as he tumbled into the mech, and he cried out as his wrist snapped. Ogroma's face fell forward, and the sharp angle of the steel jaw cut into Armas's chest, slicing clean through the armor. He screamed in terror as pain erupted all along his torso.

Seconds later, the rockslide Armas had started slammed into the giant mech, sending Armas flying again. He struck a rock, and all went dark.

EIGHT

JON

Jon stared at Armas's unconscious body. His wrist was broken. A nasty jagged red line ran across his chest, though his armor had taken the brunt of it. A purple bruise bloomed on his right cheek. His nose was mangled and his lip split. Jon pored over the screens, but the limited med scanners on the medical support ship showed he was stable. The medical officer swabbed ointment and bandaged his chest.

It was a miracle. There was no other way to explain it.

When the rocks had settled, Jon and Raimi, and Majors Barish and Zeru had scrambled down into the rubble to find Armas. At first, they found only the remains of Ogroma, their giant mech completely crushed in. His stomach twisted when Major Zeru and Raimi pulled the bodies out — all five pale, hairless, broken, and bruised, entwined in silver wires leading to augments. Whatever planet they were originally from, whatever nation, Near Side or Outer — no one could tell. They didn't have the Stiner tattoo on their neck. His father ordered the bodies and what could be salvaged of their suit to be taken to the military facility on Richo to study. He didn't ask Saul what he planned to do with the remaining Phenian prisoners; he just knew they were not returned as the king had promised under the offer of challenge.

Major Barish found Armas first, pulse faint, underneath the rubble of Ogroma, the giant mech's crushed suit managing to protect Armas's life from the fallen rocks. Jon and Raimi used their suits to clear the debris. Abe had joined them, carrying the Advocate to the ship where Saul ordered his personal medic to care for him. The commanding officers had their mechs secured on the transport ships before joining Saul onboard his transport to return to Glia.

"He was willing to die to save us," Major Zeru muttered as Jon reentered the main cabin, her arms crossed. The major was six years older than him and had achieved her rank only a few months earlier. Her cream-colored hair was cut close to the scalp, her tanned brow furrowed with concern over hazel eyes. Her bodysuit, like Jon's, was stained with sweat and dirt. She'd unzipped hers halfway over the standard-issue long-sleeve gray undershirt.

"This was his plan," Major Barish said. "For someone with no military experience, this trap was genius. And to take on Ogroma? What courage."

Jon glanced at his father. At first, Saul hadn't seemed to be paying attention, but his cheeks reddened, the lines on his forehead more pronounced.

"Yes, young Armas did take my place," his father said sharply as he stood, straightening out his uniform — he was the only one to fully shed his bodysuit and change. "But only because he insisted. I would've died for Melas. You know that."

Jon raked his fingers through his hair. Back in the valley, Saul said he was willing to challenge Ogroma, but he didn't believe for a moment his father would follow through.

"Of course, Your Majesty," Major Barish began, "but we ought to share the news with the other transports. A true hero of Melas, one who came from a simple background —"

"He's not simple," Saul spat. "He's a Perez. He comes from a line of Dahan leaders, even if they haven't been involved in recent years. If Dahan hadn't given up on strengthening our military, we wouldn't be in the position we are today. Those farmers haven't done much —"

"Those farmers have been dying for you, for this war," Major Zeru said, her fists clenched.

Fear pricked along the back of Jon's neck. It was one thing to argue military decisions in the Situation Room. Another to challenge Saul so openly in front of him. "And not only Armas, but his brothers Eliot and Shane came fighting for you, too. He's given up everything for Melas, like many of our people."

Saul's eyes narrowed. Jon surveyed those in the cabin. For a moment, he considered what was happening. A chance for change — but at what cost? What if this became a coup? *A revolution?*

Sweat beaded on Jon's brow. Abe moved to Saul's side, his hand at his sidearm. He was not only the Jamin Elder; Abe was Saul's uncle, and was not about to let anyone, let alone a Dahan major, insult the king. Jamin leaders stood at attention, waiting for Saul to give the slightest acknowledgement. The few Dahan present were outnumbered and outgunned. This was suicide.

"Seriah," Major Barish said quietly, using Major Zeru's first name. "Armas serves his king, as do you."

The Dahan major stepped back, bowing her head slightly. "Of course. We fight and die. For the king and system."

Barish raised a fist, joining in with the others as they repeated, "We fight and die. For the king and system."

Jon sucked in a breath and cautiously touched his father's hand. "Can I speak with you? Alone?"

Saul startled, turning sharply to glare at him. Jon tilted his head, silently pleading with his father to keep his cool. After a moment, he nodded, and Jon exhaled as Abe, Raimi, and the others resumed their seats. Jon led Saul to a private room at the stern of the ship.

He closed the door after his father, bracing himself as Saul yelled. "This redheaded piece of dirt comes in, has one good idea and suddenly everyone's praising him? They would've been cut to pieces out there if it wasn't for me. How many kings fight for their people in battle? How many kings are willing to give themselves up for their people? *I* am the one who fights with them, for *them*."

Jon leaned against the door. He'd seen this coming, once he sobered up and helped Armas. Jon knew that success would be attributed to the new Advocate and others would perceive it wasn't Saul's plan. Saul would become jealous and irrational, but Armas was smart enough already to know how to soothe the king's ego and wasn't the type who needed glory. Jon just didn't see Armas getting hurt — almost *killed* — and Saul *still* feeling threatened.

He had to put Saul back on top.

"Father, just remember that Armas wanted to die for you. Not for others, but for you. Because *you* are his *king*."

Saul stood straight, jutting his chin out, as if Jon had reminded him of what he'd forgotten. As if he could forget he was the king who united their home moon of Melas when Jon was a young boy, and later all the Nacaen nations. Chosen by the very prophet he later ordered his daughter to murder. Jon twisted his fingers. Armas had told him Kyla hadn't done it, and he didn't want to believe his sister would actually follow through. But his father had ordered Zam's assassination. His father would stop at nothing.

"Armas would've died for you," Jon continued, seeing how easily the words calmed Saul's anger. "He's the right advocate for you. God sent him, and I know your faith is what has led you into victory."

The words came out smoothly but left a bitter taste in Jon's mouth. Using the language of faith to placate his father, to raise him up as divinely chosen — Saul wouldn't argue with that.

"He knew I needed to survive," Saul said, his voice softer. "He knew how important it was for Melas, for all Nacaens, for me to live on."

"Right. He was just a farmer before you made him *your* Advocate." Armas had the courage to execute the plan when no one else did. Even if the shutdown command had been Jon's idea, he never would've come up with it if Armas hadn't assured him the trap would work. The lies to Saul rolled off Jon's tongue too easily. Anything to keep Armas safe, whose red hair and bright blue eyes made his heart skip a beat. "His purpose in life is to live and serve you, chosen by our God. He's not a threat. You *know* this."

Saul frowned. Jon could tell he wasn't convinced yet. The king glanced at him. "What do you think of him?"

"I — me?" The question caught Jon off guard. "I think he's a good strategist, a sharp mind. He's done nothing but serve you completely — he even had Ogroma convinced he *was* you." *What do I think of him? Handsome. Hot. I'd like to get my arms around him and* ... "He doesn't seem to hold any ill will against anyone, and Kyla likes him —"

Shit. Kyla.

He shouldn't have said that.

Saul's brows raised. "Interesting."

"Father, please. I mean, she admires him, that's all." Jon gritted his teeth, turning from his father. He'd almost forgotten the way she looked at Armas, how her cheeks flushed, how she touched his arm while they were shooting together. She did like him, quite possibly the way *he* liked him.

"The last young man she 'admired' I had sent to the front lines. Whoever she marries needs to be a good match for the kingdom. Same for you."

What if I was with him? Saul would never go for it. Marriage for Saul was all about status, privilege, and power. Which meant heirs had to be produced.

"What if ..." Jon cleared his throat. He didn't want to say it, but he had to do what he could to save Armas. "What if she married him?"

Saul scratched his jaw. "He would then be one of us. I

would know his movements, know his actions. There'd be no chance he'd be swayed to oppose me then. He would serve me well as a son-in-law."

Jon held up his hands. "Don't rush anything, Father. I'm just saying it's an idea —"

"And it's the first good one you've had for a while. Keep it up and I might restore you, as Armas's second-in-command."

Second-in-command. That ought to be an insult, but thoughts flashed through Jon's mind, of flying next to Armas, of going into battle with him, of Armas tending to his needs, the two of them alone in a deserted place …

Saul motioned to his son to move away from the door, snapping Jon back to reality. He hoped his father was calm enough to not lash out again. Jon opened it for him, exhaling as they moved back into the common area with the Elders.

Abe folded his arms. Raimi and Major Barish rose with the others, their expressions blank. Major Zeru leaned against the bulkhead, her arms crossed.

But the king's eyes gleamed. "Share the news of Armas's bravery, for all of Melas. How he, a lowly farmer, pleaded to take my place, to serve his king and all Nacaens by his brave and noble sacrifice. And God saw it fitting to spare him today and defeat Ogroma."

Applause broke out on deck, and fists raised a moment later. "King Saul! King Saul!"

A rock sank in Jon's stomach. The soldiers and Elders gave in so easily with simple words and a calm demeanor, but what if he hadn't intervened?

What would happen now that he *had* intervened, with Kyla and Armas? He'd practically told Saul to arrange their marriage.

However, a darker question probed deep in his gut. *Marriage. Heirs. Father will be planning to arrange my own life. Someday, he will be preparing me to become king. Do I really want that?*

"Your Highness," the medic said to Jon. "He is awake and asking for you."

Jon's chest swelled. His father was giving one of his usual speeches as the attention was focused on him. Jon slipped away to the private medical room.

Armas's eyes were barely open. "What happened?"

Jon went to his side, and the medic left them alone. Jon took Armas's hand in his, running his fingers over the farmer's rough callouses. "You managed to bring down the canyon on top of Ogroma, after you struck their main camera. You must've hit it dead on. Somehow, when the rocks came down and crushed the beast, their suit protected you from the same death."

"Dumb luck."

"A miracle." Jon's heart pounded. There was so much he wanted to say to Armas, but he swallowed it down. Armas moved his head, wincing, his eyes half-lidded.

"I should let you rest," Jon said, letting go of Armas's hand.

"Jon?"

He turned back to the boy who'd just saved them all, the boy who somehow changed his heart, but he dared not speak it. Not after what he said to Saul, especially what he revealed about Kyla.

"Your plan worked," Armas breathed, closing his eyes.

"It was *your* plan," Jon said. "I just aided it a bit. You're the one who led us to victory." *And should lead us into the future.*

As Jon closed the door, he recognized he meant it.

NINE

KYLA

"What can I do to help?" Kyla asked, hovering near the chief medic. Those with minor wounds had been sent to other villages on the Sim'ee continent, but the more seriously injured, and the dead, were in-flight to Glia. The medical levels and morgue were below ground in the most protected part of the fortress.

The chief medic motioned her back. "You shouldn't be here. Your father wouldn't —"

"The king isn't here, and neither is his son. Who do you think is in charge?"

The chief sighed. "Scrub up, Your Highness — you can help by stitching wounds."

Kyla washed her hands, put on gloves and picked up the liquid stitch gun. She followed the medics around, washing wounds, injecting antibiotics and sealing up the holes in the soldiers around her. She searched for Jon and Armas among the wounded, but they hadn't come in yet — if they'd survived. Saul had accepted Jon on the mission after Armas requested his presence. She had lost her chance to talk to Jon alone, to explain herself, before they deployed.

Now, she waited for what was left of them to arrive.

Word came that her father was safe and the mission a success. She heard pieces of Armas's heroic actions, but no word if he'd made it out, and nothing about Jon. Until she knew for certain, she kept herself busy and tried not to think about them. The medic closed the eyes of the soldier in front of her, ordering the gurney to the morgue.

Jon had warned her what war was like. She tasted bile in the back of her throat.

"Incoming wounded on the king's ship," the message rang out, and Kyla's heart skipped. She found the chief medic at the next bed and caught his eye. "Go," he told her. She grabbed a med kit and ran.

Kyla didn't stop until she reached the flight deck. She took a shortcut by the mech hangar, where the machines were unloaded from the battle carrier, some of which only pieces remained. When she entered the landing bay, she spotted Carmen. The Bluehawk pilot wore their hair in the traditional Sim'ee style of narrow braids close to the scalp and had the same dark skin as their father. A thin silver crescent hung on the right shoulder of their flight suit — the rank of lieutenant. Carmen had learned to fly alongside Kyla four years ago, but unlike Kyla, Carmen's father allowed them to fly combat, though Kyla knew they'd been assigned to the air patrol over Glia for this mission. Their fingers knotted in front of them.

"Any word?" Kyla asked.

Carmen shook their head. "I know there are injured on board, but they haven't said who." Carmen touched two fingers to their chest. Kyla returned the gesture, the secret acknowledgment of their shared, but outlawed, faith in Tana.

Kyla put her arm around her friend and held her breath as the medical ship hovered into the landing bay.

The Elders filed out, including her great-uncle. When Major Barish walked off without a scratch, Carmen raced to meet him, throwing their arms around their father. *Thank you, Warrior Tana,* Kyla prayed in relief.

A few fighters were carried out on stretchers from another ship, and she watched them go by, a lump in her throat. She couldn't take a step further — fear had frozen her to the deck.

Until Jon stepped off the ship. Relief flooded over her as he came right to her, and she threw her arms around him, holding him tight. He squeezed her back.

"Thank God," she said, and to herself, *thank you, Tana, Warrior of Protection.*

She pulled back slightly, knowing she had to talk to him first. "You know — I didn't ..."

Jon gave her a puzzled look. They'd need to be alone before she could tell him everything about Zam. Kyla tore her gaze to the transport. "Is he ...?"

Her hand flew to her heart. Armas clutched his arm to his chest, his clothing torn and bloodied, but he was walking off the ship with Major Zeru's help.

"He got knocked out, but seems to be okay," Jon said, but his words fell behind as she rushed away from her brother's side.

"Come with me," she ordered, surprising herself as she reached for Armas's uninjured hand. "You need to be examined."

"There's worse injured —" Armas's blue eyes seemed unfocused.

"He was knocked out," Major Zeru informed her. "The flight medic attended him, but he needs more attention. He insisted on walking off himself."

"I've got him now. Armas, you need to see the medic."

He relented, and she led him through the corridors and ramps back to the medical ward, to the private room they kept open for any injured Elders or royal family. Kyla motioned for him to sit on the bed.

Armas winced as he sat, favoring one side.

Kyla leaned out the door, her heart beating fast. "We need help in here, now!"

The chief medic rushed across the room, pausing at the door. "He's not an Elder."

"Father's orders," Kyla replied. "He's the Advocate and the king *needs* him."

"Did you lose consciousness?" the medic asked, examining Armas's head and flashing a light in each of his eyes.

"Yeah. They said *possible* concussion, but I haven't been dizzy or throwing up or anything."

Kyla helped the medic peel off the remnants of Armas's shirt. "Definitely bruised ribs," the medic said. "Good thing you had your armor. Let me see your arm." Armas grimaced and held out his arm, obviously broken at the wrist. "Looks like a clean break." He gestured to Kyla. "Get him cleaned up, then take him for imaging and bone refusion."

The princess nodded as the medic left. She faced Armas, focusing the gash on his chest — not deep but needing to be cleaned and rebandaged.

"Hold still," she said, catching her bottom lip under her teeth as she set one gloved hand on his bare shoulder, her fingers grazing his auburn locks at the nape of his neck. She dabbed at the wound. Her heart pounded in her chest and her hands shook as she finished cleaning the gash, though she tried not to show it.

He flinched as the antiseptic stung along the edges. "Sorry," she muttered, as she took a gauze pad from her bag to dab the gash, before finishing off with the liquid stitch gun, one hand still on his shoulder. She straddled his leg to get a better angle, bringing her body close to his, until the stitches set. Kyla had kept her eyes on his wound the whole time, but she slid her gaze to his, and blue eyes were locked on hers, no longer cloudy.

"How's the injured?" her father called from the doorway. Immediately she pulled back, her cheeks flushed.

"He's fine. Just took care of the wound. I'm taking him for imaging and bone refusion."

"Good." Saul said, entering the room as Kyla put the med kit away. "I need a minute alone, then you can take him."

She stripped off her gloves and dropped them into the biotrash. She didn't glance at her father while she passed him by, instead turning over her shoulder to call back to Armas. "I'll be right back."

Armas gave her a long look. Heat coursed through her from head to toe, leaving her light-footed. She practically danced out of the room. He was alive, he was safe.

One of her father's guards shut the door behind her. She frowned. *Maybe there's a vent on the other side so I can listen.*

She turned the corner and bumped into Jon's shoulder. "Hey!"

He set his hands on her shoulders; his expression puzzled. "Your face is all red. What's gotten into you?"

Kyla let out an exasperated breath, and Jon wrinkled his brow.

"Is it him?"

"I don't know what you're talking about."

"It *is* him." Jon held her forearm, pulling her down the hall away from the med bay to a maintenance closet. He glanced in both directions before opening the door and pulling her inside, shutting the door behind him and leaning against it. "You have to be careful, Ky."

She rolled her eyes at her brother. "Never mind that." She didn't want to talk about her crush with her brother. "Do you believe me? About Zam?" she whispered.

"Where is he?"

"Safe."

"You don't trust me," Jon scoffed.

"It's not that." She gazed at her feet. "It's just better you don't know, in case Father finds out."

"I won't tell him, I swear."

Kyla stared at her brother. Dark circles hung under his eyes. He probably hadn't slept in days out on the battlefield. While she'd fretted about Armas, the thought of losing Jon was more than she could bear. She threw her arms around him again.

"Hey," he said, first patting her back gently, then pulling his arms around her.

"I was so afraid," she whispered.

She felt his chest tighten. "At least I'm alive," he whispered back.

"Father ordered me to kill Zam, but I didn't," she said. Jon released her. She wiped a tear from her eye. "I had to make it look good."

"It was convincing."

"What would you have done, had Father ordered you to do it?"

Jon's shoulders slumped. "I don't know." She squeezed his hand, and he continued. "There were moments, out at Zek, where he seemed like a different person, like he used to be. For a moment, I thought he was actually going to do it, you know. Sacrifice himself to save everyone else."

Kyla hugged her arms. "If he had, you'd be king."

Jon shrugged. "I would've argued with him. Just as I argued with Armas when he went out there. But it was Armas who saved us." Her brother's eyes fixed on hers. "Saul hates him now. He's going to do everything he can to keep him under his thumb."

She shuddered. Father was in there, alone with him. "We'll have to do what we can to keep him safe."

Jon shifted his weight. "Ky, I — Father knows you like Armas."

"WHAT?"

She shoved his chest. Jon winced as she forced him against the wall. "I may have said something," he squeaked.

"What the hell did you say?"

"He asked me what I thought about him, and I told him all these great things about Armas, and I said you liked him — I meant, like him like a person, but Father —"

"You asshole." She let go of him. "Father's in there with him, alone."

"Shit."

Kyla pushed her brother out of the way and opened the

door.

"Ky, I'm sorry ..." Jon called after her, but she quickened her pace, running back to the med bay and to the reserved room, where her father's guards stood watch. She knocked before slowly opening the door. To her relief, Saul was sitting on the stool near Armas, his palms resting on his thighs, in a pleasant mood.

"Everything all right?" she asked.

"Yes, my dear," Saul said. "Just having a chat with Armas, about his role as Advocate, and how he has helped save all of Melas and the system."

"Sire," Raimi called from the hall, "You are needed in the Situation Room. New intel coming in from the battle."

"Ah yes. Duty calls," he said to Armas. The warm expression from Saul's face faded for a moment, and Kyla caught a glimpse of coldness between the two men.

"Kyla," her father added by the door. "I think it would be wonderful if you would begin instructing our new Advocate here on flight basics. He was a natural picking up the mechanized suits. You can start him on the transport ships once he's healed."

Kyla watched her father leave the room with Raimi. Whatever had passed between her father and Armas, she couldn't make it out.

She scoffed. "I'm not starting you on a transport ship. We'll try out one of the old Sparrowings first. The flight division has all the Bluehawks up north, but we can get you started soon ..."

Armas sat precariously at the edge of the bed, his bandage betraying the slightest shade of pink. Kyla frowned. Her father's expression faded from memory as she rushed over to examine his wound. "I don't think I did this right," she whispered as she pulled the adhesive off. He swore, pulling back slightly. "I'm sorry, I need to redo it," she apologized.

He caught her hand with his. "No, it's fine. It's only a little blood. It's not that bad; it was going to bleed through a bit anyway."

Kyla trembled as Armas's thumb brushed over her knuckles. His soft eyes searched hers. The knot in her stomach eased from fear to longing. With his other hand, Armas reached up to cradle her head, pulling her close. She closed her eyes and moved forward.

She had wanted this, dreamed of this moment almost since she met him, but his kiss was tentative, barely pressing against her lips. Perhaps he was in too much pain right now.

Kyla pulled back, biting the corner of her lip. "You need to rest and heal." She moved to clean up the med kit, tossing most everything into the biotrash. It was silly to be focusing on a kiss when he was injured, especially when her father was just in the room.

Armas grimaced as he pulled himself to stand.

"Wait," she said, moving to his side and brushing aside her thoughts on the kiss. "You need help."

"I'll be fine," he said, his voice low, triggering a muscle in her stomach to twist tighter. He tucked his hand behind her ear and pulled her in again, setting his mouth against hers more firmly. It took her a moment before she sank in, running her hands carefully around his neck as he deepened the kiss, parting her lips.

All her concerns fled as warmth spread throughout her body. Everything was okay. It was *better* than okay; it was amazing. Everyone she loved made it out of Zek alive.

Zam was safe, Jon was safe, and Armas was safe with her.

TEN

ARMAS

(EARLIER)

The king waited until the door closed, before turning to Armas.

"You saved us, out there. Well done."

Warmth spread across Armas's chest. "Thank you, Your Majesty."

"You did so well the people are calling out your name, shouting it from the rooftops," he chuckled. "The word has gotten out you took my place."

Armas beamed. "Your Majesty, I'm your servant. I wasn't sure I'd make it, but it was an honor to fight for you. That's what I'm here for."

"I know," the king spat, and his eyes grew stern. Armas swallowed his smile. "That's what Zam said," Saul continued, "and I believed that old fool, but perhaps he was right, and you have more ways you can serve me." The king pulled the stool over to Armas's bed, sitting down and facing him. "What do you think of my daughter?"

Armas leaned back, not following. "I beg your pardon?"

"My daughter. The one who rushed to tend to your wounds, the one who can barely speak a word in front of you but can't shut her mouth elsewhere. She's quite taken with you."

Oh. That. Wait — what? Armas wracked his brain, trying to discern what the king meant. Kyla had been kind to him, cared for him — but *taken* with him?

"I — I didn't notice, Your Majesty."

"Jon told me she likes you." Saul's voice echoed in the room. Armas sat there, dumbstruck. He remembered the moment he first saw the princess in his own home. That moment in the barn when she told him he was perfect. The way she complimented his shooting.

"This is an interesting development," the king said. "You see, the people love you. They say your name with more acclamation than mine. Some — some," he repeated, laughing, "even say you should be king. That you would make a better king."

"Your Majesty, I —"

"There is no king but me," Saul said, all laughter gone from his voice.

Frost trickled down Armas's spine.

"Of course, my King. I am here to serve you."

"If you love me as your king, if you wish for the best for Melas and all the Nacaen Group, you will become my son-in-law."

What? Armas's jaw dropped open, and no sound came out. He couldn't have heard that right. "Your Majesty, I don't understand —"

"Pursue my daughter," the king persisted. "You have my permission."

He barely knew Kyla, barely knew anyone here in Glia. He knew Jon only slightly better.

"Marry her; have my grandchildren," Saul continued. "In this way, you serve your kingdom and king best. No one can see you as a rival then. Instead, you will be my devoted son-in-law. I'll announce your engagement at the victory celebration. Jon retains his position as heir, and there is no need for rivalry between us."

"I don't know —"

"Then I'll explain it to you plainly, country boy," the king snarled. "There is only one king. And if you get in my way — if the people begin to look to you — you become a *threat*. Don't be a threat," he said. "You know what to do. Follow my orders, obey my commands, marry my daughter, and you will do well, *son*."

Someone knocked on the door. Saul's stern gaze faded as his daughter entered the room. His fists uncurled.

"Everything all right?" she called.

"Yes, my dear. Just having a chat with Armas, about his role as Advocate, and how he has helped save all of Melas and the Nacaen Group." The king flicked his eyes back to Armas. Fear crawled through his chest.

"Sire," Raimi Nadab called from the hall. "You are needed in the Situation Room. New intel coming in from the battle."

"Ah yes. *Duty calls.*" The king's eyes flickered. Armas gulped, understanding Saul's command.

"Kyla," the king added, nearing the door. "I think it would be wonderful if you would begin instructing our new Advocate here on flight basics. He was a natural picking up the mechanized suits. You can start him on the transport ships once he's healed."

The king left Armas alone with Kyla again. He didn't know what to say. He'd known her just over a week, and in that time his trust in her had been all over the place, though it wasn't her fault. What was he supposed to do now?

My pledge is to the people, to the crown, and to my God.

Kyla rolled her eyes. "I'm not starting you on a transport ship. We'll try out one of the old Sparrowings first. The flight division has all the Bluehawks up north, but we can get you started soon ..."

The princess's lips turned down, her gaze faltering. Did she know what Saul had said? She hurried over, setting her hand on his chest.

"I don't think I did this right," she said, tugging on the adhesive.

He gasped. "Shit." It stung where it pulled on his chest hair.

"I'm sorry, I need to redo it."

Armas grabbed her hand, stopping her. "No, it's fine. It's only a little blood. It's not that bad, it was going to bleed through a bit anyway."

He didn't let go of her hand, so soft and smooth in his own. No callouses. He ran his thumb over her knuckles, pondering Saul's words. To keep his position, to keep alive, the easiest way would be to do what Saul said. To fall in love with Kyla. And to do so quickly if their engagement was to be announced at the victory celebration.

There was no time to second guess. Saul had given him an order.

He had no choice.

Armas reached with his good hand, running his fingers through the bit of hair that had fallen from her braid, grazing her ear. She closed her eyes and leaned in, trembling.

He pressed his lips to hers, lightly. She pulled back, biting the corner of her lip. "You need to rest and heal," she said as she went to clean up the med kit.

He was too tentative. He was exhausted, sore, and his head pounded, but he needed to figure this out. *Now.* How to make it seem real even if he wasn't there yet.

Armas grabbed a hold of the bed rail, grimacing as he attempted to stand. Kyla almost dropped the med bag.

"Wait!" She rushed to his side, helping to brace him as he stood. "You need help."

"I'll be fine," Armas said. Then he threw caution out the door and threaded his fingers in the loose hair behind her ear, pulling her in for another kiss. She tensed for a moment, and then she responded, moving her mouth against his. He parted her lips, and a soft moan escaped. He ran his hand down her back, pressing her closer, and his own body grew warm and firm against hers.

After a few minutes, she pulled back. He rested his chin on her shoulder as he caught his breath. "You need to be seen for imaging," she said. "Hopefully they can refuse the break, it will heal faster that way. And then you need to rest."

As Kyla helped him down the hall from the med bay to imaging, the pang of guilt spread in his chest, deeper than the wound she'd dressed. He didn't want to lead her on, but Jon had told the king she liked him. And he liked her, at least, what he knew of her. But all of this — even coming to Glia, serving as the King's Advocate, pursuing Kyla — all of this had happened so fast. *If I had known what I was getting into, would I have said yes?*

It was too late to back out now. The path he thought he was choosing was chosen for him, and he had no way to stop it.

ELEVEN

JON

Though everyone else in the Situation Room was seated at the table with the king, Jon stood in the far corner, his arms crossed. Armas was still in the med bay with his sister. *What did I do?* He dragged a hand across his face. He'd said too much to Saul. With the people practically cheering for Armas and now his own daughter having a crush, Jon wondered who Saul would order to take him out. *Please God, no.*

Saul hadn't thrown Jon out of the Situation Room, but acted like he wasn't there as Abe, his great-uncle, rose and cleared away the holoboard for the debriefing. "The Phenians have fled," he announced. "No additional battle carriers, no fighters."

"There could still be a fighter or two hiding out in Horeb's moons," Raimi said. "Too many rocks to search them all."

"Nonsense," Saul scoffed. "Nothing has showed up on our scanners."

"Affirmative, Your Majesty," Major Barish acknowledged. "Though we cannot be sure they haven't contracted with other Stiner mercenary units."

Saul set his hands on the table. "The battle of Melas is over. Is there any reason we need to cause our people to worry tonight?"

Jon glanced around the room at the tired faces. Raimi cradled his forehead in his palms. Major Zeru studied her fingernails.

"It's the Stiners we ought to be worried about," Jon said, pushing off from the wall toward the table. Raimi cocked an eyebrow, a warning to the prince, but Jon ignored him. "Armas took out Ogroma. That's a pretty expensive loss."

Saul waved his hand. "It's the Phenians' loss, not ours, and besides, we are beginning negotiations with the Stiners as it is."

Jon's mouth snapped shut. Negotiating with mercenaries was never a good option — Saul himself had said that before. His gut twisted. Something was off.

Major Barish spoke before Jon could. "Pardon me, Your Majesty, but what negotiations? I wasn't informed of any delegations arriving. Representative Elders from all Nacaen nations are due to be present at any such matters."

Jon glanced at Major Zeru. She scowled and folded her

arms across her chest. She also must not have known.

Saul's eyes flicked in anger but settled as a grin spread across his face. "Nothing formal yet, but soon, I assure you. Abe has been with me in all communications, and I will bring in the Elders when I know for certain we have something more concrete."

Jon slid his gaze to Major Barish. The Sim'ee representative folded his hands, his face expressionless, but Jon doubted the other Elders would stay compliant for long. If Saul was making deals without them, the fragile alliance that propped up his throne would fall. Melas had stood on its own for the last few decades, but only with the Sim'ee, Dahan, and Jamin working together. If they wanted to defeat the Phenians or any other invaders for good, they would need the entire system — every Nacaen — behind the throne.

"I assume there are no other objections? Rest tonight. We've delayed the celebration for one day, by request of Sim'ee," Saul paused to give a nod to Major Barish, "so those recovering in Zek overnight may join us."

Jon bit the corner of his lip. A small concession to Barish for leaving him out of negotiations. Milo Barish was a principled leader and would stick by Saul as long as he felt the king had his people's best interests at heart. Jon had to give it to his father — sometimes he played the political games well.

The king rose, and the Elders left their chairs and began to file out. "Jon, a word."

Jon gritted his teeth, waiting as the others left. Raimi's expression was one of sympathy as he left the room, followed by Saul's personal guards. He braced himself.

But there was no shouting, no slamming of fists against walls, none of the usual reaction from his father.

Instead, he sank to his chair at the table. "Take a seat."

Jon obliged, pulling out the chair and sitting on the edge, nervous.

Saul pulled up the holomap that Abe had cleared away, showing the Outer Systems, running along the Beta Arm of the Euphrates Spiral Galaxy. Saul narrowed in on the Bara System, nearest to the Nacaen Group. "We know the Phenians have claimed another planet for their own in the Bara System, since their homeworld is a toxic dump now. It's complete chaos there, with the Bara Republic that once held the entire system now barely grasping their little planet of Aza, and the Leki currently dealing with their own infighting among the royal family on Balec. The Modes have taken two uninhabited moons there since this damn war with the Phenians began."

Saul swiveled the map toward the Nacaen Group. The Cana Star was in the center, and the first planet of the system, Nidos, orbited on the far side with its moon Ramah. The gas giant Horeb was closer to them in this image, with its rings and moons, including Melas, Richo, and Samar. "While we were battling the Leki in Horeb's rings, our intelligence heard rumors of Phenian sympathizers on Nidos, and their mining scout ships orbiting Ramah. Why do you think the Phenians came directly to Melas with Ogroma? Yes, we may have the capital, this may be where *we* live, but Nidos would have been an easier target."

Jon shifted in his seat. All his concerns about his father's wrath faded. "So this battle with Ogroma —"

"Was a distraction." Saul spun the map of the systems, flipping to an angle Jon rarely saw in this room: the Near Side Systems, running along the central stars of the galaxy. The Galactic Ocean, a swirl of gas clouds, separated the Beta Arm's Outer Systems from the Near Side. "While the Phenians have been expanding in the Outer Systems, adding Ilistia's neighboring planet Gerar, the Airysans are expanding in the Near Side, swallowing up whole systems instead of just worlds. The Tygan Republic surrendered. The Stiners, along with the Modes, are desperate for work and for allies because they are running out of both on the Near Side."

"Why send Ogroma here, then?"

"Phenians paid them more, of course. Stiners are still mercenaries. I believe the Phenians also offered the Stiners a possible new home world as they make a play for Nidos and whatever its moon Ramah might hold. It's uninhabitable now, but when our people first arrived, they discovered caverns underneath, and then built a settlement on its surface, even a temple. I visited once, long ago. Then it was taken over by Tananites, and we bombed the settlement, but the rock may still have resources. I instructed Abe to open a diplomatic channel with the Stiners. We have plenty of uninhabited moons around Horeb, should they need —"

"You can't be serious, Father." Jon pushed back from the table. "We can't give the Stiners ground here."

A devious glint crossed Saul's eyes. "I'm not suggesting we go through with it. I'm simply offering them the idea that there may be better options for them besides what the Phenians have to offer. Besides, the Stiners have a certain skillset that might prove useful."

"You mean assassins." While Ogroma was known for striking terror, the Stiners were known throughout the galaxy as hired guns. Doing the dirty work kings didn't deign to do.

"Only if necessary. Do not worry — I won't do anything that compromises our position overall. Merely starting a conversation. But we do need to be prepared. The Phenians are just the beginning."

"Then why ignore Captain Nadab or Major Barish's suggestion about possible Phenian ships hiding out in the moons?" Jon asked, before it dawned on him. "Because you have spies reporting directly to you and not through the Elders. That's why you know about the mining scout ships at Ramah."

Saul expanded the holomap toward Jon. "The Airysans are making a bigger play than just for the Tygan System. The Modes have fled the Airysans, under their new Supreme Ruler Alton, crossing the Galactic Ocean and settling in the Bara System. It seems the Outer System Planets — this wild space everyone thought was backwater, lacking resources, too far to be troubled — are now catching the eye of the older, more established planetary systems of the Near Side. Ramaens. The Liphes Sector. Even Byloners. Our fuel mines on Horeb are now suddenly attractive.

"It may not be long," he added, wiping the system map away and standing, "before we face something much more fearsome than Ogroma. We need to root out any insurrection among our own planets, our nations. Allotments have been paid to each of the nation Elders and to the priests for assurance of loyalty, but we must be wary of resources getting into the wrong hands. We must become one system, under one throne. And we need a moment of peace, a moment of celebration. Especially for the other nations, tonight."

Jon stood, meeting his father's gaze. "You've decided

Armas will stay."

His father nodded. "We have an agreement. As you've noticed, you've been restored. Armas, however, will be my Advocate. You will serve under Armas, and Raimi will serve you."

Saul stepped over to Jon, setting his hands on his shoulders. "You are my son. And one day you will rule this system. Don't step out of line again."

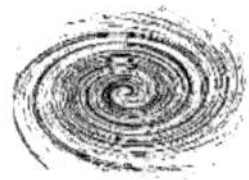

The sun through the window caught Jon's eye. It was still early; his alarm hadn't sounded.

The other side of his bed moved. He rolled quickly, a lump in his throat, before remembering. Sharda's head was on the other pillow, the dark blue sheets pulled up over her chest. He yawned and scratched his jaw. He hadn't shaved last night. Since the victory celebration had been put off to tonight, he'd planned on getting shitfaced as he usually did after fighting, but after meeting with his father, he returned to find his own liquor cabinets were completely empty. He vaguely remembered Armas helping him sober up before the battle; Jon must've asked Armas to dump everything. He was too lazy to go down into the fortress and the mess hall kitchens to find the alcohol stored there.

So instead, he'd gotten laid. That helped, but he hadn't been able to get the redheaded Dahan boy out of his mind. Nor the sense that his father's plans were not going to go as he hoped.

He slung his legs over the bed, searching for his trousers, finding them by the door.

"Jonny," the girl in his bed called, grazing his lower

back with her fingers.

He ignored her touch, gathering his clothes. "I'll check and make sure it's clear for you to go."

She sat up, running her fingers through her hair, the sheets slipping from her chest. "Is everything okay?"

"Everything's fine," he replied, tossing her underwear on the bed. She pushed aside the blankets and dressed, pulling on her coveralls. Guilt threaded through him. He shouldn't treat her so callously. He should offer to have breakfast sent up before she left. But it was later than he expected, and he was supposed to meet Raimi soon.

He opened the door a crack. Kyla's door was closed. The guards at the entrance to the palace doors wouldn't say anything, but a random servant might. Or his sister. Neither were in the hallway. "Okay, you can go now."

"Jonny, do you want to talk about this? Us?"

His head fell back against the door jam. "*Us?*"

"You know, what you said last night?"

He racked his brain, memory coming into focus. His intention last night had been to find Armas to talk to him, to find out what Saul had said, but instead he'd run into Kyla outside the Advocate's quarters, informing him "he needs to rest." When the image of Kyla and Armas got in his head, he'd messaged Sharda. He'd found her at the end of her shift and jumped her as soon as the door was shut.

She stepped closer to him, setting her palm on his cheek. "I told you this wasn't going to work, that this was all we could have."

"Oh. Yeah." Relief spilled over him, but also a stab of regret. She was rejecting him, ending this — whatever it was. It hadn't been going on long anyway.

"I'm transferring back to Richo. It will be easier if we just let this be what it was, right?"

"Yeah."

She stood on her tiptoes and kissed him — right as Kyla opened her door. His sister smirked.

He pulled back from Sharda's kiss. "All right, well thank you very much, and I guess I'll see you around."

His sister rolled her eyes as he passed by her.

Jon hunched his shoulders, shame weighing him down. He reached out, almost setting his hand on Sharda's lower back, but thought better of it. He should say something more to her, to thank her for being there for him, but his words formed a lump in his throat. Her cheeks burned as she brushed by him at the bottom of the stairs without so much as a glance, past the guards who let her slip out the palace doors into the fortress. *Coward.* Sharda deserved better.

A cough made him turn around. "I thought you'd left already, to play role of flight instructor," he called up to his sister, once the door was shut. Kyla leaned against the banister at the top of the stairs.

"I was. And I'm *not* playing — I'm *going* to teach him. Came back for my flight gloves. Armas is not able to fly right now with his wrist still healing, so he can't go up in a Sparrowing. Going to take him to the hanger and show him the different ships, go over some of the basics."

Anger pricked at his chest. He wanted to be the one with Armas, to show him how to fly, to see those arm muscles stretched taut pulling on the controls. But he'd opened his damn mouth in front of his father. He had to accept this. He could never be with Armas, and his sister could never know how he really felt. He had to give him up.

He started climbing the stairs to his room, making a plan to shower first, meet with Raimi, and go find some alcohol. "Be sure to show him the Kittiwake in the museum hanger."

"That old thing?" She wrinkled her nose. "That's ancient."

Jon reached the top, stopping to stare down at her. "It's part of the history of Melas. And it was flown by his great-grandmother."

TWELVE

JON

Jon leaned against the wall, his fourth drink in hand. He'd downed the first three quickly, and the fourth was almost empty. His head was fuzzy. The Great Hall was packed with soldiers and civilians, all gathered in celebration. But this time, Saul wouldn't need to slaughter a prisoner. It seemed more packed than ever — if it was possible. He'd lost Raimi after his second trip to the bar.

A roar erupted from the crowd as the king entered the hall. Saul was radiant, his eyes wide, smile captivating. The soldiers shouted, and the civilians rang out the chant, "King Saul! King Saul!"

"My fellow Nacaens: victory is ours!"

Shouts and whoops went up throughout the Great Hall.

"The Phenians are defeated. Our scanners show that every ship has left our system. We are free of these vultures!"

"King Saul! King Saul!"

Jon grimaced. He knew from the post-battle debriefing in the Situation Room there might be sympathizers on Nidos. His father's murderous actions the last time they celebrated a victory, and what happened to the prisoners after the battle with Ogroma, was fueling something worse. It rattled Jon's bones.

"We almost didn't survive," the king continued. His father loved this part the best, reveled in the crowd. "We almost didn't win. Surely, the Phenians would have destroyed our mechs, but we led them into a trap and caught them!"

"Ho!"

"And then, they sent Ogroma!"

"Boo!"

"And Ogroma almost defeated us!"

"Boo!"

"But God was with us! God sent us an Advocate! God sent him a vision of the trap."

"Ho!"

"I almost died. I was willing to die for you, my people!"

Jon choked on a piece of ice as he swallowed the last of his drink. *Next time, go neat. Or better yet just give me an IV of alcohol.* Anything to numb the absurdity of his father's speech, the lies he told, the fact the Phenians would soon return.

"King Saul! King Saul!"

"But at the last minute, God intervened. God sent this Advocate to take my place. I gave him my mech, to protect him, but he couldn't interface with it. So he took on Ogroma all by himself, with one pistol!"

Saul raised his Bara Sharpshooter into the air.

Jon almost dropped his empty glass, managing to only spill the ice. The crowd erupted in screams and applause.

"King Saul! King Saul!"

"And here he is, the Advocate sent to us by God — Armas Lehem-Perez, of Dahan!"

The crowd exploded, the applause and shouting becoming thunder in Jon's head. He spotted Armas, in a tight-fitting dark blue and green uniform — *Jamin colors,* Jon noticed — entering the Great Hall, with Kyla on his good arm. His other arm was in a brace, but that was the only injury visible. He looked well.

He looked *good.*

Kyla beamed. She wore a deep blue strapless dress instead of her usual uniform, and her black hair was twisted up in a crown on her head. Armas left her at the bottom of the steps and climbed the dais, joining Saul by his side, as the crowds began to shout: "Ar-mas! Ar-mas!"

His cheeks were as crimson as his hair, and Jon couldn't help but smile. The crowd loved him. A warm feeling spread across his chest and down into his gut.

"My fellow Nacaens," Armas began, but the shouts drowned him out. His father's smile was plastered on his face. *This has to hurt,* Jon thought, smirking. His father tried to quiet the crowds. Women screamed Armas's name; others raised their glasses.

Saul took control again and began describing Armas's heroics, but Jon's head swam. All he remembered was holding his hand while he lay there injured, the longing in his chest.

An elbow bumped his side. He hadn't noticed Kyla had made her way next to him. She held two drinks in her hands, offering one to him. Etho whiskey, neat.

"Thanks," he said, taking the drink from her.

She smiled wide and motioned to Armas. "What do you think?"

Jon raised an eyebrow, glancing at Armas. "He's clever, all right. He's a good right-hand man for Father."

"That's not what I meant," she said, her voice low, and Jon turned to face her. "Can I tell you something?"

"Of course," Jon said, still pondering his whiskey.

"Armas and I — we're together."

Jon dropped his glass. A servant rushed over, cleaning up the shattered mess, as he stepped aside with Kyla. "What? When?"

"Back in the med bay we kissed, and, well, after spending the day in the hangar. I really like him, Jon."

Shit. Armas must like her, too.

"And Father approves this time."

"Did he tell you that?" Jon asked.

He wanted to curse his father, but he had to curse himself. After all, he was the one who planted the idea in his father's brain. He clenched his fist. He'd done it to save Armas, to stop a coup. It was his fault.

Kyla set her hand on his arm. "It will be fine. He likes him."

Jon frowned. Saul must've said something to Armas in the med bay. His sister leaned in closer. "I need you to like him, too. For me."

Jon couldn't bear to look her in the eye. He stared at

the small scar on her forehead, above her left eye, from when she'd bumped her head in the armory a few years ago. When she was still a little girl. "Yeah. Sure."

"I mean it."

"I know you do." He didn't blink, just kept staring at the scar, a sign she'd grown up and there wasn't anything he could do about it. "Of course, I'll like him."

"Then what is it?"

Jon bit the corner of his lip. He couldn't share his own feelings that he wanted to ignore — it would break her heart. "It's nothing. I've probably drunk too much, that's all. He's really great, Ky."

He managed to hide his own anguish enough that she smiled again. "Good. I'm glad you approve. That's more important to me than Dad." She leaned her head against his shoulder, as Saul finished his speech.

"King Saul! King Saul!" the crowds shouted, and applause broke out again. Saul must've managed to get the story back to him.

Saul raised his hands for silence. "As you all know, our prophet has died."

The Great Hall went still. Jon's hands shook. *What is he doing now?*

"Until the time comes when God calls forth a new prophet, I will be your prophet. I will speak, as God has spoken to me."

"Stardust and ashes," Jon muttered. Applause waved across the room, but much more subdued than just a while ago. Controlling the priesthood *and* the army, Saul cornered all authority under himself.

"Now, let us give the offering, thanking God for our victory ..."

"Ar-mas! Ar-mas!" the crowd began to shout.

Saul smiled, but his jaw was clenched. Jon sucked air between his teeth.

This time, Armas held up his hands, silencing the crowd, and then bowed to Saul. "Our King, and our Prophet."

Smooth. The chants for Saul rose up again, and Jon noticed the king's face softening. Armas was good at this. Too good. Accepting Saul's claim to religious leadership helped appease his father.

Jon waited until the offering was given, then leaned toward Kyla. "I suppose you ought to go to him," he said, turning and winking at his sister. She threw her arm around him, and he patted her back, before she disappeared in the crowd toward the dais.

He settled against the wall, empty drink in hand, watching the women nearby. Usually, they threw themselves at him, but Armas had stolen the show. Jon wouldn't mind getting laid again, but he preferred drinking to numb his pain. Fewer people to disappoint in the morning. Still, the rejection stung as all the Elder's daughters whispered about the handsome Dahan hero. Sharda wasn't there — she'd must've already left, and she'd already left him anyway.

The fact was *he* wanted to be the one standing next to Armas, but there was no way anything would ever happen. Not now. Not after he'd stupidly confessed Kyla's crush to his father and practically shoved her to him.

Jon went to fetch another drink when Saul called for silence. "And now, I have a special announcement to make."

He tossed the shot back before the words finished out of Saul's mouth. "My daughter, Princess Kyla Kishrah, will wed Advocate Armas Lehem-Perez!"

Applause and shouts rippled through the crowds. The room was spinning. Everything was happening too fast. He didn't hear the rest as he headed out of the Great Hall.

Engagement. Wedding. *Dusted ash, what did I do? How did I mess this up so badly?*

Jon pushed his way through the corridor, all the way around the Great Hall to the atrium at the east entrance, when someone touched his forearm. He wheeled, blinking, as Lieutenant Barish let go.

"Your Highness — congratulations!"

Carmen had gone to flight school with his sister and often studied with Kyla before tests. They flew under their father Major Barish's command, and were a petite version of him, except they continued to wear their hair in the traditional Sim'ee style of short narrow braids.

Jon frowned. "What for?"

Carmen stepped closer, away from the crowd of pilots they were hanging with. "For your family, your sister — you're gaining a brother-in-law."

Brother-in-law. That's all he can ever be to me.

The lieutenant's brows raised as he didn't answer. "Jon? You okay?"

"I'm fine," he lied, brushing by Carmen and making a hard left down the servant's hall.

His breath became shallow as his chest tightened, and he unbuttoned the collar on his uniform. The door was open for the emergency stairs to let in some air. Jon leaned against the railing, overlooking the several stories drop to the alleyway below. Hard concrete. *What would it take?*

He gripped the railing so hard his knuckles turned white. He could just kick the door closed and no one would notice he was gone. Climb over the railing, be done with it.

Armas will marry Kyla. Armas and Kyla. It was never going to be me and him. Hell, he probably doesn't even think of me that way.

Jon stood there for several minutes, the sounds in the Great Hall behind him of cheering and hollering fading to the normal noise of the crowd. He loosened his grip on the railing.

"Son."

He straightened up as Saul approached him, flanked by his guards. "How are you?" His father seemed genuinely concerned, his eyes raking over him, taking in his disheveled nature.

"All right," Jon answered, hoping he wasn't slurring his words too much. He tugged on his uniform shirt, though it was barely tucked in. "Just needed some air."

"The time is coming when the next generation will step up."

Jon's eyes widened.

"It's high time you were matched and married," Saul said.

He let out a breath through his teeth. He'd heard this speech a few times over the past couple of years. Of course. Now that Kyla was engaged, he needed Jon to do the same — find a wife to have children with.

"I'm getting older," the king admitted, his eyes downcast. "Sometimes, I don't act as I should. I know I lose my temper more these days." Saul set his hand on Jon's shoulder. The king's own breath smelled of liquor. "I won't be here forever. Some days I think I'm invincible, but other times, I know I'm not. All those people in the

Great Hall? They're all cheering for Armas over me. They want *him*. I know that's what the Elders were thinking. I could've had them all killed on the transport for their treasonous thoughts."

His father leaned in closer, cupping the back of his neck. "You will sit on the throne after me. *Not Armas*. Not whatever Dahan bastard child he puts in Kyla. *You*. The seed of my seed. You understand me?"

Jon gulped, hoping his knees would hold up because he was trembling so badly. Saul wasn't being rational right now.

He's afraid of Armas. The Advocate has more power and he knows it.

"Good. I'll be looking for a suitable match for you." Saul let go of Jon, and smiled, an eerie, lighthearted smile. "Enjoy this evening. Take a girl or two with you. I know you've done it before. Get it out of your system. The future king cannot afford any 'scandals' once he is engaged."

His father left, and Jon couldn't take it anymore. He stumbled back into the servant's hall and down to the kitchens, all the cabinets open. No one questioned him as he took a bottle of gin and opened it, before he went looking for someone to make him forget what his father said. Make him forget Armas.

Hours passed, and Jon found himself on the floor of his living room, leaning against the couch. He didn't quite remember how he got there, but his door was wide open, all his lights on. The bottle was nearly empty. The room seemed blurry. He was alone.

Voices traveled down the corridor — his sister's, and someone else. She giggled, and the other voice purred. Armas.

I don't want to hear them.

Jon dragged himself to his feet to go shut his own door, but a hand stopped it from closing.

"Hey, you all right?" Armas asked. Kyla was at her own door, frowning.

"No," Jon admitted.

He pushed against his door, but Armas pushed back, overpowering Jon. He stumbled backwards, falling into the armchair near his couch.

Armas said to Kyla over his shoulder, "Let me talk with him."

"Okay." Jon watched her squeeze Armas's hand as she passed through the door into her quarters.

Armas entered Jon's quarters, carefully shutting the door behind him. "What's wrong?"

Jon rose, wobbling. "Oh, you know. You're the hero. The one who defeated Ogroma for my father. I'm just the prince who can't do anything ..."

The Advocate caught his arm. "Jon, you're drunk ..."

"You're the one who saved us from our enemies, who saved us from the Phenians — until they come back and strike again."

Armas folded his arms. "Your father exaggerated, but we'll be ready for them."

"And then he gave you permission to fuck my sister."

The hero scowled. Jon smirked, glad his words stung.

"Who would've told your father that your sister liked me?" Armas demanded.

Jon turned away.

"I don't know what's gotten into you," Armas added, his voice rising. "If you don't want me with your sister, fine. But don't go telling the king it's such a great idea, that basically now I *have* to be with her, or he'll have me killed. *You* did this."

Jon spun around, swinging his fist wildly. Armas didn't have to dodge, just grabbed his arm and pushed him aside.

"Sleep it off," Armas spat, turning to leave.

Jon sank to the couch, his elbows on his knees. "I know. God, I know, Armas! I fucked things up and this is all my fault!"

No matter how he wished them away, the tears began to fall down his face, his body overtaken by sobs.

The cushion next to him dipped. A comforting arm rested on his back. He faced his sister's suitor, as his own pulse skittered.

Jon had to be strong for so long. Strong when their mother died. Strong for Kyla. Strong against his father's wrath. Strong for his fellow soldiers.

Armas's arms slowly came around him, as Jon buried his head in his chest. He let go, letting all his emotions fall as he clung to Armas's shirt and cried. Here, in his room, with this Dahan man, for once he didn't have to be strong.

THIRTEEN

ARMAS

Armas quietly exited Jon's suite, for the prince nodded off after a few minutes. He glanced at the security camera as he crossed the corridor. No guards were coming to keep the princess chaste. He'd intended to just walk her back to her room and say goodnight, but now — he'd stayed too long with Jon, and Kyla was waiting for him.

This was what Saul wanted. He hadn't expected the king to announce it so soon. *This is my fate. I have no choice right now.*

He took a deep breath, then opened Kyla's door.

She sat on the couch in her quarters, holding a wine glass in her hand. She smiled at him, but he noticed her foot thumping hard against the floor. His own heart threatened to beat out of his chest.

She was very pretty. Beautiful. He remembered when she entered his rustic living room back on the farm. He'd been shocked to see her, the princess in his own house, like she belonged there.

But a princess didn't belong there; she belonged here, sitting on an elegant couch, with expensive rugs on marble floors. Armas wasn't so sure where he fit. *I'll have to make myself belong. Fit in. Become the king's Advocate; become her husband.*

He sat down next to her. "Wine?" She offered, and he accepted, drinking deeply. The warmth spread through his veins.

"How is he?" she asked, motioning to the door.

"He's drunk."

Kyla rolled her eyes. "Typical."

Armas bit his bottom lip. Perhaps things didn't need to go quite so fast. "Maybe I should —"

She set her hand on his knee, sliding it up his thigh. "Stay," she whispered.

Armas gulped. "Your brother —"

"Has had a lot of girls over," she interrupted. "Plenty of times. It's none of *his* business who I'm with."

Armas's stomach sank. Of course Jon would've slept with a lot of women — those green eyes would get any girl. Hadn't he watched Jon say goodbye to one of those girls recently?

Her hand was dangerously close. "Um ..." Armas said, his breath shaky. He'd kissed a few girls back on the farm, had fooled around a bit, but ... "I've never ..."

Kyla giggled. "I've never, either." She moved her hand up to his face, behind his neck, and pulled him to her.

Armas closed his eyes, kissing her soft lips, remembering how it felt before. This time, it was a little less awkward. He slid his tongue in her mouth, savoring the taste of wine there. He worried how much she'd had to drink, but she seemed to be handling herself just fine the way she kissed him back. He moved his good hand to cradle her head, his fingers slipping into her hair, then sliding to her bare, smooth shoulder. He wondered if the rest of her was that smooth.

"Are you sure?" he whispered. "We both have been drinking —"

"I'm not drunk," she insisted, "and I don't think you are, either."

Kyla managed to unbutton the top buttons on his uniform shirt before they both stood and made their way to her bedroom. His lips traced a line down her neck to her shoulder, his fingers finding the zipper on the back of her dress. Her own hands slipped under his untucked shirt, slightly tickling his side, until he drew back sharply, the ache along his ribs and the pain from the wound still raw.

"Sorry," Kyla muttered, and he stared at her, the dress falling down to her waist, her breasts bound by the strapless bra she wore.

He knew he should ask her if she was on Prevention, because he hadn't brought anything with him. But he didn't, because Jon was right — Saul Kishrah, King of the Nacaens, wanted heirs.

Wedding. Marriage. Saul had directed his future, his *life*, giving him no say in the matter.

There was no choice, not with Saul pulling the strings. Anger began to stir inside of him, a rage kindled. He'd been set up. And there was no way out.

He pushed Kyla back on the bed, tried to kiss her again, but his mind was on Saul. He pulled away, sitting up.

"I'm sorry. It's not you, it's — I can't do this."

"Armas," she pleaded. "I know."

He faced her, confused.

"I know how my father is. You're a good man." She tilted her head, her eyes brimming with tears. "I know my father just sees this as a good political match. But ... I like you. If you don't want to stay, you don't have to."

Armas's tongue stuck in his throat. She was offering him a way out for tonight, but what about the next night? What about their wedding night?

"It's not fair to you. We barely know each other," he said.

She reached for his hand, still healing from the fused bones. "Nothing is fair for me."

Armas's heart still thumped hard, but slowly, she took his hand and set it on her bare thigh. Something about Kyla wanting him to touch her broke through him. She trusted him and wanted him. *Nothing is fair, for her or for me.* The *only* way to take control of the current situation was to accept this. He would be the king's son-in-law as well as the King's Advocate.

He kissed her again, and this time, he wanted more.

She helped him undress. In the sheets, he found out just how smooth her skin was as he explored her body with his good hand and mouth, her hands roaming over his muscles and hardness. He slid his hand up between her legs and her hips bucked. Despite his inexperience, even battered and bruised, he rolled her until she was on top of him and he pressed into her, managing to make her say his name, over and over.

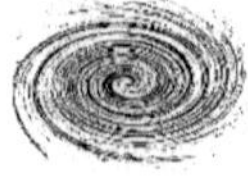

The sun had risen when Armas woke. Kyla slept next to him, but he'd tossed and turned most of the night, nightmares of Ogroma flashing through fitful sleep and utter exhaustion.

The sound of furniture shuffling on the tile floor startled him. He sat up. Kyla didn't stir, but someone was in the living room. He spied his trousers and underwear at the foot of the bed and pulled them on, careful with his injured hand, and managed to slip his shirt over his shoulders before creeping out of the bedroom. His uniform jacket had been laid over the back of the couch instead of where he left it, crumpled on the floor.

"Ah, sir," a voice whispered, belonging to a tall woman with light brown skin, blond hair plaited in a spiral design. She wore a top with the shoulders cut away, revealing a thin silver tattoo ring around her arm near her shoulder. "I set some breakfast for you both. I was told not to disturb you."

"And you are ...?"

"Laina, Kyla's maid. I've cared for her for many years," she replied, her accent lilting. Armas guessed she was Tali or Hessan — he'd heard those accents on the media before.

A thick silver medallion fell outside of her blouse as she leaned over the table. Armas saw it only for a moment before she tucked it away, but he thought it had an image of a hunter on it — the goddess Tana. He frowned. Idols were forbidden by law, so he'd been taught. He remembered when he was young, the messengers from the priests coming through his hometown of Ephra, decrying all other gods. The Serah fertility shrines were cut down. But he didn't say anything to her.

He ate a little, and after Laina left, he retrieved his boots from the bedroom. Kyla had flopped over on the bed, but her eyes weren't open; he decided not to wake her. He returned to the living room and grabbed his jacket. His chest ached from the wound as he pulled the jacket on but had difficulty buttoning it — a servant had helped him dress before last night's celebration. He managed two buttons before giving up and walking out of Kyla's door into the corridor —

— and right into the prince.

Jon's hand was on Armas's forearm, jaw dropped open, but he closed it right away. "So you did stay over."

Armas stared at the floor, anything to avoid Jon's accusing gaze. "You know I had to."

The prince let go of him and Armas dared a glance. Jon folded his arms across his chest. He'd showered, dressed in camo pants and a t-shirt, and his green eyes were amazingly clear.

Armas cleared his throat. "Are you feeling ... better?"

"Yeah. Just getting back," Jon replied, turning to enter his keycode and opening his door across from Kyla's. A nearly empty bottle of gin sat on the coffee table. The prince glanced over his shoulder. "Are you coming in, or what?"

Armas muttered a curse and followed him in. Jon grabbed the bottle. Right as Armas was about to suggest drinking wasn't such a good idea, Jon emptied the remaining contents into the sink.

"As I said, just getting back from a treatment. Went to

detox early this morning at the med bay. Decided the one-time meds weren't enough."

"Oh."

Jon tossed the empty bottle into the recycler. "I was a mess last night. I'm sorry."

Armas approached him, cautiously. He remembered how he had held Jon in his arms, before the prince fell asleep on the couch. Before he went over to Kyla's room and ... "I'm sorry for what I said, last night." He cleared his throat. "This wasn't your fault. Your father made this happen, not you."

Jon turned away, and Armas couldn't read his expression. Though he liked the feel of Kyla's kiss and her warm, smooth body, his palms became sweaty as he stood near Jon, and his heart started racing.

Ever since he woke up in the transport. Maybe even before that, if he was honest with himself. It wasn't Kyla he wanted.

"There's no escaping Saul," Jon said, his voice barely above a whisper as he faced Armas, his face blotchy. "You're caught in this now. He will destroy us."

"No." He clenched his fists. "I won't let him."

"You don't understand what he's capable of."

Armas bit his bottom lip. "Jon, no matter what — I'm on your side. I couldn't have brought down Ogroma without you. I couldn't have won without you. We're going to face the Phenians again." He dared to reach for Jon's hand. "I want ..."

Armas's words were lost as Jon cupped his face and kissed him. His lips were firm, insistent. Armas wrapped his injured arm carefully around Jon's body, his good hand tangling in his light brown hair. Jon smelled like warm rain, as when the sun came out after a storm. Jon's fingers quickly made work of Armas's uniform jacket, every touch a spark as he unbuttoned the shirt underneath. Heat coursed through Armas's blood, and he pressed against him as Jon's bare palms slid around his rib cage, careful of his bruises.

The prince rested his forehead against Armas's as they caught their breath. "No one can know," Jon said, and Armas closed his eyes, his heart heavy. Jon kissed him again, this time pushing Armas against the wall.

Armas gripped Jon tight as they kissed, fire radiating between them, the hardness of Jon's erection pressing against his stomach. But he'd just slept with Kyla. His future wife was next door.

Jon's sister!

It was all dusted up.

He pulled back slightly, but one glimpse in Jon's emerald eyes, and all his reservations rushed away, along with the blood from his brain.

When so much was decided for him, this was the one thing he could choose for himself.

Armas spun Jon around, pinning him next to the door. A hum escaped from Jon's mouth as Armas's hands slid around his waist. Armas had never felt this way before, wild and ravenous.

"I want you," he gasped, and Jon's eyes fluttered as Armas lifted his shirt off with hungry hands. He moved his lips along Jon's jaw, and just past his ear, he glimpsed the door was not fully shut, and neither was Kyla's.

He blinked, and Kyla's door was closed.

PART TWO

FOURTEEN

KYLA

"You are beautiful, Your Highness." Laina clasped the necklace of sparkling jewels around Kyla's neck. Her hair was pinned up like it was the night of the engagement announcement one year ago, but her strapless dress was white this time, with blue and green jewels embroidered along the hem and bodice.

Kyla didn't feel beautiful. A dull ache had settled in her chest. It had been a year, but she never spoke to anyone about what she saw that morning. Not even her husband-to-be. The few times he was home, the rare moments when he came to her quarters, she savored every moment: his blue eyes gazing over his freckle-dusted cheeks, the feel of his body, his scent and taste. She never told him she pretended to be asleep while he slipped out of her bed and across the hall.

Armas was often away as the Phenian Wars raged on, even after the defeat of Ogroma. The enemy regrouped, hired more Stiner mercenaries, and attacked Nidos. Last time, Armas had been gone for over a month. Each time Armas came back, he was different. He'd put on muscle. He'd added more scars. He almost lost his leg. She noted each of these with worry in the few moments she had with him.

Kyla had grown thinner in the last year, hollows forming under her eyes. Her father refused to let her fly into combat; the stress of Armas being away was enough, he said. She needed to rest. She needed to be safe. Even Major Barish relented when it came to Carmen, because every pilot was needed. But her father would not. He'd gone as far as grounding her from the shuttle.

The cage became smaller. She'd not only lost Armas, she no longer had Jon to confide in, and the only thing that gave her any sort of freedom had been taken from her. Anger, resentment, jealousy, rejection — all settled cold in her heart. *If only I was stone and could feel nothing.*

Laina lifted the veil, fastening it into the updo she'd twisted Kyla's dark locks into, bringing her back to the task at hand. Her maid wore her blond hair in long, loose curls, instead of her usual braids, her own dress a shimmery silver held by thin straps at her shoulders before flowing down to her ankles, matching the silver of her tattoo on her upper arm. "I know it is difficult, Your Highness."

"Laina, when have I ever asked you to call me that?"

Kyla replied, forcing a smile.

"Kyla," her maid said, with a slight smile. "Today is your wedding day. You are the princess marrying her prince. You should be happy."

"A prince I hardly ever see."

Laina's hands settled on her shoulders. Kyla caught a glimpse of pity in her maid's expression before she grinned. "You'll see him tonight, that's for certain."

Kyla pursed her lips. She tried to remember the joy she'd felt when she thought Armas had wanted her, the night of their engagement. Before the next morning, when everything shattered.

She faced Laina, trying to smile. "I wish it was different."

Laina adjusted the veil, placing the lace over Kyla's shoulders. "I know that sometimes, you have to take what moments of happiness you can find and treasure them. They are a gift. In a place engulfed in one war or another for decades, sometimes you have to fight for happiness, too."

Kyla gazed at herself in the mirror, shaking her head. How could she fight against her brother and his love? Against the forces that pushed Armas and Jon out the door and forbade her to join them? She was always left out: of her marriage, of the war, of any choices she could make for herself.

Laina moved around her, turning Kyla's focus from the mirror. "Might I cheer you up with my wedding present?"

Kyla's eyes widened. "A present? Laina, you don't need to give me anything. You do so much for me!"

The maid smiled at her in the mirror. "I think you'll like this." She left for a moment, returning to the room with a large white box and handed it to the princess. "Open it."

"Shouldn't I wait for Armas?"

"This is just for you. Open it," she insisted.

Kyla pulled the ribbon off and opened the box, removing the tissue paper. Inside was a large wooden carving: the mask of Serah, goddess of farming and fertility. It was exquisitely carved and painted, smooth to the touch.

"Oh, Laina, it's beautiful!"

"They're rare now, mostly destroyed by the priests, but I wanted you to have this." She bent over, her voice in a whisper. "There are Sebuj farmers on Dahan land who still carve her face into the trees, since the shrines were all cut down." Laina squeezed Kyla's shoulders. "You're supposed to place it under your bed, for luck."

Kyla's smile faded. Her maid didn't notice, as she removed the box and began putting away the combs she'd used for the princess's hair.

Would Armas stay, if I became pregnant? Would he see me as something more, if I was the mother of his child?

As Laina turned to leave, Kyla stopped her. "Armas and I barely know each other. Do you think it's possible to grow into love over time?"

"It may be possible," she replied, "but I wouldn't know."

The door chimed, and Laina checked the screen. "It's your father," she said. Kyla rose from her chair in the bedroom and walked to the living room while Laina opened the door, bowing before the king entered.

Saul wore his ceremonial dark green uniform, sword

at his side. Kyla's breath hitched, remembering what he'd done with that sword before, how he slaughtered the Leki informant, spilling his blood on the steps. "I'd like a word with my daughter. Alone."

"Of course, Your Majesty," Laina said, bowing again. She exited the princess's quarters.

Saul approached, his hands out to take Kyla's. "My beautiful girl. What a special day." He kissed her cheek, then glanced around the room. "Armas isn't here?"

"Of course not, Father," she said, trying to keep the bitterness out of her voice. "He is in his quarters, getting ready." Unless he'd snuck back to Jon's one last time, but she hadn't heard him. The last time she saw Armas was yesterday morning. He'd stayed a little later than usual in her bed but hadn't made any gesture toward intimacy. The ache of rejection gaped wide in her chest.

Saul raised an eyebrow. "I did not wish to see scandals among my children, but I am not so old as to not know what happens in my own home."

Kyla's breath caught in her throat as she sat down.

"I know he stays here, sometimes, after the late nights in the Situation Room, after working out strategy with Jon. While I would have preferred for you to wait, I'm not so old-fashioned as to know you're both young and eager."

She exhaled through her teeth. Even though this wasn't a conversation she wanted to have with her father *at all*, at least he wasn't talking about Armas's relations with Jon. As much as the betrayal and infidelity stung, Jon was still her brother, and she cared deeply for Armas. Her father would rip them apart if he knew.

"Tonight, the wedding. Tomorrow, the honeymoon. I am sorry we cannot send you to the Etho resorts as planned. It's too dangerous to send you out of the system. But Nidos is free of all dissidents now."

Kyla's eyes widened. "Are the wars over?"

Saul smiled, but it didn't reach his eyes. "For now. We rounded up the remaining Phenian sympathizers. Armas negotiated a deal with the Lubez nation to have more control."

"That's good," Kyla said in return. Laina was accompanying her and Armas, not only to serve the newly wedded couple, but also to see her family in the Tali nation on Nidos. She hoped they weren't caught up with the sympathizers.

"We found evidence of Tana worship there."

Kyla's heart grew cold. "Like what?"

Saul tilted his head. "Shrines, statues, figures of women with bows and spears. I thought we'd rid our system of that filth long ago." He smiled at her. "One God, one system, one people. That is who we are. The old national allegiances need to go, and the old gods are part of that problem.

"I know you've been disappointed, Kyla," he continued, changing the subject as he took the chair across from her. "I had to keep you safe. If I allow one child in danger, I must protect the other. But now that the Phenian Wars are over, when you return from your honeymoon, I will give you an assignment."

Her eyes widened. Finally, a chance to prove to her father she could lead. A chance to have a life other than as Armas's wife.

Saul cleared his throat. "There's evidence of goddess worship elsewhere in this system. I worry they may be hiding among our uninhabitable moons."

Kyla's hands shook. She shoved them under her thighs to keep still. There were goddess worshippers everywhere, but they'd managed to keep their practices unnoticed. Wrapped them in the worship rituals of the One God. There were communes scattered among the rocks in the system.

For over a year, she'd kept secret where Zam was hiding. The Tananites who lived under the surface on Ramah, under the ruins from Saul's destruction when he cleansed the system years ago.

"You will lead a special team to hunt them down." He leaned over, cupping the back of her neck to kiss her forehead, as he'd done a hundred times when she was a child. "Wipe. Them. Out."

He stood, reaching for her shoulder and pulling her up into an embrace as she trembled. "But don't be afraid; don't worry about those things for now. It's time for me to escort you down the aisle to your husband."

JON

(THE NIGHT BEFORE)

When the briefing ended, Armas told Saul he had some last-minute wedding details and needed Jon. The king motioned for the two to leave.

An hour later, Jon sat against the wall on Armas's bunk, shirtless and sated. The Advocate's officer's quarters were much smaller than Jon's palace suite, but closer to the king's Situation Room, and they'd opted to go there, barely getting the door closed before giving in. Afterward, he'd half-dressed, and Armas, in only his undershorts, sat down in a chair across from him and tuned his seven-string lyre.

Jon's gaze raked over his lover's body, soaking in every moment as if it might be the last time he saw him. The red scar on his left thigh where he'd almost lost his leg. Smaller scars from incisions to re-fuse bones. A jagged mark on his upper arm from a Phenian bullet that pierced his armor. His taut thighs and calves, solid arms, pectorals and abs, evidence of muscle added through conditioning and battle.

"Do you want to hear it?" Armas asked.

Jon reached forward and grazed Armas's knee with his fingers. "Of course."

Armas strummed the melody and Jon leaned back, closing his eyes as Armas's voice rolled in his head like his tongue had moments before.

> *"You are my strength, my steadfast shield,*
> *Only for you my heart will yield,*
> *You are the king of my heart.*
> *The only thing I know is true:*
> *I'd give my life, I'd die for you,*
> *You are the king of my heart ..."*

Jon opened his eyes, quirking a brow. "Who's that new line about? God, or the king?" *Or me?*

Armas shrugged. "Does it matter? Poetry can be about multiple things. Don't be so binary in your thinking."

Jon took a pillow and struck his shoulder lightly. Armas's laugh was liquor in his veins, though he hadn't had a drink in a year. He'd stuck with treatment, but the next day might throw it all away.

He didn't know how he would survive the wedding.

"We gonna talk about it?" Jon said, setting the pillow down.

Armas returned the lyre to its case, then moved to sit next to Jon, leaning into him and settling his head on his chest. "No."

Jon rested his chin on the top of Armas's head. "We have to."

"What is there to say?"

Jon sighed, letting his fingers fall from Armas's knee. "Tomorrow. Today really, at some point, this is going to end."

Armas sat up and faced him. "I've been engaged this whole time. It's not going to make a difference."

"You know it is." Jon scratched his neck. "I don't want to hurt her more than she already is."

"I don't want to hurt her either," Armas insisted, entwining his fingers with Jon's. "But she knows. She's known this whole time and never said anything."

"She also never said anything about the women who keep throwing themselves at you," Jon teased, "but you've always put on a good show of resisting them and staying by her side at all the formal events. But you, coming to my room at night — we have to stop," he added quietly.

Armas let go of Jon's hand. "Don't do this. Don't give up on us —"

"We can't," Jon said sharply. "You are marrying my sister. She is ... eventually going to have *your* children. I won't do this to her, or you."

"So you're ending *us*?"

Jon dropped his head against the wall. He'd dreaded this conversation though it should've happened weeks ago. "It has to be this way."

Armas pulled back, his eyes sharp ice. "Was this just *fucking* to you, Jon?"

"No, of course not," he insisted, taking Armas's hand again and squeezing it. "It has nothing to do with you *or* me." Jon faced Armas on the bed, placing a palm on his lover's cheek. This time Armas didn't shy away as Jon continued. "I never expected to care for you this way. The last thing I wanted was to fall for the Advocate of my father ..."

He gulped, not daring to say out loud *my sister was already in love with you before you walked off the shuttle and into my life.* But he would be brave enough to say this. "I love you, Armas. I can't imagine my life without you." He cupped his face and kissed him, his lips soft. "My heart is yours. My soul is yours. But I can't ..." Jon choked, setting his forehead against Armas's. "I can't continue this knowing I can't be *with* you. That I can never say the vows in my heart for our friends and family to witness. And if it was *just* you and me against the galaxy, against my father, I'd risk it all. But not Kyla. Even if she knows, I don't want her to resent me forever. I want her to know I won't get in the way."

A tear escaped the corner of Armas's eye. Jon brushed it away gently with his thumb, and Armas pulled back, his red locks pasted by sweat to his brow. "In some ways I wish this was just sex," Jon added. "It would've been so much easier. Or just another arranged match like my father has proposed."

Armas stroked the back of Jon's neck. "Did Saul make a decision, then?"

Jon nodded. "The daughter of the Beneur Elder on Richo. Solid political choice. There are some details still being worked out with her family before we announce. It means I'll be pulled off duty for a while. I know Father has you back at his side the minute you return from the honeymoon."

Armas snuggled back to Jon's side. "This sucks."

Jon wrapped his arm around Armas's shoulder and planted his lips on Armas's temple, running his fingers through his lover's thick auburn curls. "Yeah. But we don't have a choice. Not in this system, not in my father's reign." And not with Kyla's heart also on the line.

Armas squeezed Jon tighter. "I don't want to lose you."

"You won't." He set his hand on Armas's chest. "I will always be right here. My heart is bound to yours. My soul is bound to yours. No matter who else I'm with, know this: I will only love you."

Armas responded by pulling Jon around his side and flipping him to his back, pinning him to the bed. "I am yours. *Always*. Don't forget me."

Jon knew he should say no, but once Armas started a trail of kisses down Jon's chest to his abdomen that burned so badly, he couldn't think straight.

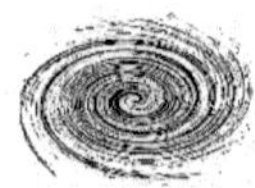

Jon hadn't slept. He stood in his father's Situation Room with Raimi, wearing his dress uniform and for the first time, carrying a ceremonial sword like his father. He hadn't seen Armas since he left his quarters in the middle of the night. The next time he saw Armas, he would be his sister's husband.

Sweat trickled down his back. He never wanted to drink so badly.

"Relax. It's your sister's wedding. Yours is still a few months away," Raimi drawled, his hands on his hips. "Miss Vellar is here, by the way, with her parents." He motioned to the door. "Already seated in the Great Hall."

"Thanks." Once the ceremony was over and the

reception began, his father expected him to mingle with Rela Vellar on his arm, even if it wasn't announced yet. Give her mother the step up she needed in assuring the Beneur nation leadership by letting everyone see her daughter with Jon.

"The king said I can serve as your personal guard once you're married, if you want."

Jon raised an eyebrow. "Do you want that job?"

Raimi ran his hands through his jet-black hair. "Jon, you and I have been through hell and back. Of course I want to, but — I miss how we used to be."

Jon's friendship with Raimi had grown distant. In the past, long nights on faraway moons meant a shared flask and card games. Raimi often covered for Jon if he'd found a woman in another unit interested in sharing a bunk. While Armas and Jon had been discreet on missions, they'd spent much more time together, and Jon's abstention from alcohol pushed him and Raimi further apart.

"I can't be that way anymore. I'm the prince. The heir." Jon folded his arms across his chest.

Raimi shrugged. "Yeah, I get it. I'll be your personal guard. For you and Rela."

Jon drew breath to speak, but the door opened. Abe Renk peeked his head in, scowling. "Where is your father?"

"With my sister. He went to have a word with her before the ceremony."

Abe swore. He was also in his dress uniform, and should be in the Great Hall, ready for the royal family to enter. "Of course I'd be left with this mess. We have some emissaries here, from the Leki."

Jon's eyes narrowed. "What are they doing here? Who allowed them beyond the force shield?"

"I did. They arrived earlier than expected."

The prince frowned, glancing at Raimi, but his confused expression shared that he also didn't know anything. With Kyla and Armas leaving on their honeymoon tomorrow, his father wasn't taking any time to relax. "I take it they're not here for the wedding." While still unusual, it was not improbable that his father would've reached out to the Leki royal family with an invitation. "So he's back in negotiations with the Leki?"

Abe gave a curt nod.

Coalition building. Saul hadn't mentioned the conversations with Stiners in the last few months, but given the Leki's prior arrangements in hiring the Stiners to attack — which Saul discovered from the Leki informant he then dismembered — Jon didn't doubt they were part of the equation. Jon stood, straightening his uniform. "Tell them the king will contact them tomorrow. And make sure they have comfortable quarters."

"Shouldn't the Advocate give that order?"

"He's about to get married," Jon said, moving to the door as the servant arrived, motioning for him to follow. "And I'm going to walk with my sister and the king down the aisle. Make sure their needs are attended to. And turn the heat up — their world is warmer than ours." He motioned to Raimi. "Captain Nadab will assist."

Raimi saluted Jon, while Abe scowled. Jon had never liked his great-uncle and the feeling was mutual.

The corridors were clear of guests as guards were stationed at every junction. Saul stood at the corner of the last corridor before the foyer to the Great Hall. "Is she ready?" Jon asked. His father gestured around the corner.

Jon turned, and his voice caught in his throat. His

sister was lovely, her hair done up, the veil cascading behind like angel wings. Laina straightened the train of her gown where it bunched up.

But even before the distance closed, Jon caught the sadness in Kyla's eyes. She'd known, and she'd kept his secret.

He leaned into her as she approached, bending to kiss her cheek. "You are beautiful."

She smiled, but it faded quickly.

Jon wanted to assure her he wouldn't be in the way, that she could have Armas in a way he never would, but he couldn't say anything in front of his father. Even if they were alone, he knew he wasn't brave enough. He'd snuck around her with Armas for a year. The damage was done.

"Shall we?" Saul asked. He kissed Kyla's forehead, then pulled the veil over her face. Laina checked to make sure it was arranged evenly, and Jon waited until the guards opened the doors to the Great Hall. He took his place behind Kyla, walking next to Laina who would accompany them until the ceremony began.

They followed Saul and Kyla into the Great Hall, where everyone stood. On the other side of the hall, Armas entered, escorted by his father and mother, and his two brothers behind him. Jon gulped. Armas's hair was as bright as flame, his eyes the ocean. He wore a white dress uniform with blue and brown edging — weaving the traditional colors associated with both Jamin and Dahan together. The parents and children met at the base of the steps, and Armas took Kyla's hand in his. Laina moved from his side, once more spreading out the train and the veil, then took her place near some of the guards who served the royal family.

Jon couldn't see his sister's expression, but Armas beamed, looking at her as if she were the only person in the world as they ascended the steps of the dais together. Armas knew how to play the part of the Advocate, of dutiful son-in-law, and now husband. He knew how to survive.

The priest stood before him in dark brown robes, allowing the guests to take their seats. Jon followed Saul to the side of the steps.

Now Jon had to play his. While the priest led the assembly in prayer, Jon glanced to his left and caught a glimpse of Rela Vellar. She wore a tight-fitting black dress with a slit up the side, her legs crossed. Her eyes were not closed, and she winked at Jon.

"Where's Abe?" his father whispered, snapping his attention back as the priest continued.

"He's settling in the Leki delegation. He came looking for you in the Situation Room."

Saul pursed his lips. "They're early."

"I figured it was best to be discreet about it and have him do it rather than anyone else from the Council. I'm assuming no one else knows they're here, and I'm assuming that was part of the plan." He raised an eyebrow at his father.

Saul placed his hand on Jon's shoulder. "We're not ready for the Elder Council yet. A few more things to negotiate."

The wedding continued, with Kyla and Armas reciting their vows. Saul leaned into Jon again as the ceremony neared the end. "I know this past year was not easy, but you did well with Armas in command. I won't be here forever, and soon, all this will be yours."

He leaned toward his father. "Certainly not for a long time."

"Perhaps. But your marriage to Miss Vellar will assure

the fate of the kingdom for future generations."

"As does Kyla's marriage today," Jon countered.

Saul tugged on the hem of his jacket. "For now."

Jon shot his father a look, but the king offered nothing more as he clasped his hands in front of him. If his father didn't like Armas, why let him marry Kyla at all? He said before he wanted to keep him in line, but Armas had done nothing except serve Saul and make sure Saul was credited with the victories.

He turned back to the dais, though his father's comment echoed in his ears. The priest looped the threefold cord around Armas and Kyla's clasped hands. "Two are better than one," the priest began, a familiar proverb as he concluded the end of the service, binding the two families together in marriage. "For two can withstand another together."

Armas shifted his gaze slightly, locking eyes on Jon. His heart skipped. Despite this wedding, for all that he wanted his sister to be happy, Armas belonged to him. He'd always be his.

The groom refocused on the bride as the priest pronounced them married. Applause and shouts filled the Great Hall as the couple kissed, and Jon looked away —

Right into his father's cold stare.

"Remember. The kingdom's future is at hand. Escort Miss Vellar tonight. Give your sister and her husband some space in the palace to be alone tonight, before they leave on their honeymoon."

The applause continued as the newly married couple descended the steps, but Jon couldn't shake the feeling his father had some other plan in place.

SIXTEEN

KYLA

"My daughter, and now my son," Saul said, beaming, as he kissed his daughter on the cheek, then his new son-in-law. "I couldn't be happier."

Kyla could almost buy his smile and cheerful demeanor. She could almost believe he wanted nothing more than her happiness, but this was Saul. Her father, whose pre-wedding pep-talk had been the promise of a mission to wipe out the people of her faith. Besides, she knew the pressure was on for grandchildren and heirs.

He'd escorted them both directly to her chambers in the palace well after midnight.

"Goodnight, Father," she said, opening the door to her

quarters.

Armas followed her in, shutting the door behind her. Jon had left the reception earlier, stating he didn't feel well. Kyla noticed Rela's look of disappointment when he left without her. *He must be waiting for Armas.* "What a sham," she muttered, entering her bedroom, unclasping the jewels from her neck and setting them on the bureau.

"What? I didn't catch that," Armas said, following her in.

"Are you going to stay here tonight?" she asked him, point-blank, hands on her hips.

He gave her a puzzled look. "Didn't we just get married?"

"Didn't we get engaged a whole year ago?" She slumped down onto the bed. "I can't do this anymore."

Armas leaned against the doorframe, loosened his shirt, and frowned. "What are you talking about?"

"This." She motioned between the two of them. "Pretending. Pretending we're happy. Pretending that you love me."

"I do love —"

"Don't lie," she said, trying to stop the tears, but they fell over her fingertips faster than she could wipe them away.

The mattress dipped as Armas sat next to her. His fingertips brushed her back, slipping over her shoulder. Part of her wanted to resist. Part of her reveled in his touch, any moment she had with him.

He pulled her close and pressed his cheek against her forehead, and she breathed in his scent, warm like honey and sweetgrass. "Do you remember the first time we met," he asked, "when you came into my living room?"

Kyla leaned back. "Of course I do. I remember

thinking this was the most handsome man I ever met, except that he did smell like sheep."

Armas's blue eyes twinkled. "I remember thinking here was the most beautiful woman I've ever seen, and she's helping my mom serve tea in my own house."

She laughed, wanting to believe him, but she knew better. "Do you love him?"

Armas pulled back, avoiding her gaze.

Kyla palmed his cheek, forcing his eyes to focus on her. "Do you love him?" she asked again.

Armas nodded. "But he and I — it's over. I promise. We can never be."

Her hand slipped from his cheek. She'd known it all along, but the admission stung like a needle in her arm.

"Kyla, I — we — never meant to hurt you."

"Did my father force you into this engagement?"

He pursed his lips, which was enough for her.

"Then you didn't love me, didn't want me."

She rose from the bed, but he caught her hand. "I knew you were special from the moment I saw you in my home," he insisted. "I knew I wanted to go with you. I can honestly say I have feelings for you, just ... different."

No matter how much she wanted to escape this hurt, he always managed to draw her back, and she couldn't resist. She let him pull her back to the bed.

"Is it possible to love more than one person?" she asked, desperate as she sat down again, keeping her eyes locked on his. "Is it possible you could learn to love me?"

His brows raised. His sapphire eyes were so full of light and wonder that Kyla dared to hope, dared to feel that even if she had to share him, she could make it through.

Armas wove his fingers into her hair that came loose

from the pins, setting his thumb behind her ear. "I don't know," he admitted, "but I'm willing to try."

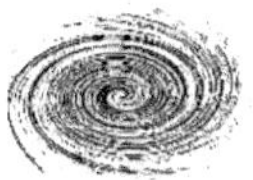

It was still dark when Kyla woke, surprised to find Armas's arm draped across her bare stomach.

She lay there for a while, snuggling next to his naked body, but couldn't get back to sleep. He'd stayed. His auburn locks hung over his face, his mouth slightly open.

He'd never looked so good.

And the way he'd made her feel — it was like their first time. Every touch, every moment full of power and passion. The way he'd undressed her. The half-lidded look in his eyes as he brought her to release, the way his hips rolled to meet hers, their bodies moving as one. Any reservations she held fell away. He was hers. He was here to stay.

But she couldn't sleep. The first night he'd stayed in months, and she kept shifting in bed. He was exhausted, after months of missions. Kyla slid out from under his arm, and he rolled slightly, but settled on the side of the bed.

She pulled on her robe and left her quarters, creeping down the marble staircase to the rest of the palace. She skirted the living area to the long corridor that ran from the west tower suite she shared with her brother, to the north tower. She wondered if her own mother had wandered these halls. She remembered her mother sometimes suffered from insomnia due to the medicine she took for her illness, which then took her life.

It was oddly quiet, with no guards, not even at the junctions which would be minimal security. Her father had mentioned to Jon to give her and Armas some privacy, but this was a bit excessive — and Jon had gone to bed before them anyway. She frowned. Apparently, her father really didn't want anyone disturbing them. *He wants grandchildren.*

Kyla shivered in the hallway. A fan must be on, somewhere. She came to a junction, where the breeze was coming from her right. From the high north tower, where her father had moved after her mother's death.

She never ventured there. Her father was usually in the Situation Room near the hangar and officer stations on the south side of Glia, where he strategized for war with Armas. His quarters were his private retreat, away from the family, away from memories of what once was.

But the door was open, and voices carried.

She couldn't make them out at first, as she crept toward the open door.

"I know you're used to the coldness of space. Melas is a warm world, but not as warm as Balec. We must keep up the appearance of hosting a Leki delegation."

She stopped, heart in her throat. *Appearances? Who are they really, if they are used to space?*

Her father's voice turned sharp.

"He was supposed to be an advocate for me — turn the people's attention to me as their king. But after every battle, more and more call his name. I told him to bed my daughter, to become my son-in-law, to get him under my control, but divisions are forming in my ranks, even among my own Elders. I do not trust the Dahan contingent, even with the marriage. Major Zeru should've been court-marshalled for her insolence months ago. But even now, Barish has let me know his misgivings on my decisions. We lose him, and the whole thing falls apart."

He crossed in her line of sight, and she held her

breath, staying in the shadows, out of view of the cameras. "There are representatives, Elders of every Nacaen nation in Glia tonight, and they have no idea you are here."

Kyla dared a step closer.

A deep voice, unknown to her, spoke. "Do we have a deal, then? You'll give us Ramah?"

She froze.

"Yes," Saul continued. "Soon word will leak out that we welcomed Leki representatives here. Keep up that façade. With their royal family split, the Nacaen Elders will assume you are one faction. They won't care in the long run, once they know what the Modes want. It would be the end of my reign if they knew I'd made a deal with *you*."

The princess took a step back, staying in the darkness.

"The Elders will be outraged at the Leki," the voice challenged Saul.

"And they will refuse all negotiations going forward with them. They will understand once and for all that we must have allies from the Near Sides, allies who need home worlds, such as yourselves, and others."

Another voice spoke, lighter. "The Modes are still angry about Ogroma. We are kin, you know, with the Modes, and losing their most valuable weapon into your hands strained our relationship."

Kyla's heart raced.

"I will return the bodies of Ogroma shortly. We now have their secrets, so I believe an agreement will be mutually beneficial."

"Indeed," the deep voice replied. "We suspect Ramah contains dendrilite. The Modes will want it for their neurolink silk. We can negotiate to keep them out of the system, and you give us a home world. No more hiring ourselves out to survive."

"If I'd known, I'd have never destroyed the settlement there, but it is yours if the mission is complete," Saul replied. "Now, your end of the bargain. Make it quick, and do not harm my daughter." His voice sounded hoarse. "I don't want her to suffer any more than she already has. But what could be more moving than the people's hero slain, the daughter of the king now a young widow? They'll demand we wipe out the Leki and welcome you *Stiners* with open arms."

Kyla bit her own lip to keep from crying out.

Tana protect us!

She moved through the shadows as quickly as possible, back through the maze of rooms and up the stairs to her own quarters. She spied the camera above her. Saul would know she left her room and came back, but when would he be alerted to it? He didn't know she'd overheard. There was nothing that could be done about the footage.

She had to act fast.

Her new husband was still sleeping, legs tangled in the sheets.

"Armas! Armas!" She shook him hard.

"Huh?" His hair stuck to his forehead with sweat.

"You have to go. My father is planning to kill you!"

He lifted his head, propping himself up on his elbows. "What?"

"You have to go. Now!"

"You're not making sense. Did you have a nightmare?"

Kyla pulled all the blankets and sheets off the bed. "Armas! You have to go. He wants to kill you. He has Stiner assassins here."

She tossed his clothes at him, and Armas sprang up, yanking on his trousers and undershirt from his wedding uniform. "Where are my boots?"

"Here!" she said, tossing them to him one at a time. "Go out the window. The archways will lead to the museum hangar."

"Okay?" he responded, more as a question than a response.

"The Kittiwake Flyer. Its transponder doesn't work and its drive signature is easy to mask. It has enough fuel to get you to Ramah — I flew it the other day and had it refueled." She'd done so when Saul, Jon, and Armas were away late last week at a briefing and planned for it to be a wedding gift. She'd needed something to do and thought maybe it would help her understand where Armas came from, and that he might enjoy a solo flight. Might think it was a sweet gesture from her. Thank Tana she'd done it then.

"Zam is there. He'll hide you." She'd have to figure out how to save the prophet again and the Tananites later.

"But I've only flown it once —"

"You're gonna have to be a fast learner," Kyla said, all the while the footsteps growing louder in her mind, though she had no idea when the assassins would arrive. "Hurry!"

Armas flew to the window, and audibly gasped. She knew the top of the archway that led from her window was ten, maybe twelve centimeters wide. Armas held onto the window frame, eyes wide. "You've got to be kidding me."

"There's no time — you have to go. You have to trust me!"

But Armas spun around and caught her face, planting

his lips on hers. Everything Kyla ever wanted from him. He pulled back for a moment, his fingers lingering on her cheek.

"I trust you."

"Promise me you'll come back to me — when it's safe. *Promise me*."

He nodded. "I promise."

"Go!"

Armas leaped onto the archway, with his hands stretched out as he tried to balance. But Kyla could not afford to watch him.

She crossed the hall and rapped on Jon's door. "Jon!"

He opened the door quickly, surprising her. Dark circles lined his eyes — he hadn't slept at all.

"It's Dad. He's trying to kill Armas."

"What?"

"There are Stiners meeting with Dad right now, planning to assassinate Armas tonight. I told him to fly to Ramah — there's a secret settlement there. Get the force shield down so he can fly out. Do what you have to do, shoot down our own pilots if you have to. Just make sure Armas makes it. He's in the Kittiwake."

Kyla didn't wait for Jon's response, crossing back to her own quarters and slamming the door and locking it. She sprang to the bedroom, stuffing some pillows down under the blankets, and covered the pillows with old clothes. Her foot bumped something under the bed. The Serah mask from Laina. It had brought her luck with Armas. She placed it on the pillow, pulling the blanket up over it.

The door vibrated once, twice, before the door pushed open. Kyla shielded her eyes, lying on the bed next to the figure underneath.

The assassins entered the room, dressed as palace guards, startled to see her up.

"Who are you? What in God's name are you doing? This is our wedding night!"

"The Leki have admitted the Advocate is in league with them. The king gave orders —"

"Well, the king will have to wait," Kyla sneered. "My husband is sick, poor thing. See?"

The guard crept closer to the bed, leaning over. Kyla whipped back the Serah mask, catching him in the face and cutting across his cheek with Serah's nose. She launched off the bed at the other guard, pulling him to the ground, wrestling the pistol from his hand.

"You wouldn't dare shoot me."

"You have permission to shoot if she moves." Her father's voice uncoiled from the shadows beyond her door.

Kyla shuddered, dropping the gun. The assassin behind her grabbed her arms.

The king's eyes narrowed. "Traitor. Where is he?"

"He's long gone," she spat. She glanced at the Stiner holding her, smug that the gash was deep. It would scar.

Saul searched the room, stopping at the balcony. "He's out the window. He couldn't have gone far!"

The other assassin jumped to the windowsill.

"It's too late," she said defiantly to her father. "Faking the Leki diplomats' arrival and framing Armas? Your plan is in ruins. You've lost."

The king's eyes were flickers of flame.

Kyla swallowed back her fears, for the courage that had filled her surged through her veins. "Zam has foretold it. Your time is over. God has removed favor from you."

"Zam?" her father repeated, frowning.

"The people will rally to Armas, and if not Armas, then Jon. You can't kill us all. You need heirs, or this has all been for nothing."

He moved over to strike her, but Kyla laughed in his face. "There's nothing you can do now to hurt me. You wanted Armas to marry me so he wouldn't be a threat to you, but the people love him more. He's already won. You can humiliate me, kill me even, but he'll still win. When he comes back, the people will be behind him, and there is nothing you can do about it."

Saul lunged for her, his hands against her throat. Kyla struggled for air. "The people — will love it — when they learn — Armas's wife is dead — heart is broken."

Her eyelids drooped, her vision becoming spotty. If this was it, so be it — she would die to save Armas, to save the kingdom.

But the tightness around her throat released. She gasped, drawing as much air as she could into her lungs.

"Get her out of my sight."

"Yes, sir."

Kyla was forced down the hall. Her throat hurt, her muscles ached. They dragged her down unfamiliar passages into the catacombs underneath Glia, into the cells where the war criminals were kept. So be it. As long as Armas was free. She only hoped he made it out in time.

The cell door slammed, and she was in complete darkness.

SEVENTEEN

JON

Jon returned to his own bedroom despite Saul's order to be elsewhere. He scanned through vids because he couldn't sleep, turning up the sound when he heard Saul's voice outside his door, escorting his sister and new *brother-in-law* to her suite. While Jon had accepted it when Armas visited Kyla's bed a few times in the last year, tonight he couldn't handle it. He paced the floor. He opened cupboards emptied long ago of liquor. He knew some of the mech techs had drugs they swore took the edge off everything. He changed out of his dress uniform and into camo pants and shirt, pulling on his boots.

However, though Saul had left, there were probably twice as many guards posted, protecting the princess and royal family. He laced his hands behind his head, counting his steps across his living area, to his bedroom and bathroom, and back. Jon didn't need alcohol. He didn't need drugs. He could survive this. He had to. He paced his quarters a hundred times.

He collapsed on the couch, sleep finally catching him.

Jon startled awake at pounding on his door. "Jon!"

He opened the door. Kyla's hair was a mess, and she was dressed in her robe and slippers, but her face was paler than he'd ever seen.

"It's Dad. He's trying to kill Armas."

"What?"

"There are Stiners meeting with Dad right now, planning to assassinate Armas tonight. I told him to fly to Ramah. There's a secret settlement there. Get the force shield down so he can fly out. Do what you have to do, shoot down our own pilots if you have to. Just make sure Armas makes it. He's in the Kittiwake."

"Ky —"

She'd already crossed the corridor and shut her door, the distinctive sound of locks sliding into place.

He's trying to kill Armas.

Jon didn't spend one more second contemplating her words. She always told the truth — even about Zam in the end, she told the truth to him. He knew his father well enough. He could only imagine how he'd decided to murder his son-in-law on their wedding night to rally the people around him and eliminate the closest threat.

He ran down the stairs, two at a time, and grabbed the railing to swing around the corner. No guards posted. Not just odd, but entirely out of protocol. Saul had ordered a doubling of the guard for the wedding — he'd been in the briefing when his father gave the order. *Where the hell were they?*

A chill ran down his back. *Why would you need guards when the enemy is working for you?* This was all part of Saul's plan.

Jon sprinted through the corridor and down the ramps to the main hangar. He ran across the deck to the round room for flight control. No guards were posted. Jon punched his code in, and the door slid open.

Two flight control workers sat at the console, one on the comm, the other bringing up the cameras from the museum hangar.

"Unidentified pilot, you are not cleared to take off," the flight control admin said.

The secondary worker said in a low voice, "Security breach, museum hangar —" Their eyes grew wide as they spotted Jon in the reflection on the screen.

Jon's heart skipped as Armas's voice came over the comm. "This is Red Lion, clearance A-2 Advocate Override."

"Negative, Red Lion. Under the king's order, no —"
The comm feed was filled with static.

"Open the launch doors," Jon ordered, sweat beading on his brow. He had no weapon to force them.

The viewscreens showing the museum hangar flashed as proton fire struck the doors, then the feeds went dark.

"Dusted ash. Perimeter breach in the museum hangar!" the secondary shouted over the security comm.

"That's the King's Advocate!" Jon shouted back. "What the hell do you think you are doing?" Both workers stared at him, the administrator's jaw dropping.

"Your Highness, the king gave strict orders that no one

—"

"You think he dusting meant the Advocate, or me? Drop the force shield."

"But Your Highness —"

A crackling sound came over the comm as the screens lit up red, the force shield sustaining the proton fire. Armas would die in a matter of seconds.

"Lower the force shield!"

Jon didn't wait for a response — he pushed the secondary out of the way, grabbed the large red sliding lever and pulled it back. The energy levels on the monitors dropped, the crackling ceasing. A white blur of a ship shot through.

He slumped to the console, watching the viewscreen as the Kittiwake slipped toward the atmosphere in the night sky. The damn thing was painted white, probably the only Kittiwake still in use in the entire galaxy. Armas would be spotted easily.

Boots on the ground raced toward him. "What the hell is going on?" Major Barish demanded. Three others followed behind, staying in the shadows.

Jon snapped his jaw shut. He didn't know how to explain this, that his father had tried to have his own Advocate assassinated.

"Sir," the flight controller saluted Barish, "Someone stole the Kittiwake from the museum hangar and shot through the doors —"

"Because you wouldn't open them for the Advocate," Jon defended. "I pulled the shield down just in time."

"What in God's name —"

"You tell me," Jon retorted. "Where are the guards? What happened to the security protocol arranged for tonight?"

"The king changed the order, according to Major Renk." Barish pulled his tablet from his pocket and shoved it at Jon. "Gave pretty much everyone except us the night off once the reception was over. Moved the guards to cover the Leki delegation that arrived."

"They're not Leki. They're Stiners."

Major Barish's jaw flexed. "That's a hefty accusation, Your Highness."

A beeping sound emanated from the control console. "Your Majesty," the flight control administrator said, bowing, as Saul's face appeared on the screen.

"I ordered you to secure the perimeter and allow no ships in or out!" Saul screamed at the administrator. Jon winced.

"But sir, the prince said —"

"Jon? *Answer me!*"

"Father," Jon said, gathering his courage. "Someone was trying to kill Armas, and so —"

"You —" Saul snapped his jaw shut, his face red, the vein in his temple throbbing. "You let him get away. The Advocate has betrayed us."

"Father —"

"He is a traitor! He ... he ... he is in league with —" Saul shook his head.

Jon had never seen his father like this. Full of rage and fury, yes, but usually tempered with cold calculation. Saul was out of control. Flustered for words. He couldn't even come up with the lie because he'd been so sure the Stiners would catch Armas and kill him. Didn't plan on both of his children saving the Advocate instead.

Every second wasted gave Armas a greater chance at survival.

The king closed his eyes, inhaling deeply. The redness

left his complexion, and the composed, determined leader returned. "Take a squadron. Hunt. Him. Down. That is an order, *Jon*."

"Your Majesty," Major Barish interrupted. "We don't have a full squadron on — your protocol dictated only emergency flight crew rotations."

"Go find him with whoever you have. If he resists, kill him." The screen blipped out.

Barish stared at Jon, his brow furrowed. "The emergency crew is on deck and ready to fly, Your Highness. I'll lead them —"

"No. He ordered me to do it." Jon bit the corner of his lip, and added quietly, "You know how wrong this all seems."

"You heard your orders," Barish said loudly to the three pilots in the shadows. "Follow the prince. Hunt down the Kittiwake."

"Milo," Jon said, holding Barish back. "Birds in the air, wolves on the ground."

Barish saluted, acknowledging Jon's coded phrase that something more was going on. "Affirmative, Your Highness."

Jon hoped the Sim'ee major understood that Saul was covering up something, but he needed to tread carefully.

He ran back across the hangar as the emergency tech crew on duty readied their fighters. Jon pulled on his flight suit, then glanced at the other three pilots, faces now lit by the hangar lights. Faces he might have to shoot down to save Armas.

Two he recognized from previous missions, though he didn't know them well.

The last was Carmen Barish.

EIGHTEEN

ARMAS

The four Bluehawks gained on him. He ignored their hail, heading into the rings of Horeb, weapons hot. The magnetic interference was already messing with his sensors; Armas hoped it would mess with their targeting systems as well.

Over the last year he'd learned to fly and had piloted Bluehawks on occasions, but he was nervous flying this old bird. *His bird.* His grandmother's fighter. He'd taken it up once before, after he'd been cleared for solo flights. Never thought he'd be fleeing Melas in it.

Rocks and gas swirled around him, clouding his visuals and messing with the dated instruments onboard.

"Red Lion, this is Dark Wolf."

A shudder traveled down Armas's spine as Jon called to him over the universal channel.

"You are ordered to turn off your weapons and return to the surface of Glia."

Armas switched channels, hailing Jon privately. "He'll kill me —"

"*I know.* Stay off the universal comm and head into the rings. Use the gravity of other moons to skip across. Cut your engines to conserve fuel when you can." Jon took a deep breath. "Armas, I need you to trust me."

"With my life."

He could imagine Jon quirking a smile. "That's what I'm afraid of."

Before Armas could respond, the rocks a few meters to his right exploded with proton fire.

"Watch out at your five — he's breaking for you!"

Armas heeded Jon's warning, rolling the Kittiwake away. He flipped, belly side up, weapons facing the Bluehawk.

"Fire!" Jon ordered Armas.

He hesitated. These were pilots that he trusted, that trusted Jon. "I can't —"

The Bluehawk fired, missing him by meters below. Armas fired back. The fighter exploded as he hit the munitions bay.

More rocks exploded above him. He couldn't tell for certain which of the three remaining Bluehawks was Jon.

"For the love of God, run for it," Jon pleaded. "You can't win this one."

"They'll follow me."

"I'll take care of them. *Trust me.*"

Armas flipped his ship over and burned hard toward the larger rock in front of him. Far off in the distance, he could make the lights of Richo. Samar, the wintry moon, was on the far side of the gas giant.

Ramah orbited Nidos, the planet closest to the Cana Star. Eventually he would have to cross open space, with no moons or rings to hide in.

Rocks exploded to his right, sending his ship in a spin as debris struck the wing and hull. "God blast it!" He glanced at the rear-view screen.

One Bluehawk had fallen back. In two seconds, the ship that fired on him was in pieces.

Armas didn't hesitate. He changed course, shifting from asteroid to moon in the rings, hiding between rocks, then cutting engines for a while to catch his breath. The two remaining Bluehawks fell back, until they were off his scanners. Jon must've convinced the other pilot to return, or he destroyed them.

Even then, Armas waited in the dark, watching clouds race across Horeb's cream-colored gaseous surface for hours, before leaving the safety of the rock he'd hid behind to burn hard for Ramah.

Nidos orbited so close to Cana that only the southern hemisphere, which perpetually pointed away from the star, was inhabited. Orbital station shields reflected light away from Cana and kept the giant shipbays, where the warships of Saul's fleet were built, safe from radiation. The Tali, Hessan, and Lubez nations had settled there, but shipbuilding was often delayed due to conflict on the planet. Armas had spent much of the last year on Nidos or in orbit defending the orbital shipyards during the Phenian wars. But he'd never been to Ramah. He knew Kyla had sent Zam there, and he'd kept her secret.

The marbled moon hung far off in orbit. Swirls of gray and dark brown rock covered the surface, along with scars from the old settlement, bombed by Saul years ago. He'd been taught by the village priests growing up that when the twelve ships first arrived to the Nacaen Group, they found water underneath its surface. The three nations that decided to stay and not continue to Horeb's moons refilled their water supply from Ramah, before they built reflective shields and converted Nidos's atmosphere.

Armas had barely slept. The ship's fuel cells were low, and he'd drunk most of the water and eaten the nutrition packet on board. He needed to set the ship down, but there was nothing on the surface indicating a landing pad.

He hesitated to send a ping, worried who would be listening, but an automated command came through. Coordinates led to a gray rocky crevasse, a gap in the surface. Armas guided the ship in, adjusting for the moon's gravity, until the crevasse widened into a metal shaft. Turning the ship ninety degrees, he entered the hangar.

He set the Kittiwake down in the middle, shutting down the power to conserve the tiny bit of fuel he had left. He scanned the hangar — there were some low emergency lights on, and dirt and debris scattered across the floor. Abandoned, or at least trying to look like it. A loud clang sounded as the hangar bay doors closed behind him. Instruments showed pressurization in progress, oxygen levels rising, and carbon monoxide and other gases disappeared. He noted the air cyclers at the hangar's far end, and a set of metal doors nearby.

He fumbled around in the cockpit until he found the personal weapons compartment. Kyla had left him an Ember 90, a pistol with a holster strap for his flight suit.

Armas popped the hatch with a hiss, keeping his helmet on for now. The gravity was lower here than the habitable moons of Horeb, and he leaped from the cockpit, landing on the hangar floor.

One of the doors opened. Two priests in gray and black robes emerged, their heads shaved, silver and black tattoos on their left arms. They tapped their chests with two fingers and bowed.

Priests of the cult of Tana.

"Welcome, stranger. Have you come to drink of the font?" one asked, her voice high and lilting.

Armas kept his weapon pointed up. "I don't know what you're talking about. I'm looking for Zam, the prophet."

The two priests exchanged a glance. "You're a God-fearer, then."

"I'm not here for a religious argument."

A cough sounded behind him. "At last, the Advocate has found his way."

Armas spun around. A door Armas hadn't noticed before was open, etched out from the rock. The old man walked hunched over, his feet shuffling across the floor. His hair had grown shaggy, and his brown robes hung disheveled.

Zam looked as though he'd aged twenty years in one.

"The tea that helped keep up my strength no longer is useful, even in the low gravity," the prophet said, before coughing again.

Armas removed his helmet. The air had a tinny smell, but the sensors on his flight suit monitor indicated the air was breathable.

"You need to refuel your ship," Zam said.

Armas had expected to feel relief, or hope. He'd thought, during the hours on the run from Melas, that here he would find direction and purpose. But before the prophet could speak again, fury raged in Armas's chest.

"That's it? You're just sending me on? You came to me, begged me to go be Saul's right-hand man. You told me I was destined for something greater. But at what cost?" He pointed his finger at the prophet's chest. "You claim to speak for God, but why would God do this? Why would God choose Saul and then have him try to kill me? Why would God do this *to me*? And now you're just telling me to go on the run?"

The prophet cast a glance behind him, and Armas followed his gaze. The two priests of Tana stood close, whispering.

"They think our ways outdated, though they're the ones who believe in a goddess of war. Our God is of peace. But no matter." Zam waved his hand and called out to the priests. "This does not concern you."

The two women bowed, tapping two fingers to their chests, before leaving through the door they entered.

"Fool!" Zam shouted at Armas. "God doesn't control you like a puppet. You make your own choices." The old man spat. "Saul was chosen by God, but then he chose to do things his own way. He didn't heed wisdom."

"He didn't listen to you." Armas folded his arms across his chest.

"He didn't listen to God, but you're right, he also didn't listen to me." Zam sighed, running his fingers down his beard. "Saul is hell-bent on preserving his reign instead of the kingdom. You are different."

"Because I don't want to be king."

"Because you're the *right person* to be king."

Armas stood agape for a moment. "No. No – I'm no king."

"You stopped the Phenian advance, and you destroyed Ogroma."

"That was dumb luck, nothing more."

"It was ordained by God, and you are the one."

"What if I'm not?" Armas threw his hands in the air. The anger dissipated into the fear woven in his sinews since he left Kyla. The fear that this was all a huge, horrible mistake. "What if I'm the wrong person? Right now, I can't even be on the same planet because the current king wants to kill me!"

Zam scoffed. "Did you expect it to be easy? Did you expect Saul would simply acquiesce to your advice as Advocate? Or did you think by becoming his son-in-law he'd accept you?"

"What else could I do? He practically ordered me to marry Kyla to be part of the family, then decided to kill me on my wedding night!"

"Perhaps you hoped that eventually, he would accept your love for his son?"

Armas's jaw dropped open. "How did you know?"

Zam ignored his question. "You fell into his trap, thinking that if you continued to bend to his will, you'd win his praise, his affection, his acceptance as the Advocate. And now, you'll be on the run until one of you is dead."

"Dusted ash!"

The prophet eyed him sharply. "There is no pleasing Saul. He can never be satisfied. And he knows more than he will let on, he's always one step ahead. Which is why you *must* go. Take your ship to Nidos and find the priests of our God there among the Hessan, they will give you shelter. Saul will look for you there, but you will escape. If you remain here ... he *will* kill you."

"What about you?" Armas asked. "Won't he kill you?"

"Despite our differences, they have hidden me well," the old man said, motioning toward the doors where the two priests had left earlier. "My time is short as it is." Zam glanced at the Kittiwake. "That ship doesn't have much life left in it, but it will take you to where you need to go."

"How do you know?"

"If what I said doesn't turn out to be true," the prophet said, "you won't be able to come back and complain about it anyway." Zam leaned in, the brief smile in his wizened face turning to sorrow. "You have no choice. You must go. Now."

NINETEEN

KYLA

The food had long gone cold on the plate, the cup untouched.

"Your Highness, please eat," the guard insisted, but Kyla leaned against the wall of her cell, sitting on the floor as there was no bed, no chair, only a commode in the corner. Still wearing her slippers and robe, she pulled the fabric tighter around herself, but she would not show fear. If she was to be a political prisoner, she would act like one.

"I told you; I will not eat until my father tells me my husband is safe."

The guard sighed, holding on to the cell's bars.

She tilted her head slightly. "Where is the king?"

"I don't know, Your Highness."

"And you wouldn't tell me if you did know, would you?"

The guard let go of the bars.

"He tried to *murder* my husband!" she screamed.

The guard's footsteps echoed down the metal corridor, and the lights in the hall went dark again. One of Saul's crueler methods was to keep prisoners of war in total darkness for days, even weeks. If Armas managed to make it away alive, Saul would attempt to turn the people against him, turn him into the enemy.

She never imagined he would turn on *her*. Her neck still hurt where his hands squeezed her windpipe, her heart from his hate.

"Zam," she cried in the dark. "Why is this happening? Why didn't you protect us?"

Hours passed. A light flickered on down the hall. Kyla squinted as the steps grew closer. "What do you want?"

Her great-uncle Abe sighed, leaning against the door. He'd shaved his head completely, losing the crown of white he usually wore, wearing his dark blue flight suit. "You always were my favorite niece."

Kyla spat. "I'm your only niece."

He rolled his eyes. "I thought you'd want to know. Jon is pursuing the traitor in the rings, and your father will have him in custody soon."

Jon won't let them find him. Thank the goddesses. "He's not a traitor. Dad hired the Stiners to kill him."

Abe smirked. "So you know. Ah well. The truth doesn't matter in the long run. You learn this when trying to rule a system. All that matters is who wins in the end, for they get to rewrite the narrative."

"How can you be so callous?"

"It's *war*. Since our people landed here, war is all we've known. War with each other. War with nations from the Bara system after their republic fell. War with the Sebuj who were on this world before we came. Know anyone who is Sebuj now?"

Kyla shifted her gaze from Abe, but he continued.

"You don't, because we wrote them out of history."

She bit her lip to keep from smirking. Laina had just told her, right before her wedding, *there are Sebuj farmers who still carve her face into the trees*. The worship of Serah had come from the original people.

They were still *here.*

"We have four naturally habitable worlds without terraforming and underpopulated," Abe continued lecturing, "although Nidos is too hot for my liking and Samar far too cold. We have dendrilite, we have unlimited fuel from Horeb, and Richo's farms produce threefold what we all need. We have all the resources. We ought to be united against our enemies. Armas is a threat to that."

"He is *not* the enemy," Kyla said, frowning, though his mention of dendrilite wormed its way in her brain. She remembered her father mentioning it before with the Stiners as a bargaining chip. She glanced back at Abe, who folded his arms.

"Your father thought he could keep him under control as his son-in-law. But you hear how the people chant his name. They want him, not only over Saul, but over your brother, and that cannot happen, not if we want to establish a legacy. We tried democratic elections with the old council, years ago when Dahan was the seat of government. It didn't work. We need centralized power that can last beyond a generation."

Kyla shifted on the floor.

"I will admit your father is more ... unsettled these days." Abe seemed to chew over his words. He scratched his chin. "When you were younger, your father would've never gone against the prophet."

"When did that change?"

Abe raised his eyebrows. "He aligned himself with the most powerful families of Dahan and Sim'ee, and outlawed all religions but belief in the One True God. Slaughtered the Tananites, destroyed the Serah shrines, burned down the wooden temples of Starre. Any remaining dissidents of Dahan and Sim'ee turned to his rule rather quickly here on Melas, and he did the same on other Nacaen worlds. Religion is a powerful tool to control."

"Zam didn't use religion that way," Kyla countered. "He believed in one God but would never call for the slaughter of innocent people."

"Your father will do what it takes — even use fear — to unite people, because it's the only way we will survive against what is coming."

"What do you mean?"

"The Leki, the Phenians, all the nations of the old Bara Republic — they all wanted not simply to destroy us, but to *take* our worlds for their own. To build an empire that was lost when Bara fell. To use our resources in preparation for war with the Near Side systems. They are building up, occupying and driving out the smaller nations and peoples. Aza is the last world of the old Bara Republic, and it's barely hanging on to independence.

The Modes already fled the Near Side ...”

Modes. Dendrilite. Didn’t her father once mention it was what the Modes used for augmentation?

“He’s going to let the Modes mine this system, isn’t he?”

Abe tilted his head. “You catch on quick. Saul should’ve made you an advisor and added you to the Elder Council. You would’ve been much more helpful than Jon. But no matter. Armas’s death by the Leki would’ve sealed Saul’s alignment with the Stiners. Framing Armas as a traitor is a setback, but one that I think can be accomplished with you also named as traitor. Saul will not withhold even his own daughter from trial and execution.”

Kyla edged away from her great-uncle. “He won’t kill me.”

“I wouldn’t be so sure,” he sneered. “But you can save yourself. Tell us where Armas has gone.”

Kyla swallowed her smirk. *He lied. They don’t know where Armas is.* “I don’t know,” she lied back.

Footsteps echoed down the hallway. Two guards accompanied her father, who wore his flight suit and sidearm. He was carrying something, but she couldn’t see what it was behind the guard in front.

“Still won’t tell you?” Saul asked Abe. He shook his head. Her father lifted up the Serah mask. “Where did you get this?”

“It was a wedding gift,” she said, shrugging, and glanced at her fingernails, dirty from the cell floor.

He threw it down and stomped on it, smashing it to pieces. Her heart thudded.

“Bring her in,” Saul said.

Kyla scrambled to her feet. Bound with her hands

behind her, a gash on her forehead, Laina was dragged by two guards. She wore loose trousers and a long flowing shirt; they had arrested her during daytime hours. How long had it been?

Her pulse raced. *He won't kill me, but he might kill her to get me to talk.*

"Let her go," Kyla demanded. "She has nothing to do with this."

"But she gave you the Serah mask, didn't she? An outlawed cult," her father said.

"It was decorative only; a wedding gift," Kyla argued, her heart racing.

Her father reached for Laina's neck, snapping the silver chain that she wore, and pulled out the silver medallion she'd carefully tucked inside her shirt. The medallion with the figure of Tana on it.

He struck her across the cheek.

"STOP!" Kyla panicked. "Don't hurt her!"

Saul stood closer, placing one hand on the bars. "Where is he?"

"I — I don't ..."

Saul pulled something out of his pocket; a figure of Tana, a faceless woman with rounded breasts and hips carrying an arrow. Kyla usually had it in her pocket. "She gave this to you," he accused. "She wore her symbol willingly and will die for blasphemy."

Kyla gulped, grasping at straws of a plan. "He fled to Bara."

The king shook his head. "You love him so much. I understand why you are lying." He pulled his weapon and aimed it at Laina. "But I also know how much this woman means to you, who cared for you after your mother died.

It's a pity that freedom comes with such costs."

He's going to kill her.

"Tell me where he is, and she will live."

It's all my fault.

"Ramah," she uttered, falling to her knees, defeated. "He's at Ramah."

Saul holstered his weapon. "You could've made this so much easier. You wouldn't have suffered." He shook his head, his eyes full of pity, before he turned to the guards. "I'll deal with them both once I return."

The guards opened the cell door, thrusting Laina inside and slamming it shut. Saul and Abe departed with the guards, leaving her and Laina alone in the dark.

Kyla scrambled to her feet, placing her palms on Laina's cheeks. "Are you hurt?"

Her maid shook her head, setting her hands over Kyla's. "Your Highness, never mind me! Are you —"

Kyla wrapped her arms around her. "I'm so sorry. Laina, I failed you."

"You never failed me." Tears soaked into the fabric on her shoulders. "You *saved* me."

TWENTY

JON

"Carmen, listen to me —"

"What the *fuck* just happened?"

"Listen to *me*," Jon demanded. The remnants of the ship he'd destroyed floated by him. "This has been a set-up to kill Armas."

"The Advocate fired on us!"

"He fired on Lion-Four because *I* told him L-Four was moving into position." Jon cleared his throat, sweat clouding his vision. "What I'm about to say to you will be considered *treason,* but you have to listen to me. All our lives depend on it."

Carmen was silent on the comm.

Jon switched on the light in his cockpit. If Lieutenant Barish's instruments had any interference from Horeb, they would still be able to target him on sight. Though it was a minor risk given he was the prince, he tried to give some gesture of sincerity.

"I trust your father. Can I trust you?"

The comm remained silent, but a light flickered on fifty meters away. Carmen's ship was pointed at his. He couldn't tell if their weapons were hot.

"The king hired Stiner mercenaries to kill Armas," he told them. "Kyla helped him escape."

"That doesn't make sense."

Jon pursed his lips. "I know it doesn't to you, but Saul sees Armas as a threat to his sovereignty." He sighed, leaning his head back as far as he could in the helmet against the headrest. "I know you and my sister are friends. I told your father, 'Birds in the air and wolves on the ground' because I know he doesn't believe Armas is a traitor and to keep his eyes and ears open. Armas saved us all — including your father and me — on the battlefield against Ogroma."

Carmen burned their engines to avoid debris. Jon did the same, monitoring their every move.

"I know you trust my sister. Please, trust me on this."

They were silent for a moment. Jon couldn't be sure because of the interference from Horeb, but he wasn't picking up Carmen's weapons lock. He held his breath and waited.

"So what do we do?" the younger Barish asked him.

Jon let out his breath through his teeth. "We tell them we lost him in the rings. Luckily my father didn't expect Armas to escape the force shield," he added, omitting his part in it though Carmen was on deck when it happened.

"They'll find the debris from the two fighters but won't be able to tell —" Jon swallowed "— that I fired on Lion-Eight." His hands shook.

"What about flight recorders?"

Jon chewed his lip. He knew everything was recorded onboard. "Destroy them. It's the small box under the comms panel. You'll get questioned about it when the flight techs discover it isn't there and report it. Say you already turned it over to security for investigations. I'll come up with a cover."

"Your Highness, they will interrogate us."

"Tell the truth, up to this point, that Armas got away, and we don't know where he's gone. That much of it is your truth. L-Eight is my problem."

I killed him.

Jon swallowed back bile and fired up all systems, rolling and flipping his ship. He wanted to buy Armas some time, so he set out in the opposite direction through the rings. "Follow me, protect my flank as you would anyone else." He shoved the guilt of the dead pilot out of his head.

"Yes, Your Highness."

"Lieutenant," Jon added, "I won't forget this. I owe you everything."

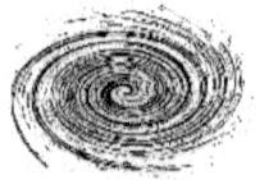

Jon led Carmen through the rings, until he was certain they'd left behind any evidence of Armas's path, before leading them back to Glia, six hours after their encounter with the fugitive. The fortress had transformed quickly. Mech units had been called up to guard the city, and after they flew through the entry shaft and into the hangar, the alert lights still blazed yellow. His father and other pilots gathered on the flight deck, some already heading for their ships. Major Barish shouted orders, his own Bluehawk being prepped.

Jon popped the hatch. His hands still shook, and he yanked his gloves off, rubbing his fingers and hoping the tremors would stop.

He'd killed people before. *Shoot down our own pilots if you have to,* Kyla had told him. It cost him. But he'd do it again, to save Armas.

He found the recorder box and yanked it off, slipping it inside a pocket on his flight suit.

"You all right?"

Jon startled at Major Zeru's voice. She stood a few meters off, wearing the dark under-armor bodysuit for the mechs.

"Yeah. We lost him," he told her, moving to the ladder.

"Dusted ash." She set her hands on her hips. "This is all wrong," she muttered, just loud enough he caught the last.

"Jon," his father called from across the hangar as he climbed down. Deck crews immediately began checking systems on his bird to get it back in the air. His legs almost gave out when he reached the deck. He forgot how exhausted he'd been, how he hadn't slept the night before.

"We lost him," Jon repeated. "In the rings —"

His father wore a flight suit, helm under his arm. Saul was going to pursue Armas himself. "It doesn't matter," the king said. "Kyla told me he's gone to Ramah. Though I destroyed that place years ago, the survivors must have gone underground."

Jon blinked. "Ramah?" *How could she —*
Saul's pained look told him everything.
He forced her to tell him.
His father had favored Kyla, but even that couldn't protect her. She stood in the way of a threat he wanted to eliminate.
Jon recovered quickly. "Father, it's just a rock, no one would —"
"It's where the cult of Tana has been hiding. I should've finished what I started, years ago." Saul set his hand on Jon's shoulder. "If he's gone there, then he's truly betrayed all we stand for. I know you've had no rest."
"I'll go with you," Jon insisted. "I'll help you."
"Your Highness," Carmen approached. Jon grew still. "I would like to continue this mission, to finish what we started."
The king nodded. "We'll bring back that traitor to justice. Twenty minutes."
Saul left them.
"Did you —" Jon began, but Carmen motioned to their pocket.
"Didn't have a chance to destroy it."
"Thanks." He leaned closer. Major Zeru was not far off, but she was talking with Major Barish and not paying attention to him. "I don't know what is going to happen," Jon whispered to Carmen. "If something bad happens — run for it. Someone needs to live through this and tell the truth."
"But Your Highness —"
"Thats an order, *Lieutenant*," Jon said sharply.
"Your Highness," they began again, "Are *you* all

right?"

He rubbed the back of his neck. "No."

Carmen glanced both ways, then pulled a small packet from their chest pocket. "Stims."

Jon took the packet from their hand. "Thanks." He knew the risks. He also knew he needed to make it through this to try to save Armas.

Carmen saluted him, then headed back to their fighter. He scanned the flight deck. Zeru was leaving, probably to head up the mech defenses. Jon wasn't sure what the protocol was right now, everything was in chaos from the wedding.

Before he could catch his breath, a familiar voice called out. "Damn, you look like hell."

"Raimi." Jon was irritated. He didn't want Raimi on this mission, not if they found Armas. How many people would Saul hurt?

Jon changed the subject. "I heard you got stuck with Abe during the wedding."

"Yeah, had to settle in the Leki delegation and missed the ceremony."

Jon grabbed Raimi by the arm and pulled him around a mechanic's transport. "Tell me the truth: you know they weren't Leki."

Raimi's brows drew together. "Of course they were. Had on their long underwear and everything, complaining that space travel was too cold for them."

Jon sucked in a breath. "They could have been faking it. Anything seem off to you?"

"Besides a bit more of a stick up their ass than usual, and besides they fact they are crawling back to us? No."

"You don't think they were ... spies?"

Raimi squinted. "Are you okay, Jon? Have you been

drinking again? Not good when flying, man."

"Forget it."

Raimi was his friend. He'd always trusted him before to have his back.

But his friend was lying through his teeth. He'd known Jon had been sober for the last year, and that Jon would never fly after drinking. Raimi was part of the cover up.

TWENTY-ONE

JON

A full squadron of fourteen launched in pursuit of Armas, with Major Barish as wing leader. Abe, Raimi, and Carmen flew along with Jon and his father. Armas maybe had an eight-hour head start on them. Not enough time. The remaining squadrons were on patrol duty of Melas's airspace.

Jon flew in formation behind Saul, stims keeping him awake, struggling to figure out a plan as they left Horeb's gravity pull and headed toward Cana and Nidos. Though the schematics they had on the moon Ramah were decades old and from destroyed settlements, the moon was small. If Armas had landed and remained there, they'd find him.

Saul didn't know that Zam was alive, that Kyla had

sent the prophet there.

What did Father do to her, to make her tell him about Armas? His stomach twisted in knots.

His father remained oddly quiet on the comm.

Jon's only hope was that in the presence of the squad, Saul would choose to take Armas into custody. Major Abe Renk flew a Heron Five, a larger fighter with a second seat and med bay that could accommodate a medic and four patients. A prisoner could be sedated and transported — if Saul didn't kill him.

"Wake up, Your Highness," Raimi called on their private channel, though Jon hadn't dozed with stims in his system. "We're here."

The dark brown and gray rock tumbled far from Nidos. "Scan for any unusual metal, any cracks too even," Abe ordered on the universal.

"If there is a colony here, why aren't we seeing any buildings, or entrances from the surface?" Jon asked.

"About a decade ago the cult of Tana took over the temple and city," his great-uncle replied, "along with all our sacred sites from the first landings in the system. They were destroyed."

"The Tananites survived here, below the surface," his father said, breaking his silence.

Jon inhaled harshly. *How can I save Armas now? And Zam, if he's still alive …*

"There!" Raimi shouted, breaking formation and flying near the surface. Jon followed, with Carmen behind him. A sliver of gray formed a crevasse, wedged deep into the surface.

Raimi's scans came across the screen, showing the crevasse and hangar doors at the end. The data suggested a landing bay deep enough for at least half a squadron. "Gray Wolf, what are your orders?"

"Dark Wolf and Wolf-Two," Saul called out to him and Raimi, "White Lion and Lion-Twelve," for Major Barish and Carmen. "You're with me and Pale Wolf." His great-uncle's call sign.

"Copy that," Jon called out. Raimi and Carmen drew behind him, while his father positioned himself directly ahead of him, with Abe and Major Barish leading the rest. They traveled into the deep crevasse. Horizontal doors opened, revealing a landing bay.

"Everyone on alert," Major Barish ordered. "Whoever it is, they're expecting us."

Jon used his landing thrusters to maneuver next to Raimi, and slipped inside, setting down in the empty hangar. The bay doors had closed, but the comm channel was still open with the remaining ships in orbit. Scanners showed the oxygen levels rising, and Abe, Milo Barish, Carmen, and Raimi opened their cockpits, weapons drawn. Once Abe signaled it was clear, Jon and his father left their ships.

The Kittiwake was not there.

The hanger reminded Jon of the other uninhabited moon stations of Horeb — constructed with hard metal, and double doors leading out from either end of the hangar to underground facilities, or up to the surface where the buildings had been destroyed.

Relief swept over him as he realized Armas was gone. There was no place to hide a ship. He'd left, hours ago. But if Armas wasn't on Ramah, he would've gone on to Nidos. The Kittiwake didn't have the fuel capacity for interstellar travel. Hopefully he'd found a way out of the system from there.

Jon removed his helmet and leaped over the side in the low gravity, almost giddy. Major Barish stood next to his ship, frowning. "Scanners showed the drive signature of the Kittiwake in orbit. It should be here."

"Unless the traitor slipped away," Saul muttered, turning to Abe. "If he went to Nidos ..."

"We'll have a hard time retrieving him if he did," Abe finished.

"Why?" Raimi asked, his helmet still on. "We just cleared out the dissidents there. They *owe* us."

Saul gave Raimi a look. "Enough. We'll cross that bridge if we have to."

Jon's eyes narrowed. *Something* happened on Nidos. The recent conflict from the Phenian Wars had been painted by Saul as a win, but Jon knew the final negotiations had not gone as expected. Something Armas was involved in, but he hadn't pressed for more information at the time.

Major Barish stepped in closer, interrupting. "Your Majesty, we should secure this facility."

"Agreed. Major Renk will remain here, along with Captain Nadab," Saul added, motioning to Raimi. "Jon and I will come with you."

"Your Majesty," Abe protested, but Saul cut him off.

"There's something here, some reason ..."

Saul didn't finish his thought. Jon frowned. If Armas wasn't here, any distraction in his father's schemes bought him time, but his father's eyes appeared glassy, lost in thought.

Major Barish took point, with Carmen checking the door. It opened easily. Dim lighting lit a narrow, curved hall on the other side. Saul moved past Carmen, walking behind the major, while the younger Barish dropped back with Jon. They walked slowly, weapons drawn.

"What do you think that was about, with Nidos?" Jon whispered to Carmen after a few minutes. The two of them lagged several meters behind the major and the king.

"You've been there, I haven't," they retorted.

"Oh. Right," he winced. While Carmen had been allowed to fly in combat, they still were kept away from the worst of the fighting.

Jon and Armas had fought on Nidos a few months ago, against some Tali resistance fighters before they surrendered. "I do know there was some sort of agreement giving the Lubez more power," he said.

"The shipbuilders? That makes sense. But what's really going on, Jon?" Carmen said, startling him. Raimi was the only other person, besides Armas, who dared use his first name.

"I don't know. All I know is Armas didn't do what he's being accused of."

Barish raised his fist, and they all fell silent. Carmen moved in front of Jon to shield him.

After a moment, the major motioned them forward. Jon followed Carmen. "There's a large room ahead, with more light. I'll go," the major said, giving a look to his child. Lieutenant Barish's eyes widened, watching their father creep forward, pistol raised.

"Clear," he called back.

Carmen led Jon and his father out from the metal hallway into a circular room, hewn out of the rock. In the center sat a stone basin two meters across, full of water. A metal pipe led from it to a large tank, with columns rising up into the stone above them. The rock walls were ribboned around them, a thin metallic substance, shimmering in the emergency light.

"What is this?" Carmen asked, rounding the basin to the other side.

"It's a well," Jon muttered, locking eyes with his father. "I recognize the pump mechanism from the museum displays in Glia." An unknown language was stamped into the side. "It's from one of the Twelve ships that escaped the Red Nebula, centuries ago."

"This was a landing site," the king acknowledged. "One of the original ships. The Lubez, Tali, and Hessan decided to remain here and on Nidos. They dismantled a ship's water pumps, according to the history records."

Jon glanced up. Above him, the ceiling vaulted into a cylinder, which led to the surface. Probably to storage units above for the ships to refill their water supply, long gone when the aboveground settlement was destroyed. As he surveyed the room, he saw markings on the walls, spaced evenly and painted between metallic ribbons. A woman with an arrow, the marks of the cult of Tana — the warrior goddess of the Hitti people, the original people of Nidos. *Originals.* That was the name given to the early Nacaens, like the Sebuj on Melas, from before the twelve ships arrived.

Laina, Kyla's maid, had a metallic tattoo on her upper left arm. She was Tali, from Nidos.

"That's old Sim'ee markings," Major Barish said.

Carmen whipped their gaze to their father.

"Are you sure?" the king asked.

"Yes. The Sim'ee first claimed Ramah but gave up the claim when more habitable moons were discovered surrounding Horeb. At least, that's what our history records state. But I recognize the writing."

"Can you translate it?" Jon asked.

Major Barish shook his head. "I'm not a scholar."

"I know this place," Saul muttered.

Major Barish glanced across the well to the king, frowning. "Your Majesty — you've been here before?"

"I was told of it," the king said, his voice softer. "When I trained as a prophet, long ago. There was once a temple for the One God on the surface. Zam trained there."

At the sound of footsteps, Jon wheeled and aimed his weapon. A woman with thin, brown fuzzy hair, and a dark gray robe stood across from them by the narrow hall. Silver tattoos lined her left arm, and an arrow was tattooed on her left cheek.

Jon scanned the walls, but couldn't find any trace of a door, any crack that indicated where she came from. *She followed us.* Even if Carmen should've been watching their trail, he should've been aware. He'd been preoccupied thinking about Armas, about all that Saul hadn't told him, and what Raimi might be hiding.

"There is no need for weapons here," she said, raising her hands, glancing at each one of them. "Have you come to drink of the font?"

"A Tananite," Saul sneered.

The woman's eyes flew open. "The killer king."

Carmen again moved in front of Jon, while Major Barish protected the king. Four more priests emerged from the tunnel, all with their heads shaved and the same silver tattoos along their left arms. The woman with the arrow tattoo on her cheek raised her hands. "We tend to the font, the wellspring of life that grants visions. We do not attract converts. We allowed you to land to see we are peaceful."

"You worship Tana, false goddess."

"*We* tend to the waters *She* gifted the people, the ice that once was at the heart of this moon, long ago. The water and the dendrilite allow us to survive."

Jon focused on the water, into its clear depths. The stone basin itself was crossed by hundreds of metallic ribbons, silver and black.

"One can see visions in the water," the priest said. "Dendrilite expands our minds to receive the thoughts of others."

The king holstered his weapon and leaned forward, staring into the water, and Jon copied him. Frowning, he remembered what his father had told him about the Modes wanting access to Ramah. They must've suspected the moon contained the mineral. Ogroma had used it for linking to their mech.

"How do you see in this?" Jon asked. How could someone see anything in water? *Folk tales*, his mother said. The memory surprised him. He hadn't thought of her in a long time. *Your father is a mystic. He believes in the old stories, even if he denies it.*

"You drink of the font," the priest answered him.

Saul pulled his glove off, setting his hand in the water. Ripples waved toward the edge. He cupped his hand.

"Father, don't —" Jon warned, but Saul ignored him, and drank from the basin, its waters laced with dendrilite. The ripples faded, the surface clear, reflecting their faces back at them.

"I see him," the king said.

Jon frowned. He only saw his reflection. He touched a gloved hand to its surface, watching the ripples form until it was smooth once more.

"I see him," Saul's voice rasped, his eyes squinting. "He was alive, all this time."

Jon stared at him. "Who are you talking about?"

"Zam. He was here."

The vein pulsed in Saul's forehead.

Jon stepped closer to him. "Are you all right?"

"Zam was here. Prophesying my demise. He sees it."

"How can you know that?" Jon asked, moving to stand next to him. His heart sped up. He knew his father had trained like Zam, years ago, but he'd never seen this. Fear crept up his spine.

"He sees the Advocate crowned king. He sees —"

Saul raised his eyes to meet Jon's gaze, his face deathly pale.

Then the king's eyes rolled into the back of his head as he fell to the ground.

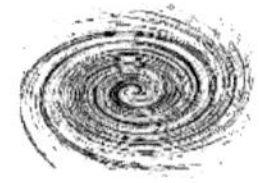

"Father!" Jon rushed to Saul's side along with Major Barish. Saul's eyelids fluttered, his arms and legs spasming.

"He has drunk of the font," the priest with the arrow tattoo said. "He has seen what is already in motion."

"The water must be poisoned," the major said, glancing at the Tananites.

Carmen kept their pistol raised, but the priests did not move.

"It is not poison," the priest retorted. "It is holy. It connects our minds."

Jon's eyes focused on the arrow mark on her cheek. It was not a tattoo, but an implant. The tattoos on the priest's arms matched the ribbons in the basin. "It's the dendrilite. It's what the Modes use for their augments. The residue in the water must have affected him."

Saul's body settled, and his eyes opened. Jon helped him sit up, and he spat.

Major Barish furrowed his brow. "Your Majesty, are you all right?"

"I'm fine."

"We ought to have you checked out on Renk's ship."

"The Advocate is on Nidos. I saw him in the vision," the king added, standing up with help from Major Barish. He turned to the priest with the arrow. "Zam was here, all along."

"The God-fearer lives among us, yes," she answered. "But he is in his last breaths."

"We must find him and Armas, immediately," Saul said to Major Barish.

Jon noted the sweat along his father's forehead, the sickly tone. "Father, listen to Major Barish. You need to be examined."

"Armas has plans to usurp me."

Jon gripped Saul's forearm, forcing him to look him in the eye. "That's not true. Father, all he wants is to serve you." He tightened his grip. "You need help. You're sick."

"He is connected to the thoughts of the dying prophet," the priest with the arrow mark said. "He cannot see outside of it."

Saul's eyes locked on Jon, cold and unfeeling. "It is far too late. The vision —" Saul shook his head, his eyes turning from icy rage to sadness. "Son, there is much I wish I'd done differently."

Jon's heart slowed. Maybe he could still convince his father to stop. "I know Armas's heart. He longs to give of himself to you, to the people, to this system." He let go of his father's arm. "Let me take care of you. Call off the hunt and return home to Melas."

Shocking him, his father nodded. "I'll return home. *You* will go to Nidos and find him. We'll set things right. You will bring him back home to us."

Jon frowned. Something was off in his father's voice. "Father — no more schemes. Armas is *not* a traitor." He sucked in a breath and whispered to his father: "There's no need to bring in any other *outsiders* into our business."

Saul stared at him, realization dawning on his face, and Jon nodded his acknowledgment that he knew about the Stiners.

"You'd do well to heed his wisdom," the priest warned the king.

"Take us to the prophet," Saul said.

The priest with the arrow mark moved to the right. A metal panel Jon hadn't noticed before hung at eye level. The priest placed her left hand on it and a door appeared, outlined in light. *Dendrilite. They must be able to connect to everything this way.*

Jon followed the priests with Carmen at his side, his father behind him and Major Barish bringing up the rear. The previous hallway was paneled with dull metal; here, the corridor widened, lit above by lines of dendrilite.

"I thought these passages had collapsed long ago," Saul murmured. "Scanners showed everything was destroyed."

"The Hitti were here long before your people arrived," the priest responded, before arriving at another metal panel, and once again placing their left hand on it. "They knew how to survive."

Jon glanced at his father. "This was never part of the surface settlement," the king said, motioning to the dendrilite interface.

"One thing your priests and ours had in common was an understanding this place was sacred and should not be abused."

Another door appeared. Jon followed the priest with the arrow mark. "Zam has been resting here —"

Jon gasped.

Zam lay in a bed, his hair and beard white as snow. Blankets were tucked around him, and wires protruded from his body, connected to medical machines. His eyes were closed, and the heart monitor showed a steady line.

"We tried to save him, but the disease progressed too quickly," one of the other priests said. "He wanted comfort measures, nothing more. He refused the dendrilite that would fuse his mind with others, and might allow for healing."

Jon's gasp caught in his throat as his father stepped forward. Saul's jaw flexed, and he blinked several times. Jon had never seen his father cry, but no tears came forth.

"Father," Jon whispered, touching Saul's shoulder. Carmen moved to stand by his side.

"Major Barish," Saul ordered, breaking the silence. "Round up the priests. They are coming with us for questioning."

"Dusted ash," Jon muttered under his breath, withdrawing his hand. Any dim hope that Saul had a change of heart was sucked right out of him.

"Leave us be," the priest with the arrow mark said. "We have not caused any harm. We have remained here in peace —"

"You conspired to hide a traitor to the realm!" Saul shouted. Jon's heart froze. "Your religion has long been outlawed. I should've wiped this place clean when I had the chance."

"Hands where we can see them," Major Barish ordered. The five priests complied, turning around.

"What about Zam?" Jon asked. "Father, we ought to leave the priests and just take Zam's body —"

"You will do as I say, *son*," Saul said through gritted teeth. "This was his home. He can rot here."

Saul ordered Jon and Carmen to lead the priests — now prisoners — back toward the hangar, while he and Milo followed behind.

"Tana deliver them," Carmen muttered.

Jon let out a shaky breath. "Keep your beliefs to yourself, Lieutenant. My father spares no one."

TWENTY-TWO

KYLA

"I betrayed him. I betrayed *them*," Kyla muttered, resting against Laina's knees, finishing off the last of the bread, now stale. Two more days had passed, but she broke her fast, knowing there was nothing she could do to stop them from finding Armas or the cult of Tana. Nothing that starving herself would help with.

The guards had turned the lights back on, allowing Kyla to wash the gash on Laina's head, now an ugly red line. Laina had insisted on helping her bathe with the towel and the water basin provided, combing out her hair with her fingers as she sat on the bench, Kyla on the floor.

"You did what you had to do to keep us alive." Her maid's voice was flat.

"How many are left at Ramah?" Kyla whispered,

though the guards were farther down the corridor and engaged in their own conversation.

"Not many," Laina replied, starting a braid at the top of Kyla's crown. "The tenders of the font have dwindled over the years. Most practice their faith in their everyday lives, like my family."

"What does it mean to 'tend the font'?" Kyla knew of the wellspring, the symbolic waters of Tana's womb that was on Ramah. The well became sacred to the Twelve nations who established it as a place of worship for the One God in their early years in the system.

"Mostly, making sure the water still flows."

Laina tied off the end of Kyla's braid. Kyla faced her, noting the dark circles under her maid's eyes, the lines on her brow. "My father mentioned the Modes were interested in Ramah for some metal, dendrilite."

Her maid's eyes widened. "Dendrilite is sacred, used to aid in prophetic visions. The high priests use it for collective mystical experiences."

"He said it was used by the Modes as neurolink silk for their interfacing."

Laina nodded, rolling up her sleeve to the tattoo on her upper arm. "Those of us with ties to Ramah are marked with dendrilite as a rite of passage, but not all Tananites choose to do so. Some find other ways of connecting to the sacred divine. Most of us find it simply heightens our awareness."

Kyla frowned. "He promised the Stiners they could use Ramah's to bargain with the Modes."

Laina clutched Kyla's shoulder, so hard she winced. "It would strip Ramah bare ... the well would be gone forever. No more visions. The water is Her blood; the dendrilite, Her veins."

"But there are other wells around the system?" Kyla asked. Laina released her, and Kyla moved to sit next to her on the bench.

"Yes, but none with as rich and pure a source."

Kyla wrapped her arm around Laina's shoulder. *So that's why Father was sending me there, after the honeymoon.* To wipe out the Tananites *and* secure the dendrilite. He knew.

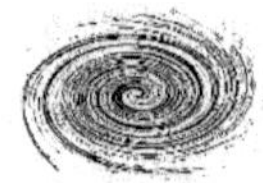

A few hours later, toward evening, a guard approached. Kyla and Laina stood, prepared to receive their next meal, but Major Zeru appeared before them, wearing her brown Dahan officer's uniform with a gold pin, three stalks of grain, signifying her rank. Her skin was tanned like Armas's, but her blond hair was almost white, trimmed short. Among the nation Elders, Kyla knew only Major Barish and Major Zeru, and them mostly at formal functions. Milo Barish had shown her kindness, perhaps because she was Carmen's friend, but Seriah Zeru was aloof, constantly biting the corner of her lip as if she had something she desperately wanted to say but dared not speak it aloud.

"I have orders from your father. You are to return to your quarters and be secured there."

Kyla folded her arms. "So still under arrest."

"The term he used was 'for your safety and security.'"

The door to the cell opened. Kyla shot Laina a look before following Major Zeru. The guards stood on either side as they marched down the corridor.

"Why is my father sending you to do this?"

The major clasped her hands behind her back, biting her lower lip. "He is calling all the national Elders to a banquet in a few days for some sort of formal announcement." She glanced at Kyla. "Your brother is retrieving your husband and bringing him home. The king has declared the Advocate will have his name cleared once he returns to Melas. Further investigation has shown there was an assassination attempt on the Advocate's life, which is why he fled."

Kyla tapped two fingers to her chest, her body shaking, not caring if her devotion to the goddess was revealed. *Thank you, Warrior Tana, for protecting Armas.* Laina placed her arm around her, steadying her.

"But —"

"Your Highness," the major interrupted, "I'm sure you haven't slept much or eaten well the last few days. Let's return you to your quarters where your maid can care for you properly."

Kyla took the hint. She didn't know Major Zeru well — she'd achieved the rank of major shortly before the Battle of Zek — but she was well-respected among her own. Though most soldiers were trained in piloting both mechs and fighters, she, like Armas, had found her strength among the mech units. Her quick-thinking had saved her squad in the previous war with the Leki, earning her promotion and place as an Elder for the Dahan nation. She didn't say much, and when she did, her troops listened.

Kyla didn't say anything until they reached her quarters. "Major, may I have a word?"

Zeru nodded to the guards, who stood at attention, and entered Kyla's quarters with Laina. "Don't speak," Major Zeru warned after she closed the door, scanning the room.

"There are no cameras —"

"There weren't before you were arrested," the major retorted. "You might be bugged now."

"Your Highness," her maid began. "Can I get you and the major tea?"

Kyla frowned. "Rest, Laina — you've been through so much."

"Your Highness, I insist."

Kyla hesitated. Her maid had been abused, struck by her own father, and had slept as little as she had. But Laina went to the kitchenette to make tea, and Kyla sat down on the couch. Zeru pulled a small black rod from her pocket, a centimeter wide and five centimeters long and flat on one side. She clicked a button, and two small antennae rose from the rod. She set it on the small table before she sat across from Kyla in a chair. "This will disrupt any spyware and listening devices. It's Airysan technology."

"Where is Armas?" Kyla asked, clasping her hands in her lap.

"The king believes he is on Nidos. And because of the agreement made to bring the Lubez into power, your father can't send in any force that might be seen as a threat by the other nations there. Diplomats only. So he's sending in the prince and Captain Nadab."

"Armas didn't do anything wrong." Major Zeru sighed. "When the king gives orders, we must follow. As it is, your father revealed there was an assassination attempt, and it threw everything into confusion. Two assassins were found dead in your quarters."

He killed them because they failed.

"Seriah," Kyla used the major's first name, "my father hired Stiners to kill Armas."

The major remained motionless.

"He's made a deal with them. He's going to allow them to settle in our system."

Zeru leaned forward. "Do you have any evidence of this?"

Kyla shook her head. "I overheard my father just in time to get Armas off-world before I was arrested. Jon knows."

"The nations will not agree to any sort of settlement with the Stiners."

"He's allowing them to mine Ramah, to trade with the Modes. Maybe some other moons."

Major Zeru scoffed. "How could he possibly hide them, even on uninhabited rocks?"

Kyla ran her hand over her braided crown, remembering her wedding reception. "I remember overhearing Jon talk to my father about a Leki delegation. They arrived just before the wedding. They must've been Stiners instead."

"The mercenaries do have capabilities to change their physical appearance, hide their ID tattoos, look like others." She swore. "Without evidence, we could be letting them right in and no one would believe it."

"He'll get the nations to agree," Kyla muttered. "The Leki have no other alliances right now, with the royal family divided." She closed her eyes. She'd always believed, until her wedding night, that everything her father did — even the cruelest actions, such as the public slaughter of the Leki informant — was because he believed it was necessary to secure the throne, even if it horrified her.

After she overheard him with the Stiners, she knew that wasn't true. Saul had lost his mind. He was selfish, unjust, and unfit to rule. Zam was right. She knew it in her heart.

"Major, I am in your debt."

Zeru leaned back on the couch.

"What I am about to ask," Kyla said, her heart racing, "will be considered treason if it gets out. Do you know of any dissident voices within the Elder Council?"

The major shook her head. "No. Everyone is loyal to your father."

"Are you?"

Zeru tilted her head. "Your Highness ..."

Kyla moved closer to the major. "I love Armas, but he is descended from the heroes of our world, of *your* people. I am asking you, as the representative of the Dahan, to protect Armas from my father."

Zeru exhaled. "I will."

"If it comes to this ..." Kyla said, her voice low. "If it comes to choosing where your loyalties lie, choose the Advocate."

"You're talking civil war."

"The next king will be Jon. Save Armas, and you save the kingdom. Zam chose him to advise the king."

Major Zeru scoffed. "The prophet is dead, by *your* hand."

"No. He's alive. He was at Ramah. If we have any luck, he would've fled with Armas." And taken the remaining Tananites with him, if he could persuade them. "My father ordered me to kill him, but I helped him escape. Zam was like a grandfather to me."

The major bit her lip again but did not reply.

Kyla sat up straight as Laina brought over tea. "Now, tell me more about this banquet," she said, changing the subject.

"All I know is he's calling for a Banquet of Reconciliation. The king said it was to clear the air regarding Armas, to show how he and the Advocate have nothing to hide."

Laina offered the major tea. Zeru took the mug, studying the maid's face, but she didn't say anything about the scab on her forehead. The major took a sip. "He then sent me personal orders to retrieve you from the cells, but no one else knew you were down there."

"Abe Renk did," Kyla said.

Zeru's eye twitched. She paused, as if choosing her words carefully. "I know my predecessor on the Council didn't approve of the king appointing his own uncle to rep the Jamin, and when he protested, he was found dead the next day." She sighed, tapping her fingers against the teacup. "Your father's first mission was to unite the nations of the Twelve. He did that well. But to hold on to power, he needs Elders who will back him, no matter what. Renk isn't the only one who will do whatever your father asks without question."

"But you don't. Maybe there are others."

She looked Kyla directly in the eye. "You've now seen the extremes your father will go to, even imprisoning you both," she added, glancing at the Tali maid. "I can't promise anything. The risks for anyone are too great. Tread carefully." Zeru set down her mug and stood. "He will be watching your every move until he is certain Armas is *contained*."

Kyla knew exactly what she meant, as the major retrieved her tablet, leaving the interference device behind. "Remember the guards are posted outside," she advised, before she exited the princess's quarters.

Laina set down a plate of Dahan twelve-grain bread, creamy goat cheese and jam. "You need to eat."

"My father is setting a trap," Kyla said, walking over to the window overlooking the balcony. She spotted the blast marks in the stone arches, where Armas fled for his life only a few days before. Panic rose along her spine. "The banquet is a trap for Armas. Jon can't bring him back here."

TWENTY-THREE

ARMAS

Most of Nidos was too hot, too close to the sun, but the southern pole was tilted away from Cana and orbital shields helped lower the temperatures in the southern hemisphere. They doubled in hiding the shipyards that constructed warships for the system fleet — when the nations that inhabited the world cooperated.

Armas had been to the surface, about two months before the wedding, as the last of the Phenian sympathizers were rooted out from the Tali nation and imprisoned, and the rest surrendered. As the King's Advocate, he'd helped negotiate the terms that secured loyalty to a unified Nacaen system under Saul's rule.

Ironic, now that he had to hide from the king among those same people.

"Unidentified pilot, please send your credentials," he was hailed as he approached Nidos. Two Lubez scout ships were on an intercept course — four-person security vessels, oblong in shape with two lower wings and a tail, packed with firepower to protect the shipyards from invading forces. Behind them, in the distance, were the massive solar shields, curved shells covering the shipyards, and the other orbital maintenance stations.

"Credentials sent," Armas replied, using the message Zam had given him.

Saul had not wanted the Lubez to have so much power. The Lubez wanted the Nacaen Group to join the Interplanetary Alliance, an old agreement with a few Near Side system nations. But they needed Nidos's ships, and the Lubez controlled the shipyards. The best compromise Armas could come up with was to put the Lubez nation in power with limits on the rest of the Nacaen Group's influence, especially the king. Saul got his ships, but at a cost.

Looking back, Armas understood it cost him more than he thought at the time.

"Welcome, Brother Marren," the Lubez security patrol sent back. "We are not used to priests piloting their own vessels, let alone an old ship such as that. It's not showing up on our registry."

"Ah, well, you know, Dahan doesn't have many priests these days. I'm the first in my family," he added for his cover, "and left the military for religious service. This ship was decommissioned and given back to the family." Zam had given him an identity of a former priest to use as a cover.

"You will be escorted until you reach Hessan

airspace," the security patrol informed him, and he confirmed the coordinates. "Note that on the surface we use local time rather than Bylon Standard." Armas confirmed that message, too, remembering his last trip to the surface — the days were shorter on Nidos.

The two scout ships flanked him as he approached the orbital shields, following the course they sent to avoid the heavy space traffic. He knew showing up in an old retired foreign ship, let alone a fighter, would raise suspicion. Given that almost any Lubez ship would be able to outmaneuver or outgun his Kittiwake, it was a risk he had no choice but to take.

The shipyards were full, Armas noted, with construction on six new Aurora-class warships resuming once the negotiations were completed. Orbiting above the south pole of Nidos was the security station, a spiral structure containing the headquarters of the Lubez nation, where dozens of scout ships launched to patrol in orbit. The scout ships were designed for space travel, not atmo, unlike the Bluehawks and the Kittiwake Fighter he flew that could handle both. On the far side of the security station was another orbital shipyard building luxury liners — the kind of ships systems like Etho would invest in, places of wealth and prosperity.

None of that matters now, Armas recognized. *Saul wants me dead.* All he had worked for, negotiated for, would benefit the people of Nidos, and in the long run, all Nacaens, but Saul had been too short-sighted to see it. He cursed Saul's name.

Armas was accompanied by the two scout ships through orbital traffic until they reached the upper atmosphere of Nidos. The northern hemisphere, mostly desert, had clear skies, but the southern hemisphere was shadowed with cloud cover. The scout ships peeled off before entering the upper atmosphere. "Continue on course into Hessan territory," they advised.

Armas frowned at the readings on the instrument panel in front of him. "My scanners are showing severe weather," he said over the comm, as the massive cumulonimbus clouds blocked his view through the glass.

"It's storm season," the security escort replied as they retreated. Armas prayed the old, beat-up Kittiwake would hold together as he headed into the thick clouds.

Though he'd been to the edge of Hessan territory before, storm season was something else. The ship rattled in turbulence until he broke through into heavy rain pattering the glass of the cockpit. The price of making the planet's southern half at least somewhat habitable after building the solar shields. *No wonder my people decided to keep looking for a home world,* Armas thought. Melas had needed little intervention over the years, besides neutralizing soil.

Armas followed the course over the rolling hills that gave way to a rocky land with short, twisted trees scattered among larger boulders. Lean-to buildings fit snug against the erratic rock formations, the traditional buildings of the Hessan villages. He followed the coordinates to a hangar carved out of massive butte and landed inside.

After shutting down the engines, he opened the hatch. Three deck technicians approached, wearing drab coveralls. "Brother Marren?" one asked.

"Yes?" Armas answered after he pulled off his helmet.

"We got word you were arriving. We'll take care of your ship."

Another tech whistled. "Haven't ever seen one of these," she said, "but we'll refuel it and give it a once-over."

Armas scratched his head. "Thanks. I — how much do I owe you?" he asked, nervous because he was certain any account access was restricted right now.

"This is courtesy of the Order," the third tech told him, running his fingers underneath the wing as Armas climbed from the cockpit and down the ladder. He had tanned skin and red hair, similar to Armas's own. "We take care of all who serve our God."

"Thanks," Armas acknowledged. He stared at the entrance of the hangar, where the rain continued to pour. Trenches diverted the water away from the entrance and into collecting containers. "Um, where do I ..."

"Just across the way, the other side of the village," the first tech pointed, out the open hatch. "You can't miss it."

Armas nodded his thanks and headed out the door. Everything ached. He hadn't bathed since before the wedding and had only eaten the nutritional packets on the ship. Exhaustion threatened to bring him down, but he only had a few hundred meters to go.

Until he reached the entrance and peered through the thick rain and fog. The village before him was constructed in a circle. Across from the hangar was a steep hill. Even in the fog, he could make out the structure at the top. The temple.

Armas put his helmet back on and cursed as he headed into the rain, crossing the village. Mud sucked at his boots. He plodded to the steps and sluggishly began to climb, almost slipping on the slab slate steps. He stopped counting after one hundred, and the fog thickened to soup.

His vision swam at the edges. He stumbled near the final step, when strong arms caught him. "Welcome, Advocate. We've been expecting you."

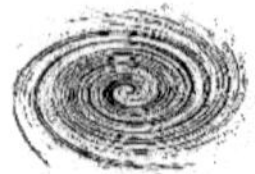

Armas woke, the crackling fire and steady hum of rain on the rooftop comforting him, the smell of baking bread filling his nostrils. *Home!* He rolled over, but something was wrong. His bed was stiff. His dog Roxy wasn't sniffing at him.

He shot up. A woman in a dark green shirt and black pants placed a log on the fire, her thick reddish-brown hair tied back. She looked to be at least ten years older, with deep brown skin. She glanced at Armas. "You've slept for a day and a half, at least, of our days. A bit shorter than you're used to on Melas."

Armas rubbed the side of his cheek, scratchy with stubble. He wrinkled his nose at his own smell.

"Toilet and shower are through that door," she said, pointing.

"Thanks."

"I'm Mel."

"Brother Marren —"

"You don't remember me, Armas?"

He squinted, trying to make her out in the dark. She wasn't wearing her uniform with its crimson sash, but suddenly he recognized her. "You — you're Mel Diez, Elder for the Hessan people."

She nodded, crossing her arms.

"Did Zam tell you I was coming?" Armas asked, swinging his legs over the side of the cot. His flight suit had been removed and hung on a post nearby. He was wearing the same clothes he'd managed to pull on when he left Kyla's room, a few days ago now.

Mel raised a brow. "The old man sent a message a while ago, predicting you'd come here. Said you might need to lay low for a while." She motioned again to the door. "I don't mean to be rude, but you could use a shower."

"Thanks."

After Armas had bathed, he wrapped a towel around himself and peeked through the door. Mel was gone, but a fresh change of clothes was set on the bed. He dressed, and his stomach gurgled. On a table against the far wall from him was a bowl of vegetable stew and some bread. Armas scarfed it down, though the bread was light and airy, not the full grain he was used to from the Dahan farms.

Once he finished, sopping up the thick broth with the last of the bread, he took note of the sparse room he was in. The priests back in Glia had comfortable quarters, similar to what the officers had. This was bland in comparison. The walls were stone and slab, the roof slanted, and the flooring made of wide, gray boards. Across from the cot he slept on was the stone fireplace. A short wall separated his cot from the doorway outside.

Feet stomped — probably to remove muck from boots — and the door opened. Mel shrugged off a long, dark gray waterproof cloak and hung it on a hook while slipping off her boots. Another person entered, their curly hair cut close to their scalp, a shade of brown lighter than their skin. They looked to be a year or two younger than him. "This is Erdan. They're a priest."

"It's wonderful to finally meet you," the young priest

said, bowing. "I've heard so much about you."

"Zam has sent messages to our people, ever since he came to Ramah," Mel explained, "though I met you on Melas, and of course, during the Nidos Accords."

Armas gritted his teeth.

"Even when we felt the decisions you negotiated were not necessarily in our best interests at first, we came around to understand," Mel added.

"Understand what?" Armas questioned.

"With the Lubez having more official control and a steady relationship with King Saul, we've been able to recruit more easily among the Hessan. Your negotiations were brilliant. The king can't send in any more military expeditions. It's given us a bit more sovereignty to —"

"Wait — what do you mean 'recruit'?"

Erdan raised their brows at Mel. "He doesn't know?"

Mel pointed at Armas. "When Zam proclaimed you as Advocate, we all hoped you might reason with the king and get him back on track. His torture and execution of a prisoner in public, along with the assumption of prophetic duties, is a violation of our beliefs. I wanted to pull Nidos out of the united system, but we knew Saul wouldn't give up the shipyards. He might even destroy them rather than see us leave."

"But when you married his daughter," Erdan said, "we knew God had placed you in this position for a purpose. You are the one who will unite us. You are the one who will lead us."

"We want you as king," Mel finished.

Armas almost fell over. "You *do* know I'm a wanted man. I'm considered a traitor to the throne, to the *actual king*. I'm here with fake credentials to hide out." He leaned against the short wall.

Mel shook her head toward Erdan. "I told you he wouldn't believe us." She motioned to Armas. "Come join us in the temple. You'll see."

Armas pulled on his boots and took a spare cloak from Mel, zipping it closed and pulling the hood as far as it would go in front of his face as Mel opened the door. The rain no longer pounded but still came in sideways due to the wind. Erdan flicked on an electric torch and Armas followed the two into the dark. From what he could make out, they were at the top of the steep hill lined with rows of slanted houses like his, probably as simple in design. In the center was a large structure, with a roof at a steep angle, rising at least three stories above him.

Mel opened the door to the temple and Armas's eyes flew open. The temple was constructed in a trapezoid shape built out from the rock with the narrower end in front, and a thick wood roof rising up at an angle, pointing toward the sky. A stone altar was carved out from the rock underneath the structure, the wooden floor of the dais surrounding it.

The temple was packed — standing room only. Most wore similar rainproof cloaks, but there were families with young children, along with soldiers and pilots, some with the crimson and black uniform of the Hessan army. A chant rose up from the crowd: "Ar-mas! Ar-mas!"

Armas's head was a mess. "What — what does this mean?"

Erdan slapped his shoulder. "You're the one we've been waiting for. Our people have been pushed to the brink: starving, forced to live in hardship while the Lubez take the best of everything. But our war isn't with the Lubez. We know Saul will use Nidos for whatever he needs, and our people will suffer. Even now, the supply allotment apportioned by the Elder Council goes only to the priests. We've shared what we can with the people, but it's not enough."

Armas gazed over the crowd chanting his name and muttered a curse. He'd no idea that people had suffered. He knew some nations received a supply allotment, but never questioned how much was given or how it was used. He'd never seen their poverty. *Oh God, what if other worlds are just as bad?* Outside of the occasional Elder's estate, he only ever saw the military bases, not where the civilians lived on Richo and Samar. He'd negotiated the accords that left these people with nothing but also kept Saul from messing with their local leadership. He'd managed to make deals on behalf of Saul, doing all he could to keep the system together, but at what cost? If Saul truly made back-door alliances with the Stiners, everything he fought for were just surface victories designed to keep the people in line, not actually help them.

"The people believe in you," Erdan said. "They will stand with you."

Armas turned to the young priest. "How? Your people have suffered. The Tali as well."

"The Lubez will need convincing, now that they have the power," Mel added.

Armas crossed his arms. "You know that won't be easy."

"But you'll do it? You'll be our king?" she asked.

Armas closed his eyes. "I never wanted this." What he wanted was Jon, and he couldn't have him. He wanted Kyla to be safe. Who knew what Saul had done to her when he discovered her betrayal?

What would Saul do to his parents, to his brothers? "I can't do this." Because this was insane.

But the shouts of his name only grew louder.

"Armas," Erdan warned. "They're hungry, not just for food, but for justice."

He ran his fingers through his curls. Under Saul's reign, there would be no justice. Just manipulation, greed, power, and control.

It could be different. *I could lead differently.*

Armas glanced at Mel.

"Welcome to the revolution," she replied, and he knew there was no choice.

To live, he must choose war.

TWENTY-FOUR

JON

Jon didn't know how much longer he could keep going on the edge of exhaustion. Saul and his great-uncle had conversed in secret before announcing a mistake had been made in the investigation. Armas would be given a chance to clear his name by returning to Glia within three days, at which time the king would host a celebratory banquet with the Elder Council and the Advocate. He ordered Abe to take the Tana priests aboard his ship to the military prison on Richo with two other pilots escorting in their Bluehawks. Milo, Carmen, and most of the others returned with the king to Melas.

Raimi was ordered to accompany Jon to Nidos, to ensure that the Advocate understood that he must return home to assure transparency, to correct the story.

Something had been off with Raimi for a while. Jon suspected Raimi was part of the plot his father had hatched surrounding Armas but didn't know how far back it went. Raimi had helped Abe secure the "Leki" guests during the wedding reception. He might have helped Saul orchestrate the assassination attempt. Or quickly moved on Saul's response that Armas was a traitor and helped spread the word among the other pilots. Jon didn't know. He had no evidence.

But his gut was rarely wrong.

"You have your orders," Jon said over the comm after they departed Ramah. "We are to approach with the news that Armas is pardoned. No aggression on our part. We will escort him back safely to Melas for the king's banquet."

"Affirmative," Raimi responded.

A buzzing had started in Jon's ear, and he knew it wasn't his comm. It was the stress and exhaustion setting in.

"Did you know they were Stiners?" Jon asked.

"I didn't quite catch that, Dark Wolf — can you repeat?"

Jon closed his eyes for a moment. "The Leki delegation. You knew who they were."

Raimi didn't respond for a few seconds. "Jon — I was under orders."

"You knew they were there to assassinate Armas."

"No, I ... I mean, I didn't know until ..."

Jon gritted his teeth. Regardless of when he found out, Rami *did* know. The timing was irrelevant, either before or after.

"Jon, I didn't —"

"Let's keep the comms free of chatter. We're

approaching Nidos security."

Two scout ships approached, hailing him. "This is the security force for the Lubez nation guarding Nidos," the security detail said, having pinged Jon's transponder ID, "Please send your verification credentials."

"Verification sent."

"Your Highness," the security officer said again, their voice wavering on the comm. "We were not expecting an official delegation. To what do we owe the pleasure of your visit?"

"Classified. But it will require your assistance."

"Please follow us to the command center, Your Highness," the security detail requested.

Jon followed, with Raimi on his tail. The scout ships accompanied them to an orbital station directly above Nidos's southern pole, a spiral shaped structure spinning to generate its own gravity. Jon landed as instructed.

Stardust. They were following royal protocol.

All hands were on deck, lined up, saluting as he opened the cockpit. There were rows of guards in light blue uniforms trimmed with gold. He pulled his helmet off and glanced over at Raimi, who shrugged. He climbed down the ladder out of his Bluehawk, and a tech approached, offering to take his helmet. Jon obliged and unzipped his flight jacket. He knew he looked like hell, but it couldn't be helped. His stomach churned slightly, a result of the station's spin gravity.

"Your Highness," the captain of the guard said, the two gold bars on his shoulder giving him away. "We weren't expecting you. According to the Nidos Accords —"

"This was an unexpected visit, Captain. Apologies for the inconvenience." He motioned to Raimi. "Captain

Nadab and I are trying to track someone down who came this way within the last forty-eight hours." He stifled a yawn. *Get it together.*

"Another Phenian sympathizer?" the captain asked, escorting Jon and Raimi out from the hangar.

"No," Jon said harshly, giving a pointed look at Raimi. "This is someone who is important to me." His tongue felt swollen. He shouldn't have said that in front of Raimi. "He's important to the king," he corrected.

The captain led them to a room filled with workstations, screens mounted at desks and on the walls. "This is command central, to guard our shipyards," the captain told him. "All three nations are involved, but with the agreement in place, we have more Lubez nationals on our stations."

"I see," Jon acknowledged, noticing very few purple uniforms of the Tali nation and no crimson signifying Hessan soldiers.

The captain motioned for him and Raimi to a station. "All vessels that have arrived in the last forty-eight hours will be listed here along with all passengers."

Within two seconds, Jon found the record of a retired Kittiwake and a "Brother Marren," heading to the Hessan nation.

"That's him," he said, while thinking *dammit, Armas, you didn't even try to hide your ship. It's like you want to be caught.*

"Your Highness, we are prepared to help you retrieve him," the Lubez captain said.

"No need, Captain. Just show us the way and we'll take care of it. He is not hostile." He flicked his gaze to Raimi. "We'll recover him and be on our way —"

"Captain," Raimi interrupted. "We hate to intrude, but

we would request one more thing — lodging for rest. His Royal Highness has not slept —"

Jon waved his hand. "I'm fine —"

Raimi gave him a look and Jon snapped his jaw shut. He was right. The stims were wearing off and it was all he could do to hold himself together.

"It is our pleasure to assist you, Your Highness. We are glad to be part of the Unified Nacaen Forces, under your father's reign."

Jon acknowledged him with a wave of his hand. Armas had accomplished a great feat in bringing about the accords for Nidos — and to the Lubez, loyalty to Saul — but he wondered how far that loyalty extended, beyond the brass.

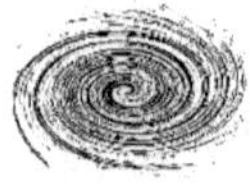

Raimi insisted they rest twelve hours before resuming the mission, and Jon stopped arguing. Exhaustion had caught up to him. As much as he mistrusted Raimi, his friend's concern for his well-being reminded him of how things used to be. Armas had changed everything.

Even when he could finally rest, Jon's sleep was troubled. As he and Raimi entered Hessan airspace, his mind flashed back to his dreams. Armas, tortured and killed by Saul. Kyla, grieving her dead husband. Sharda, crying out for him from Richo. He'd thought of her the other day, during the wedding reception, and wondered if she was all right.

Ice rain pelted the hull of his Bluehawk. He'd last been to Nidos during the dry season, and never to Hessan land.

"Dark Wolf, you got a lock?"

"Affirmative," he replied to Raimi, his thoughts back on track to landing in this soup. Though the Hessan didn't report to Lubez security anything within their own borders, there was only one major temple in Hessan territory, making it easy to find. *Why didn't you hide somewhere more discreet, Armas?*

Jon didn't know what Raimi's true motives were, and that frustrated him more than anything. He knew his father's. He was certain the valiant announcement he made before departing Ramah was all fake. All the words about clearing Armas's name, holding a banquet to celebrate — he *knew* it was a trap, but how Saul would do it, with everyone watching, Jon didn't know.

Raimi was there for insurance, to make sure he followed through on persuading Armas to return. Would Raimi understand what he had to do to *save* Armas?

Jon led Raimi over the hills in Hessan territory to a village hangar, setting down his Bluehawk while Raimi landed next to him. Three deck technicians approached as Jon climbed down and removed his helmet. He scanned the large, empty hangar with a curved roof. A large tarp covered stacks of crates in the corner.

Large enough for a Kittiwake to be hiding back there. Jon palmed his face at the utter foolishness.

"Prince Jon," a technician greeted, and all three bowed. "We noticed your call sign on your Bluehawk."

The Dark Wolf leaping at the nose did make his fighter stand out. Raimi raised a brow.

"Where is he?"

"Who?" the technician asked.

"Whoever came here recently and whose Kittiwake Fighter you're hiding over in the corner," Jon said flatly.

"That is Brother Marren's," the second tech said, a

woman. "He joined the Order for the One God."

"Where can we find him?" Raimi asked.

"The Hessan temple is at the top of the hill," the red-headed tech said. Jon did a double-take. The man was shorter, and his facial features different, but the red hair was even a similar length as Armas's. Might be a Dahan transplant.

"Thanks," Raimi said before Jon could speak.

Jon followed Raimi out of the hangar and into the cold rain, though it was lighter now than when they flew in. As they walked into the rain, the dismal conditions of the village caused him to stop in his tracks. Most of the buildings were lean-tos built against large boulders, shacks with repurposed siding from old ship hulls. They might keep out the wind, but most likely were cold and damp. He glanced over his shoulder. Even the hangar, though better constructed, had patches in its metal roof. The trees were twisted and small.

"Jon? This way," Raimi called to him, for he must've gone on ahead and realized Jon hadn't kept up.

Jon caught up to him. "I had no idea things were this bad here."

"You should see the Dagael nation on Richo."

Jon grabbed Raimi's arm. "What do you mean?"

Raimi frowned. "You're engaged to a member of the Beneur Elder's family. You can ask her. But the Dagael live out in scraps of old ships while the Beneur all have mansions."

Jon let go of Raimi's arm. Sharda was Dagael. He hadn't even thought about it when his marriage was arranged, that Rela Vellar and Sharda were from the same world.

Didn't know that Sharda's own people lived in poverty.

They climbed the slippery steps up the hill to the top. A circle of buildings, also with peaked roofs but constructed of wood and stone, surrounded the large temple building. The buildings here were sturdier, probably where the priests that served this temple of the One God lived. Jon considered how his father had built the Great Hall in the fortress of Glia to become the main center of worship, but each nation kept their own temples, a reminder that Nacaens held differences in practice.

Try as his father might, his way of rule was conformity, easily mistaken for unity.

Voices carried from inside the temple. Jon exchanged a look with Raimi before they pushed open the doors together.

Hundreds of people gathered in small circles, sharing food. On the dais at the front, where the roof peaked, priests handed out loaves of bread and bags of goods to greedy hands.

"Are they giving away their allotment?" Raimi pointed to the priests.

Jon swore. Part of how his father maintained some order was giving each nation an allotment through their Elder representative, along with the priests of the One God. It was one thing to share discreetly with a few people in need, but most of the village must be here.

"They must be desperate if they ..." His voice trailed off.

Someone was singing. He scanned the room, locking his gaze on a robed priest handing over bags from the dais, the voice reaching him:

*"How long — will we live in hiding,
How long — must we bear the pain?
Our song — will lift up our voices,
The people will rise again!"*

Other voices joined in.

*"Our song — will rise over mountains,
Our song — will carry the sea,
Our ship — will sail the horizon,
Until we all are set free!"*

The priest slid their hood back, revealing their signature red locks and freckles below those icy blue eyes.

Jon's heart caught in his throat.

"It appears we have visitors," Armas said, his gaze cold. The crowd grew quiet. "His Royal Highness, Prince Jon Kishrah, and Captain Raimi Nadab."

Jon's hand went to his side, as uniformed Hessan soldiers faced him and Raimi.

"By order of the king, stand down," Raimi warned.

"Let me hazard a guess," Armas said, his voice deep and threatening, his tone one Jon only knew briefly from the war room or the few negotiations he'd been allowed to attend. "You are here to escort me back safely. That the king's wild accusation that *I* am a traitor to the Nacaens was a misunderstanding. That he recognizes *I* am the one whose life was almost taken by assassins, had it not been for my wife's daring intervention. That he knows he couldn't send a squadron after me without being in violation of the very accords *I* negotiated."

"Armas, please —" Jon began, but the freezing stare

from Armas cut him off. *I wasn't part of this. You know that,* he pleaded inwardly.

"We're here to bring you back home to your wife and family," Raimi said. "And as a gesture of goodwill the king has declared a banquet in your honor. All the nation Elders are invited," he added, as Jon spotted Mel Diez, the Hessan representative Elder.

He swore again. The priests dispersing their allotment was one thing, something that could be argued was within their rights. The nation's Elder among them, when she had access to government resources ...

Jon spied the bags being passed around. Some were open, and he saw flashes of silver, bars of credits. His eyes drew to the Hessan soldiers near him, the bulges on their sides.

His stomach fell. *Some of those bags must contain weapons. They're building an insurgency.*

"Can we go somewhere? I just want to talk," Jon pleaded, raising a hand slightly to Raimi who'd taken a step closer.

Armas's gaze slipped between him and Raimi and back. "Come with me." Armas motioned for Mel to follow him.

God, I hope you know what you're doing, Jon thought, as he and Raimi put their helmets back on. They followed the Hessan Elder and the Advocate out of the temple as they pulled up their hoods.

Out in the rain, they made their way to a smaller building. Raimi pulled Jon aside. "You know we *have* to report this and bring him back."

"Let's hear him out —"

"Jon ..."

He ignored Raimi, pushing past him to follow Armas

inside a cabin. A blast of heat met him as the door opened. He noticed the Advocate's flight suit hanging at the door, the sparse furnishing inside. He hadn't been here long. Jon pulled his helmet off, his cheeks warmed from the crackling fireplace.

Mel removed her cloak and hung it up, then leaned her hip against the back of a chair. She carried a weapon at her side.

"When did you get here?" he asked.

"Six days ago," Armas said, yanking off his cloak and tossing it over another chair before turning to face the fire. "Nidos days, that is, so about four-and-a-half standard?"

Jon's stomach flipped. This wasn't right. He wanted to go to him, get his hands on him and know he wasn't hurt. But he couldn't. No one knew, except Kyla, and they couldn't be public now without losing everything.

"I'm not going back," Armas continued, crossing his arms and shifting his focus to Jon, then Raimi. "So you can finish delivering whatever message you were instructed to, then return to the king and let him know that if he leaves me in peace, I will remain here and continue to uphold the accords."

Raimi scoffed. "We saw the weapons, the credits." He turned to Mel. "Your days are numbered on the Elder Council. Your stockpiling is tantamount to treason."

The Hessan Elder shrugged, scratching her trouser leg just below her holstered weapon. "With the Lubez holding power, our people have nothing. This is merely so we can defend ourselves against whatever promises the king made to the Stiners."

Sweat gathered along the back of Jon's neck; it was so

stifling hot in there.

Raimi's hands dropped to his sides. "What are you talking about?"

"The princess told me before I left," Armas said. Jon noted how he didn't mention she'd helped him escape, only that she protected him. Still trying to protect her, somewhat, from any implication she might've aided a terrorist willingly. *Terrorist. That's what everyone will think he is if he doesn't come back.*

"Saul hired Stiners to try to kill me," Armas continued. "He made a deal with them." He nodded to Mel. "The Elders have been kept from those negotiations."

Jon's chest hurt. *Armas, play the game. Don't let on you know so much.*

"When the king brought up resuming relations with the Leki to the Elder Council, I was suspicious," Mel said. "Why would they want to come to the table with us, when we had defeated them in Horeb's rings, and the king had killed one of their representatives? Then I learned the king quietly paid them off. Still, the Leki are a small nation with a divided royal family, barely holding down their world and moons in Bara. They don't have anything to offer us." She glanced at Jon. "We heard that delegates arrived during the wedding."

Diez's admission of what she knew, what other Elders might know, confirmed that Armas wasn't going to play Saul's game.

God protect him.

"They were the Stiner assassins," Jon admitted. "You can't come back."

Raimi's brows drew together. "Jon —"

"No." He faced his companion. "It was a mistake to come here."

"*Your Highness,*" Raimi emphasized, "we have orders from the king to bring him in."

"Stardust. Don't do this," Jon warned.

Raimi drew his weapon. "We have no choice, Jon. He has to come with us, or he has to die."

Mel moved to draw her weapon, but Jon was faster. He didn't think. In a fraction of a second, Jon pulled his Sharpshooter and fired at Raimi.

His former friend's eyes grew wide in recognition, hand moving to his chest. Jon grabbed him as he slumped over. If they'd been in mechs, they would've had chest armor, but not in their flight suits.

"Goddammit," Raimi swore, blood pouring over his hand.

"God damn this whole thing," Jon added, holding on to Raimi. "I'm so fucking sorry."

Raimi gasped once, twice, and then his body was still.

The prince laid his captain on the ground as life left him. Jon's whole body shook. A loud, guttural, animal sound escaped from his chest as he screamed.

Familiar hands braced his shoulders. Armas dropped to his knees next to him. "My love," he whispered, cupping Jon's face.

Jon grabbed Armas's shirt, balling his fists, holding on to his lover as he continued to shake. "What have I done?"

He could only watch as Mel went to Raimi, checked for a pulse and shook her head. She pulled her cloak over his body, touched Armas's shoulder once and slipped out of the room.

"You saved *me,*" Armas insisted, drawing his lips to Jon's and kissing him. "You did what you had to do.

"You're not safe here," Jon managed to whisper

between kisses.

Armas grabbed the zipper on Jon's flight suit and unzipped it. Sweat drenched Jon's flight shirt. "God, Jon, you're burning up."

"Forget about me. You have to go. My father will hunt you down. If you don't come back, he'll find an excuse. He'll convince the Lubez. They know I — we — came for you," he added, glancing once at Raimi's body.

"You didn't have a choice," Armas said, motioning to Raimi. The Advocate's eyes were ice. "You had no choice, Jon," he repeated, cupping the back of Jon's neck. "Saul did this. Saul set all of this up."

"Which is why you must leave the system. Go to Bara. You have to disappear."

Armas shook his head. "My family — my parents —"

"I'll get them out," Jon said. "I promise you." He wrapped Armas in his arms, forehead to forehead, despite the heat flaring in his temples. "I'll do anything for you."

"Jon ... they want me to lead." Armas's eyes twitched. "They want me to be king."

"You should."

Armas shook his head. "You should be king, it is your right —"

"Listen to me." He palmed Armas's cheek. "I've known, ever since the battle of Zek, you were *meant* to lead. You were destined to become not Saul's Advocate, but *our* advocate — to all the system, to the universe that wants to destroy us. Zam knew it when he chose you. And I will serve you, right beside you, when the time is right."

"What are you saying?"

Jon shifted on his knees, turning further away from Raimi as he held Armas close. "I will do all I can to support you, but I can only do that knowing you are safe. But my hand, my heart, my soul are yours." He kissed Armas hard. "I live for you, die for you, *kill* for you. I'll do anything. You are *my* heart, *my* king." He took Armas's hand and placed it over his own heart.

Tears beaded on the corners of Armas's eyes, twin seas Jon could drown in. Despite the fever rising, despite his twisted gut at having to shoot Raimi, he loved Armas even more deeply than he ever imagined he could. He brushed the corners of his lover's eyes with his thumbs. "Find a way off-world, out of this godforsaken system. Leave the Kittiwake here." Jon breathed out hard. "I'll make it look like you and Raimi killed each other."

"Jon," Armas whispered, "tell Kyla —"

He pressed a finger to Armas's lips. "I'll thank her for saving your life. And I'll tell her she needs to move on." He gave Armas a stern look. "There's no need to break her heart further."

"What are you going to do when you return to Saul's banquet without me?"

Jon kissed him again, a chill now falling over him. "Stay alive."

TWENTY-FIVE

KYLA

Another week had passed since Major Zeru escorted her and Laina back to her apartment. Though she wasn't in the dungeon, she wasn't allowed to leave, and the guards refused to answer questions. All communications were cut off from her rooms, so she had no idea if her father had returned, if they'd gone to war, or if the banquet had taken place without her. It might be more comfortable, but it was still a prison.

She didn't know if Armas and Jon were still alive.

The door opened without the chime, and her father entered, wearing all black. Kyla stood, then stepped back as she recognized the color of mourning. "Oh no. No."

"I'm afraid it's true."

She grabbed the edge of the table, the room spinning.

"Zam is dead."

The words were jumbled in her head. Not Jon. Not Armas. *Zam*. She breathed out.

"How long have you betrayed me?"

His words startled her. *Which betrayal: Armas? Jon? Zam?* It didn't matter. The moment her father killed the Leki informant, she'd sworn not to follow his path.

"I couldn't do it," she said, standing tall. "He was like a grandfather to me."

"We left his body to rot on Ramah."

Kyla frowned. "Then why the black uniform?"

A muscle in his jaw twitched. "I mourn him, traitor though he was." He motioned to her bedroom. "Get dressed. The banquet will start in an hour."

Saul left her quarters. She slumped into a chair as Laina emerged from her bedroom. "Your Highness, are you all right?"

"Zam is dead," she said, her voice flat. She'd known the old man's health was failing, the medicinal tea couldn't keep his strength forever.

"And your brother? Your husband?"

She rested her chin on her palms as Laina stroked her back. "I don't know, but I have to hope they are alive."

Kyla chose a black dress: long sleeves and a collar buttoned up her throat, a long narrow black sheath over black boots. If her father would mourn openly, so should she. Laina twisted and pinned back Kyla's black hair.

Her great-uncle greeted her at the door to her quarters, also in black. "Fitting," she said, as she took his arm, "that you would be my guard once more."

"Be glad your father has softened toward you," Abe said, his voice low, as he escorted her down the marble staircase. "Some species devour their children. You may be the one who escapes with only a few scratches."

She glared at him. "Where's Jon?"

He scowled. "Your father didn't tell you? He arrived with a special message."

Kyla bit back her smile. Like sister, like brother — Jon must've found a way to help Armas escape from her father's wrath.

Abe tugged her to the right, toward the doors out from the palace and into the rest of the fortress. "Aren't we going to the formal dining room?"

"This is a special banquet," Abe said, motioning to the guards at the palace doors. "Your father invited all the Elders and decided to hold it in the Great Hall, so it could be streamed to the entire Nacaen Group."

Kyla's heart stuttered, her smugness shattering. *He knows something. Oh Goddesses, he will make a show of us.*

A long, wide table dominated the center of the Great Hall, with holoscreens set in the middle. Seven chairs lined either side — one for each of the twelve nation's Elders, along with one for Jon and one for Kyla. At the head was a large chair carved from Dahan hardwood — the same kind of tree used for Serah masks. At the foot was a matching chair.

"The king insisted we set a place for the Advocate."

Kyla said nothing, her heart threatening to escape her chest as Abe led her to her chair and took the one beside her as the Jamin representative. The other Elders mingled with drinks already in hand but came to the table to take their seats. Her father and Jon had not yet arrived. Major Barish bowed to her slightly before taking his seat.

She recognized others — Mel Diez in her black dress with a crimson sash from the Hessan nation, among others.

"Where is Seriah?" Kyla whispered to Abe, as an unfamiliar Dahan representative took the major's place.

"She resigned her post."

Kyla's hands trembled in her lap. If Major Zeru had left, was there any hope of resistance within the Council?

Everyone rose as Saul entered, flanked by Jon. Her brother wore his green dress uniform, apparently not getting the memo about mourning colors. He sat across from her, glancing once before looking away, folding his hands in front of him. Shadows layered below his eyes.

"Jon," she whispered, but Abe hissed at her.

"It's better if you don't speak."

"Please, please, take your seats," the king said, his voice sounding amused.

The Elders sat, and servants placed napkins in their laps and bowls of Sim'ee-style greens and dressing in front of them.

"Before we begin the meal, we have a few announcements. Two days ago, Seriah Zeru resigned her position as Dahan Elder representative along with her post in the Melas Unified Military under the United Nacaen Forces." Her father's eyes flickered for a moment, betraying his anger.

She must've found a way to leave before he knew it, or he would be announcing her death, Kyla thought.

Saul continued, faking a smile. "We have a special guest tonight in her place."

Kyla glanced at the new representative, a short man with red hair, wearing the brown and tan uniform of the Dahan. His hair reminded her of Armas. She shifted her gaze back to Jon to see if he noticed the same.

Jon looked horrifically pale. Kyla dropped her fork.

"Oh yes, you may have also noticed the Advocate is not with us. Sadly, in the confusion following my daughter's wedding and the arrival of Stiner assassins, our intelligence gave conflicting messages. We've since sorted everything out. I sent my own son to retrieve our Advocate, to clear his name, and yet Armas Lehem-Perez is not here, and neither is Captain Nadab."

"Jon," she whispered again, but her father caught her eye.

"Ah, darling daughter. You who roused your husband from his sleep to escape — do you know what he has done? Who he has become?"

An image popped up on the holoscreen in the middle of the table. The Elders at the table grew still.

Armas was at the center of the vid, as crowds of people shouted his name. Mel Diez was standing with him. Every head swiveled toward the Hessan Elder. She snapped her jaw shut and shook her head.

Any hope Kyla held shattered like falling stars. Saul had set everything up, baited the trap, but it wasn't Armas alone he hoped to catch.

Jon. Mel. *Anyone* who had ever helped the Advocate. Kyla's breath grew ragged.

"Welcome to the revolution," the traitorous representative of the Hessan people said on video, as the crowd's shouts proclaimed Armas as king.

Saul waved a hand, pausing the video, as guards approached, hauling Mel Diez out of her chair. "Take her to the cells. Until the Hessan can put forth a delegate who will swear allegiance to the Nacaens and forsake the insurgency, we will leave the Hessan seat vacant."

Whatever Mel planned to say, her voice was muffled by the gag placed over her mouth as she was taken from the room.

The Elders were stunned into silence, fear pricking Kyla's skin. The servants stood off to the side, nervously fidgeting, carrying baskets of Dahan breads, but uncertain whether to continue dinner service.

Saul continued as if this was all a normal interruption to dinner. "We are grateful to Dege Edmon, a mechanic in Hessan territory who reported to us that a new insurgency was forming on Nidos."

A messenger approached the man who sat in Seriah Zeru's seat, bringing him a silver case. "Your payment for your loyalty," Saul said, "which is more than I can say for my son."

The image on the screen shifted to one of Jon embracing Armas. A body lay at their feet, and Kyla gasped in horror, recognizing Raimi. Dead.

Captain Nadab, who'd served with Jon ever since he went to flight school and mech training — *Jon must've killed him*. Raimi was the one who covered for Jon when he did something reckless. Raimi was the one who always had his back.

He must've tried to stop Jon from saving Armas.

On the screen, Jon kissed Armas, and Armas fumbled with Jon's flight suit zipper. *Oh Goddesses, no.* It was not Jon and Armas's love that caused her face to redden; it was her father's blatant shaming of his children, of equating their love with betraying him.

Saul swiped the air to stop the video. "We've seen enough of this garbage. My son, the prince, having an affair with his sister's husband. Murdering Captain Nadab, a trustworthy servant of the throne and of all Nacaens. Disgraceful." Saul motioned to the guards. "Take him out of my sight."

"Father!" Jon pleaded, and Kyla's heart tore apart. Tears streamed down her face, but she couldn't move. She couldn't do anything to save her brother.

Saul paid no attention to her as the guards forced Jon out of his seat and away from the table, most likely to the same dungeon she had been held in.

"Ky!" her brother shouted at the doorway, her heart shattering before he was dragged out of the Great Hall.

"It is clear we are no longer a united kingdom," Saul said gravely to the remaining Elders, frozen in their terror.

The room began to spin. Kyla gripped her chair, trying to maintain focus and not pass out.

"There are rumors that I've made an alliance with the Stiners." He glanced at each person at the table. "I want you to know," he added, pausing at Kyla, but refusing to meet her eyes, "I have made no such deal. Stiner mercenaries have attacked us far too often, first with the Leki, and then with the Phenians. In the confusion over the Advocate's betrayal, I did hire a *few* Stiner mercenaries. I will admit this was a bad call, but I didn't know whom among our own soldiers we could trust. There is *no* agreement with the Stiners at large."

The princess shuddered at how easily the lies slid off her father's tongue, how he twisted the tiny bit of truth to feign his sincerity.

"However, there is an alliance I do believe would be beneficial to our people. One we must consider, but of course it must be agreed upon by all of you first."

He swiped the image of Jon kissing Armas away from the screen. Spikes of terror traveled down Kyla's spine as an image of a man, paler than any she'd seen, appeared on the screen. His head was shaved, his eyes dark, his expression stern. He wore a black fitted jumpsuit. A silver hexagon pinned on his chest was the only adornment.

"The Supreme One of the Modes, Alton of Gallim, wants to normalize relations with us."

Gasps and whispers echoed around the table.

"The Near Side systems are falling. The Airysan Union is creeping its way through the center of the galaxy, and we must forge alliances."

An Elder objected. "But we can't! They're pirates!"

"Members of my — *our* Council — have already betrayed us." Saul rose from his seat, placing his hands on the back of Kyla's shoulders.

She sat still. *I will fear no evil.* Armas once sang a song to her with those words, a song he wrote after the Battle of Zek.

Her father squeezed her shoulders, harder than necessary. "I have made no agreements with them and will not do so without the full support of this Council. My loyalty is to all nations who are committed to the promise of a united kingdom. Therefore, we will send a delegation to them, to learn from them, and to present any agreement to you. I plan to send Abe Renk of the Jamin, along with my own daughter, Kyla. After all, she acted to save her husband, as any dutiful spouse would, and had no idea he was plotting a revolution against her own people."

She tried to stop the tears, but one more escaped down her cheek. Her father held her in her chair, not allowing her to bolt. He was sending her to the people who created Ogroma.

Monsters.

"Your Majesty," the Reshar nation Elder said, "with all due respect, both of those representatives are of your family. Perhaps you should send another?"

Saul arched a brow. "I was planning to send Major Barish," he said, acknowledging the Sim'ee representative, "but I am moving him to the mech division after Major Zeru's resignation."

"Your Majesty," Major Barish interjected. "If it would please you, send Lieutenant Barish in my place. They can attend to your daughter as her personal guard."

Saul nodded. "Excellent idea." His hand moved to the back of Kyla's neck, reminding her of when he almost choked her to death.

"I know this is much to take in," he continued, letting Kyla go as he motioned to the servants. They hurried to the table, setting out the baskets of Dahan bread, and others carrying the main course, curried Jamin-style beef with mushrooms, and root vegetables in a cheesy roux. "But the banquet will go on." Saul moved back to his seat and raised his wine glass. "Elders, we may be entering a period of war none of us wanted or imagined. Let us pray it is over swiftly. Let us pray that we learn the Modes will be friends rather than foe. May we secure a lasting peace for all our peoples, the Nacaen Group, together."

"Long live the king!" Abe said, raising his glass.

"Long live the king!" the remaining Elders responded.

Kyla took her glass of wine and downed it, shoving her fears down her throat. She could not worry about Jon. She could only hope Armas was truly safe.

Right now, she would have to focus on surviving the Modes and finding a way to stop Saul.

PART THREE

TWENTY-SIX

ARMAS

Three weeks after he left Nidos, Armas paced the spaceport terminal in orbit above Balec, the Leki home world in the Bara System. A year ago, he'd never been off Melas. Now he stood before the viewscreen on an interplanetary spaceport, an orbital station above a blue-green world of swirling oceans and small swatches of the remaining tropical forests. Tall buildings lined the coasts of continents and islands, and bulbous mining pods dotted the seas. Carbon collectors floated below in lower orbit, trying to stall the effects of climate change.

The orbital station was the junction of long shipping routes to the Near Side Systems, and the remaining stars of the Outer Systems. Between the Near Side and the Outer Systems was the Galactic Ocean, a vast expanse of dust and gas difficult to cross and communicate through, unless one traveled via Jordan Station, a dead rock in the middle of it all.

Armas knew this because his great-grandmother had immigrated on that same path.

The Outer Systems were often referred to as wild space, and for a reason. The Leki royal family, consisting of twenty-some royals with rival titles, sometimes fought among themselves. Given that Saul ended the war with them by paying them to withdraw and killing the informant who tried to bribe Nacaen Elders, and that he'd tried to frame them for Armas's death originally in the botched assassination attempt, Armas was uneasy with being recognized here.

Mel Diez had arranged for his travel, along with a dozen Hessan rebels, smuggled aboard a decommissioned fuel tanker. Armas cut his hair, dyed it black, and attempted to blend in with the other multiplanetary travelers, trading out his military clothing for the loose trousers and tunics, browns and tans and grays, of a no-name people from some no-name world. The other Hessan rebels who'd hidden aboard the station with him were scrounging up resources and contacting sympathetic Leki officials within the divided royal family, while Armas wandered the interplanetary terminal. He'd received a message from Erdan, the Hessan priest, that a contact from Dahan would meet him there.

Erdan also let him know Jon had been arrested and Mel disappeared, presumed dead.

He swiped away the messages, encrypted and using a code they'd worked out before he left, and opened the screen for the details of a large cargo hauler due at the station in four days.

"Any word?" one of the Hessan rebels asked, dressed in the same nondescript backwater world uniform.

"Not yet. Waiting for Erdan's contact," Armas replied, checking the time. "Take some of the guys down to the lower-level docks, see if you can get some unloading work with the shift change."

"Yes, sir," the Hessan man whispered.

Armas grabbed his arm. "Keep quiet, but see if you can find out anything about a large freighter from the Liphes sector coming in."

Armas let go of the man quickly, keeping his head down as two Phenian soldiers in light blue uniforms walked by, masks over their noses and mouths, and weapons at their sides. Phenians had long adapted to the polluted air of their home world Ilistia. Even on the Leki orbital station, the pumped-in oxygen was too rich for their blood now.

"Can't believe the Leki have sided with them," the Hessan rebel whispered after the soldiers had passed. "You hear the Leki lost two moons to the Modes while they were backing the Phenians against us?"

Armas nodded. "That's why the Leki royal family is divided. Some sympathize with us. But the system is falling apart." He motioned to the rebel. "Go check on that freighter."

The Hessan rebel slid his hands into his pockets as he walked away.

We won't last long, Armas thought to himself, *if we don't start building broader coalitions.*

But he couldn't worry about the Leki and Phenians now. He was no longer the King's Advocate. He was a fugitive, probably doomed to be shot on sight since he hadn't returned with Jon, and Raimi killed in the process. A terrorist. A rebel.

He continued through the terminal toward the lifts, stopping now and then to read the screens that posted ships with room for passengers. The Leki citizens on the station wore thermal underwear, visible underneath the sheer silky fabrics their people were known for down on the surface of their tropical planet. But most of the people passing by wore the colors of dust and ash, the basics of most backwater worlds.

It wasn't hard to disappear in plain sight, speaking the Galactic language, even with Melas's flat accent. No one paid him any attention, and he began to hum a tune, a song he'd started working on during the voyage away from Nidos.

That's why he was shocked to his core when Seriah Zeru called his name.

He whipped around, eyes wide at the figure in the dark red cloak standing near an empty terminal station. "You must master the art of subtlety, and probably, not sing in public," she said, smiling, as she drew back her hood. She wore her cloak over dark brown trousers with black boots and a cream-colored top. "And I figured you'd recognize my voice enough you wouldn't be clamoring for your weapon," she added, noting his hand was tucked into the pocket of his coat.

"I wasn't," he insisted, drawing his communication device instead, though he did have a pistol in his other pocket. "I wasn't sure who was going to find me first."

"You got the message from Erdan?" she asked.

"Yeah." He pursed his lips. "How is ... the prince?" he whispered.

She shook her head. "We've had no direct contact since he was taken into custody, but he's been spotted with the king."

Armas's heart sank. He couldn't imagine Saul killing Jon, but Saul might try to use him to lure Armas back. He squeezed his eyes shut.

Zeru touched Armas's arm, and he opened his eyes. She pressed close to him to whisper. "Saul has sent a delegation to the Modes."

Armas pulled back. "I thought he was making an alliance with the Stiners."

"We all did. None of our spies had that intel."

Armas swore. "He's always a step ahead. Always has an alternative plan." He cleared his throat. "How long have you been part of this?"

She gave a casual glance around the terminal, before beckoning him to follow her. "There's been some unease in certain ranks for a while. But it's all been separate — no one national group knowing what the other was doing. Keeping it decentralized in case someone got caught."

Armas stopped, his chest growing cold. "The Hessan priests —"

"If they didn't leave, they are as good as dead."

Armas sucked in a breath as Seriah continued walking. The terminal corridor came to a junction, and she led him down a corridor. Armas hurried to keep up with her longer legs. "When Saul ordered your arrest, on your wedding night, and called us all back to duty, I knew it was wrong. I knew what he accused you of was a lie." She paused for a moment. "The princess asked me to help you."

Armas closed his eyes at the mention of her. Kyla had known about him and Jon, and still she remained faithful to him. "Major —"

"Just Seriah now. I formally resigned my post before Saul could take it from me."

He shook his head. "I can't repay you for what you've

done."

"You were chosen by Zam," she said, her voice sad. "We found his body on Ramah and buried him there."

Armas gritted his teeth. He'd sensed Zam was near death when he saw him last.

"The prophet was organizing people for the last year, ever since he went into hiding. He was in touch with priests not only among the Hessan, but among the Dagael, Maire, Ildan, and other nations. Including Dahan. When I decided to leave Glia, there was a network waiting for me." She reached for his arm again, tugging him down a side ramp to a lower deck level for charter ships. "I told them I'd come find you."

Armas's brows drew together. "Who, exactly?"

The former major didn't have to respond, because waiting for him at one of the terminal stations were his parents and brothers. They all wore hats and heavy cloaks, carrying a few possessions in their bags. They had the harried look of refugees, trying to hide and yet still standing out.

But it was Roxy who jumped toward him first. He sank to his knees as his beloved sheepdog covered his face in kisses. His older brother Eliot pulled on Roxy's collar as Armas's father hauled him to his feet.

"Thank God," his mother said, wrapping her arms around him. Armas closed his eyes tight, fighting off tears. He'd just seen her at his wedding, she was so happy for him. Now, Nita sobbed in relief in his arms.

"Son, I ..." Jesse began, but he choked. Eliot let go of Roxy, who proceeded to put her front paws on Armas's thigh. He turned from his mother's embrace, wrapping his arm around his father's shoulder. Shane stood off to one side, hands in his pockets.

"We have to get you out of here," Armas said, patting Roxy's head. He worried anyone looking for them would know who they were. The wedding photos had been all over the networks in the hours before Saul tried to kill him.

"It's taken care of," Seriah said. "I had Eliot issued a new ID before I resigned, and since he's been flying transports, we were able to get a ship."

"Due to Grandmother's heritage as Diboni, we have status as refugees," Jesse said. "The atmosphere cleared up there about fifty years ago. She never wanted to go back, I remember her telling me as a child, but I'd like to see where she came from."

"It's going to take us a long time, but it's our best option," Eliot added. "At least, until we can return."

"Couldn't we stay here with you?" Nita asked. Armas slung his arm around his mother's shoulder, knowing this was too much change for her in such a short amount of time.

"Saul will eventually track you down," Seriah said. "It's still dangerous, even here. The king will target anyone he can to flush Armas out of hiding, and if the Leki know anyone here has a bounty on their head, we're all done for."

Shane continued to stand off to the side. His golden hair had been cut short, military-style. Armas had barely spoken to him at the wedding reception. He lifted his gaze, with the same blue eyes as his own. "I want to stay and fight with you."

"Shane —"

"It's not right that you're left to handle this alone," his brother said quietly.

His mother buried her face in his chest. Armas stroked her back, soothing her as her tears soaked the front of his shirt. He cleared his throat. "It's not likely we'll —"

Jesse shook his head in warning to Armas. *No more talk of death.*

"The ship is waiting," Seriah interrupted. Nita pulled away from Armas and leaned back into her husband's arms. "You must make a decision now," she said to Shane. "Eliot's been hired on as the pilot, the transport has enough fuel and supplies to make it to Jordan, and from there you can resupply and get to the Noma System and your new home world. If you stay ... there's no choice. You fight with us."

Armas knew what lay under Seriah's threat. So much had already been risked to get them off Melas, she would not let them throw the revolution away.

"I'm staying," Shane said, moving to stand by Armas. "I'll fight with you."

"I'll get them to safety," Eliot said, shaking Armas's hand. "You — don't die."

Armas pulled his older brother in for a hug, then hugged his parents one last time. Shane followed suit. The two younger brothers watched as Eliot and their parents picked up their bags, and Armas scratched Roxy behind her ears one more time before Eliot pulled on her leash. The family entered the airlock to the private ship. "God, keep them safe," he prayed, blinking away his tears as he waved one last time.

Shane hauled his bag over his shoulder and raised an eyebrow. "You know, *rebel* has a nice ring to it. Sounds like something I'd do, anyway."

Armas chuckled. He'd never gotten along with Shane, but there was something in the look in his eye that caught his attention. "What?"

"You've really changed, you know. Not just the farm

kid. Not just the shepherd. Not even the Advocate." Shane tilted his head. "I was so jealous when you were chosen. Then you almost died at Zek, and so many missions since then. You didn't do this for prestige. You did this because it's *who you are*. You've got the king of the Nacaens against you, and yet you still seem determined to find a way to win this for everyone else. Not just survive, but ..."

Shane dropped his bag and threw his arms around his brother. Armas slowly brought his arms around him, squeezing his eyes shut to stop the tears.

"When the prophet came to our house, I thought he was just a crazy old man," Shane admitted, pulling back from Armas. "But everything he said was true. And I don't think he intended for you to be the Advocate. He wanted you to be the king."

His brother dropped to his knee.

"Shane," Armas hissed, yanking on his arm to make him stand. "Don't be ridiculous."

Armas gasped when Seriah touched his shoulder, looking at him with reverence. "You are our true king," she whispered. "We must fight to get you your throne."

Armas raked his fingers through his hair as he pulled away from both of them. "Stop it, both of you, before someone sees you. I didn't just come here to hide out and wait."

He drew his comm out of his pocket, swiping to the screen he'd studied before Seriah found him. "I've been tracking the freight docks on the lower level." He handed his comm over to Seriah. "There's an unusually large freighter, the *Behemoth*, arriving in four days standard. The dockhands are talking about how they're basically clearing out all the berths on one side for refueling."

The former major frowned. "Liphes sector? Shipment

of steel?"

"I think it's a front. Everyone knows Airysan is superior now and the Leki have the money for it. Check out the specs on it."

Seriah swiped through and her eyes widened. "Except for the extra drive cones, and odd cargo boxes ... stardust, it's an Airysan mech transport, isn't it?"

Armas nodded as she handed his device back. "Disguised like an old Liphes freighter but too big. Fake drive cone on the keel."

"I remember when the Airysan hauler came to our system. Docked at Nidos, then unloaded onto the mech transports in units. But we have a separate military orbital."

"So do the Leki, but for some reason they're landing here."

Seriah scratched her ear. "That doesn't make sense."

Armas crossed his arms. "It does if someone in the Leki royal family ordered them and didn't want the others to know."

Shane frowned. "So what does this have to do with us?"

Armas smirked at the former major, and they looked at Shane at the same time.

"We're going to steal it."

"*He* thinks we can steal it."

"We can intercept it before it arrives here," Armas countered.

Seriah stroked her chin. "With a crew that's largely trained for cargo freight, because no one would be stupid enough to try to hijack an Airysan mech transport, probably double-hulled Airysan steel, with the usual defense cannons and shields. Not even the Modes would attempt it — especially since the Airysans developed a patch to fix the hole that you and Jon used to bring down the mechs."

Armas couldn't help but smile at the memory. It was the moment they'd come up with the plan that he'd felt that spark for Jon — and he knew Jon had sensed it, too.

Seriah's eyes gleamed. "Do you have a plan?"

"Working on it. I've got twelve Hessan fighters here of various skill levels. You?"

"I came here with your family. Too suspicious to ask anyone in the Dahan units to come with me, but after I left, the Dahan mech units defected, and so did some of the Ildan and Maire pilots and fighters. A few are hiding scattered in the moons of Horeb, some others may be hiding here. At least one Leki royal princess is willing to hide priests and civilians as asylum seekers. Most of our fighters are in open space on transports outside of scanner range, but they'll run out of supplies in a few weeks. We surprisingly got a Tali labor crew to take the *Darkangel* for us right out of the dock."

Armas was impressed. The *Darkangel* was one of the new warships negotiated by Saul.

"It won't get here in time," Seriah said, crushing any hope of using the firepower, "and besides, a warship showing up on Balec scanners will trigger a large-scale response we can't afford." She chewed her lip. "Know anything about the royals Saul negotiated with before?"

"Just that they don't all like each other."

Seriah pulled out her own comm and looked up a name. "When Saul paid them off, he sent Captain Laban Carmel, who is Jamin, and his wife Abby. Laban Carmel is somehow related, I guess through his grandparents, to the grandnephew of the Leki king, and they set up residency here with his citizenship. Abby is Ildan."

"Doesn't sound like he could be persuaded to help us against Saul."

"*She* might," Seriah countered. "The Beneur on Richo have the most power there and are in the pockets of Saul. I know Zam visited the Ildan in the last year. She might be more interested in helping her people."

Armas recalled that Jon was engaged to Rela Vellar, the daughter of the Beneur Elder, deepening the alliance with Saul. He pushed those thoughts aside. "If this is going to work," he said, "we need to arrange for a meeting with her in the next twenty-four hours. See if she can get us access to a transport that could intercept the *Behemoth* and supply us with some weapons."

"Even if we get her to help us, even if we get the ship and the weapons, we've still got the problem of approaching the hauler unnoticed," Shane said. "You said it has the usual defense cannons. Won't they just shoot us?"

Armas's hope deflated. "You're right. We don't have the Modes' tech for stealth or hacking into their scanners."

"But we might have an in," Seriah said. "Laban stayed here because of his family connection. He's now the head inspector for imports on this very station. We could ask him what he knows about the large cargo vessel coming into port."

"And risk tipping him off?"

"Or if he likes money as much as the royals he paid off do." Seriah shrugged. "It may be our only shot."

Armas didn't like the plan, but he didn't see any other way forward. "All right. Let's set this up."

TWENTY-SEVEN

KYLA

Kyla stood on the bridge of the *Sinai,* an Aurora-class warship Saul had recently commissioned from the Lubez. She finally wore the Jamin flight suit she'd coveted for so long — dark blue, with a special holster for her Bara Sharpshooter and a few other weapons tucked under her flight jacket. She stood next to the captain's chair in the center of the semi-circle shaped bridge, the large viewscreen curving in front of them, with the navigation and weapons stations forward, engineering and communications to the right and left. Laina sat on the bench seat at the rear of the bridge, wearing civilian flight coveralls in a deep purple, the color of Tali uniforms, her hair braided back like Kyla's. Carmen Barish sat next to her, in the same dark blue flight suit but with the lieutenant's thin crescent insignia pinned on their shoulder, and Kyla's great-uncle sat next to the captain in the first officer's seat. Her father had finally given her a mission, and to her relief, not to hunt goddess worshipers.

It had taken a week to meet up at the rendezvous point the Modes had given her father, on the edge of the Bara system. The warship had the capacity to hold a full squadron of Bluehawks, but currently had only six on the flight deck. Though the ship was armed with the usual ion cannons and torpedoes, they didn't want to look like a threat, and besides, Saul had recalled all other ships. Carmen told her their father heard rumors of dissent and defection among some of the nations.

How many deserted? She and Laina had been confined until they were transported from the fortress to the warship in orbit, but on board she heard whispers. Abe played down the rumors, but she'd heard the entire Dahan mech unit had left the system.

"How long?" she asked again.

Abe cocked an eyebrow. "They'll know we're coming before we do. Their technology is far more advanced —"

Klaxons blared, yellow lights flashing on the bridge. "Proximity alert!" the communications officer shouted, turning to Abe, the ranking officer on board.

Abe moved to the center of the bridge. The screen still showed only the stars, and the blackness between them.

"Where are they?" Kyla asked, stepping closer to her great-uncle. "I don't see anything."

"They are probably interfering with our systems so we can't see them."

The communications officer frowned. "That's not possible, we ..."

Whatever words they had to say fell off their tongue.

Kyla gasped.

The dreadnought filled the entire screen, seeming to swallow up stars as it appeared. "The Modes have lived their entire lives in space," Abe said, his voice calm. "Once solo ships, they wreaked havoc on entire worlds in the Near Side by holding their systems hostage for ransom, shutting down warships. They could've been an empire." Abe's voice had a hint of admiration. "But they lacked one thing: unity. They were pirates, attacking each other, working solo. Until Alton of Gallim came to power. When the Airysans began taking over worlds, he cut their losses on the Near Side.

"The Airysans may think they won against the Modes, but Alton saw possibility in the Outer Systems, and Bara's uninhabited moons. With the Leki and Phenians fighting us, he sent ships there and managed to capture two moons without incident."

"To settle?"

Abe shrugged. "Most likely mining for the materials they need."

A chill traveled down Kyla's spine as the outline of the dreadnought before them came into view. The Modes' ship was at least six times the length of theirs and thrice as wide. Two "arms" — the only way Kyla could think of them — jutted forward from either side of what she assumed was the bridge, though the shape was hard to make out. The ship grew like a shadow, darkening the starlight within its outline, a cloaking technology she couldn't fathom.

"We're being hailed," the communications officer said.

"Delegation from the Nacaens: I am Alton, the Supreme One," a cold voice slithered over the comm. The screen brightened, and Alton stood on the dreadnought's bridge. He wore a black flight suit with the silver hexagon, but what made Kyla shudder were the visible augments on the side of his skull at his temples, a thin silver rectangle curving around the back of his shaved skull. They had been missing from the picture her father had shown, and his eyes had been dark. Now, his gaze held thin rings of silver.

Minimal augments were legal in some systems: implants that modified one's senses, some that filtered out toxins in specific environments, with heavy security against viruses and hijacking. From what she knew, the Modes used augments to hack and control other computer systems, ships, even people. It had never been explained to her how the Modes' augments worked, how they interfaced with one another and their ship. Severely modified humans were forbidden from citizenship of most worlds. How the Modes got their name — they adopted the slang term for modified people.

Alton leaned forward, his silver eyes seeming to drill right through the viewscreen.

"Supreme One," Abe said, bowing slightly. "I am Major Abe Renk, commander of the Unified Nacaen Forces, second under His Majesty, King Saul Kishrah."

Kyla bit her lip to keep herself from speaking. *Armas is second.* But with Armas on the run and Jon now imprisoned, she had no idea what her father might do.

Abe continued the formalities. "This is Princess Kyla, daughter of King Saul. She has accompanied me in good faith as promised."

"Your formal delegation may come aboard. We have the contract ready with our services as your king requested."

Kyla shot her great-uncle a look. "What contract?" she

asked.

Abe held up his hand. "Merely a formality," he muttered to her. "Yes, we have the king's payment. Six of us will be arriving in the shuttle: myself, two guards, Princess Kyla Kishrah, her maid, and her personal guard for this mission, Lieutenant Carmen Barish."

Alton gave a curt nod. "Very well. We will bioscan the craft before allowing entry onto our ship."

The screen darkened, returning to the image of the dreadnought. "It's time," Abe announced. "Gather your belongings, we may be on board for a while."

Kyla followed her great-uncle off the bridge, along with Carmen and Laina. When Carmen diverged to their quarters, Kyla pulled Abe aside. "What is going on?"

"What do you mean?"

"What contract? What payment? I thought we were beginning the negotiations." Kyla took a step back. Her great-uncle's smug expression betrayed everything, and a cold feeling unwound in her stomach. "Father already negotiated. It's already done. This is the final piece."

"You should know your father's ways by now. The Elders need assurance their voice still matters, but with your husband amassing a rebellion in his name, time has run out."

Kyla gasped. "It's all true, then." Though her father had been tight-lipped, Laina had been allowed to gather supplies for the trip and had heard rumors of Dahan desertion. For the first time in weeks, her heart beat with hope.

"Do not think the Advocate is coming to save you," her great-uncle warned. "Your best hope for survival is to do as I say and not ask questions. The Modes could decide to terminate the contract — and us — at any moment.

They know they hold the advantage. But if they agree to our terms, we have a permanent solution to our problems in the Outer Systems. A way to eliminate the Leki, the Phenians, even the Stiners."

"The Modes work with the Stiners, don't they?"

Abe raised a brow. "Don't bring up Ogroma when we are on their ship. They're still not happy about it, but they fully blame the Stiners for losing their favorite weapon, even if it was the Phenians who hired them from the Stiners."

"But — we won't be staying long, will we?"

Her great-uncle brushed past her. "Keep your mouth shut and we might make it through, not only alive, but with an unspeakable power in the galaxy by our side. But we might have to stay a while. Be prepared."

A half-hour later Kyla sat on the shuttle with Laina, Abe, the two guards, and Carmen as pilot. Kyla had changed to more formal attire — the same black dress she wore to the banquet. It seemed fitting — if Alton wore black for this formal meeting of negotiation, so would she.

The shuttle docked in one of the dreadnought's arms, and a blue light transversed the shuttle. "Bioscan," Carmen informed them. "Probably to make sure we have no transmissible diseases. From what I know, the Modes themselves have remained isolated on their ships. Ogroma was an exception."

And one that cost them.

The airlock hissed open, and Kyla rose from her seat. Laina followed behind, pulling two rolling cases. Abe strode out in front, flanked by the two guards, and Lieutenant Barish departed the shuttle last.

The corridor was so dark Kyla almost bumped into her great-uncle. "What is going on?"

Soft lights began to glow in a line above them, giving shape to the corridor of the ship. The hallway was hexagonal, and the lights lit up in sections to their left.

"That's dendrilite," Carmen muttered, pointing to the lines of silver and black above. "We saw this on Ramah."

"This way," a voice called, seeming to come from all around them, but no one was in the corridor. "We do not need light to see, but understand your inferior manner needs it."

Laina touched Carmen's arm. "Do not mention that place again."

"Why?"

"It is sacred and holy; look what they do with it."

Kyla glanced at Carmen. What did they know about the use of dendrilite?

But she dared not speak it out loud. Instead, she followed Abe as the corridor lit ahead, section by section, winding through the massive ship. "They may not need light, but at least they use standard artificial G," she said quietly, glad to not have to dig out her magnetic boots.

The corridor turned, arriving at another airlock that hissed open. The lights behind them faded out. "They must keep parts of the ship cold to conserve power," Abe muttered as Kyla shivered before entering the airlock.

Kyla stepped into a large room, the light adjusting. Several Modes were there, all wearing black, with various augments. She tried not to stare. One had a red light where an eye should have been. Another used an entirely mechanical arm. Still another wore a black skull cap, with thin silver wires traveling down their neck. There were variations in skin tone, though most were pale, appearing almost blue. Another Mode glanced at her, goggles over their eyes appearing to zoom in on her. They had light freckles on their cheeks.

The freckles reminded her of Armas.

Alton stood in the middle in front of a large hexagonal table, ringed by comfortable chairs. The rest of the room appeared dark and blank, except for lines of dendrilite that ran along the walls and the ceiling, giving a soft glow to the room.

"Welcome, delegation of the Nacaens. Please, take a seat." He flashed his palm in a gesture of welcome, and Kyla noted his entire hand was threaded with silver and black.

Abe motioned and Kyla took the seat next to him, Carmen on the other side of her. One of the Modes motioned to Laina to follow her. "I will show you your place of rest." Kyla gave her a reassuring nod, though the whole thing terrified her. She shoved down the thought of staying any longer than necessary.

"We will bring you refreshments. I'm afraid we mostly rely on synthetic protein, but we know how those of you who have remained biologically intact still need supplements. And even among us, well, taste buds come and go." Alton smiled, his teeth an unnatural white.

Kyla suppressed a shiver.

"We have agreed to your terms," Abe began. "Your ships will defend us against future threats from the Bara System. We also ask for aid in defense against civil threats."

Alton quirked an eyebrow — he did have them, though they were thin. "This was not part of the agreement." The other Modes in the room glanced at each other. Kyla wondered if they could communicate with each other in silence. *They must be able to, as they are reading each other's expressions.*

"It's a complication that has arisen," Abe said smoothly. "The Advocate of the king has rebelled, and so our forces are divided. We believe he has taken a remnant to Balec, the Leki home world."

Kyla shot her great-uncle a look. She hadn't known where Armas had gone after Nidos. They must've tortured Mel Diez and others for the information.

The Supreme One leaned back in the chair. "Does he not wish for us to destroy them along with the Leki?"

"The king ... did not suspect so many would go with the Advocate. He wants the Advocate dead, the Leki royals held accountable for harboring him there, but for the rest to return to our system."

Kyla tucked her hands under her thighs, trying to keep still.

"Such complications," Alton mused. "This operation would require more of our ships than previously discussed, ships that are currently configured for mining the moons we have taken from the Leki in Bara."

"We have a much richer source of dendrilite than all their worlds combined," Abe said, passing over a data stick, a small plastic circuit board one centimeter across and three centimeters wide.

Alton palmed the stick from the table and immediately smiled. "Ah yes. That will do nicely." He tilted his head slightly, responding to Kyla's puzzled look. "My palm interface can read it immediately. This moon Ramah has all the dendrilite we will need for generations." He turned to two of the Modes that stood to his right. "We can spare some ships from the current mining operation."

Kyla glared at her great-uncle. "That was not to be part of the negotiation," she whispered.

"Plans change," he whispered back.

"Abe, no," she said, setting her hand on his arm, but he pulled it away.

A rock settled in her stomach. She'd known this might happen for some time, ever since she put together what her father planned for her the night of her wedding, to eliminate the Tananites and take their dendrilite. One small comfort in the aftermath was that she hoped her father had abandoned those plans.

Instead, he'd been plotting this, all along. Once he learned Ramah had dendrilite, he'd shifted his focus to an alliance with the Modes. She'd have to break the news to Laina and tell her the most sacred place for their faith was about to be stripped.

Kyla had failed her again.

"Very well," Alton said. "We accept this amendment. Do you submit to the retina scan?"

"I do," Abe said as he stood, and the Mode with the red eye circled to the table to Abe. "Scan complete," the mode said, her voice almost robotic.

"Then it's done?" Kyla said, standing.

"Yes. Major Renk, you may return with your guards to your ship. Princess Kyla, I will escort you and your guard to your *new* quarters."

"*New quarters*? Surely, I'm not staying that long. You're coming to the Nacaen group."

Alton's eyes flicked to Abe. "She doesn't know."

"Thought it would be easier this way."

"Know what?" Kyla said, raising her voice. Carmen stood, hand near their weapon.

"Your weapons are useless here," Alton said, standing and pacing around the table. "We have already magnetized the mechanism on your pistols so they will not fire." He motioned to Kyla. "What your great-uncle has failed to tell you is that your father has agreed to my marriage proposal to you."

Kyla gripped the chair's arms. "You can't be serious. I'm already married."

"Your father mentioned your husband had deserted you and so he deemed the marriage failed. He offered your hand in marriage to legitimize us as a nation and not simply a, what do they call us? Band of augmented pirates. Don't worry, I see the ridiculousness of that argument in your expression."

He leaned into her space, and a sickly feeling spread throughout her stomach.

"No, the truth is we modified humans have difficulty ... reproducing. We sometimes graft on to others to bring them into our society, but we've found better integration from our own offspring. Sadly, it is rare for us to produce offspring. Five of us were able to give birth two decades ago. Being born of all modified human parents, they were integrated to each other from their very beginning."

Kyla's heart raced dangerously fast.

"You've already concluded the outcome. Ogroma was our greatest achievement, and our most devastating loss. The Stiners promised to care for them. And they lost them." Alton slammed his fist on the table. "To your husband."

And it was my father who refused to return their bodies. But Alton didn't know that.

He cupped her face, grazing his thumb over her cheekbone. "I see the fear in your eyes. I will not harm you. But you are now my wife by contract. An agreement that binds the Nacaen royal family with the Supreme Leader of the Modes, bridging our two peoples together."

Alton gestured to Carmen. "Your services are no longer required, and you may return to your ship with your major and the others."

Carmen puffed out their chest. "I am here to serve Her Royal Highness. I will not leave her service."

Alton bowed his head. "Very well. We will arrange for your quarters." He turned back to Abe. "You may take your leave. We will move our ships into position at Balec. If King Saul's last report is correct, then the rebels are unaware they will meet their defeat."

Her great-uncle took a step closer, but Kyla leaned away from him. "You may not understand now," Abe said, "but this is a choice to save you and your people. You've never had to make the hard choices."

She spun around, but her great-uncle caught her fist in his hand, then pulled it behind her, forcing her against his chest. Carmen lunged toward him, but two other Modes caught the lieutenant by their arms.

"Your father protected you as long as he could," Abe whispered in Kyla's ear. "He did this because he knows he can count on you. That you won't fail when the time comes."

"I chose Armas," she retorted.

"*One* mistake. How many did Jon make? He's your father's weakness," Abe spat. "Your father will always relent when it comes to him. He knows you will eventually follow his ways. In the end, you *will* serve your father."

She gathered up all her courage. "I serve my true *husband*, and Armas will come for me."

At this, Alton's laugh slithered through the air. "I hope he does. I would love nothing more than to defeat the man who destroyed *our* children. I would love for him to see you by my side."

Abe let go of Kyla, and she stumbled out of his grasp. "I need to return to Saul's service," her great-uncle said. "Supreme Leader, may you be blessed by our God in your marriage and service to our crown."

Alton gave a slight bow. "We offer the king our blessings from the God of Everlasting Life."

Kyla stared in surprise. She did not know the Modes worshiped a god.

The major left with his two guards, leaving Kyla and Carmen alone with Alton and the other Modes. "Come, have some refreshment with me in your private accommodations."

A numbness filled Kyla. Her father had used her like he did so many others in his service. She followed Alton in silence, with Carmen trailing behind her, through the dimly lit hexagonal corridors and wondered when she'd finally have the courage to step out for herself.

They reached a door, and Alton motioned to her. "Set your palm there. It will read your biometrics and allow you entry. If you choose to become like us, once you are modified, you won't even realize you're thinking of opening a door before it opens."

Kyla raised her hand, and the door slid open. Her jaw dropped. The room was brightly lit, unlike the corridors and the meeting room she had seen. Holoprojections on the walls were set to various scenes on Melas. On one wall was a view of Glia from a distance. Another projected the shores of the southern ocean, facing the Sim'ee continent. Above her, the ceiling showed the rings of Horeb.

Laina stood near the entrance to the bedroom. "I have set out your things, Your Highness," she said, her voice slightly betraying her nervousness.

Two comfortable couches faced each other across a low table. Two glasses of wine, a glass of water, and a plate of bite-size morsels were set there: small bits of bread and cheese, some sort of seafood in a white sauce, a bowl of greens and root vegetables.

"Barish, your quarters are next door," Alton motioned.

"I'll go with Her Highness's leave," Carmen said, clasping her hands behind her back.

He's not going to kill me, she wanted to say, but didn't know how to form a more diplomatic way to say it.

Nonetheless, she recognized it was true. The panic that had overtaken her now cooled into rage against her father, fueling her mind. As much as she detested this entire setup, a plan sparked. Alton and the Modes *needed* her, both politically and biologically. She'd been promised to them — that was out of her control — but not *how* she fulfilled her father's bargain.

With all that had been taken from her, there were some choices neither her father, nor Alton, could foresee.

She could use this position to help Armas. It was her father who set this civil war into motion, not her husband. And despite what her father or Alton said, she would remain true to the one she loved.

She would remain true to *herself.* It was her only choice. Take whatever limited power she had in this position and use it.

"You may go," Kyla said to her guard. Carmen's eyes widened, but they bowed slightly before taking their leave. "You too, Laina," she added.

Her maid's eyes flew open. "Your Highness, is there

anything —"

"I am all right. I wish to enjoy this food with my new husband."

Laina's mouth snapped shut.

"There is food and drink for you in your quarters," Alton said to Laina, before he turned to Kyla. "All you need to do is call her name, and the ship will alert her to come to your side."

"Thank you," she said.

Laina set her hand on Kyla's arm, but Kyla gave her a reassuring nod. "I'm fine. I want to be alone with him."

Her maid bowed once before leaving.

Alton faced her as soon as they were alone. "Let us be honest with one another, Princess Kyla. I can detect deception rather easily. The games and scheming you will attempt are a product of your lesser biological impulses."

He reached for the two wine glasses and offered her one. Kyla drank deep. The wine was rather good, surprising her.

Alton seemed pleased at her reaction. "I do want you to be comfortable here. Whatever you desire, we will do what we can to make it happen."

She sat down on the couch with her wine glass, uncertain of how to get Alton to help her. "Tell me about your god."

"The Everlasting God?" he asked, sitting down on the other side of the couch, seeming pleased with her question. "We know that among all the peoples of the galaxy, there are many gods worshipped. We believe those false, and only ours answers our prayers. The Everlasting God has shown us the way to eternal life through modification. Do you know how old I am?"

Kyla shook her head.

Alton leaned back. "I am one hundred and forty-three, and still in my prime."

Her jaw dropped open. He gave a slight smile. "I don't seem it, do I? We all started as you once. Then we went through the modification process, perfecting it over the years. The Everlasting God is always changing, showing us the new way forward."

She took another drink, deciding to simply be up front. "If I'm going to be married to you, will I eventually become augmented?"

"Marriage is a concept we have not dealt with for the last few hundred years, but we know it is how political alliances are forged. Which is why I agreed to your father's proposal. But we do not force our augments on others. We know this is considered an abomination to your people."

She set down the wineglass. If she was going to get out of this, if she was going to help Armas, she didn't see another way through.

Alton had told her if she chose to be augmented, she'd be able to open doors without even thinking of it.

I need that power, if I'm going to help Armas. If I'm going to help Laina and Carmen.

If I'm going to save myself.

"I want to get started."

Alton was taken aback. "Are you certain?"

She moved closer to him on the couch. "Not me. I'm fascinated by how you ... interface." She set her hand on his arm.

Alton frowned. "Your change in behavior betrays your plotting."

She dropped her hand. "You're right. I can't scheme. What I can do is this: set me up with an augment. Help me to understand you and your people. You do that ... I'll have your baby."

The Supreme One tilted his head, trying to read her. "Offspring are already part of the contract. However, I will not force myself or others upon you, if that is what you are afraid of. We would simply extract your ovum to carry out the procedure in one of our own who is willing." His eyes brightened. "I will accept your conditions and arrange for your modification. When would you like to begin?"

She took another drink of wine, gathering her courage. "Right away."

TWENTY-EIGHT

JON

Jon sat in the rear of the cargo area with his forehead cradled in his hands. His helmet was next to him, his feet shackled together. Major Barish had spared one glance his way, a look that expressed pity. It was all he could afford to give the prince.

Jon didn't see any way this didn't end in terror.

Saul had transferred his call sign to this cargo ship, signifying a diplomatic mission to the Lubez security, who allowed him to pass through without an escort. He knew Saul lounged in a comfortable compartment above, along with Dege, the Dahan mechanic turned informant. The cargo hold was pressurized, hiding two dozen troops arriving to wipe out the insurgency on Nidos.

Mel Diez hadn't been seen since the banquet. She was never brought to the dungeon where Jon had been kept the last two weeks. Rumor among the guards was that she'd been taken to a private cell where Saul extracted what was needed and then beheaded her.

None of it surprised Jon, not since Saul slaughtered the Leki informant and ordered his sister to kill Zam. Even the brief period of peace when Saul arranged the engagement between Armas and Kyla.

His father was a monster.

The pressure shifted as the ship entered the atmosphere. "Helm's on," Barish ordered. "That includes you, Dark Wolf."

Jon obliged, though it was pointless given his feet were shackled. His father had not spoken to him, only the guards who informed him that Saul wanted him there when he confronted the priests.

Dege must've directed them to a different location than the hanger Jon had met him in, for when the ship landed and the cargo doors opened, they were on a flat plain. A few twisted trees dotted the view.

Barish ordered the rest of the troops out, before coming to Jon and kneeling at his feet. "Your Highness, your father has instructed that you accompany him." The major inserted his electronic key, releasing the magnetic shackles that fell to the floor of the cargo hold.

Jon followed the major off the ship, without a weapon. There was a light drizzle, but it was not nearly as windy as when he found Armas here. His chest ached at the memory. The last time they'd held each other. How he'd killed Raimi. How Dege must've bugged Armas's cabin.

Dege stood on the other side of his father. Violence curled at the edge of Jon's tongue, but he held it. It would do no good to accost him now.

"This way," the betrayer said, pointing toward a low

ridge against a dark gray sky. "The temple is on the other side. They won't be expecting us.

Major Barish led the troops forward with Dege, while the king stayed back with Jon at the rear of the unit with two guards assigned to him as prisoner. They marched toward the ridge, the drizzle turning into a steadier rain, dripping down Jon's helmet and flight suit.

"I'm surprised you haven't pleaded with me to turn back," Saul said. When Jon didn't respond, the king stopped. "How long were you and Armas together?"

Jon tried to brush past him, but Saul grabbed his arm. "Did you love him?"

The prince was caught off guard by the question. He stared through his helmet's visor, unsure of his father's motives in the moment.

"You do love him, still."

Jon yanked his arm away. "When has love ever mattered to you? Kyla loved him, and you still tried to kill him. The people loved him more than you, and you — you'd rather destroy everyone than allow one person to have something you can *never* have."

Saul grabbed him again. "You know nothing of what I have sacrificed for you and your sister. You know nothing of your mother ..."

He let Jon go and marched ahead without him, trudging toward the ridge.

Jon and his two guards caught up when they reached the ridge, climbing the slope. There were no stairs on this side, but stunted trees lined the top of the ridge, hiding them from view. The temple and the circle of cabins were a few hundred meters away.

"Why are the people here in such poverty?" he asked his father.

It was Saul's turn to be caught off-guard. He was silent a moment before answering. "When the Hessan were in power before the Nidos Accords, they controlled almost all the crops. That's why the Tali had so many sympathizing with the Phenians. The enemy promised them food. The Lubez wouldn't help unless they had the warship contracts, but we couldn't get a contract negotiated while the Hessan and Tali were fighting. Armas and Milo helped the Lubez gain power over the labor force, but in doing so, Armas gave most of the farms east of here, which lie outside of the worst storm patterns, back to the Tali in the accords."

Jon caught Saul's grimace even through the thick face shield of his helmet. "I wasn't happy with how the Nidos Accords were negotiated," his father added. "Punishing people by removing food is barbaric. It's not what we do."

The prince was stunned. He'd not seen a compassionate side of his father, not like this, in some time.

The thought rattled in his head while he followed Saul into the thick brush and stunted trees. When he'd last seen Armas, he was helping the people here. With weapons, yes, but also with food. His father had known then and hadn't helped them.

Saul still tried to shirk responsibility for the people.

The troops crept toward the temple as the rain fell sideways, pelting into them. "You don't have to do this," he muttered to his father.

"Are you always so blasted sentimental?" his father snapped. Saul turned to the two troops guarding him. "Don't let him do anything foolish."

"Father —" Jon began, but Saul wheeled on him.

"Do not interfere. I brought you here so you might

understand, what *you* will have to do someday."

Fear burned up Jon's chest.

Saul left him behind, marching up to the front with Major Barish and Dege. Jon felt absolutely helpless, hopeless, as the troops ran across the open ground to the temple.

As the doors were flung open.

As the troops rounded up the priests who led prayers.

As children and parents screamed and clung to each other.

It all buzzed in his head as Dege pointed out the priests who'd hidden Armas and smuggled weapons. Saul ordered Major Barish to line up four of the priests and some village leaders and shoved them to their knees.

"I am your king. I am your prophet. You betrayed me; you betrayed our God. For that, you will die."

For all his talk of compassion earlier, Saul didn't blink as he gave Dege his own weapon and called upon him and the troops to shoot them in the back of their heads.

As the first priest's body fell, Jon fell to his knees.

When the second hit the ground, Jon yanked his helmet off. His guards attempted to pull him back up, but he shrugged out of their grasp.

At the third, his own screams clawed out of his throat, matching those of the families — the *children* — who were witnessing this atrocity.

The screams in his head rang so loudly.

"Shoot me!" he shouted, long after the gunfire stopped. "Shoot me!"

The fourth priest was still kneeling, but Saul held his hand up to stop the assassination.

"Kill me," Jon insisted. "I'm the one who helped him escape. Kill me. Please."

The king walked over to him, removing his own helmet. "Get up."

"No. I am as guilty as they are. I deserve to die as they did."

Dege stood next to Saul, holding out Saul's own weapon.

"Don't ask me to do this, son."

"Kill me," Jon whispered, tears streaming down his face. "I love him. I won't stop loving him. There is nothing you can do that will make it stop, so end it, now."

He closed his eyes. There was no way his father would live down this humiliation, the prince kneeling before him and admitting his love for his father's enemy.

He sucked in a shaky breath, waiting for the sound of weapon fire.

Jon didn't know how long he knelt there, how long the tears fell, before his father's knees bumped his own, his arms wrapping around him. "You're my son. *My* son. There is no other. It is you who will sit on the throne."

His father's hand came around his neck, and he pulled him closer. "I couldn't bear it when I saw how you looked at him. Such admiration. Such *love*. I tried to ignore it, arranged a marriage for you, married him off to Kyla, but I knew if there was anyone you would betray me for, it would be him."

Jon gripped his father tighter.

"Come back to me, my son. Serve me. Serve this kingdom. Serve our God together. I love you. I cannot rule without you. Help me pull it back together."

"Father ..." Jon said, pulling back as Saul cupped his face. "I'm here. I serve you."

"Then foreswear him. Reject the Advocate and pledge your loyalty to me. You are the crown prince. You will sit on the throne. Maybe the deserters will come back, if we show them we are united."

Jon bit his lip so hard it bled. It was the only thing he ever wanted: his father's love. His acceptance. But could he do this? Could he sever his heart in two, and leave his promise to Armas?

He knew he could never betray Armas.

He also knew the only way he could stop Saul from killing the civilians was to give him what he wanted.

"I — I serve you, my King," he said. "I pledge myself to the people, to the crown, to my God."

His father kissed his forehead, then rose, pulling him up. Through blurry eyes Jon spied the bodies scattered on the ground. Barish's appearance was ashen.

"Let them go, Father," Jon whispered.

Saul looked puzzled.

"The children, the parents. That priest," he added, for the priest still knelt, their whole body shaking in terror. "They've suffered enough. These people have all suffered far too much."

"Your Majesty," Dege said. "The weapons are gone, along with the credits and food stashes. We ought to search the village."

Major Barish's stare grew cold. "They've gone," he spat. "We already violated the Nidos Accords by coming here. Assassinating villagers is not what we do."

Jon tensed. The major was on dangerous ground in addressing the king this way. He reached for Saul's arm. "He's right. We ought to go. We can explain to the security forces this was a small operation. Compensate the villagers well and they will corroborate. Don't risk more unrest."

Saul nodded. "Major, see that it's done. Dege Edmon,

you have received your reward. You may return to us, as I doubt you will be welcome here."

"But, Your Majesty, I'm sure we can find more —"

"That's enough. *We're* done here," the king ordered. He turned back to Jon. "Walk with me."

Jon walked with his father out from the temple of blood and back into the rain. It had tapered back to a drizzle, but neither put their helmets on.

Saul gripped Jon's arm. "You saved me today, son."

"How?"

"When you — when you asked me to kill you," Saul began, a tear forming, "I finally saw how you see me." He paused, wiping his eye with the back of his hand. "You and your sister both. You see me as a monster."

Jon shook his head, but Saul pulled him into an embrace. "There's no need to lie. As I saw you on your knees, I saw your face in everyone I have killed. Everyone who was a son, daughter, child of someone. I am a monster. But you don't have to be." He let go of Jon.

"Come," his father beckoned. "There is one more thing I must do before we return home."

TWENTY-NINE

ARMAS

"This is not going to work," Shane muttered.

"It *is* going to work," Seriah argued, "because the Advocate is going to turn on the charm that he does so well."

Armas wasn't sure it would work.

Seriah's small transport she'd flown from Melas, with Armas's family on board, was cramped and racking up docking fees every day, but so far, they hadn't been evicted from the station. She found him some clothes from an Etho merchant — a silky black top with sleeves that rolled up, showing off his forearms, and trousers that fit but were a tad tight. The collar was unbuttoned, a little further down his chest than he would prefer, but Seriah said it would give him that "Etho" look. When he glanced in the mirror, he didn't recognize himself with his black dyed hair and clothes. Seriah lined his eyes with kohl. "You know that Etho fashion at one time included holographic tattoos. Be glad those have gone out of fashion."

The former Dahan major had also changed her appearance, wearing a wig of long dark brown hair with gold streaks, and a light blue dress with heels. She lined her eyes with sparkling purple shadow, one of the latest Etho trends.

"You sure they'll be there tonight?" Armas asked.

"I made an appointment with his office administrator and said we would like a casual meeting rather than a full-out business proposal, and to include his wife." Seriah hesitated. "Definitely made it sound as if we might be interested in bribing him." She put her makeup kit away. "I don't know what her husband knows about soldiers defecting in the Nacaen Group, but Saul has a bounty on your head, that I'm sure of. Definitely keep quiet on any recent politics."

Shane slid his gaze from Armas to Seriah. "You two will make an interesting couple."

Seriah slunk her arm through Armas's, as he shook his head. "We'd decided on a brother-sister relationship, remember? Jude and Diana, refugees from the previous wars to Etho, interested in a business venture."

She swatted his arm. "Sure, whatever." She let go of his arm to straighten her wig and insert her ear comm before turning to Shane, who wore the nondescript travel garb of most other small worlds. "Remember: stay out of sight. Casual surveillance. If something goes down, get the hell out."

Seriah handed Armas a tiny communication device for

his ear.

"The Hessan troops are on standby," he told Shane. The decommissioned fuel rig was now at the maintenance docks, where they'd blended in with the work crew there.

"Got it," Shane replied. "Don't mess this up."

Armas shrugged. "Should be relatively straightforward. I'll go up to Abby and say, 'Hey, you're Nacaen, right? Want to help the rebels?'" But he wiped his palms on his trousers again before looking at Seriah. "Ready?"

Seriah lined her lips, then placed the lipstick in her purse, flashing the small Ember 75 pistol she hid there in case things went bad. "Let's go."

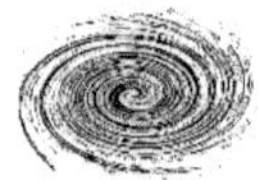

Balec was a truly interplanetary station. Besides all the travelers Armas spotted on the terminals, the restaurants and lounges on the orbital station's commercial level served food from all over the galaxy. Local seafood from Balec, rice dishes from Ilistia with various toppings, including a spicy glaze similar to Jamin beef and noodles on Melas. Jeweled fruits and crisp vegetables, and a million kinds of alcohol from Etho to Ramaen and other Near Side systems. Armas almost stopped at a sing-along lounge, but Seriah nudged him along. "That would blow your cover." She was right, but still — he was intrigued with the new "starwave" sound that was becoming popular in some of the Near Side systems.

The interstellar lounge took up several hundred square meters of space, with an area for gaming, a central bar, and several small tables and lounge chairs. Small holographic fake fire pits lined the floor, but the heat was real, allowing the Leki citizens to ditch their thermal underwear and dress in their more revealing sheer fashions. Holoscreen tables littered the room, where one could order their food or beverage, or escort services for the night. The Leki liked to share their indulgences. Armas understood why Seriah had him dress the way he did — he blended right in with his tight clothes. Even if he didn't look Leki, he looked like the kind of tourist that belonged there.

"Captain Laban's assistant said he would meet us here," Seriah said before she went to one end of the bar. Armas chose the opposite side, managing to flag down the bartender first. "Etho whiskey, neat." It's what Jon used to order, before he stopped drinking.

While Armas waited, he caught the glances of those sitting nearby. He ran his fingers over his hair, blushing. He knew Kyla found him attractive, but it was Jon who told him he was irresistible, often pointing out the people who blatantly flirted with him that had gone over his head. It had taken a year for him to go from inexperienced and shy to recognizing the pull he commanded when he walked into a room.

A woman with smoky eyes and silky black hair ran her fingers along his arm. The sheer fabric of the Leki fashion barely covered her chest. "You dress like you're from Etho, but you don't look like it. Your skin has no sparkle."

"I ... uh ..."

"They're here," Seriah said through his ear comm, and Armas swiveled his gaze, ignoring the woman at the bar.

A man wearing a gray civilian-fleet captain's uniform entered. He had a trimmed brown beard and mustache and a light tan complexion. Except for the blue wave pin on his shoulder marking him as a Leki official, Armas wouldn't have known and couldn't have guessed his nationality.

In contrast, hanging on the captain's arm was a woman in a sleeveless red dress, with gold bangles at her wrists, part of the Ildan fashion as he remembered from when he visited Richo's military base. Her deep brown hair cascaded over bronze shoulders.

The captain escorted his wife to an empty table, then went to the bar where Seriah was sitting. The bartender placed the glass in front of Armas and he picked it up, right as the man on the other side of him, wearing his sheer shirt unbuttoned all the way, squeezed his bicep.

"Nice," he said to Armas, winking.

Armas stepped away from the grasp of horny strangers. He'd become used to being flirted with, but the groping annoyed him. He then tossed back the entire glass, allowing the whiskey to coat his throat, before setting down the empty glass on a table and making his way over to Abby Carmel's table.

Time to turn on the charm.

"Mind if I join you?" he asked.

Her eyes widened. "Well, um, my husband is getting my drink —"

Armas waved his hand. "I'm not here to proposition you or anything. Forgive me, but *your* look — Ildan?" He motioned to the gold bangles at her wrists.

She leaned forward. "Yes! Have you been there before?"

He grinned. "A long time ago. My sister and I — we fled to Etho when we were children, as refugees."

She smiled wide. "I thought your accent sounded different. Melas?" Armas nodded, and she continued. "It's rare to meet people who've visited the Nacaen Group, and I think I've met two other Nacaens my entire time here. But then again, I've mostly been aboard the station, and not places our people have settled."

He motioned to her husband at the bar. "You're married to a Leki national? I recognized the pin."

She sighed. "He's Jamin as well but came here on a diplomatic mission and used his citizenship to work here. Thought maybe I'd escape the hardships on Richo, see the universe, you know. The sort of stupid thing you do when you're young."

"You still seem young to me," Armas said, leaning closer.

"Yeah, well, spending the last year aboard an orbital makes the days much longer than you think." She shook her head before returning her gaze to Armas. "My name's Abby."

"Jude," he said.

Abby arched a brow. "That sounds like a Near-Side name."

Armas laughed, and at that moment the captain and Seriah came to the table, both carrying two drinks. "Ah, I see you've met my wife. Abby, this is Diana, and you must be Jude," he said, setting down a drink in front of Abby while Seriah set one in front of him. "Diana was telling me about your time living as refugees in Etho. What a shame. I hear there is unrest again back home. I thought King Saul would have everyone in line by now."

"If nations like the Leki would leave us alone and not try to take our resources, we might not be in this situation," Armas said.

Seriah gave him a pointed look. "Of course we know the Leki wish to make peace now," she added quickly. "Which is why we are interested in expanding our business here."

"I was on Melas when the last war broke out," Captain Laban said. "Glad it came to an end without further losses."

Armas glared at the captain, for it was the Leki who'd hired Stiners originally to attack the system — though Saul had tried to frame the Leki with the Stiner assassins the night Armas fled. The king was always trying to outplay others. He swallowed the drink, this time feeling the whiskey burn.

A server brought over more drinks and food. Seriah asked the captain about the sort of imports Balec received, and the size of ships, but wasn't getting the information they needed. Armas noticed that Abby kept quiet, only speaking when talking about the Nacaen Group, but the captain often interrupted her, coming back to what he wanted to say. Armas gave Seriah a knowing glance as the man reached for his fourth round.

After a while Seriah casually asked if the captain knew anything about a large freighter arriving in a few days.

"Yes. I'll be heading out to inspect it before it docks. It's unusual to have that large of a freighter arrive from the Liphes sector, but a faction of the Leki family has some major construction projects in the works and apparently required an incredible amount of Liphes steel."

"Seems odd, doesn't it, since Airysan is the better quality these days," Seriah said casually before taking a sip of her drink.

Laban's face flushed red. "My thoughts exactly. If it was Airysan, it would bring in a higher import tax. Which is why I suspect corruption." He lowered his voice, but Armas worried just about anyone could overhear the drunk captain. "My family's faction would very much like to know if it is Airysan. I think your *king* might want to know, too."

It was Armas's turn to shoot Seriah a look. Shane swore on the comm, and spoke through the earpiece: "Do you think maybe he's trying to make a deal to smuggle mechs to Saul?"

"I bet the king would be interested in that," Seriah confirmed.

"You know," the captain said, setting down his drink and motioning to the bartender for another round, "there was some kerfuffle recently — I'm not certain — but it sounds like King Saul discovered an insurgency was developing. He and the prince stopped it. There was a public execution."

Armas's stomach flipped. *Jon, I hope you know what you're doing.*

Seriah, for her part, didn't flinch at the news, but Abby seemed distraught. "Ever since the nations were united, the king has dispatched with more cruelty."

"It does seem that way," Armas muttered, before taking a drink.

"That's what happens with the Twelve, they can never agree that the king is sovereign," Captain Laban said, using the old slang name for the Nacaen nations and continuing his drunken spiel. "They're always picking fights with people. Problem with backwater worlds like the Twelve. You know they used to be called the dust of the universe, because it wouldn't take much to dust those four little worlds ..."

Armas set his glass down a little harder than he meant to. Seriah frowned in warning.

Abby stood from the table. "That's quite enough, Laban. You've had too much to drink tonight."

"Oh, love, you know I didn't mean it that way, I'm Jamin as well for God's sake ..."

Anger sparked in her eyes. She wheeled, running from the lounge.

Armas didn't think, he just jumped and ran after her. He didn't call her name until they were well away from the lounge, heading toward the lift that would go down to the freighter ship docks.

"Abby, wait —"

She turned, a single tear having traveled down her face. Armas touched her forearm, clasping it gently and pulling her off to the side.

"Jokes about genocide from my husband. Can you believe it?"

Armas crossed his arms. He'd never been out of the system before this, but he'd heard the stories of how Nacaens were treated when they left as refugees. Years ago, on Dibon, where his great-grandmother was from, refugees from Melas had been accused of all sorts of crimes, and many were murdered simply for being Nacaen. The Twelve. The dust of the galaxy.

"I'm so sorry."

Abby wiped her eye with the back of her hand. "He'll sleep it off."

"He's an ash-duster," he said, referring to Laban.

She laughed, wiping her eyes again, and she touched his forearm. "Thank you, Jude. You and your sister have been very kind."

Armas caught his bottom lip under his teeth. She was vulnerable, and something twisted inside him because he knew this was the moment to get her help.

But he didn't see any other way around it. *God help me, Shane was right, I'm gonna mess this up.* He touched his earpiece, clicking it off.

"My name is Armas. I'm the king's former Advocate."

Abby's eyes widened as Armas told her pieces of what happened — how he'd served the king faithfully, but the king tried to kill him, hiring Stiners to frame the Leki — and how he'd gone on the run. He didn't mention his relationship with Jon, or the rebellion beginning to take shape. "We need your help. When Laban goes out to inspect the *Behemoth* before it docks, we need to get on board. We need to convince him to take us along, something about making sure his cargo inspections are thorough ..."

Please let her trust me. Please let this work. Because if it didn't, all she had to do was decide to turn him over to Laban, or to any authorities here on Balec Station and he was as good as dead once they shipped him back to Saul.

Abby stood straight, lifting her chin. "I understand." She exhaled slowly. "If you truly are planning to lead and unite our people, to lift up all the nations and their citizens with equal access to resources — then I'm in. But Laban will never allow extra passengers with him."

Armas swore. "We need those mechs."

"Mechs?"

"That's what we suspect is really on board. He basically confirmed it with the Airysan steel talk tonight, as it's only used for military defense. And King Saul might be interested in it, meaning Laban may be planning to impound the cargo and then sell it off."

Abby considered, dropping her hand to Armas's forearm. "He'll take me with him, I've gone along before. I'll do what you need me to."

"Abby ... this could be very dangerous." A plan outlined in his mind. "If you were able to shut down the scanners and the proximity alarm, we will take care of the rest."

He searched her eyes, knowing that he was putting his life and Seriah's into her hands.

"He'll do the inspection and then he'll pull the captain of the ship in for a 'briefing' which usually involves drinking. I can do it."

Her eyes widened and she dropped her hand. Armas followed her line of sight. Her husband lumbered down the corridor, calling her name. "You should go," she said, her voice sad.

"Abby ... we'll get you out of this. I promise," he vowed.

THIRTY

JON

I hate politics, Jon thought as he waited for his father.

After arriving at the Nidos security station in orbit and ordering several shipments of supplies to be delivered in a "humanitarian effort" for the Hessan, the king and Major Barish were pulled aside by the chief of Lubez security. Jon remained on the observation deck, looking out at the shipyards. Three berths had recently emptied with the promised Aurora-class warships delivered to Saul: the *Sinai*, en route to the Modes; the *Starhawk*; and the *Firedawn*. Still under construction in the berths were the *Shiloh* and the *Galilee*. Those ships should've been built a year ago, but conflict between nations had held them up, including a delay from Major Barish as Elder of the Sim'ee because they wanted the same guarantee for their Bluehawk construction.

When Saul and Barish emerged from the conference with Lubez security, he learned two things: one, Lubez security had agreed to keep their mission in Hessan land secret, and two, the *Darkangel,* the sixth ship promised to Saul, had been stolen right out of port by Tali construction workers loyal to Armas.

His father quietly asked Jon to arrange for a shuttle transport for them and two guards, leaving Major Barish and the remaining troops to deal with the aftermath of the temple executions and to cover up what really happened. *All in a day's work in the life of service to King Saul,* he thought grimly.

Jon turned his thoughts toward Richo. He had only been to the Beneur nation and the Vellar estates. He knew Armas had been to the military base before, but he never had a reason to go. He wondered if Sharda would be on duty. He hadn't bothered to reach out after all this time. Probably best to leave her be.

How many hearts will be broken when this is over?

Every time he thought of Armas, and a sliver of hope that somehow, he could declare boldly his love for the man who'd captured his heart, the hope shattered as he thought of his sister, now off negotiating with the Modes. His father had been tight-lipped except to say that Abe had accompanied her along with Carmen Barish and Laina, and that she would be away for some time to heal her broken heart.

Despite what he'd said on Nidos, Saul was still king, still scheming for power. Jon may be saved for now, but he didn't doubt for a second that anyone else who stood in his father's way would face his wrath.

On the way to Richo, Jon wondered if his engagement to Rela Vellar had been called off in the aftermath of everything. He thought better of asking his father during the shuttle flight. They slept on board the shuttle, arriving in Richo's orbit as dawn approached the central continent. The world was a bounty of natural resources: a thickly forested southern continent providing most of the lumber used for construction in the system, an equatorial continent of farmlands and orchards where the Vellar estates were located, and two large islands in the north peeking through shallow seas, one with a mixture of pastures and plains, and the other, the military base.

A sprawling complex of steel and stone, the military base covered the island, with runways for their Bluehawk and Sparrowing fleet, and gold and green colored mechs guarding the perimeter. Jon noted they were mostly Liphes steel. Their own mech units had been depleted in the wars with the Phenians, and he wondered if his father had a plan for replenishing them.

The base followed protocol, with troops in standard formation to greet the royal delegation as the shuttle exited the hangar. "Your Majesty," Major Ngo greeted them. The Ildan military leader with straight black hair, dark eyes and a sharp jaw cutting across his light brown features served as head of military forces on Richo. However, he was not the representative to the Elder Council. Like some of the other nations, they kept military and political leadership separate. He wore a dark green uniform, with a thin gold bangle on one hand along with a gold triangle pinned to his shoulder.

"At ease, Major," Saul said, as Jon walked next to him.

"I'm here on an unusual visit."

"Your Majesty, I am of service."

"I wish to speak to a prisoner."

A muscle flexed in the major's jaw. "The one you had brought in from Ramah?"

Jon's chest grew cold. The Tana priest with the arrow mark on her cheek that Saul had taken into custody. He hadn't dared ask his father what he'd done with her.

If the dungeons in Glia were harsh, they were nothing compared to the military prison at Richo, according to the rumors. Part of Ngo's role on Richo was also to serve as warden. As he led them down into the depths of the island fortress along with four guards, Jon discovered the rumors were true.

Saul liked keeping certain enemies close by, such as the Leki informant, certain war prisoners, even his own children. Richo was where Saul put prisoners he wanted everyone else to forget.

Two levels down were medical labs and the prison morgue. "This is where we performed the autopsies from Zek," Ngo muttered.

Ogroma. Jon still shuddered thinking about the hairless bodies, the various ports and cords that had connected them. He once again thought of Kyla and prayed she was okay in the hands of the Modes.

On the third level stood two open cells, probably left open to intimidate those who came down. They were a meter and a half wide and deep — one would have to sleep scrunched in the diagonal, unless they were short. No sink. No window. Holes in the ground. "The remaining Phenian prisoners from Zek were held here," Ngo informed them.

"But none are alive today," Saul questioned, and the

Ildan major grunted in confirmation.

They descended another ramp, and the lights grew dim. There were guards at every floor previously, but as they reached the lowest level, there were none.

There was only silence.

"She's down here. Your Majesty, if you recall my report —"

"I've noted it, Major."

Though the hallway was dimly lit, there were no lights in the cells. Which is why Jon's chest constricted when he spied an eerie glow from a cell at the corridor's end.

"Unlock it, and leave us, Major. You and your guards."

"Your Majesty, I strongly advise —"

"She did not fight us when we detained her before. Besides, my son is armed." Saul had returned Jon's Bara Sharpshooter pistol to him on board the shuttle.

"As you wish, my liege." The major swiped an electronic key against the door and bowed.

Saul waited until the major began to climb the stairs. When he opened the door, Jon gasped.

There were lines of dendrilite running up the walls, glowing in a rhythm. They gathered against the wall where the Tananite priest sat, her eyes bloodshot. A gaping wound on her cheek marked where the arrow had once been, her arms ripped and red.

"You tore it from your own body," Saul muttered.

"You cut me off from my siblings, from my goddess," the priest responded. "We did nothing to harm you, Killer King. You hunted us down, like you did the worshippers of Serah and Starre. We did nothing to you, but you said we were a stain that must be wiped clean." She spied Jon in the shadows. "Why are you here?" she said, angling her face back to Saul. "I thought you put people here to forget about them."

Saul knelt on the floor. "Tell me, is it true: you can talk with the dead?"

A chill spread over Jon to the point he shivered. *What is he doing?*

The priest laughed. "Oh, this is something. The king who tried to wipe us out, said we were blasphemous, that there is only one God, is now asking me, a priest of Warrior Tana, for help to summon their own dead prophet. What, is your own God no longer answering you?"

Saul remained motionless.

The priest shifted to her knees, crawling toward the king, the dendrilite pulsing with her breath, Jon realized with a shudder. "Ah, it's true. The king who declared himself prophet and priest has found his God silent. Perhaps it's the warmongering. Perhaps all the bloodstains have begun crying out. Perhaps your God chose another in your place, but you did not heed your own prophet."

A lump grew in Jon's throat.

"Can you speak with him, or not?" Saul demanded.

"Your prophet, Zam, the one who died in the womb of Tana. He died surrounded by dendrilite. I can reach him. But what will you do for me?"

"I will have our best medics —"

"You will return me to Ramah, where I will be buried."

Saul nodded.

Jon set his hand against the door of the cell, feeling weak.

The Tana priest closed her eyes and began to hum. The dendrilite veins lining the wall began to pulse. "You know why I did this?" the priest asked, opening her eyes a slit toward Jon.

He shook his head.

"There's actually dendrilite on the other side of these walls. This island is full of it. We never knew. The people who lived here before you, the Rito, worshiped Starre, building altars and temples to her in the south. Starre is a sister to Tana. We never bothered each other, allowed each other's people to thrive."

"You're not Nacaen?" Jon asked. He'd assumed she was Hessan or Tali.

"The Hitti were the *original* Nacaens, living on Nidos and Ramah before your people came, among where the Tali settled. Nidos was a harsh world, but the orbital panels made it possible for us to come out of our caves. We welcomed the Tali, embraced them, taught them about Tana. On Ramah, the Sim'ee welcomed us and brought us to their continent on Melas."

Jon remembered the old Sim'ee language markings on Ramah.

"We knew the Sebuj people who worshiped Serah, living on the very land you now claim as your own —"

"ENOUGH!" Saul shouted. "Bring me Zam, now!"

"Hush, king. He's coming. It's hard to reach through Airysan steel walls, but it can be done."

Between the lines of dendrilite on the walls, an image appeared, an old man in robes, appearing as he had when Jon last saw him on Melas.

This has to be a trick. Some sort of holographic projection. Faked the way his first death was.

"Why have you disturbed me?" the old prophet's voice wavered, as his image flickered.

"You have to help me, please," Saul said, not moving from his knees. Jon was surprised at the groveling tone his father had taken, that he believed the image in front of him to be real. "There is a gathering rebellion. Most Dahan units have fled, along with the Hessan, some of the Tali, others — the numbers of desertion have grown. This wasn't supposed to happen —"

"God has turned away from you."

Saul fell silent, his head bowed.

"It is as I told you, that day back in the Great Hall. God chose another. He came to help you, but you rejected his help, only used him as a pawn when it was beneficial. I told you then it was too late, but you would not listen." The image shifted slightly. "Everything you have done has set what is to come in motion."

Jon's hands began to tremble. He folded his arms, tucking his hands in his elbows. *This can't be real. This can't be ...*

"What is to happen, Zam?" Saul pleaded.

"I see dimly in your world now. Where I am is bright, the brightness of dawn. But I see the Phenians returning in yours. While you've been busy trying to kill the one person who would've helped you, you've divided your own kingdom. You are weak, your defenses drained. The Phenians are vultures. They've been watching and waiting this whole time, rebuilding their forces on Ilistia and Gerar. They picked you apart at Nidos with the Tali. They're about to come picking again, but this time you don't have Armas on your side to stop them."

"No," Saul muttered, weeping. "Zam, tell me a good word! Tell me how to make it right!"

"Soon, you will be with me," the vision of Zam said, before it faded into darkness.

The priest slumped over, the dendrilite peeling from the walls, the light pulsing lower until it went out.

"You will soon be with me," the priest muttered, her own voice wavering. She opened her eyes and looked directly at Jon. "As will your son."

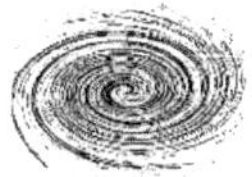

It was a long while before Jon could persuade his father to get up from the floor of the cell. The king had cradled the dead priest's head in his lap, sobbing. Jon had panicked, shouting for the guards, but no one could hear him down there. Finally, his father rose, and Jon braced him, helping him down the hall until they reached the ramp, climbing to the next level of the prison where Major Ngo and his guards waited.

"What happened?" the major asked, his face grave.

"The priest died," Jon told him, not mentioning the strange vision they had beheld. "She is to be taken back to Ramah for burial."

Ngo looked at Saul for confirmation, but all he did was nod.

"Please prepare a room for him to rest. He's had an ordeal," Jon said. "Please keep this private, of course."

"Certainly, Your Highness," Major Ngo replied. The two guards that had accompanied Jon and Saul on the shuttle waited at the entrance to the prison, and they escorted Jon and Saul to the private officer's quarters in the base.

Jon didn't allow the guards into the room. He closed the door as Saul slumped on the bed. Jon found a washcloth in the bathroom and wet it, then went to Saul, kneeling before his father. He washed the priest's blood from his hands, the sweat and dirt from his brow. He removed his father's jacket and boots, before helping him lie down.

"Son ..."

"Dad," Jon said, his voice hoarse. He never dared to call him dad until now. "You need to rest."

"What the priest said, what Zam said. I'm so sorry. I'm so very sorry about all of this."

"Get some rest," Jon said, tucking his father in.

He shut the light out and left the room, the two guards from Melas outside the door. "I will come for him in the morning. He needs sleep."

"Where are you going, Your Highness?"

Jon sighed, raking his fingers through his brown hair. "I need to speak to Major Ngo. I'll be back later."

A guard escorted Jon from the officer's quarters to Major Ngo's office on base, where Ngo led Jon to the command center. He asked for any intel reports on ships in the system, but nothing came up on the scopes from Nidos, the satellites in Horeb's orbit, the scanners from Bega. "What are you looking for?" the major asked.

"Phenians. We have a hunch they are making a play for us, again."

Major Ngo gave him a skeptical glance. "You all routed them out of the system a few months ago, including the last sympathizers on Nidos. Why would they try again?"

"Don't know. Just a hunch." Jon cleared his throat and changed the subject. "Sir, this is an awkward question, but I was wondering if I could see a roster of your mech techs."

"Certainly, Your Highness. Are you looking for a specialty?"

"No, just someone who used to be stationed at Glia." He smiled slightly. "Someone I once knew."

Major Ngo gave him access to the roster at a

workstation. He scrolled through the screen, but he realized he didn't even know Sharda's family name. "Do you have a way to search by nationality?"

The major frowned. "Most of us here are Ildan. The Beneur have been exempt from military service ever since Elder Vellar was elected."

"Of course." *I hate politics. I'd make a terrible king.* Once again, he dreamed of an alternative universe, where Armas and he could reign together, but he would serve as his second. Let Armas handle the messy political sphere. "But what about the Dagael?"

"There are some in service here." Major Ngo narrowed the search, and Jon immediately spotted her name. Mechanized Suit Technician Ley, Sharda. Discharged eight standard months ago.

Jon scratched his chin. "Major, what I'm about to ask ... can you be discreet? Can you give me a location as to Technician Ley's whereabouts?"

Major Ngo gave a slight frown. "The name is not familiar, but I don't work directly with the techs." He swiped through the system and found the address. "Here. The Dagael mostly are on the southern continent. Do you require a ship?"

"That would be very kind of you, and I would owe you a favor."

"Nonsense, Your Highness. Glad to help."

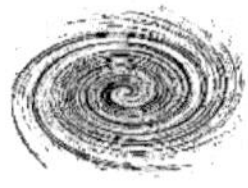

An hour later, Jon, having managed to convince Ngo he didn't need a security escort, flew the borrowed shuttle south from the base island, skimming the ocean near the equatorial continent. He remembered how Kyla flew

Saul's shuttle because it was the only thing she was allowed to fly, and now he was fortunate to be able to fly at all.

He hoped she was okay, wherever she was. He shuddered thinking she was meeting with the Modes. *Please keep her safe,* he prayed. Jon had never been as religious as Armas, something they talked about on occasion, or as zealous as his father, but the experience with Zam's spirit left him cold. What the priest said before she died, that he and his father were coming to their end. It was nonsense, surely. Just a play to get back at his father at the end of her strange, twisted life.

But it made this trip seem even more urgent.

Another hour passed, and he neared the edge of the southern continent as the Cana Star hung low in the sky. The tall conifer trees waved like long needles against pale pink clouds. Strips of bare hillsides showed the result of massive logging operations from years past. Small towns with little houses and compartment homes — old cargo containers from ships that had been converted into lodging — dotted in between the trees and clearings, with landing pads. The coordinates the major gave him drew him to a village near the crest of a hill.

He set the shuttle down on the landing pad, killed the engines, and glanced at himself in the reflective screen. During the Phenian Wars, he'd cut his hair military style, but it was starting to get shaggy. He'd changed into one of his father's spare dark green uniforms, as they were the same size. His face was thinner, his cheeks hollow. The recent events had taken a toll on him. Nonetheless, he saw his mother in his face once again, remembering her tenderness and good heart.

Help me to be more like you, Mom.

He stepped off the shuttle. This village was made up of a few compartment homes, along with some houses constructed of wood. He knew the Dagael had similar roots to the Jamin, starting off as hunters when they first came to the system. He wondered if that was why they opted for the compartment homes, easily packed up and taken to the sky on a cargo hauler. *Or am I just trying to excuse the fact they don't have the same resources as the Beneur?* Raimi had slipped once about the Dagael living conditions. He shoved that thought away. He'd never had a moment to grieve the friend he lost, the one whose life he took.

Some villagers had come out from their homes. Most of them wore simple trousers and shirts, some sweaters as it was approaching autumn there. "Excuse me," he approached an older man with thin gray hair. "Do you know Sharda Ley?"

He grunted, pointing toward a compartment home, a long rectangular shell from an old freighter, painted blue. Jon thanked him. As he walked to the compartment home, his feet weighed heavy. *What do I say after all this time? "Just wanted to see you? See how you are doing? See if you missed me?"* What do you say to your ex? Was she even really an ex?

Right as Jon reached the door, it opened. Her once long blond hair was cut just above her shoulders. Dark circles lined under her eyes. The last time he saw her, she was wearing her tech coveralls, but now she wore gray slacks and a green shirt.

But Jon's eyes drew to the baby on her hip. They had a tuft of brown hair, similar olive skin tone as his own. Chubby rolls on the thighs and arms and cheeks, wearing a footed blue all-in-one outfit. He wracked his brain.

How long ago was it? More than a year ago. It ... couldn't be.

The baby's green eyes confirmed it was.

"Jonny," Sharda said, her eyes wide in recognition as he tore his gaze back to her. "What are you doing here?" She tucked a strand of hair behind her ear, shifting the baby on her hip.

He opened his mouth and shut it, unsure of what to say. He finally settled on, "I had to see you."

"After all this time?" She shook her head. An awkward silence hung between them. She looked past Jon and rolled her eyes. "Get in here," she hissed.

Jon glanced over his shoulder. The villagers had drifted over to stare at the man in the Jamin uniform standing outside the single mom's home.

Shame flooded him.

He followed her inside, and she shut the door. "Can I get you something? Tea?" she asked him.

"No, please ... what can I do to help?"

She faced him, shifting the baby to the other side. "You don't need to help me. I'm fine. From the moment I knew I was pregnant, I knew I wanted to do this on my own. I know what kind of life he could have, and there's no room in that world for me."

"Sharda —"

"No." She stared at him, cold determination on her face. "You're doing this out of guilt. I could've called you at any moment. Granted, I'm sure your father would've had a way to hide all of this, clean it up, but still. I knew how to reach you, and I chose *not* to."

Jon caught his bottom lip under his teeth, turning away from her dark eyes. The compartment home, though small, was cozy. A simple kitchen, table and four chairs, one with an adaptation for a baby to sit in it, though the baby seemed too small to use it yet. A couch and two chairs with a holoscreen. A door from the living area to what Jon presumed was a bedroom. A plush rug drew across the floor with baby toys strewn about. It was simple, and somehow perfect. Like she'd been for him when he needed her.

Someone who listened, gave him what he needed, and never asked for anything in return.

"What's their name?" he asked.

"Seth," she said. "Named him after my father."

"Can I?" he asked, reaching out his arms, but Sharda stepped back.

"I think it's better if you don't. Jonny, we were never gonna get married. He was never going to be *your* son. Don't do this now. It will just break your heart and his when you can't come see him. When you're married and ruling as king and have royal children to care for."

"Don't tell me what I don't *want*," Jon snapped. "My father's been dictating my life for far too long. I came to see you because I've been thinking about you. I didn't treat you well the last time I saw you —"

"You didn't —"

"Please, just let me finish," he said, raising up a hand. "I'm still trying to figure out what I really want in life." He wanted to scream at her, *you didn't give me a choice — you took this choice from me, just like everyone else!*

But what would he have done in her position?

He exhaled, calming himself. "You're right — I never imagined marrying you. Let's just leave it at that. But now that I know — I want to help, however I can. I'd like to have him registered with me as the father. I'll legitimize it, so he will receive inheritance. At least let me do that for him."

A tear emerged from the corner of her eye. He knew he should let it be, but he walked over to her anyway, wiping the tear with his thumb, and tucking the loose strand of hair behind her ear. He then cupped his son's face and kissed his forehead.

Sharda hinted at a smile, setting her free hand on his chest. "You're a good man, Jonny. You always were. Don't let anyone take that from you." She stood on her tiptoes and kissed his cheek.

He blinked back tears before turning and reciprocating by kissing her cheek. "I have to get back." He had to leave before his own heart shattered.

"I know. Goodbye, Jonny."

He ran his hand over her hair once more, bringing her forehead to his, allowing his son to grasp his finger, before he pulled away and walked out the door.

Jon didn't look at the villagers as he made his way back to the shuttle. He didn't know if any of them recognized him as the prince, though his face was known in the system. Coming dressed in an officer's uniform, flying a private shuttle — dusted ash, it looked bad. He shouldn't have come like this without warning. He only hoped he didn't cause her more trouble.

When he entered the shuttle, the communications lights were blinking. He'd left his personal comm on board.

He pressed the button as he fired up the engines. "This is Dark Wolf."

"Dark Wolf, this is Major Ngo. I'm with the king. Phenian ships are on a direct course to Melas. You must return immediately!"

THIRTY-ONE

KYLA

"Your Highness," Laina muttered, wiping a tear from her eye. Carmen stood against the bedchamber door, her arms folded, her expression cross.

"Laina, how many times do I have to tell you to call me Kyla? And don't cry. I chose this."

She sat in a chair, staring at the reflection screen. Her long locks were gone. Laina helped to style the remaining hair over her scalp and down one side, cutting an angle at her chin. The other side was completely shaved. Thin strips of silver lined from her temple to behind her ear — the first augment. Alton said it would take a few hours for the dendrilite to fuse as neural silk and integrate with her brain stem, but then she would be able to access even more aspects of the ship than she could by simply using her palm at door sensors. At her wrist was an entire band of silver, penetrating her vein and sliding over her palm — it would eventually grow and connect to her neural implant, allowing her to interface directly every time she touched someone or something, like the ship.

"Why?" Carmen asked, folding their arms. Their eyes were dark, brows drawn together. Kyla had never seen them so angry.

Kyla gave Laina a look, and Laina went to her personal bag, retrieving the interference device Major Zeru had once used in her room. Laina set it on the table, pressing the button for the two antennae to emerge.

"I have no idea if the device will work here," Kyla said, "or if they can override it with their abilities, but it's worth a shot."

She bit the corner of her lip, then leaned forward toward the lieutenant. "I did this so I can learn as much as I can about them," she replied to Carmen. "I did this to help our people."

Carmen took the chair in front of her and leaned forward. "Did he force you —"

"No." She reached forward and set her hand on Carmen's knee. "This was my choice."

Carmen's gaze softened, and they gave a slight nod, understanding.

Kyla turned to Laina. "I promise you, I will do all I can to protect Ramah."

If Alton was able to hear, or somehow process what she said, she hadn't revealed anything he didn't already know or figure out. He'd have to know she had ulterior motives for becoming like them.

"You've sacrificed too much for me and what I hold

dear," her maid said.

"I haven't done enough, Laina. I've complained about my life like it was a cage, until it actually became one. I took on your religious practices knowing that even if my father caught me, he wouldn't kill me. When he hit you — " Kyla touched Laina's arm "— I knew I'd failed you. I'd lived in a bubble my whole life, and, while it may have been confining, it was safe. Even now — my father knew Alton wouldn't hurt me or touch me." *Though he did try to claim my reproductive organs*, she reminded herself. "The only time I risked any of that was for Armas."

"Kyla," Carmen said, using her first name, "you ought to have suggested me. You didn't need to risk yourself."

"This is a decision one must make for themselves; no one else can. And if anything went wrong, I couldn't live having seen either of you do this." She changed the subject. "How long until we reach Balec?"

"We're still two standard days away."

"Alton told me it would take a few hours before the augments — whoa." Her head drooped, as a wave of darkness and nausea rushed over her.

"Kyla!" Laina bent down, clutching her hands. Carmen touched her forehead. Kyla could still see them, feel them and hear them, but something else was overtaking her. The thoughts and feelings of hundreds of people on board.

She'd assumed, from the little she, or anyone else knew, that the Modes were a collective. What they'd understood from the autopsy of Ogroma, even though she hadn't had access to the full report, was that the Modes were interfacing on a regular basis. That they'd given up some of their individual identity to be one.

A horror such as none she'd experienced before

clutched at her heart. Thoughts became voices ringing in her ears. "*Help us. Free us. End it now. He won't let us. He's draining us. Using us. I've forgotten who I used to be. He's taking away who we are.*" Light ran through them like a chain, connecting them, pulling them all toward one.

The Supreme One.

"They're all enslaved," she whispered, her lip quivering. "Alton controls them all."

Suddenly all the thoughts and feelings stopped. She was in the room, alone with Carmen and Laina who looked like ghosts. The interference device had caught her signal and blocked it.

"Kyla," Laina said, her voice grave. "Are you all right?"

She shook her head. "The interference device is working. It's blocking whatever signal there is through collective control. But they're all still individuals, trying to get out. I don't know how he does it." Kyla's chest tightened. "They were never united before Alton came to power because he did something. He altered how they interacted with each other. Before, they were simply individuals who chose to join the Modes and be modified. Now, they have no choice, and he is trying to expand his control."

Her eyes flew open, as she understood. The brief time she was connected she saw the light running through the ship, running through their veins.

"By using more dendrilite than they've ever used before." She turned to Laina. "Tell me everything about how the Tananites use it."

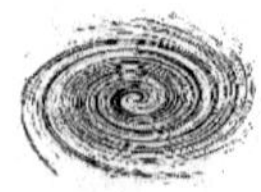

Laina spent the rest of the evening explaining how the ancient Tana worshippers discovered that dendrilite in the water brought enhanced visions, and how they built the sacred well on Ramah. Then, they started extracting small bits and using it in their bodies. They found ingesting it directly was often deadly, but small amounts opened them to mystical experiences. The art of tattooing it into one's skin allowed for it to be absorbed into the body at a reasonable rate, but they'd never connected it directly to the brain stem. "That sort of thing led to madness, from what the legends say."

Her maid shared that in larger amounts, they created mystical connections with each other. Sometimes a shared experience, such as a vision, or shared dreams. When Laina received her tattoo on her arm, right before she left Nidos, it was a reminder of where she came from. "Sometimes, right when I was falling asleep those first few nights on Melas, it felt like I was home with my family. I could see a glimpse of them, and I could feel their love and joy. From what I understand, I'd be too far away to make that connection, and I don't think there was any dendrilite in Glia, so maybe I imagined it."

Kyla tilted her head to Carmen. "Do you understand how the interference device works?"

"It simply blocks communication signals. I would imagine that all it is doing is blocking you from receiving those communications and from you sending them."

"So the feelings, voices I heard — they are the people trying to communicate." Kyla turned to Laina. "Have you felt anything, since you have a dendrilite tattoo?"

She shook her head. "But I haven't tried to."

Kyla frowned. "What do you mean?"

"In the first weeks I was on Melas, it was easy to do so because I longed for my family, longed to communicate with home, and then I could see them. But as I said, I probably just imagined it. I gave up after a while, and I no longer saw them or felt them."

Kyla stood. She didn't want Laina to risk herself trying to connect and becoming entangled in this. "I wonder if there's a way to block them —"

A sound came at the door. She glanced at Laina. "Put away the device."

"But your augments —"

"If I'm controlled by him ... we'll deal with that." She whispered to Carmen. "If something happens and I'm compromised, you need to find a way to stop him."

Carmen's eyes grew wide, but they simply nodded.

As soon as Laina pressed the button on the device, the feelings rushed back in, the darkness and nausea sweeping over her. She fell into the chair.

The door opened, and Alton rushed in. "I didn't think you would connect so soon," he muttered, moving to kneel in front of her.

Kyla saw him approach, his pale skin, his augments, the way he silenced all the other voices on the ship. The nausea left her, and she could see clearer, sharper. He touched her cheek, his fingertips skimming the augmented device.

"Is she all right?" Laina asked him.

"For the first few standard days, the body tries to reject the augmentations," he said. His silver eyes searched Kyla's. "You've heard them. The voices of dissent. As you adjust, you'll no longer hear them, only the voices that collaborate together. Everyone who wishes to join us has the choice, but once you are part of the Modes, you are together. The body becomes one. When part of the body tries to reject others, it becomes a cancer. The cure is conformity."

He leaned closer, whispering into her ear. "Your body right now is trying to reject all of it. This is normal. I will use my connection to suppress those voices that tell you to leave, so you will embrace and heal."

Kyla could almost see him doing it, ordering all the others on the ship into submission. The ship appeared to her like a body, the dendrilite everywhere the veins, the Modes the cells. It was terrifying and beautiful all at once, what Alton had built since he left Gallim, their home world on the Near Side, annexed by the Airysans. It was like what Laina had said about the Tananites, how they were connected in a mystical way, but here the dendrilite was connecting them all along with their ships. They were no longer separate ships of people working together to steal and take control. They were one. They *were* the Everlasting God.

They were all becoming Alton, he a puppet master and all of them puppets on strings. There was a thread to everyone, it seemed, except for Carmen and Laina.

But there *was* a thread to Laina. She felt it now, a dim light connecting her, the dendrilite on her arm. But Alton did not perceive it; she was certain. *Why does he not see it when I can?*

She swallowed that secret away.

"You need rest, my wife. Rest and healing. Which is what I thought you were doing when I left you alone," he added, an edge to his voice toward Laina and Carmen.

Kyla turned to the two of them. "He's right. I need to sleep. But I will call for you in a few hours."

Laina raised a brow, but Kyla dismissed her maid anyway, hoping against hope that Alton would not discover Laina's dendrilite connection.

"Your Highness," Carmen said, bowing, but touched Kyla's shoulder gently before leaving the room.

Alton took Kyla by the arm and led her to her bed. "Do not worry. As I said before, we will have no relations, *unless* you want them."

She got into the covers, resting on the side of her face without the augments, gazing at him. "Do you want them?"

He tilted his head. "You're trying to play games with me. I know how you look at me, how you look at all of us. You chose this because you thought this would help you find a way to stop me, to stop who we are. Eventually, you will be one of us, and this conversation will not matter."

"Does anyone ever touch you?" she asked, taking her fingertips and gently grazing them down his forearm.

He pulled away quickly.

"Tell me something. Why did you let Ogroma leave the collective?"

His hands clenched, and a vein pulsed in his neck as he pivoted away from her. "It was their choice. They were the first we made interlinked from birth. They had such incredible power together. They saw themselves as one, but *not* one with us. They became their own mind. Though we'd made arrangements with Stiners before that were mutually beneficial, Ogroma wanted to go with them."

Alton glanced back at her in the bed. "This is why, when I became commander, I interlinked every one of us. So we'd understand who we are, why we need each other

— why we can never be apart."

Kyla's stomach twisted as he left the room, the light leaving with him. He'd kept his promise, and their thoughts and feelings were out of her head for now. While he was blocking them, he also blocked himself from her.

She knew she needed to sleep but she relished the brief freedom she had to think through the few things she knew for certain right then:

The interference device would help for a short time if necessary.

She *was* connected to Laina, somehow.

She had to stop Alton before he attacked Armas.

She breathed out heavily as sleep began to overtake her, remembering her wedding night, being in Armas's arms, and the promise he made as he fled through the window.

"Promise me you'll come back to me — when it's safe. Promise me."

He nodded. "I promise."

THIRTY-TWO

ARMAS

"This is suicide," Shane said. Three days earlier, they'd confirmed with Abby the timing of the *Behemoth's* inspection rendezvous.

Armas grunted as he checked the rounds in the weapons for the third time, squeezing around the Hessan fighters who'd joined up and were pulling on environmental suits. Though there was more room on the decommissioned fuel tanker, the shuttle was easier to explain as a vehicle off-course if they were caught. They trailed the massive freighter in their radiation exhaust so they wouldn't be spotted, in case Abby hadn't managed to turn off the proximity alarm. But the ship hadn't turned its defense weapons toward them. "It's still our best option," he replied to his brother as he pulled on his own suit.

Shane had gone over the schematics and discovered *The Behemoth* held a current complement of thirty-six crew. The freighter had let crew off at their previous port, giving them a lighter load for the last run.

"Thirty-six of them, plus Laban and whoever else he brought with him besides his wife, verses fifteen of us," Shane said, crossing his arms. "Not the best odds, but not bad."

"Have to assume a good number are trained for combat and to resist people like us," Seriah said, checking the magazine rounds on her own Ember 75 before slipping it into the pocket of her environmental suit and picking up a sharpshooter pistol.

Abby thought it too risky to communicate directly with them once she left Balec's orbital station but gave Armas approximate timing of when Captain Laban would arrive, and that the captain's shuttle planned to dock at the port side shuttle airlocks of the *Behemoth* in twenty hours. Armas and his crew left ten hours after Laban did to give plenty of distance to not be spotted by Laban, with sufficient time for him to do his inspection and perhaps start drinking with the *Behemoth's* captain before they caught up to him.

Seriah hadn't lied when she said she'd stocked the shuttle — the amount of weaponry she'd managed to get was tantamount to a small arsenal he'd once visited on one of the guard outposts on Samar. They'd spent the last day on Balec's orbital trading for some tools and environmental gear. Seriah and Shane together figured out the best place to magnetically lock onto the freighter and to drill into the airlock. The downside was that once the airlock popped alarms would go off all over the place.

The three of them skimmed through the holoscreen schematics. Seriah scratched the back of her head. "Okay, we release the pressure from the airlock, the alarm goes off, and by the time we are open and through, we'll have at least twelve guns on us."

"We'll take them out," one of the Hessan soldiers said, but Seriah gave him a look.

"We'll have casualties. And they could just seal the deck and space us."

Armas set his hands on his hips. "Just great."

Shane rubbed his jaw, a bit of stubble having grown in. "What we need is a diversion. Get them to go to the wrong part of the ship while we get in."

Armas raised a brow. "That could work. The alarm would go off, but they'd at least be divided, or distracted by the first alarm."

"How do we do that?" Seriah asked. "We can't be in two places at once ... No. Don't you even think about it."

"What, I'm not thinking anything," Armas lied.

"You're a terrible liar and I know that look." She turned to Shane. "He ever tell you how he almost lost his leg at Zek and told everyone he was fine while having his ass carried out of the canyon?"

"I think that's where we first met, at Zek," Armas reminisced. "But yes. This is the plan: I'm going to suit up and after we're attached to the ship, take a walk on the hull, and create distraction number one right there," he said, pointing to the port aft side, underneath where Captain Laban's shuttle was currently docked. "The rest of you can enter at the starboard side shuttle airlocks as that will be a much easier breach, and go directly to the bridge, take the captain into custody and commandeer the ship."

"And you think the remaining crew will just let us take the ship without casualties?"

"I'll go alone and get caught on purpose. They'll see who I am, take me into custody for the reward — I'm assuming my face has earned me a reward — and then to save his own life the captain will tell the crew to stand down, we're simply hitching a ride to Balec. Once we're in close comms range, we'll contact those who have fled to Balec and get them to help with the rest."

Seriah rolled her eyes. "It's a terrible plan."

"But it's going to work."

"It's a terrible plan," she said, swiping away the holoscreen schematics.

"It is a terrible plan," Shane added, "because you've got it wrong. Let me be the distraction."

"They might shoot you on sight," Armas said.

"They might do the same to you. Don't assume your pretty face will save you." He leaned toward Seriah. "I'm actually the good-looking one."

Armas chuckled. He'd washed the dye out of his hair that morning — glad to go back to his normal red locks and stop pretending to be someone else. It was true, when they were growing up Shane always got the girls with his golden hair. "Stick with Seriah. She'll have your back. If it's not my looks, it will be my good-natured charm. Or the dusting huge bounty on my head."

There were no counter-maneuvers made by the *Behemoth* when Seriah locked the shuttle onto the hull. All fifteen of them were suited up, and armed to the teeth, with Ramaen blasters, proton rifles, pistols, and Shane wore a belt of grenades. All stupidly useless outside of a pressurized cabin, and stupid to use inside one. Armas carried the tools necessary to open the emergency airlock, where he hoped to God he would get caught at the right time and that they didn't just shoot him or rip his helmet off and space him.

After they checked each other's helmets, Seriah led Armas through the aft airlock of the shuttle, having him double-check his magnetic boots. "Good luck," she called over the comm as she depressurized the airlock.

"You too, sir," he said, saluting as if they were both still serving in the Melas Unified Military.

When the outer door opened, he carefully stepped over the edge, turning at a ninety-degree angle to keep the wall of the shuttle as his floor. "I am not afraid. I am not afraid," he repeated to himself, a song he'd started writing after the battle of Zek. "I'm in the place of death, but I am not afraid, for You are with me."

He took step after careful step, treading onto the *Behemoth's* hull, walking over the ship and avoiding the fake cone drive on the keel. He made his way through the maze of empty outer cargo containers until he reached the other side and turned again at a ninety-degree-angle, until he found the emergency airlock.

The light was red.

"Dusted ash," he said over the comm.

"What?" Seriah asked, sounding annoyed.

"The airlock is pressurized." Meaning the other side of the airlock was open.

She swore as well over the comm.

"There's nothing to be done. I set off the alarm

immediately as soon as I fiddle with the door pressurization and then we have a real hull breach. They'll cut off that deck. You all can get your door open and haul ass."

"Armas ..." she sighed heavily over the comm. "Affirmative."

He took the drill from his belt and found the magnetic hinges. Armas then moved away from the door, drilling at a perpendicular angle, so if the thing blasted off at him, he had a chance of not getting loose and being sucked away.

"Do you have the door —" Seriah said over the comm right as the door blasted off the hinges, taking the drill with it. Armas clung to the side of the hull with his magnetic gloves and boots.

"Hull is breached," he said over the comm, watching as all loose materials inside the uncontained area ejected into space.

"Copy that," Seriah said. "Countdown started."

Once Armas was certain the debris had cleared, he climbed through the hole from the door. The inner hull door was missing — probably sucked out with everything else that came off the ship. Red lights flashed overhead, signaling the hull breach. He pulled the Ramaen Blaster off his back, though he knew the assault rifle was useless in the moment. Still, he scanned the entrance with his weapon raised.

He crept through the empty hall. "All clear here. Looks like the deck's been sealed. Will try to find another way through."

"We're almost in," Shane replied on the comm.

The hallway was a magnetic compound, making it easier for him to continue to move around in zero g with his mag boots. There were no signs, nothing that could indicate what was on this level. If his memory of the schematics was correct, the other side of the wall should be the upper level for the cargo hold, where the mechs were waiting. Every few meters stood a doorway on his right, but they were all locked. Armas swore. He'd lost the drill out to space.

The hallway curved, and he came to an airlock, probably where the deck was sealed. The light indicator was red. He opened the door easily, and pulled it shut behind him, pulling down the latch to seal. Instantly his suit registered oxygen rising and pressurization.

"I think I'm in," he said.

There was no response.

"Seriah? Shane?"

Stardust and ashes.

When the light turned green, Armas slung the Ramaen Blaster over his shoulder and unfastened the seal on his helmet and pulled it off. Sweat gathered at the back of his neck. He tore off his gloves, then pulled his weapon back into place. He clicked off his mag boots. Artificial gravity was on.

He opened the second airlock door. The hallway in front of him was the same as the one behind him, except yellow lights flashed. He stepped carefully down the hallway, as doors continued to appear every few meters on his right.

Armas knew the ship was massive, on the specs and even on the screen when they approached in the shuttle. But walking the length of the damn thing had him frustrated. If there were thirty-six crew on the ship, where were they? Had they caught the others already?

His stomach sank. *Did Abby turn them in?* He'd probably been a fool to trust her.

As he neared another curve in the hall, the sounds of boots clicking on the deck made him freeze. There was nowhere to hide. He dropped to his knee, Ramaen Blaster ready to fire.

"Armas?"

"Abby?" he said, not lowering his weapon until she came into view. She wore dark gray coveralls, her brown hair tied back. The signature Ildan gold bangle hung on a chain around her neck, like a medallion.

"They're —"

A blast shook the hall. Instinctively, Armas dove, wrapping himself around Abby as debris flashed around them. The lights above continued to flash yellow.

"You okay?" he asked, uncoiling himself from her and helping her stand.

"Yeah. The guards are fighting your friends. I got the proximity alarm off but didn't realize there was another alarm for the shuttle airlocks. They assumed this side was a distraction."

Another blast sounded, but the hall didn't shake. Armas slung the Ramaen Blaster away and pulled his Bara Sharpshooter from the holster. "It was a stupid idea to bring the blasters," he said. "Why'd you come this way?"

A slight smile grew on her face. "I had a hunch it was you."

He moved in front of Abby, but she grabbed his free hand. "This way," she said, pulling him back to a door on the right. She let go of his hand to scan a keycard, and the door slid open. Inside was a narrow hallway, a meter wide, with dim lights. "This is the maintenance shaft.

They won't look for us here," she added, as the door slid back into place behind her. Abby again took his free hand, leading him through the passageway.

"Where are we going?" he whispered.

"The bridge."

He pulled his hand out of her grasp. "Abby …"

Her eyes were deep brown and bright, even in the dim light of the shaft.

She reached up and touched his cheek. "You've been incredibly kind to me." Her fingers caught the edge of his red curls, and a soft smile spread across her face. "Laban is on the bridge with the captain and third shift crew, and he's drunk off his ass."

Armas swallowed hard. "Okay. Let's go."

They continued in silence, heading down one set of steep stairs, crossing to another section, then up two flights before coming to an end, where a ladder rose up another floor. "This is it — we're at the shaft that leads up to the bridge."

She pressed her lips to his cheek, right next to his mouth. "Good luck." She slipped her keycard into his hand.

He climbed up the ladder. At the top, there was a door with a window, leading out to the hallway connecting the bridge to the rest of the ship.

Weapon in hand, he slid the keycard. As soon as the door opened, he burst through it onto the deck.

"Everyone's hands where I can see them," he shouted.

The bridge crew immediately put their hands in the air — navigator, engineer, and communications officer. "Don't even think about sending a distress call," he warned, as the comm officer's hand moved.

In the captain's chair was Laban, a bottle in hand, his eyes closed.

"Where's the ship captain?"

"He went to investigate the shuttle breach," the navigator said.

"Order the rest of the crew to stand down," Armas said. "Do it now!"

The comm officer nodded quickly as their hands trembled. "This is the bridge. All crew, stand down. Repeat: stand down."

Abby stepped onto the bridge. "Crew of the *Behemoth*, you will not be harmed," she announced to the bridge crew. "Do as these people say."

"What are your orders?" the navigator asked Armas.

"Comms quiet. No harm will come to you, and we'll give you the shuttle to get to Balec."

"Who are you?" the comms officer asked.

Armas spun around with his weapon ready as voices sounded from the hall. Two crewmembers, disarmed, entered with their hands raised, Seriah behind them with her Sharpshooter pistol drawn.

"Where's the rest of the crew?"

"We've captured half of them, the rest are dead," she said, her voice grave. "I'm sorry, Armas. Shane didn't make it."

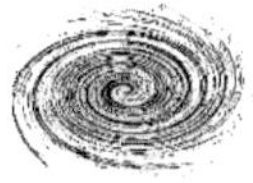

Armas sat on a couch in the ship captain's quarters, his environmental jumpsuit in a heap on the floor, wearing only a short-sleeve shirt and insulated pants. Seriah had taken him to his brother's body. He hadn't wanted to leave him, but Seriah insisted Armas needed to rest. She'd found Abby, who led them here. The captain's quarters were similar in size to his old officer quarters back on Glia, with a couch, a chair, a small table and a desk. On one wall stood a closet, and the other, a double bed, with a plush comforter and pillows lined in Etho dark blue silk.

Seriah poured him a glass of Ramaen vodka from the captain's liquor cabinet and set it before him. "I'll make sure we get Shane home," she said.

Armas stared at the glass, not acknowledging her.

"We've got the captain and crew locked in a storage room. Laban hasn't regained consciousness — I suspect alcohol poisoning. He's in the med bay."

Armas grabbed the shot and tossed it back. Seriah poured him another. "We're monitoring communications. I don't trust the comm officer — they may have managed to send a distress call — but so far we're not seeing anything on the scopes. Two of our Hessan crew have some experience in piloting larger ships from Nidos's shipyards, but it might take them overnight to learn the nav system."

He took another drink. Seriah poured another. "I'd stop after that if I were you, but I'll let you be." She rose, setting her hand on his shoulder for a moment. "I'm sorry. I have a brother, too. I can't imagine losing him."

She left him alone.

Armas had never lost anyone like this before. His grandparents all died of old age. Even in combat, though there were people around him who died, he was never close to them. Even Raimi — he knew Jon's heart had broken but he'd done it to save him.

Shane should still be alive. *This is all my fault.*

The door opened, and Abby slipped in, closing it behind her. She sat down next to him. "I'm so sorry."

Armas gritted his teeth. "He shouldn't have come along. He should've gone with my parents to Dibon."

She set her hand on his arm. "He wanted to help you. It's what brothers do."

He sighed. "We were never that close. Even when he re-enlisted, I hardly ever saw him. He was mostly on guard patrol at Glia. I think he spoke three words to me at my wedding reception."

Abby began to stroke his shoulder, and a tear slid down his cheek. She brushed it away gently with her thumb. "I'm so sorry. His sacrifice will not be forgotten."

He buried his face in his palms.

Abby wrapped her arms around his shoulders, holding him while he cried. Her palm slid around his neck, and as he wiped his face, she kissed his cheek.

Then she kissed his mouth.

His chest pounded. He broke away. "What ..."

Abby's lip trembled. "I'm sorry. I thought ..." She took his hand gently, and his fingertips skimmed her pulse. He searched her eyes. "I know how it is to feel lonely, Armas. I know you are hurting right now. It's so lonely, out here in space," she said as she leaned closer, her hand sliding up his chest to his neck. He knew he should stop her again, but she pulled him down for another kiss.

Armas's head buzzed with all sorts of confusing thoughts, but his body responded with need. He deepened the kiss, and a moan escaped her lips. Her hands went around his neck, thumbs tucking under his ears. His hands slid around her waist and up her back. The alcohol and grief made everything fuzzy. When he drew back for air, he threaded his hands in her hair that had fallen out of its clasp. "Abby."

She hushed him with another kiss, climbing into his lap.

He unzipped her coveralls as her fingers grazed his rib cage under his shirt. He didn't remember lifting her up, but somehow, they stumbled to the soft silky bed. They left each other breathless as they traded kisses and removed clothes, fingers wandering over pulse points and smooth curves and solid muscles. All the guilt, shame, sorrow, and rage coursing through his blood broke through in waves of heat along his skin as he explored every inch of hers. He slid into her warmth, building into a steady rhythm as her ankles wrapped around him. She arched her back, calling out his name, and he braced himself for the waves of passion before collapsing on her in release.

A tap came at the door. Armas blinked. Abby's head rested under his, her arm on his chest and leg slung over his hips. He peeled himself away from Abby and found his thermal pants, pulling them on.

"Armas," Seriah said on the other side of the door.

He slid on his boots and opened the door. She raised a brow as he pulled his shirt over his head. "Sorry, I fell asleep."

"I, or we?" Seriah crossed her arms.

Armas leaned back against the door, feeling the heat rise in his cheeks, but didn't respond.

"Doesn't matter," his former major said. "You've been through a lot." Seriah cleared her throat. "Laban died in his sleep last night. Cardiac arrest. One less liability."

Armas drew his hand across his face. "Stardust."

"There's worse news."

He lowered his hand.

"I just got in touch with our allies on the *Darkangel*." She motioned for him to follow her down the corridor from the other crew quarters. "They've been hanging out of range of Nidos monitoring communications. It seems Saul's made a deal with the Modes, and they're on course to attack Balec." She had a keycard and opened the double doors in front of her, leading to a balcony with a railing.

"Ashes," Armas swore in awe. In front of him was the massive, cavernous space of the cargo hold. Lined up, in six rows of twelve, stood the Airysan steel mechs he suspected were the real cargo. They were unpainted, unmarked. Crates lined both walls, labeled with ammunition types and weapons. Armas whistled, momentarily forgetting all the troubles and complications.

"They've been patched, right?"

Seriah nodded. "I went over the schematics. No shutdown code or virus will work on these beauties."

"We might stand a chance against the Modes."

"Armas, there's more." She handed over her comm device. There was a message loaded, and he clicked it.

Saul's face appeared.

"When did this come in?"

"A few minutes before I came to get you. It was sent on universal."

He played the message.

"To all Nacaens: we are in grave danger. The Phenians are planning to attack Melas. We do not have the forces to withstand them.

"To Armas Lehem-Perez: we need you. *I* need you. Bring your forces and come to our aid."

The message ended.

"Trap?" Armas asked, handing Seriah her comm.

"Not this time. Encrypted in the message were signal codes they'd cracked for the Phenian fleet. The enemy has sent their mech drop ships, fighters, warships — everything. Their route is direct to Melas."

"Stardust and ashes." He closed his eyes, leaning on the railing. "How far are we from Balec?"

"Seventeen standard hours. But if we leave now, we can go directly to Melas and escape the Modes who are en route to Balec. But we won't beat the Phenians to Melas."

"Who all do we have on our side?"

"Most of the Hessan fighters, some Tali, our mech fighters and pilots from Dahan. A few units from the nations of Samar. Probably a fifth of all Nacaen forces, scattered throughout the Nacaen Group and interstellar space between here and there." She bit the corner of her lip. "But we have civilians and priests on Balec, in sanctuary, in danger from the Modes."

Armas swore again. "Saul needs us."

"Not him," Seriah said. "*Our people* need us. They need *you* to lead."

He pushed away from the railing. "If we leave Balec —"

"The Modes may destroy the Leki and our people in asylum."

"Hundreds of thousands of innocent lives caught up in it."

Seriah nudged the floor with her toe. "I told you it was worse."

Armas wove his fingers together behind his head. "We just commandeered the mechs that could provide Saul — *our people* — with the defenses they need *right now.*"

She shook her head. "We don't know we'll be able to defeat the Phenians, even if we haul ass there. We may be too late."

"Are you saying we cut our losses, and try to go up against the Modes to save the Leki and those on our side?"

"No. I'm saying I serve you, Armas." She set her hand on his shoulder. "It's your decision."

THIRTY-THREE

KYLA

Alton gave Kyla a tour of the ship, at her request. She changed her clothing to a black jumpsuit that clung to her body, similar to what other Modes wore on the ship. The massive dreadnought was about half the size of Glia's fortress. The hexagonal passages were a maze at first, but eventually Kyla could sense them through her implant. Alton was easing up on the block. She could feel others, but the cries for help seemed dulled and distant. She wanted to assure the voices that she would help, but she dared not let Alton find out. They had twenty-four hours before they reached Balec's orbit, before they attacked Armas and the rebels with him. Every minute had to be spent gathering information to stop Alton.

All the Modes had individual rooms for rest and where

they received synthetic nutrition, sometimes by mouth, other times by intravenous methods. The massive ship was powered by similar trifusion drives as other ships in the galaxy, but dendrilite connections allowed engineers to make adjustments from wherever they were on the ship. Navigation controls were still quicker from the command consoles on the bridge. Communications, however, all ran through Alton. "Before I became the Supreme One, we had communications officers for each ship. Now, all the ships talk to me. I direct them where to go in the galaxy."

"Even at this distance?" she asked.

"Much faster than your universal communications channels," he said, smiling slightly. It seemed to please him that she asked so many questions.

"You can just think, and send the message along?"

"Not quite. I still use dendrilite through the ship's communication system. While I can control most of the ship on my own, it is easier on my body when I am interfacing at my station on the bridge."

When Alton brought her to the bridge, she gasped. The space was wide and dim, and eerily silent. He was still muting her power through the augments, but she was surprised no one used verbal communication at all. Engineers and navigators and weapons, including cyberweapons to override commands of enemy vessels and steal ships, were all at sparse console stations arranged in a hexagon, all facing inward to the Supreme station — the large chair and console in the center.

The entire chair was crossed with lines of dendrilite.

She waited until they left the bridge before asking him, "Is the chair the only place where you can control the whole ship?"

He raised a brow. "Still plotting, are we?"

She tensed. She remained silent for the remainder of the tour, until he came to her quarters.

"Where are your rooms?" she asked.

Alton tilted his head. "You wish to see them?"

She nodded.

"I'll show you."

She shuddered. He hadn't opened his mouth.

"I can speak in your mind now. Don't worry. I'm not prying for all your secrets. Yet. It takes some easing into."

She touched the side of her face. His expression transformed to worry. "Does it hurt?"

"It was a sharp pain, now it's gone." *More like a cold worm sliding in,* she thought to herself.

He winked at her.

She exhaled, working to clear her mind as he led her around the maze, to a room just below the bridge. The map of the ship unwound in her mind, and she could see every passage, every way to move around.

Alton's quarters were the same shape as the bridge, a large hexagonal room. But while hers was bright, with screens full of scenes from home, his was dark, dimly lit by the dendrilite on the walls. It glowed a bit brighter as she entered.

In the center of the room was a six-posted bed. She'd never seen anything like it. Dendrilite spiraled down the posts.

"The bed helps to keep me young," he said. "I know you've wondered how I have kept my one-hundred-forty-three years looking like I'm barely forty standard."

She scratched the back of her neck. "I did wonder."

"This is the other place I can control everything. If

there is an emergency, I will awake here and immediately call our ships to come to our aid."

Good to know.

"You think you'll kill me here."

Her eyes flew open in surprise.

"I can read you so easily. Same as I can the others," he added with a smirk. "I've sometimes wondered if I should cut my losses and kill them, be done with it, but it's such a waste of potential. And we don't take others on board who do not consent at first, so it would take a long time to replace them."

"Learn how to silence them, to refuse them, and you will find peace. But I will continue to suppress their voices for now," he said in her mind, and she suppressed the urge to shudder.

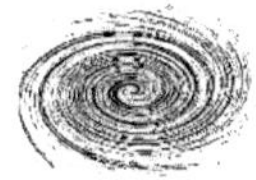

When Kyla returned, Carmen was working with Laina to figure out if the interference device could be useful. They tried it again when Alton was out of the room, and it completely silenced any communication through dendrilite.

"Do you think we could use this somehow to stop him?" she asked Carmen.

"I doubt we will find the materials we would need to build something on this ship large enough to interfere with all his power. He's also figured out a way to use dendrilite to signal across the galaxy — if he's also controlling the ships mining in Bara."

"I wonder if I could attempt to communicate, with the dendrilite in me," Laina asked.

"No. Don't even try it," she warned her maid. "It's too risky and he might discover you, find a way to connect you to the collective."

"But what if — what if I try, just you and me. We can reconfigure the interference device to allow for communication within a small space."

Carmen's brows raised. "That could work. The device, I mean. I have no idea if there's enough dendrilite in your tattoo. But the device can be used to allow a close-range communication."

"No."

"Kyla," Laina said, taking her princess's hands in her own. "I know you feel guilty about what happened to me. I've made all my choices, same as yours. I was offered the position to serve as your maid after your mother died, and I said yes. I chose to leave my home. I also chose to teach you about Tana, because I know, on your mother's home world of Samar, they carve images of Starre in the ice. I chose all these things. I chose to come with you when your father did not give you a choice. I *choose* to do this."

Kyla closed her eyes. Laina's fingers were wound around hers. Even though she'd grown up, Laina's hands still seemed larger than life, there to comfort and protect her.

"Trust me, because I trust you."

Kyla let out a breath. "All right. Let's give it a shot."

Carmen set up the device to only allow for communication signals inside the room. When Kyla opened her eyes, she could feel nothing for a moment, like the first time the device blocked the dendrilite. Then, slowly, she reached out in awareness.

Though she could see Laina physically across from her, she could sense light in her, too. "I feel you."

Laina's mouth opened. "I — I feel you, too. It's strange,

like the smell of your hair when I'm braiding it ..." She covered her mouth.

Kyla smiled, touching the remaining shorn locks on the side of her face. "It's okay. But yeah, your dendrilite works. Which is why you must keep the interference device on you."

"But —"

"It will keep you safe —"

The connection broke. Laina stood in front of her, but she could no longer feel her through the dendrilite. She raised her brows at Carmen. "What did you do?"

"Nothing — I didn't do anything. What's wrong?"

"I can't feel her at all. I am just wondering if the interference device is cutting off the signal between us."

Carmen pulled off the cover. "No, it's still set. Maybe try again?"

Kyla closed her eyes again, concentrating on Laina, trying to remember how she sensed her —

The princess found herself on the floor, Carmen helping her to stand. "What happened?"

"I — I can't explain it," Laina said, holding her palms in front of her. "I didn't do anything, but it felt like an energy pulse."

"Is there something different about your dendrilite?" Carmen asked, staring at Laina's tattoo, as Laina had her sleeve rolled up.

"No," she said, shifting her sleeve down — and the medallion she often wore fell out of her blouse.

"Your medallion," Kyla breathed. "Is it dendrilite?"

"No, it's just a silver varnish ..." Laina sounded doubtful. "The king returned it to me before we left. I was shocked because I was certain he destroyed it."

"Can I see it?"

Laina obliged, removing the medallion from her neck and handing it to Kyla. There was an energy pulse, but softer this time, as she touched it.

Carmen bit the corner of her lip. "May I remove the varnish on the back?"

"You don't need to," Kyla said, a wave coming over her again. "The core is concentrated dendrilite, in the shape of an arrow. It's Tana's arrow."

"You can tell?"

"Not only can I tell what it is, I know how to use it." She turned to Laina. "You told me that too much dendrilite can be deadly if ingested. Apparently, when concentrated, it acts the same way with my augments. When I reached out to you the first time, we could sense each other. I believe the arrow somehow picked up on the interference device and magnified its power, it's so densely packed. So when I tried again — boom. You threw me off the chair with that much power concentrated."

"The arrow magnified the signal disrupter," Carmen said, then glanced at Laina. "How did you get it?"

"My mother gave it to me. Passed down from my great-grandmother, who was Hitti, an original of Nidos."

"The priest on Ramah, she had an arrow implant," Carmen said. "I wonder if it magnifies power in a similar way for her."

Laina touched Kyla's hand. "You could use it against him."

"If I time it right," Kyla said, "I can use it to bring down the whole thing."

They approached Balec's orbit. Alton had not come for

her, and when she had gone in search of him and the bridge, her access was denied. She could sense the ship's hallways, the crew's quarters, the drive — but the way to the bridge was blocked. As if it was erased from her mind. She tried using her palm interface but to no avail. Alton was keeping her out.

Kyla was almost out of time.

She inhaled and bit her lip, having to do the thing she dreaded most. *"Are we there yet?"*

A snicker echoed in her mind. *"Patience. We are having to direct our energy toward breaking the communications firewall at Balec."*

"They have you blocked?"

"Like any system, it does not take us long to hack in and take control."

She swore, and then prayed. *Holy Tana, give me courage. Give me strength.* She felt the medallion, tucked into her back pocket, with the interference device zipped inside of her jumpsuit on the front.

Armas was running out of time. If she was going to save him, she had to do this.

"I want to see you," she said, putting as much meaning behind it as she could, all the longing for Armas toward Alton.

She sensed him, in her mind, saying nothing. As if he was considering her, or searching for what she hid behind those words.

"You may come to the bridge."

"No. I want to go to your bedroom."

Silence again, but she found the pathway to the room underneath the bridge was as clear as the path to her own bedroom back in the fortress on Glia. She made her way through the hexagonal sections, the dendrilite pulsing with light, getting stronger as she neared his room.

He was already inside, waiting, when she entered, the doorpad responding to her touch. Her pulse pounded with every step she took forward.

"If you mean to try to trick me, or trap me to save your former husband, you have already failed. We're almost into Balec's system. Their defenses will fall at any moment."

She held her head high, refusing to be swayed, hiding her fear, directing all her passion for Armas toward Alton. He stood before his bed, shifting his weight from one foot to the other.

"How long has it been since you felt the touch of another?" she said, laying on the seduction in her voice. "Not just to take their energy, but to share? To give?"

She strode up to him, and reached for his hand, turning it over to his palm. She slid her palm interface over his, and a spark jumped.

He quirked an eyebrow. "You *do* want me."

"I want you," she affirmed in her mind, reaching up to his face and pulling his mouth down to hers, her tongue sliding between his lips.

Alton responded, his hands cupping her face, fingertips running along the augment from the side of her skull down her neck. Her breath hitched at his touch. She shoved any thoughts of who it was in front of her and thought only of the one she really loved as Alton unzipped the front of her jumpsuit.

His hands were cold under her breasts, causing her to shiver as his mouth moved to her neck. She pushed him toward the bed, and he fell back. The dendrilite pulsed in the room, pulsing down the six bedposts, and she straddled him, reaching to pull back her jumpsuit, and secretly unzip the compartment with the interference device, palming it carefully as she shrugged out of the top of her suit.

She ran her augmented hand over his jumpsuit, unzipping the front, and gasped. His torso was so white he was almost blue, with silver lines of dendrilite threaded along his ribs. But the hard length of him pulsed beneath her. Her heart raced along the rhythm.

"Do I frighten you?"

She shook her head. "Nothing frightens me anymore."

He reached for her, thumb behind her ear, stroking the side of her augment as he kissed her, tongue sliding over her teeth. With one hand, she slipped the medallion out of her back pocket.

Suddenly Alton jerked back. "What are you doing?"

"Saving my husband," she said, as she slammed the medallion against his chest and clicked on the interference device.

A bright light burst forth from his chest, blinding her as she flew upward. Her shoulder caught a bedpost and she slammed down hard, falling off the bed onto the floor.

The room went dark.

"What's going on?" "We are free!" "Oh thank the gods!" "Someone stop her!"

The last voice jerked Kyla awake. The room was dimly lit. She picked herself up off the floor, battered and bruised, but nothing seemed broken —

She stepped back in horror at Alton's body, the blackened shape of an arrow on his chest. His eyes were wide open, but there was no pulse, no movement.

The dendrilite no longer pulsed from the bed.

"Listen to me!" she called out, as she pulled her jumpsuit back on and zipped the front. *"I know some are*

loyal to Alton as Supreme One. We have to stop the attack on Balec!"

She reached out, and the ship responded, showing her the way to the bridge. She connected to the shipwide comm system. "Carmen! Laina!"

"Yes?" "How?" "Where are you?"

"I'm on my way to the bridge. Alton's dead. Carmen, grab our weapons." She easily found the holoscreens in both their rooms through the map in her mind. "Here's the pathway to the bridge," she said, sending it to their room comms. "Follow the dendrilite glow."

The confidence she'd felt since she bravely walked into Alton's room surged. There was so much she could see and do now. She was connected to everything, and it was so complex yet so simple. She knew every aspect of the ship, every system, instantly. She could help them. She could lead them.

Kyla reached the bridge, and the door opened. Two engineers held a third in a headlock. One of the navigators swung his arm at the other. Two other crewmembers seemed to be trying to turn off each other's console stations with their minds.

"Enough!" she said verbally, right as Carmen and Laina entered the bridge. Carmen tossed her own Bara Sharpshooter and Kyla caught it easily with her augmented hand, raising it right to eye level. "I'm pretty sure whatever lock Alton had on our weapons is down and I'd rather not put bullets through you. I'd rather tell you that you are free again."

A navigator lunged for Laina. Kyla didn't flinch, her pistol firing the moment she thought it. Carmen shot the engineer that moved toward them.

The remaining crew on the bridge froze.

"I know there is chaos right now. I do not wish to kill you, but we must stop this attack."

"Princess Kyla," the Mode with the red-light eye said verbally to her, standing at a console. "You have freed us. We are in your debt. We are receiving confusing communications from the other ships. No one knows what to do."

Kyla walked over to Alton's chair and sat down, shifting her pistol to her other hand and placing her augmented palm on the chair's arm. Immediately, the cool dendrilite connections flowed into her veins. It felt like her body was here, but an arm was at another world in Bara, where there were mining ships, and her foot was on the other side of Balec in orbit, having hacked through the firewall and waiting for the signal to take down Balec's orbital defenses.

"Hold your position," she communicated to the other ships. *"Do not proceed. I will explain everything in a minute."*

She had no idea if they would obey her or not. She did not know how to control, only how to communicate the desire in her for peace.

Kyla hoped it was enough.

"Put Balec on screen."

The ship obeyed, bringing up an image of the blue-green orb that Kyla had seen before on Armas's screens the few times he worked from her apartment. It was a beautiful planet, considered the jewel of the Bara system.

"Open communication with the majority ruling Leki royal family," she commanded.

Their hail was responded to by a short, stocky man, visibly shaken. He wore a white silk uniform with a blue wave pendant and several ribbons on his chest.

"Who — who is this?" he asked, seeming to forget all protocol.

"I am Princess Kyla Kishrah of the Nacaen Group. I have assumed command of the Modes Fleet, temporarily. I don't know how long I will be able to hold them."

"Princess," the Mode with the red-light eye said, "Their orbital weapons are targeting our ships."

Kyla sensed the tension within the entire fleet. *"Hold for now. Please,"* she added.

The weapons on board the other ships did not fire.

"We're withdrawing our assault. I beg of you, please do not fire on us. I know you have nothing to go on but my word. We've taken down your defenses, but we are not firing." She turned to the Mode with the red light. "Retreat from their defense systems. Show them we are telling the truth."

The Leki man conferred with another off-screen before returning. "Princess Kyla, we are ... surprised."

"Yeah, I've changed my hair," she said, relief washing over her. She could sense from the other Modes on the bridge that the orbital defense weapons of Balec were powering down.

He bowed to the screen. "I am Crown Prince Zik Lagan."

"I know my father has dealt with you in the past. I believe a Captain Laban Carmel is in your employment."

The crown prince scratched his head. "Princess, Captain Laban is dead — he died two days ago, aboard a ship he was inspecting that was hijacked — by the King's Advocate."

Kyla's mouth dropped open.

The mode with the red-light eye — *Farra is her name,* somehow Kyla knew — sensed her shock.

"The other ships are standing by."

Kyla closed her mouth, straightening in the chair. "Why would he steal a ship?"

The crown prince's face turned red. "I ordered a shipment of Airysan mechs to arrive to defend our world. Laban told us the Nacaen Elder Council would not support Saul engaging in another war, but I was afraid he would find a way."

He almost did — by framing the Leki and trying to kill Armas.

"The Advocate stole the mechs?"

"He and his fighters took over the ship, sent back the remaining crew with Captain Laban's body. His message conveyed sorrow in leaving us defenseless, but that he was taking our mechs to Melas, because they were about to be attacked."

"From who?"

"The Phenians."

PART FOUR

THIRTY-FOUR

JON

The Phenians had been waiting for this, plotting for a long time. In Horeb's grand orbit around the Cana star, they were at the point when ships leaving Ilistia and Gerar in the Bara System had the shortest distance to cross interstellar space, lining up with Melas perfectly.

Jon knew if Armas hadn't been caught up in all of Saul's plots trying to kill him, the Advocate might have discerned the possibility, warned Saul, and they would've been prepared. He was smart like that. Smart and amazing.

The prince knew he would probably never see him again.

Four days after the word had come to Major Ngo of the Phenian advance, Jon sat in his bedroom in Glia. The order had been given for all available mech fighters to head to the mech hanger before sunset. All mech techs were working overtime, patching up any old Liphes suit they could find and prepping the few Airysan suits they still had for battle. Major Barish was leading four squadrons of Bluehawks, made up of Sime'ee, Jamin and Ildan pilots, to try to take out the bombers before they reached the city perimeter. Saul ordered the civilian evacuation of Glia and other cities, including New Ephra in Dahan land. Armas's family farm was near there. Thousands of people — in transports, cargo ships, even Dahan cattle haulers — left for Richo and Samar.

The five Aurora-class warships from Nidos were in Horeb's rings, crewed mostly by Lubez personnel, to take out the Phenian assault ships before they reached Melas or decided to change tactics and go after Richo or Samar. Nidos was on the other side of Cana; perhaps the Phenians would spare that world this time.

But the Phenians had never brought their entire force before. They'd come to wipe out Glia once and for all.

The alert came again on his personal comm: "All mech fighters are to report to the mech hangar immediately for deployment."

He shut the alert off and turned his comm to record.

"Armas, there's so much I want to say to you, but I don't have time. Saul sent Kyla to the Modes. Abe said she's remaining on board with their Supreme One, Alton. I haven't been able to contact her. The Phenians are here — I've got to go suit up. I don't know if we'll make it through the night." He sighed. "If I could say anything to you, it's this: You have my heart. My soul belongs to you. You mean everything to me."

He raked his fingers through his hair. "Also, I want you to know I have a son. His name is Seth. His mother is Sharda Ley; you may remember me talking about her. She lives on Richo among the Dagael. She doesn't want anything. I haven't told Saul — you know how complicated that is." He laughed. "Complicated is one way to say it, given how he's tried to kill you. But I wanted someone to know. I wanted *you* to know."

His comm beeped again with the action stations alert. "I have to go. I love you, more than I can ever say."

Jon ended the vid, rushing out the door and down the marble stairs of the palace. He ran down the familiar corridors, the ramp near Saul's Situation Room that led down to the lower decks. Ten weeks ago, he raced there to get the force shield down so Armas could escape. Now he prayed to God it would hold.

Others were still running to the hangar, though most of the mechs had marched out the open door to the south. Jon's black mech was next to his father's dark gray, the metal gleaming in the hangar lights. He pulled on the armored bodysuit that hung with his gear, fastened his boots and helmet, and climbed inside. Immediately he was connected to his fellow mech fighters.

All seventy-three that were left.

Forty-five were seasoned mech fighters. Twenty-eight were various soldiers, old militia guard, and even a few mech techs who volunteered to be trained in the last forty-eight hours.

Jon shoved aside his anger. He didn't fault Armas, but Major Zeru's resignation made him bristle, even if the consequences were unintentional with all the Dahan mech units defecting.

She'd left them vulnerable.

His father was among the last to arrive, accompanied by Abe. Abe helped him into his bodysuit armor — what was once Armas's job — and he climbed into his mech, replaced after the battle of Zek with a newer Airysan model, but the same electromagnetic sword on his back lit up against the dark steel. Abe then powered up his dark green mech.

"All units. The Phenians are upon us," his father said over the comm. "There is but one mission: protect Glia. The force shield is strong. We will protect her perimeter.

"Make no mistake: the Phenians are coming to destroy us. They tried to take Zek from us and our Bluehawks on the Sim'ee continent. They tried to take the shipyards from Nidos, even had some of the Tali sympathize with them. They know we are weak right now. I've sent out a plea to those who have rebelled to return. I do not know if they will answer.

"You may be what stands between the Phenians and any future for all our people. Fight for your life, because under Phenian rule, we will be lost. One God, one system, one people. That is who we are. Don't fight for me. Fight for each other. Fight for yourselves. Fight with your life!"

If only you'd given that speech before, Jon thought, *maybe we could've held it together.* Too late to think that now.

Jon followed the mechs charging out from the hangar. Twilight had fallen, the edge of Horeb lit up in a thin arc across the sky, the rings visible tonight.

To the west, dark shapes appeared in the sky.

The Phenian mechs descended from their drop ships, the dark orange paint gleaming in the dim light like blood dribbling from the sky. Phenians didn't have fighter ships like Bluehawks, only bombers that Jon recognized from their oval outline. "Dusted ash. Gray Wolf, the bombers are behind the mechs."

"Copy, Dark Wolf. Glia's defense cannons are on them. Focus on the mechs," his father ordered.

"They're firing," Abe called out.

Proton rifle fire peppered the ground nearby. A dark green mech fell to his right, blasted in the arm by cannon fire. Jon opened the arms of his mech and fired back, taking out one.

"What's the report?" he called out.

"Ninety-nine mechs," Barish chimed in from his Bluehawk. "Seventeen bombers. Gray Wolf, some have diverted south, and we are not chasing them. Repeat: we are not chasing the ones south."

"Affirmative," Saul grunted.

Which meant Dahan land. Jon prayed they'd evacuated. Even if they hadn't left for Richo, there were bunkers in the southwest mountains. They'd survived previous wars before. They *had* to survive now.

"Enemy mechs coming through," Abe called, and Jon saw the eerie green gleam of his father's sword not far to his left.

"Take them down," Saul called, leading the charge. Jon yelled and followed, blasting with his shoulder cannons. Two more fell while he followed after his father. The Phenians were not as well trained as the Nacaens, but there were more of them. In the long run, Saul's forces were far outgunned.

In the corner of his screen Jon saw the oval shape blip through Barish's forces above him. "Bomber at the perimeter!"

The blast shook Jon to his knees, but he held on. His

father hadn't wavered at all, continuing to slice through energy shields and mow down the Phenians in front of him. Five, six, seven.

"Force shield is holding," Abe called out.

An orange light flitted at Jon's side. He leaped out of the way, just in time as an electromagnetic sword swung through the air.

"Thought my dad was the only one," Jon muttered as he fired back at the mech, then kicked as his cannon reloaded, knocking it away.

"Gray Wolf," Barish called out on the comm. "Scanners from the *Firedawn* are picking up Phenian assault ships. Heat signatures suggest baratanium warheads."

Dusted ash. Baratanium was made in the Bara System and had been used in previous wars on Dahan land. The half-life was so short it cleared out quickly. Nice way to take out your enemy and take the land for yourself if you were willing to wait a couple of years.

"How many?"

"Eight. Six heading our way, two toward Nidos. The *Firedawn*, *Starhawk*, and *Sinai* are intercepting. The *Galilee* is holding position near Richo. *Shiloh* has lost navs."

Stardust. They'd pulled the *Shiloh* from the construction dock on Nidos before she was completed.

They were going to lose the shipyards at Nidos. Worse, the solar shields. An environmental disaster of mass proportions. But Jon couldn't focus on that now. He could only try to save Glia behind him.

Barish and his Bluehawks managed to take out three bombers before they reached Glia. Two others broke through, but the force shields held. Instead, they were losing mechs left and right.

Hours passed but the Phenians kept coming. Horeb slipped over the horizon, the darkness pierced by yellow cannon fire. Bursts of red light filled the sky as the force shield over Glia was struck, and the gleam of electromagnetic swords of every color crashed against energy shields on the battlefield. Every now and then Jon checked the screen for flashes of green light, the knowledge his father was still alive by the light of his sword. Jon had used up two-thirds of his proton rifle rounds, falling back to the perimeter of Glia with the others. A fiery crash plumed to the west, the result of Barish and the thirty-nine remaining Bluehawks who'd managed to take out three more bombers.

But the Phenians were relentless, and the bombers kept coming. A yellow flash to Jon's right half-blinded him.

"Perimeter breached. Force shield is at critical," Abe called out.

Jon knew going into this battle that things were bad, but he hadn't felt hopeless until the shields over the city spiraled red and then vanished.

"The force shield is down. Repeat: the force shield is down."

Jon fired at the Phenian mech in front of him with his shoulder cannons and grabbed another on his left, thrusting the mech to the ground and jamming the blade from his mech's elbow into its knee.

Bombs began raining down on the fortress walls in flashes of white and yellow.

"Fall back to the East Gate," his father ordered, meaning only one thing: things were so bad they were protecting the last evacuation route out of Glia. Bad enough his father had given the order himself.

Jon didn't have time to stop and mourn that his city was about to burn. Instead, he fought like hell.

"We've got incoming ships," Major Barish called out.

"More Phenians?" Abe swore. "We're done for."

"Wait …" Major Barish broke in. "It can't be! It's Major Zeru!"

"About dusting time," Jon shouted on the comm. "Tell me she brought the mech fighters who left with her."

"Even better," Zeru herself said on the comm, and Jon dared a glance at the camera view above.

A massive beast of a ship loomed overhead, stars winking out as it passed. Dropping from the sky were dozens of dark shadowed mechs. Unpainted, unmarked, they fell until their landing thrusters engaged, and they fired upon the Phenians. At least a dozen carried electromagnetic swords, glowing purple, and they cut through the Phenian lines.

The enemy stopped its advance, confused by the arrival.

Jon broke through the mechs in front of him, using up the last of his proton rifle rounds and switching to his shoulder cannons and blades. The power cells on his unit had been running at maximum, but he pushed forward, thrusting his elbow blade into the neck joint of the mech in front of him. He switched to a private connection with Zeru.

"Is Armas —?"

"He's a few hours behind — some mechanics from the Hessan brought in the Kittiwake and a few Bluehawks. He'll back up Barish."

"Two Phenian warships are heading to Nidos —"

"We got them on our scanners. The *Darkangel* is heading to intercept."

One of the new Airysan mechs under Zeru's command landed near him and tossed him a proton rifle, fully loaded. "Thanks," he said.

"Watch out," Zeru called from above, moving toward him on her thrusters.

Jon turned, catching the Phenian mech's arm before its electromagnetic sword sliced him. He shoved his new rifle into the enemy's chest. "Die, ash-duster."

The blast shoved the enemy backward, but Jon spotted the other mech coming on his right, too late.

He went down on one knee as the proton rifle fire caught the joint of his mech, right where the Airysan steel was the weakest. Jon aimed his rifle, but the enemy grabbed his arm before he could fire. He was tossed in the air, landing hard on his back. He wheezed, the wind knocked out of him, his neck and shoulders throbbing.

The power cells blinked out on his mech. *Dusted ash! I don't have time for this!*

"Zeru I need help!" He rasped on the comm. Panic threaded up his back. He had no feeling below the waist.

She landed twenty meters away, firing at the mech that had attacked him. He tried to reboot his system, but it was no use. Except for life support and comms, he was in a metal can. No weapons.

"Zeru, if I don't get out, give this to Armas," he said, sending the message he recorded the day before.

"Dark Wolf, on your left!"

Jon grunted, managing with the strength he had left to roll his mech, in time for the orange light of the electromagnetic sword to fill his rebooting screen.

THIRTY-FIVE

KYLA

The Modes ship was faster than any she'd known, efficient because of dendrilite. Kyla understood why the use was taboo. She'd never known such incredible power, to move the ship where she wanted it to go, to call upon all the other Modes on board to do what she needed.

It frightened her.

The Modes had started out as pirates, modifying their bodies and using dendrilite for interfacing with the ship, but only Alton used it to control others when he came to power. With Alton gone, Kyla left the other ships and their crews to make their own decisions. Most returned to the worlds they were colonizing in Bara. One was still debating among themselves whether to stay or return to the Near Side systems.

Everyone left on the dreadnought chose to go with Kyla, to help her as she had helped them.

"Princess Kyla," Farra, the mode with the red-light eye, said as they approached the Cana star, "The ships are divided."

Kyla brought up the screen, and with the help of navigators interfacing with her, discerned that most of the Phenian forces had attacked Melas. "My Goddesses," she breathed, as the ship's scanners showed the debris field growing in Horeb's moons. Busted fighters, broken bombers, cargo and transport ships caught in the crossfire.

"The Nacaen warships are split: three defending Melas, one defending Richo, another at Nidos." Farra paused, sadness crossing her expression. "A sixth — the *Shiloh* — has gone down on the southern continent."

Kyla closed her eyes, trying to shut out the emotion. She understood a bit now why Alton desired to control everything. Being able to sense emotions from the other Modes was overwhelming.

Or maybe it was her own sadness that affected Farra. She couldn't tell.

A comforting hand wrapped around her own, and her eyes snapped open. "I'm here," Laina said. "We're with you."

"The *Darkangel* has sent out a distress call," one of her navigators said out loud. "They are defending Nidos from two Phenian assault ships. They have no other fighters to defend them."

Carmen stood by the navigation console. "The *Darkangel* can't hold them much longer. Nidos's shields might fall."

A lump formed in Kyla's throat. She knew Carmen wanted to help their dad defend Melas. Kyla's heart wanted to go there as well. To find Armas, and Jon, and somewhere inside her, she knew she didn't want her father to die.

"Princess," Farra said softly. "You are conflicted."

She shut down her emotions, attempting to block her link to Farra and the other Modes. She couldn't allow her own personal desires to interfere with the mission at hand. "No. We must go to Nidos and defend the people there. If we don't, they'll die."

The dreadnought swung around the far side of Cana, to where Nidos gleamed in Cana's brightness. Above the orbital shields, sharp flashes of yellow and white: torpedoes and cannon fire.

She didn't have to give the command. The dreadnought moved with her thoughts, shields configuring to confuse the scanners of both the Phenian ships and the *Darkangel,* knowing the Nacaens might fire on them. As soon as they were in range, Kyla gave the order: "Hack into the Phenian shields."

Farra and others on the bridge worked to bring the shields down, but Kyla's own interface sensed distress aboard the *Darkangel.* Traveling across the distance, she could see the navigation system failing, and their shields at sixty percent.

"Is it possible to strengthen the *Darkangel*?"

Farra tilted her head. "We've never hacked into a ship to *help* it, but it's possible."

Kyla closed her eyes. "Their drive core is overheating. We need to get in and shut it down."

"We're trying," Farra said. "Trying to access three ships at once is beyond our usual capability —"

"Do it."

Farra nodded. "Breaching the *Darkangel's* firewall,

and —"

A bright flash of gold and yellow filled the screen in front of them.

"What *happened*?" she screamed.

"Direct hit," Farra said, a tear emerging from her clear eye. "We — we didn't move fast enough to stop it."

It was there, right in her mind like a blueprint. They'd found a way through the firewall, found the shield generating systems. They'd attempted to divert power, but in the microsecond the firewall was down, the Phenians had fired at the same time. It was bad luck.

The *Darkangel* was gone.

Kyla's anger surged through her veins, through the dendrilite in the ship, as she saw right through the firewall on both Phenian ships. *I need more power.* She pulled from every centimeter of dendrilite on the ship, but it wasn't enough.

I need more.

Farra snapped her attention to Kyla.

"Princess, no!"

Kyla found the connections, the veins in each person on board she could connect to and pulled hard.

"FIRE!"

Kyla's arms ached, as if it were her own arms that released the ship's full capacity of cannon fire toward the enemy. Blasts that tore through the hulls of Phenian ships and emptied decks of personnel into space. Bulkheads pulled apart, steel turning to dust, as the screen lit up in blue light.

Strong arms pulled her out from the chair, snapping her attention to the bridge. "Stop this, Kyla! Stop it now!" Carmen held her wrists, pinning her. Two of the Modes at the weapons consoles collapsed onto the floor. Laina clutched the console, as if she was fainting.

Kyla could barely breathe.

"What happened?"

"You drained them," Farra said, her voice quiet. "Like Alton used to."

"I — I don't understand. I was just firing on ... oh Tana."

The enormity of what she had done brought her to her knees. She never doubted the need of the enemy to be stopped. She did what she had to do. Same as when she shot the Mode who attacked Laina. Same as when she killed Alton with Tana's Arrow.

It had to be done. It all had to be done.

But the cost of destroying the Phenians was not something she'd considered. She'd just — done it. Like Alton did.

Her head cleared, now that she was away from the chair. Carmen had her pinned against their chest. "I've got you," the lieutenant whispered into her ear.

The two Modes began to stir on the floor.

Tears overtook the princess. Carmen lifted her in their arms, hugging her close. "It's okay. You saved us. You saved Nidos."

"Laina —"

Carmen released Kyla as Laina rubbed Kyla's shoulder. "I'm okay. You just started to reach me and stopped. You didn't hurt me."

The princess threw her arms around Laina. "I'm so sorry."

Farra and the other Modes on the bridge helped the two who'd collapsed into chairs. "Princess," Farra said after returning to her console, "the orbital shields are intact. The shipyards suffered minimal damage. No large debris is entering Nidos's orbit."

"Thank the Goddesses." She wiped her face, glancing at the center chair, the dendrilite woven all around it. She would not sit in the chair again. She dared not reach out, at least, not now, for she did not wish to accidentally draw on their power. Instead, she turned from Carmen and Laina, facing the rest of the Modes.

She thought of her father, Jon, and Armas — it wouldn't be long before she'd see him again. She wondered how he'd react to the sight of her. She knew when she explained why, he'd understand. So much of war had changed her, but she was still Kyla, his wife. And whatever struggles they'd had before, if they both survived this war, they could survive anything.

"Any status report from the rest of the fleet?"

"The weapons fire has ceased. It appears the Phenian assault ships were completely destroyed."

She glanced at Carmen, noting her friend's relief, but also understood they wanted to make sure their father, Major Barish, was safe.

"Farra — all of you. We owe you our lives." She could sense Farra's hesitation, and she raised her hand. "I may have helped free you from Alton, but you have saved me from becoming him. I have one last thing I wish of you, before you decide to go wherever you wish to go next.

"Take us to Ramah."

THIRTY-SIX

ARMAS

Armas couldn't see through the billowing smoke as dawn broke over Melas. A quarter of Glia was on fire, the shields having fallen before they arrived. He'd arrived late to the battle and stayed in the skies to help Barish.

The Kittiwake wasn't nearly as fast as the Bluehawks, but the maneuverability was still spectacular. The mechanics on Nidos had refitted the old flyer with ion bombs and he, along with the fighters who returned with him, reinforced Barish and took out the remaining bombers.

The universal comm was full of celebratory chatter so he switched to a private comm with Barish.

"Skies are clear, White Lion," he said to Barish.

"Affirmative, Red Lion. The *Sinai* is in pursuit of the

remaining Phenian assault ships.”

Armas let out a whoop and pounded the top of his cockpit.

“Glad you came home, and just in time.”

“What's our status report?” He wasn't sure where he stood in terms of chain of command.

Barish didn't seem to care, taking a more concerning tone. “Major Ngo reports *The Shiloh* went down on Richo. The warship lost navs, crew overcorrected, and it entered atmo. Went down somewhere on the southern continent. Civilian casualties reported.”

“Stardust. What about the base?”

“They're fine. Ngo reports no losses there.”

Thank God.

Through the smoke and wreckage, Armas spotted the new Airysan mechs among the colorful older Nacaen machines. There were a handful of Phenian survivors, outside of their mechs, being rounded up by the Nacaens.

He scanned the battlefield for Jon's black mech, probably hidden among the other dark Airysan steel mechs, and switched back to the universal channel. “Dark Wolf, do you copy?”

There was no response.

“Gray Wolf, please respond,” he called, knowing there was still a score to settle with Saul when this was done. “Pale Wolf,” he called to Abe.

“Red Lion,” Seriah said, her voice shaky. “Get down here. East Gate.”

“Affirmative.” He pushed the stick forward, flying directly toward the smoldering city wall, setting down where he could find a clear spot. Wreckage from mechs lay strewn all around.

Fear crawled up his spine. He popped the hatch and

tore off his helmet. Immediately his lungs burned from the smoke, but he didn't care. He tossed the rope ladder out of his cockpit and climbed down.

"Seriah, where are you?" he called out on his handheld comm.

"North of the East Gate."

Armas ran, skirting the wreckage. Nacaen mechs, both new and old, pushed debris out from the East Gate. Some fighters had exited their machines, pulling helmets off, hugging one another and cheering.

He found Seriah's mech signal a hundred meters north. As he drew closer, he spotted Saul out of his mech, kneeling on the ground, while others stood at a distance.

"Where's Jon —?"

Jon's body lay at an unnatural angle, his head in Saul's lap.

The world began to spin.

Seriah had climbed out of her mech and caught his arm. "My Lord," she muttered, but he pulled away, falling to his knees.

Dirt streaked across Jon's beautiful face. His eyes were closed, but Armas pictured them, shining emeralds in the light. Saul gave him only a brief glance before carefully lifting Jon's head and allowing Armas to cradle him in his arms.

"My love, please, wake up."

Tears began streaming down his face. He didn't care what anyone saw, what they thought.

"Jon, please, you have to wake up."

His fingers found Jon's wrist, but there was no pulse. He pressed his ear to Jon's chest.

The prince had fallen.

Armas's whole body shook, sobs overtaking him as he held Jon to his chest. "My love!"

A hand gripped Armas's shoulder. "My Lord," Seriah whispered.

He shrugged her off.

She leaned close to his ear. "Now is your chance."

Saul sat on the ground, his hands in his lap. He stared at his son's body.

Armas caught a glimpse of the weapon in Seriah's hand, the Ember 75 pistol she carried. "I'll take care of it," she said.

He ignored her, placing his palm on Jon's cheek. *God, this cannot be. He can't be dead. God, please, I'll do anything, just bring him back to me.* "Bring him back to me," he muttered out loud, laying Jon on the ground, raising his hands to the sky.

Seriah stood, stepping around him, gun in hand.

"Bring him back to me," he said again, wiping his tears.

The former major shifted, and her words echoed in his ear: "*I'll take care of it. I'll take care of it. I'll take care of it …*"

His head snapped up.

"Seriah, no!"

She raised her weapon. Saul stared at her, blinking.

"For the true king," she whispered.

Armas rushed her, knocking her to the ground. He pried the gun away from her grasp and tossed it aside. She kneed him in the groin, flipping him over to his back.

"What are you doing?" Seriah shouted. "We *had* him. *This* is the time to end it. You are the true king."

He tried to escape her grip, but she pinned his wrists above his head.

"How many times has he tried to kill you?" she said through gritted teeth. "Don't let him get away with this. It doesn't matter how you felt about Jon — this is the man responsible for all of this. Responsible for Jon's death!"

"She's right," Saul said, jerking Armas's attention. The king had risen, stepping around his son's body, moving toward Seriah's pistol that lay on the ground. He knelt, picking up the Ember 75.

Seriah let Armas go. He scrambled to his feet. "My king." His chest pounded so fast it hurt. "We don't have to do this. We can rebuild. We can start over."

Saul nodded, surprising Armas. "You do the rebuilding. I have nothing left." He glanced down at Jon's body once more, then raised the pistol to his own head and pulled the trigger.

THIRTY-SEVEN

ARMAS

Armas sat on the stone bench in the courtyard. Nearby, most of the arches that ran from what was once Kyla's bedroom above remained standing, but the walls behind him were shattered, the Great Hall collapsed.

"My Lord," Seriah said, approaching slowly.

He lifted his gaze, acknowledging her presence, ignoring the strange formality she was using with him.

"Major Barish reports the skies are clear of Phenians. We are still sorting through the scanner data on Nidos." She let out a breath. "All the enemy assault ships were destroyed, but along with the *Shiloh*, we lost the *Darkangel*."

Armas rested his elbows on his knees, hands clasped together, pressing his forehead into them.

"Major Ngo is leading a search and rescue on Richo from where the *Shiloh* went down, but we don't expect to find many survivors. Samar is the only world to report no casualties."

Seriah cleared her throat, continuing. "There's no sign of Abe Renk. His mech is out there with the others, but it doesn't appear to be fatally damaged. A number of Jamin mech fighters and Bluehawk pilots are also reported missing. Do you want me to order a search?"

He ignored the question with one of his own. "Did Jon say anything to you, before he fell?"

Seriah pursed her lips. "No, my Lord."

"Are their bodies taken care of?"

"We've moved them to the morgue, along with others. Most of the underground levels are still intact, including the med bays. But my Lord," she added, again being more formal than he was used to, "we need to pursue Renk. With Saul and Jon dead ... he may be making a claim for the throne as the surviving member of the royal family."

At that, Armas sat up straight on the bench. "Kyla is still alive. Find out where Saul evacuated her to."

Seriah shifted her weight on her feet. "My Lord ... Armas. She was sent to the Modes."

"What?" He stood, brows drawn together. "When?"

"When Saul sent his delegation, he sent Abe Renk and Lieutenant Barish, along with the princess and her maid. Renk returned alone."

"Contact Major Barish and ask if he's heard from Carmen."

"My Lord, I believe we ought to move quickly, to crown you as king, in case Renk tries to establish himself."

Armas closed his eyes. He'd started to imagine himself as king, but in those fantasies, it was Jon by his side.

"Very well."

"Armas ... I think you should do so with Abby as your wife."

His eyes narrowed.

"When Saul sent Kyla away, he made it very clear your marriage was ended. She was sent to become the wife of Alton of Gallim. This was reported at the last meeting of the Elder Council. I wasn't there, of course — I resigned, and Saul replaced me with Dege Edmon, the betrayer. I heard this later."

Armas dragged his hand down the side of his face. "Why didn't you tell me this before?"

"Because I feared you would want to chase her down, and we couldn't afford to do that. We *needed* you. We wouldn't have defeated the Phenians without you. The people — *your* people — love you." Seriah stood in front of him and placed her hands on his shoulders. "Take the throne, now. Marry Abby so the people are assured a possibility of heirs. You said right before Saul died that we could rebuild. It's time to build, now, before the foundation becomes too fragile."

Armas's chest hurt. He didn't know what to say, how Seriah had kept from him Kyla's whereabouts or Saul's schemes. All he wanted was to hold Jon one more time.

But what he wanted was impossible.

"All right."

She clapped his shoulder. "I'll have them clear the rubble from the Great Hall —"

"No. We'll go south." He waved his hand toward the ruins of Glia. "Saul was right. We can't rebuild. We must build something new." Armas gazed back at her. "We'll go home, to Dahan land, and build there."

She straightened her back, a smile creeping across her face. "As you wish." She turned on her heel.

"Seriah?"

She glanced back, raising a brow.

"You will be my general, commander of the Nacaen Military. Use that authority wisely."

She bowed. "Your Majesty," she added, acknowledging his kingship, "it is my honor to serve you."

THIRTY-EIGHT

KYLA

The dreadnought contained two small shuttles in the aft section, sleek and made of the same dark metal as the large ship. Inside were chairs and consoles but with more hard-wired lighting than the dreadnought and minimal dendrilite. Farra, Laina, and Kyla were in one; Carmen and two other Modes piloted the other.

"Before Alton, we were sparing with our use of neurolink silk, only using it for our augments and very little for ship processing. That all changed, of course," Farra said as they left the dreadnought, hanging in orbit far from Ramah.

"Because of Ogroma," Kyla assumed.

Farra nodded. "Alton was the one who insisted the interlinking would not only be safe but would advance us all. When their minds developed and they wanted to leave us, he was furious. But he was not the Supreme One, then. Most voices consented to their choice." She paused, adjusting the trajectory of the shuttle to line up with the small canyon on Ramah. "After Ogroma was defeated, some questioned whether interlinking our minds was harmful. He became relentless in his pursuit of power. Despite our conviction as Modes that consent matters, he found ways of bending others' wills to his own. The only way to do that —"

"Was to consume more dendrilite," Kyla finished for her.

The landing bay doors opened at the end of the sharp canyon. The two shuttles landed inside. Carmen exited the other shuttle, meeting her as they descended the small steps from the shuttle doors. "Your father had the Tana priests rounded up. He took the head priest back to Richo. I don't know what he did with the others."

"Not all of us were taken."

Kyla wheeled. A priest stood before them in the dim light, having spoken in her mind.

"Yes, we, too, know our minds are linked. The Modes corrupted what we call sacred."

"We're not here to take from you," Kyla said, holding her hands up. "We have come here so that our sibling Modes might learn Tana's ways."

The priest arched an eyebrow. Dendrilite ran along her arms, a small star above her eye. "The Modes have used our dendrilite to control machines, to even become more machine than human. That is not our Warrior Way. Tana calls us to become more connected with one another, to understand our indwelling."

Farra glanced at Kyla, before turning to the priest. "We have heard the stories of Tana, and we wish to join her Way. She told us about the font." Laina had explained it earlier, and Carmen shared what they had learned when they came here with the king beforehand.

The priest smiled. "Come, then, and drink of the font, and behold what vision She desires for you."

The priest led them through the tunnels. "Did any others survive?" Carmen asked the priest quietly.

"We always have places to hide in our mother's womb," the priest said. "However, the body of our sister priest was returned to us, recently, by soldiers from Richo." She gently laid her hand on Carmen's shoulder. When she did so, Kyla could sense through the priest the guilt and sorrow on Carmen's heart.

"They feel they should've stopped the king. That their father could've done something more," the priest told Kyla.

The princess's eyes snapped open. Carmen had said little about their time on Ramah before and had never said anything to question Major Barish's judgment. The lieutenant also didn't have any dendrilite that Kyla knew of.

"You have this capability, too. You do not need the augments to feel what another does. The dendrilite simply amplifies another's thoughts when you touch them."

Kyla stole a sideways glance at Laina. Perhaps that was why the maid had always known her moods, seemed to be able to guess what was on her mind — her tattoo.

The group made their way through the passages until they reached the well. "The font will give you a vision from Warrior Tana. For the one without dendrilite," she paused, glancing at Carmen, "the vision may be surprising. For those who do, it will confirm something you already know."

The priest turned to Farra. "Do you wish to drink of the font?"

"I do."

The Mode that Kyla had come to see as her friend went forward, knelt, and drank. She grasped the side of the font, and Laina went to her side to hold her. "I see a world, no longer stripped of metal and materials, but formed and shaped to sustain life. I see our new home world in Bara."

The other Modes went forward and beheld similar visions. Laina drank next. "I see my family on Nidos. They are safe, alive."

Kyla motioned to Carmen to take the next drink, and both she and Laina stood by their side, for Carmen had told them how Saul fainted after he drank.

Carmen touched the water to their lips. Their eyes rolled back, but they didn't lose their grip on the side of the font. They trembled.

"What is it?" Kyla whispered.

Carmen leaned close to the princess. "The path I have walked in my father's footsteps comes to an end with you."

Kyla shook her head. "I don't know what that means."

"It means my father has made a choice I cannot follow."

Once Carmen assured her that they were fine, Kyla stood at the edge of the water, the dendrilite fused at the bottom of the cistern. She noted the artwork and writings that Carmen had described before they came here.

"It will be all right," the priest assured her. *"You already know what Tana will tell you."*

The princess had known this, since her wedding night. She touched the water, and it rippled, like the train of her wedding dress. The moment she betrayed her father to help Armas escape. The moment she told Jon to go after Armas.

She cupped her hand, and remembered how her father threw her into prison, then married her off to Alton. He'd tried to take fate into his own hands.

She brought the water to her lips, remembering how her father revealed to everyone that Jon had killed Raimi to save Armas.

She saw her brother's body, her father's hand on the gun.

In the end they'd all sacrificed themselves to save Armas, to give him a future. Even her father. She saw herself weeping before Armas, for all the loss. He wore a crown on his brow. She didn't understand.

They made their way back to the shuttle, the Modes sometimes talking out loud, sometimes through their connections, about their hopes and dreams for their new home worlds and the shrine they planned to build for Tana there.

Kyla tried to pay attention to their words, both spoken aloud and in their minds, but all she could see was her brother and father on a battlefield, dead. She was certain there was more to the vision of Armas wearing a crown, but Carmen had caught her before she fainted, and the vision had escaped.

She'd seen enough. Still, she hadn't told them, and the priest did not reveal it.

The Modes chattered excitedly about their vision, and how ready they were to embrace Tana as their goddess, after Alton's Everlasting God failed them. Farra told Kyla they had plans to dismantle the command chair and Alton's bedroom, to repurpose the dendrilite for those who wished to join them, but not for control.

"What will you do with his body?" Kyla asked.

"We will bury him on our world but not mourn him." Farra turned to Laina. "We will retrieve Tana's Arrow to return to you."

"Keep it," Laina said, offering a smile. "May it be a reminder that evil can always be overcome."

"You will return to your home?" one of the Modes asked Kyla.

"Yes, once we have contacted the ... king." She was certain now that Armas had assumed the throne.

The priest stopped at the door to the shuttle bay. "Someone else has arrived."

Confusion ran through the shared connection of the Modes. "We did not sense anyone."

"We use signal disrupters, so that our priests remained safe during the killer king's reign," the priest muttered.

Kyla pushed by the priest, and gasped.

Four Bluehawks and two transport shuttles had landed, filling half the landing bay. Kyla didn't even need her dendrilite to know it was her great-uncle exiting the fighter.

"Princess Kyla," he said, before taking a knee. "No, you are now Queen. All hail Queen Kyla!"

The other Jamin soldiers followed suit.

"What do they mean?" Carmen asked Kyla.

"My vision is true. It means my father and brother are dead."

THIRTY-NINE

ARMAS

The coronation took place outside, in the copse of tall needle trees where Armas's great-grandparents were married, and beyond in the fields, soldiers of all nations except the Jamin were present. Dahan was not spared from the bombing, but Armas's family farm was intact. He knelt on a rug woven by the Ildan as a gift and wore a new dress uniform: all black. Pinned to the left side of his chest was a woven circle entwining all twelve primary colors of the Nacaen nations. Armas had it commissioned, using it as a new symbol of how the nations needed each other, and were one.

"You have been chosen by the people of Dahan, chosen by the Nacaens, and chosen by God, through God's prophet Zam, to rule as Advocate and King," the new prophet said, placing the golden crown upon Armas's fiery locks. Seriah — General Zeru — had found Nate, who agreed to serve the new king as the religious leader for the Nacaens. The new prophet wore forest green, like the leaves of the trees around them, instead of the brown robes the old priests wore.

The prayers were spoken, the vows said, and Armas rose to shouts of acclamation and praise. Bluehawks streaked above the sky, led by Major Barish, to commemorate the celebration.

The moment the official benediction was given, Abby, wearing a black dress and a pendant similar to his circle pin, walked over to him and pulled him aside. They'd been married the night before by Nate, and Abby given the official title of consort.

"I took a test this morning and confirmed it," she said, grinning.

Armas's jaw dropped. "Really? I — wow."

"I know. I wanted to tell you but thought 'wait, he might have enough on his mind having just gotten married and now crowned King of the Nacaens.'" She kissed his cheek. "Are you happy?"

"Of course I am," he said, though his insides were squirming. Fatherhood had been the furthest thing from his mind until Abby started getting sick on recent mornings. He'd hoped it was just a virus.

I'm not ready, God. Not for the crown, not for a new marriage, certainly not to be a father.

But he smiled for Abby, pushing his own unease aside that he barely knew her. When she'd questioned why Nate called her consort instead of queen, he'd explained that because she wasn't from a royal family or national Elder, she couldn't have the title.

Not because Major Barish had reminded him in private the other day that he was still married to Kyla, who was still alive as far as they knew, and that the best way for unity was to find the princess and bring her back, make her queen. "It will appeal to the Jamin, show unity here on Melas, and help bring peace." He knew the major was also worried about his only child, who'd been sent to escort the princess, and had not been heard from since.

He trusted Milo Barish, ever since they planned the Battle of Zek together. And he trusted General Zeru, so when she found him and Abby kissing in the shadows of the trees, and impatiently cleared her throat to get his attention, he knew it was important.

"Excuse me," he said. "Apparently the General needs me."

"But of course, my king," Abby said, offering a curtsey.

He raised a brow as he watched his pregnant wife walk away.

"You really do have a way of charming them," the general muttered, also wearing the new black dress uniform, though she wore a five-pointed leaf, the new symbol for her rank, above the colorful circle emblem of the Nacaens.

"I'm assuming you didn't pull me aside to compliment my swagger." Armas folded his hands.

"No, Your Majesty. It's Renk. The old man sent this out right as the ceremonies started." Seriah pulled out her comm and played a message.

"To our beloved Nacaens, we grieve the death of our beloved King Saul, and his son Prince Jon. Which is why we, the remaining family of Saul Kishrah, were shocked to hear that the Advocate, Armas Lehem-Perez, who betrayed the king, took forces away from us and allowed the Phenians to defeat us. Then he decided to return to play hero and has now been crowned king. This is an outrage, especially when his own wife, Kyla Kishrah, now our beloved Queen, still lives."

The screen panned to Kyla, and Armas gasped. Her hair had been cut short, and there was something odd about her face, though he couldn't quite make it out. *Has she been tortured?*

Seriah paused the video. "He's only showing that side of her face, because we suspect she's been augmented."

"Dusted ash. Alton did that to her. Saul forced her to go to Modes."

"They're at Ramah. And I believe ..." Seriah's voice trailed off.

"What?"

"We now know the same ship brought down both the Phenian assault ships attacking at Nidos and the *Darkangel*. It was the Modes dreadnought. The Modes attacked both of them."

"What are you saying?"

Seriah played the rest of Abe's message. "Before the king died, he sent me and Queen Kyla to the Modes as a delegation. Queen Kyla has confirmed a treaty has been signed with the Modes, establishing peace between our peoples. She herself was aboard the dreadnought when Supreme One Alton died, and the new leader, Farra, has promised peace with our people."

A Mode with a red light for an eye appeared on the screen. "We are glad to establish peace with the Nacaens, and we promise to uphold our end of the treaty. We have disbanded under supremacy and ask for your help in securing peace for our new home world in Bara, as we will not tread into Nacaen space again."

The screen went back to Abe Renk. "For the sake of all Nacaens, we are willing to come to an agreement: accept Kyla Kishrah as queen and me as queen's advisor and pardon all Jamin. The treaty with the Modes will be secure, and there will be lasting peace."

Armas removed his crown and ran his fingers through his hair. "Find her and bring her home."

"She is responsible for the *Darkangel*. For all the lives lost!"

"You don't know that for certain, and you are making dangerous accusations."

"Your Majesty," Seriah said, her voice quiet. "I'd advise that you let me take care of them."

Armas blinked, but Seriah stood, her shoulders back.

"You did not just say what I think you said," he accused, though he was absolutely certain she offered to assassinate his wife and her family. "No," he snapped, stepping closer to Seriah's face. "You are to bring her to me alive, as well as whoever else may be with her. You are never again to suggest such things to me. That is not who I am."

"Of course, Your Majesty," Seriah said, bowing. "I will follow your orders without delay."

She turned to leave, but he caught her arm. "Tell her that when she comes home, we will have a funeral. Mourning in all twelve nations, for both her father and brother."

Armas had delayed the funeral under Seriah's advisement, trusting her judgment that the people needed assurance of a new king first. Now he knew he had to take charge and rule, or others, like General Zeru, would make decisions for him.

FORTY

KYLA

"I never should've let you send that message," Kyla said, as she walked off the transport shuttle in Ramah's landing bay, carrying a bottle of Bara gin she'd found in one of the cupboards. Her great-uncle had Farra assure the Nacaens of peace before they returned to the dreadnought, leaving the Nacaen Group for their new home world. But Abe had recorded his own message without her permission and sent it.

She swallowed down her anger with a shot of gin. Her grief was complicated. Her father had repeatedly harmed her with his choices and by his actions. Jon was the one who persuaded Saul to marry her to Armas, even though he loved him, too. Her chest was hollow. Her brother was gone. Her father had taken his own life. Armas was now king. Deep down, she'd known he'd be a better king than either her father or brother. Jon never wanted it.

It was strange to not be there for the coronation, but she understood the haste. Slimy weasels like Abe would try to worm their way into the gap. If Armas hadn't been crowned king so quickly, she had no doubt Abe would've claimed the throne and told her to leave with the Modes.

"Patience, Queen." Abe followed her off the shuttle. "When they arrive, we'll discuss terms of joint rule —"

"No. No way are you ruling —"

"I didn't mean me, of course, I meant you and Armas. I'll stand back, merely be an advisor."

Kyla crossed her arms. She still wore a black fitted jumpsuit from the Modes, though she wore her Jamin flight jacket over it. She was tired of the staleness of circulated air and longed to be home on a breathable world.

"You'll do no such thing. You and every other man in my life keep making decisions for me. No more! You're done, Abe." She tossed back the rest of her drink and marched over to where Laina and Carmen were talking with the priest.

"What's wrong?" her maid asked, touching Kyla's shoulder.

"My great-uncle has apparently made a deal with Major — General Zeru now — that I'll go back to Melas to be queen with Armas as king, and he'll be an 'advisor.' All other Jamin who fled will be pardoned, and the Jamin will drop their case that Armas has an illegitimate claim to the throne."

"Are we to leave, then?" Carmen asked.

"They're coming here."

The priest pursed her lips. "What will they do about us?"

"I will do everything I can to make sure that Ramah is left undisturbed," Kyla vowed. "The Modes will not come for you. There will be no mining treaties for this moon. I am certain Armas will do this for me."

Carmen's eyebrow arched. They opened their mouth but shut it quickly.

"I will go underground, then, and tell the remaining sisters. We are forever in your debt, Queen Kyla," the priest said, tapping two fingers to her chest. Laina and Carmen responded as well with the gesture, and the priest left them.

Kyla pulled the lieutenant aside. "Something wrong? I —"

She didn't finish asking because the moment she touched Carmen, her dendrilite showed her Carmen's vision. Major Barish stood before Carmen, shouting in anger, as Carmen tore their rank from their flight jacket and marched out the door.

Kyla let go of her arm. "I'm sorry, I didn't mean —"

"You saw, then."

"I didn't see everything. I didn't realize —"

"I wanted you to see," the lieutenant admitted. "Something is about to happen where I will leave my father, but I don't know *why*, except he does something I don't agree with. I thought maybe you would know."

Kyla shook her head, thinking of her own vision, remembering her grief. But at the end of her vision where Armas was crowned king — it wasn't in Glia, that she knew. There was something familiar about the place, but it wasn't the Great Hall.

An alert began to go off on Abe's comm. "Proximity alert. They're here."

The Jamin soldiers, Abe, Kyla, Carmen, and Laina entered the safe chamber on one end, while the landing bay was depressurized, and the doors opened. Two Bluehawks landed, along with a shuttle, a lion painted on the side. Just like her father's old shuttle with the wolf that she used to pilot.

Major Barish climbed out of one of the Bluehawks, wearing his light blue flight suit. He ignored everyone else and ran to Carmen as soon as the landing bay was repressurized, sweeping them up in a hug. "I've missed you so much. I was so worried."

"I missed you too, Dad," Carmen said, holding onto their father.

Kyla worried what was to come for them.

Another pilot Kyla didn't recognize exited the other fighter. The shuttle doors opened, and General Zeru disembarked from the shuttle, wearing a black flight suit and flight jacket with a five-pointed leaf. Zeru's hair was cropped short as usual, so blond it was almost white, striking against their tanned skin.

"Abe Renk," Zeru said, not bothering with his rank, "I am here as agreed to take the princess home."

"You mean *Queen*," Abe sneered. "You will address her properly as royalty."

"As far as the Nacaens are concerned, she is not queen until she has her coronation," Seriah countered, and her tone seemed to indicate an "if."

"General Zeru," Kyla said, snagging Seriah's attention. The general's eyes widened at the sight of her, and Kyla became self-conscious about her augments. She'd become so used to them. Her hair was growing back, but they were still visible. "We accept the terms. Please, escort us home."

Zeru gave a slight bow.

"We do *not* accept," Abe said, pushing himself in front of Kyla. "You have given us no guarantee that we will be included in the Elder Council and other leadership positions. I want my rank and position restored as Jamin Elder."

Seriah folded her arms. "You can object all you want, but as of right now, there is no Elder Council. King Armas is going to do things differently. Abe Renk, you have no position or rank. If your grand-niece wishes to employ you as an advisor, that's up to her, but you are *nothing* to the king."

All of Kyla's anger at Abe, how he hid the agreement with Alton, how he gave her no choice but to go along with it — surged in her veins. She grabbed Abe's neck with her augmented hand. "You are nothing to me, Renk. You have used me as a pawn for your own gain one last time."

Abe clawed at her hand, but the augments enhanced her strength, and she squeezed. "If I let you go, you will do whatever the king has ordered, and you will not be in my presence again."

Abe nodded, unable to speak. His face was turning blue.

Kyla let go, and he fell to the floor.

"General, let us be on our way," Kyla said, passing by Seriah to enter the shuttle, with Laina on her heels.

"You married Dahan scum, you're the dust —"

Kyla spun around as the shot rang out.

Abe lay sprawled on the hangar deck, a gaping wound at his chest. The general held her Ember 75 at eye level for another moment before lowering her weapon.

"No one disrespects the king," the general said quietly.

Kyla slept on the shuttle, having had not much rest the days before. It surprised her when Seriah killed Abe, but she didn't mourn his death. One way or another, he would've tried to disrupt Armas's reign, find ways of trying to manipulate her as Armas's wife.

Wife. Husband. A life she'd longed for.

Had it only been three months since her wedding? She'd lived a lifetime, it seemed.

The shuttle was as spacious as her father's had been. Carmen and Laina sat at one table while Kyla spied breakfast laid out at another — berries with Dahan goat yogurt, Sim'ee pork sausage and a pitcher of currant juice.

"What happened at Nidos?" Seriah asked, sitting down across from her.

"The Phenians were attacking the *Darkangel*. I was on board the Modes dreadnought." She didn't know how much she should share with the general about how much she was involved, how she was able to connect through the dendrilite, pull on the Modes power. She shuddered as she remembered. "The Modes tried to bring down the firewalls of the Phenian assault ships, but the *Darkangel* was failing, shields draining and their reactor too hot. We — *they* tried to hack into the *Darkangel*'s systems to help, but it brought their shields down unexpectedly. At least, that's what we think happened."

"*We.* So you were on the bridge when this happened?"

"Yes."

Seriah crossed her legs, sipping her coffee. "So the Modes just decided to eliminate all threats, then."

"That's *not* what happened," Kyla said, rising to her feet. "We were there to help! When the *Darkangel* exploded, we destroyed the Phenian ships. We broke through their firewalls, and I fired every cannon —"

"So it was you," the general said, taking another sip of her coffee before setting the cup down. "Was this before or after you murdered Alton to gain control?"

"I —"

"General," Carmen interrupted, moving to stand by Kyla. "She saved our lives. If she hadn't killed Alton, he would've wiped out Balec."

Zeru folded her hands. "The king was certain he'd left them defenseless. It seems, then, your actions saved innocent lives."

"Then why are you questioning me like this?"

"Because it's my job, Kyla." The general stood, towering over her and Carmen. Only Laina matched her height. "It's my job to protect our king from any potential threats. This kingdom is walking on eggshells right now. I know you had no love for your great-uncle, but I had to make sure you weren't still somehow working for Saul's schemes." Her eyes narrowed. "And because you have those things on your head, I don't know how much I'll ever be able to trust you."

"General," Carmen began, but Kyla cut them off.

"Lieutenant, it's okay. The General has made her intentions clear, and I respect that. I would remind the General that my *husband* is the one she currently answers to, and that I will be telling him *everything* that happened."

Seriah sat back down and refilled her coffee. "I look forward to hearing your report."

The shuttle pilot called out over his shoulder. "Everyone should buckle in. We have a lot of debris to maneuver around."

Kyla frowned, taking her seat and strapping the belt. "This is all from the battle?"

"Wreckage of more than a dozen Phenian bombers and about half of our Bluehawks," Seriah said, her voice soft.

"It must've been brutal."

"It was." The general bit the corner of her mouth. "We lost a lot of good soldiers that day. Including your brother."

At the mention of Jon, Kyla unbuckled her seat. "I'll return to the private suite," she said, nodding to Laina and Carmen.

"Stay safe," the General said, as Kyla held on to the bulkhead, making her way to the door and shutting it behind her.

She collapsed on the bed, tears overwhelming her. If Jon had lived, she wondered what would happen now. Her father would not have died, and the civil war would've broken wide open. Factions would've continued to form. Perhaps, though, Jon would've thrown his support with Armas. She would've showed up with the Modes and their support. Maybe the three of them could've ruled together. Her tears turned to laughter. Zeru wouldn't know what to do with it all.

Kyla sat back up, fastening the seatbelt as the shuttle maneuvered through the orbital debris, and clicked on the viewscreen in the suite, glancing at her reflection. Her hair was parted mostly to one side, with the shorter hair still growing out around the augments. Sure, she looked like a Mode, but she looked like herself, too. Her bronze skin and dark hair were different than any of the other Modes. She wasn't one of them. She was Nacaen, Jamin by her father and Maire by her mother.

She swiped the screen away. She didn't need Seriah's approval. But what was the General going to tell Armas? Could she turn her husband against her? The console for the viewscreen was right in front of her. She set her palm down and immediately accessed the ship's onboard computer. Seriah's comm was linked, and it wasn't hard to see her way through the maze of passcodes.

Kyla pinched the bridge of her nose. She shouldn't be doing this. This was exactly what Seriah was accusing her of — being a Mode. Being someone they couldn't trust. Hacking in and bringing down the *Darkangel*. She moved along the pathways and found the navigation systems, quickly leaving them behind. *Don't touch anything regarding the ship.* She went instead to Seriah's comm interface.

The General's files were all there, easy access. She sifted through the labels, ignoring most of them. She really didn't want to snoop. But a file in her messages caught her attention.

A file from her brother.

She downloaded it and left Seriah's files behind, slipping out of the shuttle's system and back to herself, removing her hand from the console before she played the message.

Jon has a son.

She covered her mouth as the tears began to fall, intermixing her joy and sorrow. *Jon has a son named Seth, on Richo.*

"Kyla?" Laina's voice came at the door. "We're through the debris. The General thought you might want to see."

"See what?" She unbuckled from the table, wiping her eyes, and opened the door.

She gasped as they entered airspace above the northern continent. Glia was in ruins.

"We weren't able to save the city," the General said, her voice grave. "Phenian bombers had brought down the shields by the time we arrived. Your father and brother were protecting the East Gate. Everything underground remained intact, so we were able to save the workers that remained, and the medical units were surprisingly still functioning on generator power. Though many lives were lost, it was a miracle we saved as many as we did."

The shuttle banked to turn, with the two Bluehawk escorts, heading south.

"Where are we going?"

"To your new home. On Dahan land."

FORTY-ONE

KYLA

By the time they reached Dahan land, night had fallen. Kyla recognized now where Armas had been crowned king: not far from the farmhouse where she first met him. The shuttle set down in one of the unused pastures.

As they exited the shuttle, Laina pointed to the north of the farm, a small grove of trees. "That's Sebuj land," she said. "The carver I met was from here. Armas's great-grandmother helped negotiate their return to their ancestral home."

Kyla's heart soared. She could almost feel him, as if he had dendrilite himself. General Zeru led them to a small copse of needle trees. There were armed guards at the perimeter.

"He's waiting for you, there."

She raised a brow at Seriah, walking past her and the guards.

On a bench in the middle of the copse sat her beloved, his back to her. She let out a sigh. He turned, his eyes widening as he stood. A thin crown rested atop his auburn hair.

"I'm so sorry," he began, but she cut him off by running right into his arms.

Goddesses, she'd missed him. She wrapped her arms around him so tightly she was almost afraid she'd hurt him, but she shut down her implants and just let herself be. Tears fell, streaming against his uniform — black, with the new emblem on his shoulder. He smelled like grass, like the leaves of the needle trees, everything the Modes ship had not been. He was hers, now. And Jon was gone. She sobbed against his chest.

His hand ran down her back. "I'm so sorry I didn't come for you."

"I've missed you so much," she said, finding the beat of his heart just beneath her own.

After a while, he took her by the hand and led her over to a bench. "This was the old temple here," he said, "that my great-grandparents were married in. The farmhouse is that way," he added, pointing to the east, where the outline of the barn was dimly lit.

"I know," Kyla said. "I remember."

He ran his fingers through the length of her hair, just grazing the edge of her augments. She shivered at his touch.

"I'm so sorry this happened to you."

"You didn't do this," she said, clasping his hand that cupped her face. "I chose this. I did this to help you."

"I don't understand."

She told him everything that happened on the ship, how she allowed herself to become modified, and killed Alton.

"You saved the Leki, and for that I'm in your debt. They probably won't try to go to war with us for a while now." He sighed, running his hand along her arm. "I'm glad you are here now."

Kyla smiled through her tears. "So, where do we go from here?"

"We're going to build a new palace and city, just to the north. It's all very new, we're just in the designing stages, but something that will show the grandness of all Nacaens. But for now, I'm staying ..." He exhaled. "Kyla, I'm ... I've married another."

She didn't follow. Her brows drew together as she searched his deep blue eyes. What he said did not make sense. Jon was dead.

"I'm married to a woman named Abby, and she's pregnant with my child."

Kyla dropped his hand. "I don't understand."

"You and I — we were married because your father made us, you know that. It was a political thing. But now I have to have heirs, and I met Abby when I was —"

She abruptly stood, his words finally making sense in her head. "You *married* someone *else*?"

Armas held up his hands. "Saul married you off to Alton —"

"Whom I murdered to save you!"

He got to his feet, but she took a step back. Armas held up his hands. "I know this is a lot to take in —"

"A lot to take in?" All the love, longing, hope she'd clung to shattered in a million pieces, fusing together in a rage burning through her chest. "Goddesses, my father put me in prison because I saved your life! Jon risked his life to save yours. I became augmented to stop the Modes from hunting you down and destroying you! And you just went out and ... found another wife?"

"I know you've done everything for me!" Armas shouted back.

The guards started to move into the shadows. Kyla's rage surged in her augmented arm, the power building. She could choke one of the guards, steal their gun and shoot the others. The plan was all there in her head.

But Armas waved them off. "I wish it hadn't happened! I wish your father hadn't pushed us together to keep me under control and then tried to kill me right when I accepted I'd marry you —"

Her eyes widened in horror, hand covering her mouth. "You *accepted* you'd marry me. Because you couldn't marry Jon."

"You know how I felt about Jon," Armas said quietly. "I loved him."

"Armas ... you promised you would come for me." All the rage simmered beneath the surface, but her heart ripped open, as all hope she'd clung to, every desperate thread when she'd been thrown into prison, when she'd been augmented on board the dreadnought, all slipped through her fingers. There was nothing to hold onto anymore. The devastation overwhelmed her in tears running down her cheeks. "You promised."

He didn't make a move toward her.

She took in a ragged breath, turning away from him toward the trees. "When did you meet Abby?"

"I don't know, six weeks ago? When I was at Balec —"

She spun back to him. "Wait — you've known her just

over a month and you've married her and made her pregnant?"

Armas rolled his eyes. "You weren't there — stardust, my brother had just been killed! It was complicated. I felt ... lonely."

Kyla grew quiet. She wiped her eyes with the back of her non-augmented hand. "I've been so lonely. All I could think about, when I was in the dungeon cell, when I was on board that ship, having these augments implanted — when I had to ... get close to Alton to kill him — all I could hold on to was that someday you'd come and rescue me. You'd come find me. And when you didn't, I held on to the hope I'd find you."

An uneasy silence fell between them. "You did find me."

"You sent General Zeru to get me. Not you."

"I can't exactly just take a shuttle these days by myself —"

"This is pointless," Kyla said, and Armas's eyes widened. "You've moved on and married someone else."

She had to go, now, before she did something she'd really regret.

"You can't go," he said. The guards moved in, cutting off her escape.

Kyla rolled her eyes. "You can't be serious."

"You are to be my wife. You are Saul's daughter — while the Jamin want you to be queen, the other nations will accept you as princess consort. It will be a title in name only."

She sniffed, thinking of her only remaining family. "And what about Seth?"

"Who?"

Kyla faced him. "You don't know, do you?"

"Know what?"

Both pain and anger swept through her as she walked back toward him. "Jon recorded a message for you. He sent it to Seriah before he died."

Armas froze. "What?"

"He sent her a message. He has a son, Seth, living on Richo with his mother Sharda. I'm pretty sure I remember her. Dagael mech tech, long legs and blond — always Jon's type."

"Stop —"

Kyla pulled out her comm device and set it on her palm so she could show him the message she'd stolen from Seriah, displaying the hologram vid in front of him:

"Armas, there's so much I want to say to you, but I don't have time. Saul sent Kyla to the Modes. Abe said she's remaining on board with their Supreme One, Alton. I haven't been able to contact her. The Phenians are here — I've got to go suit up. I don't know if we'll make it through the night." Jon sighed in the vid. *"If I could say anything to you, it's this: You have my heart. My soul belongs to you. You mean everything to me."*

She blinked back her tears, hearing her brother's voice again. *"Also, I want you to know I have a son. His name is Seth. His mother is Sharda Ley; you may remember me talking about her. I was with her before you. She lives on Richo among the Dagael. She doesn't want anything. I haven't told Saul — you know how complicated that is."* Jon laughed on the recording. *"Complicated is one way to say it, given how he's tried to kill you. But I wanted someone to know. I wanted you to know."*

A beeping sound interrupted, the action stations alert

that called Jon away. *"I have to go. I love you, more than I can ever say."*

Armas fell to his knees. "She didn't tell me. She didn't tell me any of it."

For a brief moment, she wanted to go to him, to console him in their shared heartache, but it passed. He deserved no compassion from her, not after what he'd done. What he'd failed to do. He'd broken his promise. Her heart began to knit back together, but in shards, like Airysan steel.

Kyla slipped her comm back into her pocket and folded her arms, focusing on what little power she had left with the man she once hoped would love her. Her old life with Armas was behind her, cut off forever.

She would leverage what she could to start over.

On her terms.

"I will make a deal with you. I will remain married to you on two conditions: one, you allow me to go to Richo and find Seth and Sharda. Two, you and I are done." She recognized the finality as she said it. "No children, no *relations*. No contact unless absolutely necessary."

"We haven't had the funeral yet," Armas said. "We have preserved their bodies, but I wanted you to be here. You'll need to appear with me."

She let out a shaky breath. At least he didn't take that from her. She gave a curt nod, understanding that for the state funeral, they would need to appear as husband and wife.

"As for Seth and Sharda," his lips trembled as he spoke, "The *Shiloh* went down on the Dagael continent. Most of the forests burned. Major Ngo has been leading the recovery effort, but there aren't many survivors."

Her heart clenched in her throat. "Then let me go, right away."

Armas got back to his feet. "If they're alive, bring them back here. They will live in my house."

"They will live with *me*," she insisted. "They're *my* family."

Armas crossed his arms. "They can live with you, but I get to see him, provide for him and support him. I'll declare him Jon's heir, though the crown will remain with me. I can do at least that much for him."

Kyla hugged her shoulders. "I will agree to that."

"I need someone to accompany you."

She squinted. "I've taken care of myself without you this long and never tried to usurp your power once. You can't —"

"If Seriah kept Jon's son from me, I have my suspicions about what she might do to anyone else related to Saul."

She tilted her head. "That's the first sensible thing you've said this evening." She paused, taking one step closer to him. "She killed Abe."

"What —?" he said, then slid his palm down his face. "Of course she did. She sees anyone in Saul's line as a threat to me."

"I think she may have killed Abe to protect me. He wanted me to guarantee him a place of leadership, and I refused." She dug the grass with her toe, covering her own suspicion that Armas was right, and Seriah killed Abe because she'd hoped to rid Armas of all Saul's relatives, including herself. "Send Lieutenant Barish with me — they've been guarding me all along. Being Major Barish's child, the General shouldn't have any objections."

"Done."

The light from Horeb slipped into the copse, brightening his face. His freckles sparkled with tears below his sky-blue eyes. She walked over to him, and touched his hand, but didn't clasp it.

"You know, when we first met," she said quietly, "I remember being so caught off-guard by you that I couldn't even breathe. Couldn't think. Zam was convinced you were God's gift to the galaxy, and I believed it. After you came back from Zek, I knew you were the one I wanted to spend my life with."

"Kyla —"

"I've never been more wrong," she admitted as she took a step back, though there was no triumph, no satisfaction of her words. It was simply the harsh truth. "I wish I'd kept breathing. Kept finding my own way."

She turned from him, one last time. "Goodbye, Armas."

FORTY-TWO

ARMAS

Armas sank to the bench, waiting for the shuttle to lift off, taking Kyla to the house they'd secured for her to live in. He'd send instructions tomorrow for Lieutenant Barish to take her to Richo and find Jon's son. *God, please let him still be alive.*

Before Kyla arrived, Armas sat Abby down and explained that Kyla was still his wife. She'd seemed to understand, but he could tell this was going to be difficult, navigating the two. He'd thought of Jon in that moment and laughed, wishing he could explain his women problems to him, while wrapped up in his lover's arms.

Now, he wouldn't have to worry about going between Abby and Kyla. Jon's only concern, all along, was that he not hurt his sister.

I didn't want to, Jon. It's the last thing I wanted.

A familiar shadow passed through the grass in front of him.

"General."

"My King, are you all right?"

He stood, squaring his shoulders. "Why didn't you tell me about Jon's son?"

She stiffened. "How did you know?"

He rose, the anger flowing through his veins as he took a step toward his general. "Why. Didn't. You. Tell. Me?"

Seriah took a step back. "Your Majesty ... we had to establish your legitimacy to the throne, as the one chosen by God, and also by the Dahan. Our nation sacrificed enough over the years only for the Jamin to keep taking it. I had to be sure your reign is secure."

"Have you found him?"

She set her hand on her heart and knelt before him. "My King, I've been in touch with Major Ngo on the search and recovery mission. They were badly burned in the fire afterwards. Sharda Ley did not make it. Her son has severe injuries and is in the military hospital, but they believe he'll live."

"Why didn't you tell me?" he asked again, his fists clenched.

She stood but did not look at him. "You'd lost your brother. You had just lost Jon. If I told you Jon's son was alive only to lose him — do you want to go through that pain again?"

"Don't act like you're protecting me, Seriah." He brushed past her. "You may be my General, but any blood you spill is on your hands. You will not harm any of Saul's family again," he added over his shoulder.

"I will do whatever it takes to see you secure on the throne," she responded.

Armas swore under his breath. He'd trusted Zeru since he met her, but now he knew he'd have to be as cunning as she was; otherwise, there might be no one left.

"Be careful that your need for revenge doesn't lead to your own death," he warned her, before his guards escorted him back to his family home, where Abby waited for him.

EPILOGUE

KYLA

The servants assigned to help her dress couldn't figure out where to place her own crown with her augments; they kept trying to part her hair on the wrong side to cover them. Laina had to take over, arranging her hair in a round braid.

"Don't hide them," Kyla told her. "They're part of me."

Laina finished the plait and fastened the crown, leaving her augments visible. Kyla's dress was long, black, and form-fitting. Her maid gave her a soft smile. "I'll go get Seth and meet you there."

Carmen arrived to escort her, their hair undone from their braids, crowning their face in short ringlets. "I hear the plans are to make this the new capital," they said, leading Kyla to the covered walkway before a constructed platform.

Kyla nodded. "Peace City is what they plan to call it."

Carmen tugged on their uniform, plain black, with no rank or insignia. Kyla frowned. "Why are you dressed like that?"

"I'm part of the royal guard now, assigned to you."

Kyla took Carmen's hand and squeezed it. "I'm sorry."

"Don't be," Carmen said, squeezing her hand back. "I chose this." They leaned in as if to say something more, but pulled away as Laina arrived, carrying Seth.

"He just fell back asleep," she said softly, and Kyla took her nephew into her arms. He'd just come off oxygen the other day. His legs were badly damaged from falling debris when the *Shiloh* went down, but he'd survived. His skin tone, the tuft of brown hair, and the soft green eyes that fluttered open for a moment were all signs that something of Jon, something of her own mother, had survived. He nestled his head against her shoulder, arms around her neck. *I've got you. You're not alone.*

The king stood on the constructed dais wearing his new dress uniform, with the new colored ring symbol of the united kingdom pinned to a woven sash across his chest, and a thin gold crown rested on his head. Behind him at an angle sat Abby, his new wife. Her eyes narrowed at the sight of Kyla, then flew open as she spied Kyla's augments.

She responded by simply arching an eyebrow. Kyla shifted Seth in her arms, but he didn't wake.

"How is he?" Armas asked, turning her attention back

to him.

"Better," she replied. "But sleeping."

"I'll go sit with him," Laina said, and Kyla obliged, handing over the sleeping child. Her maid carried him to a chair opposite Abby. Carmen remained just a step behind her shoulder, as Kyla took her place next to the king and waited for the funeral procession to arrive.

The convoy of mourners wound through the streets of Ephra, an unfamiliar city, the bodies carried by soldiers from all twelve nations, ending at the dais. *All of this is wrong.* Her complicated feelings about her father notwithstanding, he should've had a royal procession in Glia. Her brother should've been crowned king. But even as she dreamed an alternate vision, she no longer saw herself by Armas's side.

He reached for her hand, but she pulled it back. "I'm here for them, not for you," she whispered.

The prophet Nate climbed the steps to stand next to them. As he led the liturgy, chanting the prayers, Kyla's senses went to the hum of the energy force shield protecting them, the blue and red flickers only she could see. She closed her eyes.

She could sense the small thread that connected her to Laina with her dendrilite, the new force shield being set around the city, the signals broadcasting the funeral service to the other worlds of the system. She reached, searching for any signal from Ramah, but of course there was none with their signal disrupters. No sense of dendrilite, though she knew it was all there.

Nate finished and Armas stepped forward, cleared his throat, and began to sing:

"You were my strength, my steadfast shield,
Only for you my heart would yield,
You were the king of my heart.
You were beloved to all men,
Fallen in war; never again;
You will live on in my heart ..."

Tears formed at the corner of her eyes. She brushed them aside.

She reached, as far as she could. *"Farra?"*

She must be too far away.

But there, at the furthest edges of her mind, she could feel her, she could feel all of them who'd been aboard the dreadnought. A sense of joy of touching soil, tasting with their tongue, the heat of the Bara star upon their necks. She opened her eyes, thrilled for their safety, their peace. *Holy Tana, protect them.*

When the service ended, the prophet Nate drew closer to her. "My condolences again, upon the loss of your father and brother."

Kyla bowed her head in respect, but her gaze focused on the crowd that had pressed in, mostly women, some shouting for Armas. Even now — at her father and brother's funeral — Armas didn't stop them. He waved to the crowd.

"A word of advice, prophet." She faced him. He was only a few years older than her, with thick brown hair and bronze skin. "Even the best kings — what seems to be their greatest strength — can also be their weakness."

She stole a glance at General Zeru, on the other side of Armas, scanning the crowds for any threats, then turned her attention back to Nate. "The last prophet in your position risked his life for the kingdom over the king. Are you willing to do the same?"

Nate's eyes narrowed, glancing briefly at her augments, and the silver dendrilite that traveled down her arm. "I serve the One God, and the people on God's behalf."

Kyla smiled, touching his shoulder. "Then I pray you do well."

Carmen escorted her away from the dais, with Laina carrying Seth behind her. On impulse, she reached for Carmen's hand, intertwining her fingers with theirs. They squeezed back and didn't let her go.

THE END

ABOUT THE AUTHOR

Melinda Mitchell grew up in Alaska and has lived all over the United States, currently residing in Wisconsin with her husband and son. Raised by parents who were fans of science fiction and fantasy, the *Stardust and Ashes* series was born out of a late night/early morning D&D session during her time in seminary. Melinda has co-authored two academic papers on the intersections of science fiction and theology, and has also written numerous articles on theological themes found in popular science fiction and fantasy. She likes to think the greatest truths are in the stories we tell, whether or not the stories are true themselves.

www.melindamitchell.com

ACKNOWLEDGMENTS

"The soul of Jonathan was bound to the soul of David, and Jonathan loved him as his own soul." – 1 Samuel 18:1

"I grieve for you, Jonathan my brother; you were very dear to me. Your love for me was wonderful, more wonderful than that of women." – 2 Samuel 1:26

To the Creator, Redeemer, and Sustainer: my eternal gratitude, love, and devotion.

To the following, thank you for cheering on this series: Laura Anne Gilman, Amanda Cherry, Kelli Staci, Anita Peebles, Erik Scott de Bie, Jerrod Hugenot, and so many others that I know I'm forgetting some, but I appreciate you! Raven Oak, thank you for that meetup so many years ago that helped me consider pursuing this as a series. Thank you to Tammy Deschamps and Emily Papel who read very early drafts of Fortunate Son, giving me thoughtful feedback and encouragement.

Thank you to Cascade Writers. I brought the first few chapters of Fortunate Son to the 2018 workshop and am forever grateful for the feedback and encouragement I received in my critique group. Thank you to Spencer Ellsworth who helped encourage this series, and a special thanks to Jill Webb who read early drafts of Fortunate Son along with several other stories that haven't been published (yet!). Thank you for saying yes when I needed encouragement! Thank you to Matt LaWall-Shane for being a thoughtful critique partner and encourager while I was on deadline. A big thank-you to LaShawn Wanak and Paul Schneider for beta reading and providing essential insight into the final development, and for your friendship and encouragement.

Thank you to Ryn Richmond for her editing, thoughtful questions, and general cheering on of the Stardust and Ashes series as a whole. To Benjamin Gorman, thank you for your genuine enthusiasm for this book and series.

To all my readers and all my friends who have supported me—so many I can't name you all—I simply offer my gratitude.

To my mom Sarah: Thank you for always encouraging me to pursue publishing for Next of Kin despite all the setbacks before my dream was achieved, and for encouraging my love of reading at a very early age.

To my son AJ: You are the piece of my heart that lives outside of me. I love you.

To JC, my love: thank you for all your support and encouragement. You're an amazing partner and friend in this life, and I'm glad to share it all with you.

In loving memory of Pat Mitchell, my mother-in-law, who died a month after I finished writing this. You are missed and loved.

9 781956 892789